Praise for
The Killing Moon

"Gripping . . . thoroughly enjoyable . . . Hogan's theme of a small town harboring dark secrets is an addictive one that allows the reader to swallow the book in just one sitting."

—Richmond Times-Dispatch

"Hogan delivers plenty of excitement. . . . At his best, Hogan will remind readers of Lee Child and Stephen Hunter."

—Booklist

"The story displays a full array of compelling crime-story elements—forensics, sexual predation, methamphetamine dealers, romance, and even septic tanks."

—Boston Common Magazine

"Convincingly and movingly brings alive the dying Massachusetts community of Black Falls. . . . Strong characters and a memorable setting."

—Publishers Weekly

"The Boston area has long been fodder for quality crime fiction, including Robert B. Parker, Linda Barnes, Dennis Lehane, and Chris Mooney. Chuck Hogan . . . cements his bid for inclusion on this literary family tree with a thoughtful, moody thriller about small-town secrets."

—Baltimore Sun

Praise for nationally bestselling author Chuck Hogan's
crime-fiction blockbuster
Prince of Thieves

"Hogan excels at creating the over-the-top adrenaline rush of heists, heart-stopping chases, and gun battles . . . this book finds a place in my list of favorite books ever."

—*The Boston Globe*

"First rate."

—*The Washington Post*

"A rich narrative of friendship, young love, and mounting suspense. On each season's fiction list, if you are lucky, there are one or two books that live up to the advance hype. *Prince of Thieves* is such a book."

—Stephen King

"[A] moody, resonant thriller."

—*Booklist* (starred review)

"Engaging reading . . . grittily realistic action sequences."

—*Publishers Weekly*

"Chuck Hogan is a superb writer, and his *Prince of Thieves* is a grand novel peopled with believable characters in heart-wrenching scenes that throb with masterful suspense. This is simply great fiction that should not be missed."

—Ed McBain

"Smart, speedy, and stylish—a literary *Pulp Fiction*."

—Jeffery Deaver, author of *The Cold Moon*

"A fine literary effort . . . [with] layered characters and nuanced prose. . . . A story fueled by human relationships."

—*Rocky Mountain News*

THE
KILLING MOON

A NOVEL

CHUCK HOGAN

SCRIBNER
New York London Toronto Sydney

SCRIBNER
A Division of Simon & Schuster, Inc.
1230 Avenue of the Americas
New York, NY 10020

First Scribner trade paperback edition January 2008

SCRIBNER and design are trademarks of Macmillan Library Reference USA, Inc.,
used under license by Simon & Schuster, the publisher of this work.

For information about special discounts for bulk purchases,
please contact Simon & Schuster Special Sales:
1-800-456-6798 or business@simonandschuster.com.

Set in Galliard

Manufactured in the United States of America

1   3   5   7   9   10   8   6   4   2

Library of Congress Control Number: 2006045080

ISBN-13: 978-0-7432-8964-1
ISBN-10:   0-7432-8964-1
ISBN-13: 978-0-7432-8965-8 (Pbk)
ISBN-10:   0-7432-8965-X (Pbk)

To my partner in crime,
and our three unindicted co-conspirators

THE
KILLING MOON

PART I
BLACK FALLS

1
HELL ROAD

A CRACK, A SPRAY OF FLAME, and he dropped onto his back on the side of the dirt road.

Nothing made sense at first. Not the trees overhead, nor the dark sky. The gasping that would not fill his lungs.

He heard hissing and felt a great pressure easing in the center of his chest, a sensation like deflating, like shrinking back into boyhood.

His fight-or-flight response failed him, blunted by years of false alarms. In the end, his brain was unable to differentiate between legitimate trauma and the fire drill of another cheap high.

The forest was fleeing him on all sides. Light came up in his face that he did not realize was a flashlight; a bright, beaming presence he thought might be divine.

TEN MINUTES EARLIER, he had been so fully alive. Pushing his way through the snagging branches of the Borderlands State Forest, jogging at times, giddy as he followed the full and smiling moon through the treetops. *Intensely* alive, every part of him, as he had not felt in weeks or even months.

He was two full days beyond sleep, yet his thoughts remained hyperfocused and particular, his mind blazing pure blue flame (no flickers of orange tonight, no air in the line). The thrill of risk, of danger, was his spark and his fuel.

He knew these haunted woods so well because it was he who had once haunted them.

Running the Borderlands had been, back in high school, a weekend dare for popular seniors with new driver's licenses: speeding their parents' cars along the ungated fire road that sliced through the state forest like a nasty scar. A midnight rite of passage, marquee entertainment in a town full of nothing-to-do, this tiny rural map-smudge in the northwest corner of Massachusetts, a fading and forsaken hamlet named Black Falls.

He had longed to participate, to be included as a passenger among a carload of screaming teenagers tearing through the forest. Stopping short on the access road, cutting the headlights, soaking in total blackness for an extra thrill. The stuff of roller coasters and horror movies.

But he was a strange young boy who had grown still stranger in adolescence. An outcast. One whom the others would never, repeat, *never* invite.

And indeed, he was different. More than any of them knew.

That was how he got the idea.

He still had loads of makeup left over from Halloween. He knew a thing or two about theatricality, about costumes, about the importance of performance. The mask and the reveal.

Word of the black-haired ghoul on the fire road blazed through school that week. Darting out of the trees with screaming eyes and a gaping black smile. The thrill seekers who returned the following weekend were disappointed by a no-show, until the creature's notoriety exploded full force the weekend after that, with a dramatic reappearance said to have fouled the undergarments of a varsity running back.

The next week, no apparition, only the discovery of a blood-soaked shirt dripping from a low tree branch. Two more weeks passed, kids racing their fears with no payoff, until the demonic ghoul appeared yet again, this time hurling a severed human head (a hollowed-out cantaloupe larded with a mixture of Karo syrup and red food coloring) into a passing windshield, where it exploded with gore.

The legend of Hell Road had been born.

He camped there on weekend nights when the Thing in the Woods materialized, and even some nights when It didn't: watching the headlights shoot through the Borderlands, his classmates alive to the danger, begging for some appalling shock to jolt them out of their tedious small-town existence. But they were merely flirting with death, whereas he was downright smitten.

Never once had he been afraid in these woods. He found only calm here. A haunted teenager sleeping in a haunted forest, he felt consoled.

That was how he navigated this night without flashlight or fear, following one of his old tree paths to the impending rendezvous on Hell Road. He had suffered all day in anticipation of this moment, opening himself to the forest now, to whatever this night would bring. The secret of the mystery man about to be exposed.

He had even worn his costume, updated through the years, including his hair. The night heat was oppressive, but he had no choice in the matter. It was not a disguise he wore, but a manifestation.

Not a mask, but a reveal.

Secrets were a thing he fed upon. A blood meal to him, a thing he craved. That sustained him.

But to Maddox he had made certain promises, some of which he might even keep. He was trying to be good. He actually was.

Illicit, not illegal, the midnight encounter of two like-minded souls of consensual age in the deep, dark forest. Adventurous, yes, and mysterious, and spectacularly dangerous—but perfectly legal.

He was hopeful, always. Of meeting a true soul mate. Of finding one person out there who understood him. His whims and eccentricities. He did believe, from their chats, that this mystery man in fact knew who he was, and evidently was okay with that. Which was a start. It would save him from getting beat up at least. Mystery Man even referred to their rendezvous point as "Hell Road," so he had to be a local.

Regardless, it had given him something to dream about. Something to look forward to. A reason to go tripping through the forest yet again.

Night, bring me what you will.

THAT WAS WHAT he had been thinking as he emerged onto the hard dirt pack of the moonlit fire road. And what he thought now as the light flooded his eyes, and he expelled a final, gusty sigh, settling deeply and comfortably into the ground as though it were a child's soft mattress. He reverted to his best self, that innocent and unbroken young boy, exhausted at the end of another endless day of summer, surrendering to the moonlight and his secret dreams.

2
RIPSBAUGH

IT WAS THE BLUE LIGHTS that drew him.

Kane Ripsbaugh didn't go around seeking out beauty in life. He had no poetry in his heart, no language for pretty things. He owned a septic service company and ran the town highway department and was loyal to his difficult wife. But police blues pulsing against the dark night: he doubted there was ever a more beautiful sight than that.

Ripsbaugh stopped his truck and killed the engine. He left the headlights on and looked out at the road in a squinting way that had nothing to do with the strange scene his lamps revealed. This was the way he looked at the world.

The cop out there, the new hire, Maddox, had his revolver drawn. He glanced into the headlights, then backed off from the big deer dying in the road.

Ripsbaugh climbed out and down, his boots hitting the pavement. As the head of Black Falls' highway department, a hurt deer blocking the road was as much his business as anyone else's.

"You all right?" he asked Maddox, walking up on him slow.

"Yeah," said Maddox, looking anything but. "Fine."

Ripsbaugh watched the deer try to lift its head. Its hooves scraped at the pavement, blood glistening on its muzzle and ears. The stick casting a jagged shadow near its head was not a stick at all but a broken antler.

Some fifty yards down the road, Maddox's patrol car was pulled over onto the shoulder. The driver's side door was open.

Maddox started to talk. "I was driving past the falls. The spray washed over my car, so I hit the wipers. The road ahead was clear. All of a sudden, *bam!* Car jerks left—not a swerve like I was losing control, but like the car had been shoved. I realized I hadn't hit anything. Something hit me."

He talked it through, still trying to piece together what had happened, the memory of the incident and its impact as fresh to him as an echo.

"I slam on the brakes finally, stopping down there. Red smoke everywhere, but it was just road grit swirling up in my brake lights. I get out. I hear this sound like scraping, a sound I can't understand. The dust settled . . . and here it is."

Ripsbaugh looked into the trees. Edge Road was so named because it traced the treeline of the Borderlands State Forest. "How's your unit look?"

"Rear right passenger door's pushed in." He was starting to shake off the shock. "I never heard of that. A deer broadsiding a moving car?"

"Better that than getting up into your windshield."

Maddox nodded, realizing how close he had come to death. His turn to look into the trees. "Something must have spooked it."

Ripsbaugh looked him over, his blue jeans and hiking boots. The town couldn't afford regular uniforms anymore, so the six-man force wore white knit jerseys with POLICE embroidered in blue over their hearts, and black "BFPD" ball caps, making them look more like security guards than sworn lawmen. Snapped to Maddox's belt were a chapped leather holster and a recycled badge. He held an old .38 in his hand.

The deer resumed its scratching, bucking its head against the asphalt. "Aw, Christ," Maddox said, knowing what he had to do.

Maddox had grown up in Black Falls but he was no farm boy. He'd left to go to college some fifteen years ago and never returned until his mother passed away. That was six months ago now. No one had expected him to stay more than a day or two beyond the funeral, but here he was, a part-time auxiliary patrolman, a rookie at age thirty-three. That was about as much as anybody knew about him.

"All right," Maddox said to the gun in his hand, and to the deer in the street.

Sometimes the mercy part of the kill shot is less for the suffering animal than for the man who can't stand to watch it suffer.

"In the ear," Ripsbaugh advised.

The animal flailed, sensing its impending execution, trying to get away. Maddox had to brace its strong neck with the tread of his hiking boot. He extended his gun arm with his palm open behind it.

The shot echoed.

The deer shuddered and lay still.

Maddox lurched back like a man losing his balance coming off the bottom rung of a ladder. He holstered his gun as though it were burning him, the piece still smoking at his hip. His hand wasn't shaking, but he rubbed it as though it were.

Ripsbaugh walked to the deer. Maddox's patrol car blues flashed deep within its dead round eye. "That was a good stance you had."

Maddox breathed hard and deep. "What's that?"

"Your stance. A good cop stance."

"Yeah?" he said. He wasn't quite present in the moment yet. "I guess."

"They teach you that here?"

Maddox shook his head like he didn't understand. "You a shooter?"

"Just going by what I see on TV."

"Must be we watch the same shows, then."

Ripsbaugh eyed him a little more closely now. "Must be."

He gave Maddox a minute to get used to the idea of grabbing the deer's hooves with his bare hands, then together they dragged the carcass off into the first row of trees, leaving a blood trail across the road.

"I'll come back in the morning with my town truck," said Ripsbaugh, "take him to the dump."

Maddox eyed Ripsbaugh's company rig. "You working late?"

"Fight with the wife. Came out to drive around, cool off."

Maddox nodded, about the only way to respond to that. He was wiping his hands on his jeans, coming back more fully into himself now. "Well," he said, "just another night in Black Falls."

Ripsbaugh watched the amateur cop head back to his patrol car, silhouetted in flashing blue. He returned to his own truck, checked the bundle rolled tightly in the tarp in the rear bed, and started for home.

3
BUCKY

Bucky Pail—at sergeant, the highest-ranking member of the Black Falls Police Department—leaned forward against the counter, stretching his back as he looked out through the front windows of the station, past the people gathering on Main Street to the coursing blue stripe of the wide-running Cold River. The sun sparkled off its surface as though the waterway were a vein of blue blood conveying shards of broken crystal through the county. As though anyone going wading in it would shred their legs of flesh. Would find themselves standing on shins of pure bone.

This was what Bucky was grinning about when Walter Heavey walked in.

Heavey looked surprised to see Bucky up at the front desk. He hesitated a stutter-step before continuing forward, the man's skin fishy white, his hair clown orange. He wore the same red jersey he always wore, bearing the three-oval State Farm Insurance symbol of his employer.

"What's up, Walt?" said Bucky, not bothering to straighten.

"I'm here to report something."

"Okay. Shoot."

Heavey had wanted someone else to be there, anyone else. Knowing this, seeing the dread on Heavey's face, gave Bucky a little lift.

Heavey said, "I heard a gunshot overnight."

"Okay." This was going to be good. "When-abouts and where?"

"It was last night. Late. Out in the Borderlands, behind my place."

"Borderlands, huh? Woke you up?"

"It did wake me up, yes. But I wasn't dreaming."

"Mrs. Heavey had a bout of the gas, maybe?"

Bucky took Heavey's shocked stare and savored it, anger blushing the man's ridiculously fair face, further whitening his white eyebrows. Appearances alone, Bucky had zero respect for this guy.

"Okay," said Bucky, Heavey too flustered to respond. "So. A gunshot."

"I got kids in my house, Sergeant Pail. Three boys. I'm not . . . this isn't fooling around. What's it got to take for you to look into these things?"

Bucky nodded and kept up his grin. Kids. Kids weaken people. Not that Heavey had all that far to fall in the first place, but now the entire world was a white-hot threat to his precious offspring, all broken glass and sharp edges. Three tubby eight-year-old boys, identical triplets, all clown-heads like him. Piling out of the circus ambulance minivan with their Fat Lady mother huffing after them.

A comedy. A sideshow. And when something strikes you as funny, you smile.

Bucky said, "Is it that witch back sniffing around your boys again?"

Heavey was stewing and stammering now. "I never said it was a witch. I said she looked like a witch."

Kids are a sex-change operation. Turn a man right into a woman.

"Maybe," Heavey went on, "what I need to do is call the state police."

Bucky grinned again, harder this time, curling it a bit. Relishing Heavey's attempt at moxie. "See, it don't work like that, Walt. We don't answer to the staties, they're not our bosses. Completely different thing. I bet they couldn't even find Black Falls on a map." Bucky straightened, using the step-up height advantage of the front counter. "But you go ahead and call them if you want, with your complaints about gunshots and witches trying to steal your kids—"

"*Complaints?*" Heavey looked around like he was on a hidden camera. "Shoe prints in my yard? Gunfire in the woods? These aren't complaints. These are *reports*."

Eddie wandered out of the back hallway behind Bucky, chewing on an apple. "What's up?"

Eddie was two inches taller and two years older than his brother, but it was Bucky who was in charge, and had been ever since they were kids. Eddie's hair was straw blond to Bucky's dirty brown, but facially, especially in the tight eyes, there was no mistaking the Pail brand. Eddie ate green apples one after another like a horse, in big, choking bites—core, seeds, stem, and all.

Eddie would never have bothered showing his face out here just to help. He knew something about this. Bucky said, "Walt here thinks he heard something in the Borderlands last night."

"Not 'thinks,'" said Heavey. "It was a gunshot. The crack of a handgun. I heard it carry."

Chock-hunk. Eddie said to Bucky, his mouth full, "That was Maddox."

Just hearing the name changed the weather in Bucky's head from overcast to threatening. "What are you talking about?"

"Hit a deer last night." Eddie examined the apple like it was a kill. *Chock-hunk.* Bucky hated watching his brother eat. "Had to put it down in the middle of the road."

Bucky also hated these rare occasions when Eddie knew something Bucky did not. "What road?"

"Edge Road. Out by the falls."

Heavey was shaking his head. "I heard it in the woods behind my house."

"Sound carries," said Bucky. "You said so yourself. You live on Edge."

"At the other end from the falls. The shot I heard came from the woods."

Clown Man wasn't going to budge. Why was Bucky wasting his time with this anyway? "Okay then, Walt. We'll be sure and follow up on it."

"How so?"

Bucky stopped. He cocked his head at him. "What's that, Walt?"

Heavey backed down, just a little. Just enough. "I asked how so?"

Bucky said, referring to brother Eddie, "Patrolman Pail here will swing by Edge Road after the parade."

Eddie took another apple bite, *chock-hunk*. "No, I won't."

Bucky said, "Enjoy the parade, Walt."

Heavey turned, livid, and pushed out through the screen door to the front porch, starting away. Bucky imagined him doing so in big, floppy clown shoes.

"Heavey on the rag again?" said Eddie.

Bucky looked at him chewing. "Most people don't eat the stem, you know. They leave that last little bit."

"Gives me something to chew on," he said, as Bucky started past him down the back hall. "Hey. I don't actually have to go out there to Heavey's, do I?"

Bucky's focus was on Maddox now. "I don't give a fuck what you do."

He banged out the rear door, slowing at the top of the back steps, finding the others gathered around Maddox's patrol car in the center of the dirt lot.

Without looking, Bucky was aware of Maddox standing apart from them, and also aware that Maddox was aware of him. A reverse magnetism had developed between them.

"What's this, now?" said Bucky, coming down off the steps.

Mort Lees, who was third in seniority after Bucky and Eddie, straightened near the rear left passenger door. He and Eddie had run around together all through high school, Mort being the tougher of the two. "Buck, check this out. Deer rammed Maddox's unit."

Bucky went around the patrol car. The door was pushed in good, but he didn't reach out and feel it like the rest. He wouldn't give Maddox the satisfaction.

He looked over at the part-time rookie, and just by the way Maddox was standing thought he seemed more confident. Like Maddox was becoming one of the boys. Bucky felt camaraderie blooming here.

He would not ask to hear Maddox's thrilling deer story. He didn't fall in love so easy. Instead he focused on the trunk of the spare patrol car behind Maddox, which was open. "What do you think you're doing?"

Maddox had a box of road flares in his hands. "Moving my stuff into the extra car."

Bucky shook his head nice and slow. "For emergencies only."

Maddox stared like he didn't understand. "Mort took it when his windshield glass got that thread crack in the corner."

"See, that's a safety issue there. Windshield. Yours is just body-work, cosmetic. Bang out that dent if you want, but do it on your own time."

The police department budget was a joke. Black Falls was a piss-poor town struggling to afford Bucky and Eddie full-time. No money existed for their uniforms beyond T-shirts and ball caps; no paid vacations for anyone; no overtime and no paid details. Bucky and Eddie were the only ones who rated health insurance coverage, which both of them had declined, opting to leave their contributions in their paychecks, their salaries measuring out to a measly $7.85 hourly wage.

But there were other advantages to running a town. A smart cop could more than make up for the pay discrepancy on the side. That was where the real benefits of the job were: out on the fringe.

The patrol cars were puttering '92 and '93 Fords. Bucky's had more than 140,000 miles. And since February they had been paying to gas up their own vehicles. They already bought their own weapons and ammo. And anything that broke inside the outmoded station was theirs to repair.

But then Maddox swept back to town, and old man Pinty strong-armed his fellow selectmen, somehow finding enough money in the budget to hire on another thirty-six-hour-a-week cop with no qualifications whatsoever. Because Maddox was a legacy, because the man's father had been Pinty's partner once upon a time and, oh yeah, had been stupid enough to get himself killed in the line of duty in such a sleepy town as this.

That Maddox was Pinty's special hire here was a little too obvious. Transparent, the old man trying to hold on to the police force, forgetting that he had retired ten years ago and that his time had long, long since passed.

"Heavey heard Maddox's deer shot," Eddie announced to the others. "Dumb cluck thought the gun went off in his own backyard. Wants round-the-clock surveillance."

Bart Stokes, the fourth cop, thinner and dumber than the rest, said, "Guy needs to buy himself a pair of long pants and some balls."

Bucky asked, "Where's this deer now?"

Maddox's eyes and mouth were tighter as he responded. "Off the side of the road. Ripsbaugh said he'd pick it up today."

"*Mmm,*" said Ullard, the fifth cop, the joker of the bunch, rubbing his chubby hands together. "Venison stew all week at the Ripsbaughs'."

Stokes said, "Five bucks he mounts the head. Trophy of a retarded deer."

Ullard said, "You'd mount a retarded deer for five bucks."

Stokes reached out to push Ullard as the others laughed. All except Bucky. And Maddox.

Bucky said, "Show and Tell's over. Maddox, you got some forms to fill out."

"Forms?" he said.

"Vehicle damage report. And discharge of a firearm. Tell you what, why don't you write me up a full report on the whole thing."

Maddox checked this with the others. "Write *you* the report, Bucky?"

"As your senior-ranking sergeant." Bucky didn't like the look he was getting, the attitude. "And for future reference, deer hunter? 'Bucky' is what friends call me. You can stick with 'Sarge.'"

That woke up the others. Bucky was pretty much done waiting for Maddox to get bored of working his three-a-week, twelve-hour graveyard shifts all by his lonesome. Done waiting for him to sell his dead mother's house and move the hell out of Black Falls. If Maddox was entertaining any real-cop dreams and thinking he might catch on here full-time, then maybe he was stupider than Bucky knew.

But no. Maddox was anything but stupid. That was the thing. Maddox was too smart, he was too sure, and he kept things inside. Most of all, he had a knack for being around when things happened. The sort of knack that could get a man into trouble.

Bucky looked at the others. "The parade extravaganza ready?"

Maddox was in the dark about that. No one had told him about the parade plans.

"Ready, Bucky," said Stokes.

The way Stokes accentuated the "Bucky" was exactly what Bucky wanted to hear. Rally these idiots, keep the station house lines drawn. Chase Maddox off the force, and then run this town exactly as he pleased, with no one trying to peek over his shoulder. Better careful than sorry.

Bucky said, "Maddox, you're on parade duty. The rest of us? We got some marching to do."

4

HEAVEY

GAYLE UNFOLDED HER OVERSIZED sunglasses and said to him, "Walter, please. We came for a parade."

And she was right. Here he was snapping at his boys, taking it out on them. The parade was about to start, and why should he let the Pail brothers ruin the town holiday, such as it was?

Because that pair of no-brains had laughed at him.

Neanderthals. With their trademark Pail eyes peering out from deep inside their skulls, tramp eyes, Bucky with his oh-so-clever grin and Eddie with his toothy smile. Menaces. In any other town, those two would be pumping Walter Heavey's gas or mowing his lawn.

Imagine if a protected species like a bald eagle or a spotted owl knew it was protected. Knew it could peck at your eyes and ears and turd on your face and there was not a damn thing you could do—because if you so much as raised a hand against it, into jail you would go. Now give that protected species loaded guns and powers of arrest.

He reached for his sons' whiffled heads, Wallace, Walker, and Waldo, their orange fuzz bristling. If those Pails ever tried to humiliate Walter Heavey in front of his boys . . .

"The gall of that punk, Gayle. By God. Something's got to give."

Her hand fell to her side, her charm bracelet and its three identical silver heads jangling as she communicated her aggravation with a sigh. "So let's move then, Walter."

She lobbed this bomb at him every once in a while, but she was the one who could never part with the house, having sunk so much time and energy into decorating it to her liking. But he played his part. "Move where? Where else are we going to find a house as big as ours with as much acreage as we have for what we'd get in this market? At this tax rate? Take it from a man who knows," he said, thumbing his State Farm Insurance shirt.

Gayle put her hand on his arm, the immediacy of her grip meant to silence him.

A black ball cap and white jersey moving up the sidewalk. Dark sunglasses. A Black Falls cop coming their way.

Walter Heavey felt his wife pulling the boys back from the sidewalk's edge. It just wasn't right. A family shouldn't be wary of their own police force.

It was the new cop, Don Maddox. Maddox's hiring had been little more than a bad joke, indicative of the whole sorry state of affairs here in Black Falls. Maddox was about as qualified to be a law officer as Walter Heavey was. The POLICE jersey he wore, a pair of sunglasses: Was that all it took? If Heavey traded shirts with Maddox, would Maddox be able to draw up a whole-life policy? Would he be able to decode an actuarial table at a glance? Walter Heavey was his company's top performer in the region, remarkable when you factored in that State Farm didn't even offer insurance products in his home state. His region encompassed southwestern New Hampshire, southern Vermont, and eastern New York State, a customer base he had built up over the past fifteen years—fifteen years while Maddox was doing . . . well, what, exactly?

Maybe Maddox could put on surgical scrubs and take out Walter Heavey's appendix while he was at it.

Pinty was the one who had helped him catch on part-time with the police—another head-scratcher. If Pinty and Maddox went back such a long way, why would Pinty drop a friend into that pit of vipers?

"What now?" said Heavey, as Maddox came up. "You come for a chuckle too?"

Behind his dark glasses, Maddox acted confused. "I heard you heard a shot last night."

"I know, I know. You put down a deer in the road, that was the shot I heard. Only, it wasn't. The one I heard came from the Borderlands behind my house. The other direction."

"You remember the time, by any chance?"

"I do. It woke me up and I checked the alarm clock. Nine minutes after midnight."

Maddox looked around as though concerned someone might overhear their conversation. The turnout for the parade wasn't amounting to much—a combination of hot July sun and general apathy. "The shot was all you heard?"

"All I heard, that's right."

"No voices, no yelling?"

"Nothing. And I listened."

"Well, the timing seems about right," said Maddox. "This deer, it came streaking out of the Borderlands, broadsided my patrol car headfirst. Going that fast, I figure something must have spooked it."

This took a moment to settle in: Maddox believed him.

Maddox noticed the three boys looking up from behind their mother's shielding hips. He bent down closer to their level. "Hey, there, guys. You ready for the parade?"

The boys crowded closer as though trying to climb back inside their mother.

Maddox straightened, his smile bearing a trace of regret. "Anyway, enjoy the day, folks," he said.

Heavey said, "You're going to check into it?"

"I'll take a ride out on the fire road, I guess. Beyond that, I don't know."

"What about the shoe prints?"

That stopped Maddox from leaving, brought him back. "What shoe prints?"

"They didn't tell you?"

"I work just three overnights a week, Mr. Heavey. They don't give me a whole lotta help on the shift change."

Heavey told him briefly about the woman in black. He liked the concern he saw on Maddox's face. Liked it very much.

"Those shoe impressions still there?" said Maddox.

"Some, sure."

"Think you can keep your boys from trampling them? I could stop by at the beginning of my shift tonight, before it gets dark."

Heavey was speechless. A Black Falls cop actually listening to him. Willing to act.

Parade music started up, a prerecorded band march. Maddox glanced around again, leaving Heavey with the distinct impression that Maddox did not want to be seen talking to him. All to the better.

"Just you, then," Heavey said. "I don't want any of those others on my property."

5
PINTY

THEY SAY RIVERS USUALLY divide towns, but not Black Falls. The town had grown up around an east-west crook in the south-flowing Cold River, forming a natural crease between the low farmlands to the south and the foothills rising in the north. The town got its name from a pair of waterfalls just up the river, the site of a massacre—so bloody the water was said to run black—of Pequoigs in 1676, at the height of the Indian Wars. The town was not officially incorporated until 1755, the criteria being a population financially capable of building its own Congregational church and supporting its own Congregational minister. A state law in 1831 separating church from state prompted the construction of a new town meeting site, a white clapboard building renovated in the mid-1960s, now resembling a side-by-side two-family house, the town offices on one side and the police station on the other.

That building, symmetrical beneath a round attic window like an always open, always staring eye, stood at the head of the T-shaped intersection of Main and Mill. Main Street represented the top bar of the T, accompanying Cold River in either direction. Number 8 Road, the fragment of an old Hartford-to-Montpelier mail route, shot northward from the western bar, narrowing as it snaked into the hills above town.

Mill Road ran south, being the trunk of the T, first as a low iron bridge spanning the summer-swift Cold River, then as a paved road hooking around the old Falls Paper Incorporated pulp mill, rotting on its river stilts.

About half of Black Falls' 1,758 residents were clustered in the town center, in the old mill houses crowded along Main and Mill, crumbling brick tenements and company-built three-deckers with sagging roofs and slumping porches. The shuttering of the paper mill almost twenty years ago was largely to blame for the town's current state of affairs. Black Falls had evolved from a trading post town in the eighteenth century to a farming town in the nineteenth century to a mill town in the twentieth. But even its proudest citizen had to admit that the twenty-first held little promise. The town wasn't dying so much as it was disappearing. No supermarket. No traffic lights. No ATM. Mobile telephone reception was one bar at best, broadcast television reception almost nil, and the wait for cable television was currently twenty-five years and counting. As "globalization" evidently required paying customers, the modern world appeared willing to leave the town behind.

The town was hurting, financially, geographically, every which way. The community as a whole was depressed beyond simple economics. It was in the grip of a spiritual malaise from which there seemed no relief. The Mitchum County Chamber of Commerce guide referred to Black Falls as "once historic," and Pinty didn't even know what that meant, though the wording somehow seemed right.

Stavros Pintopolumanos leaned forward on his cane, the silver English grip familiar and smooth to his hand. With the bridge and the Cold River at his back, he looked across at what he considered to be the current source of the town's ills. To Pinty, everything started and finished with the police department, the institution which had employed him most of his life and which he had helmed at the time of his retirement almost ten years before. He looked at the big flag atop the pole in front, its colors vibrant even when furrowed on a windless day. As a source of inspiration and a symbol of hope, it buoyed him. He had lived in the same small town all his life, with the notable exception of three years of service in the Korean War, and whenever he laid eyes on the flag hung properly and high, he felt a breeze lift his heart.

This was parade day, after all. Two hundred and fifty years of incorporation, and that wasn't a birthday to let slip by unacknowledged. His hope that such an event might invigorate the town had already been dashed: the parade had started, and the center of town still didn't seem ready for it. So many bare patches along the sidewalks that families should have been filling. But then the Cub Scouts came marching, with their troop flag and their den mothers, and all Pinty could do was smile.

The other two selectmen followed: Parker Harris, the elementary school principal, pulling a boom box in a red Radio Flyer wagon, playing a Sousa march; and Bobby Loom, known as Big Bobby, proprietor of the Gas-Gulp-'N-Go, the minimart filling station a half mile west on Main. Big Bobby was scattering wrapped bubble gum and Dum Dums to the children. Pinty would have been out there with them as the third town selectman, were it not for his hips. He tap-tapped his cane nub on the sidewalk as they marched past.

Pinty saw Donny Maddox coming toward him along the sidewalk and felt a lift similar to the one he'd experienced looking up at the flag. Hope, mainly. But Pinty had learned in life not to hope too hard.

Donny stopped next to him, facing the parade. "Not up to it today?"

"Today's a good day," said Pinty, patting his hip. "Not a bad day."

"How about a chair?"

"Never would get up out of it."

"I'd have built a float for you, if I'd known. Sit you up there on a throne."

"I would like that. That's about my style."

"This town should throw you a parade. They will, someday." Donny crossed his arms, implacable behind his sunglasses. "They better."

Pinty smiled, not at Donny's words, but at his respect. "Two hundred fifty years," he said, gesturing at the parade like a symphony conductor demanding more out of an orchestra. "Older than the country itself. A hell of a long time."

"Maybe too long," said Maddox.

"Think of what all this land looked like to the colonists and trappers who first walked down from the hills."

Maddox said, "Think of what the colonists and trappers must have looked like to the Pequoigs already settled here."

That was Donny's habit, his role, the town contrarian. Pinty never took it seriously, this rebelliousness Donny had held on to since his teens. Donny always thought he was too big for Black Falls. And when he was younger, he was right. He'd won the college scholarship, and everybody expected big things. Now, fifteen years later, he was back, and nobody knew what to make of him.

The town plow sander came rumbling along, sputtering its diesel exhaust. Black Falls' two major municipal purchases in the past decade were: the new flag and pole, after 9/11; and the fork-bladed plow. No town in the Cold River Valley could survive winter without one of these immense road clearers.

Above the BLACK FALLS HIGHWAY DEPT. stenciled into the driver's side door sat Kane Ripsbaugh, his bare, sun-chapped elbow jutting through the open window as he kept the angry-looking plow at an even five miles an hour. The word "highway" used to be defined as any public way, and showed that the department and its facilities—the garage farther east on Main, the salt and sand sheds, the town dump—dated back to the early days of the automobile.

Ripsbaugh was the one-man highway department, a position he had held for the last three decades. Some, such as Donny, would say that Ripsbaugh's longevity was due to the job offering hard, physical work for little pay and zero prestige. But Pinty viewed Ripsbaugh's role as an honorable one, and knew that Ripsbaugh did too. A town like Black Falls could not get by without a Kane Ripsbaugh. He was as day-to-day instrumental in its upkeep as was Pinty, though the two men could not have been more different. It was funny, to Pinty, how withdrawn Ripsbaugh was, that a man so devoted to his community could be so indifferent to his neighbors at the same time.

So it was indeed possible to love a place and not necessarily adore its people. This was something Pinty needed to communicate more successfully to Donny.

Donny said, "You notice who's missing this morning?"

Pinty turned right away, looking down to the end of the parade route, the junction of Main and Number 8 Road. The house on the corner there was divided into twin apartments upstairs and down, with the upstairs tenant, who was also the owner, having the advantage of a large balcony built above the front door.

That was where Dillon Sinclair usually stood, leaning against the iron rail, dressed all in black like an undertaker, smoking hand-rolled cigarettes and watching the town pass below him.

Pinty noted the look of concern on Donny's face. Pinty said, "It's not like him to miss a parade."

Black Falls was currently home to nine registered sex offenders, four Level 2s and five of the more dangerous Level 3s. This was a regional concern. Publicity generated by the sex offender registry was effectively chasing offenders from more populated, organized, and affluent towns into smaller, remote communities. Nine out of the top ten Massachusetts communities in sex offenders per resident were rural towns far west of Boston. Out of 351 total cities and towns statewide, tiny Black Falls ranked eighth.

Dell Stoddard went rolling past in his prized 1969 yellow Mustang convertible sponsored by Stoddard's Auto Body, playing loud surfing music that in no way jibed with the mood of the moment or of the town. Two women in sun hats made their way along the sidewalk toward Pinty, Paula Mithers under a wide, curled brim of straw, followed by her grown daughter, Tracy, sporting a beat-to-hell cowgirl-style number. The mother wore a gardening shirt, Bermuda shorts, and muck boots fresh from the barn. The daughter wore an oversized T-shirt knotted at the waist and cutoff jean shorts, her knees and elbows grayed with dry mud.

The Mithers women raised llamas on a little farm over on Sam Lake. Middle-aged Paula had a face most would describe as handsome, etched with deep lines by sun and divorce, while twenty-two-year-old Tracy was sun-freckled and slim, petite yet somehow leggy, blond hair washing out of the back brim of her cowgirl hat.

"Hi, Chief Pinty," said Tracy.

"Not 'Chief,' Tracy," said Pinty, correcting her gently. "Just Pinty."

She nodded and turned to smile at Donny. "Hi."

Pinty said, "You know Donny, right?"

"I know Donny," she said, and they shook hands, a loose-gripped, formal up-and-down. Donny was the first to let go, but Tracy was the first to look away.

Paula waved for Pinty's attention. A deaf woman, she signed angrily, hands picking apart the air as though arranging her words letter by letter on an invisible board.

Pinty turned to Tracy, who looked sheepish and almost teenager-disappointed in her mother. She translated flatly: "'Aren't you going to do something about this?'"

Pinty looked back at Paula. "About what?"

Then he heard the Indian cry. It was the Black Falls Police Department come marching. Bucky Pail led the way, showing off an antique musket to the crowd and exhorting their cheers, while brother Eddie and the three others followed in tow, each gripping one handle on a rescue stretcher bearing a cigar store Indian. It was the wooden statue that greeted customers at Big Bobby's Gas-Gulp-'N-Go, adorned now with a headdress of turkey feathers and bandaged in ketchup-stained gauze.

Some spectators joined in the jeering salute, though most, like Pinty, watched in stunned silence. He felt Donny stiffen next to him and reached out to hook his arm just as Donny started to move, holding him back.

"Don't," Pinty said.

Maddox held still, watched them pass. Pinty released his arm and returned both hands to the grip of his walking stick. He absorbed the ridiculous display because he had to, using it to feed his inner resolve, as he knew it was feeding Donny's.

How had things gone so wrong since his retirement? The police department's troubles began in earnest with the passing of Pinty's successor, Cecil Pail, who looked like Johnny Cash but died like Elvis Presley, of a massive coronary inside the station john three years ago. Pail was by and large a good man, but foolish and half blind when it came to his sons, Bucky and Eddie, whom he indulged. He had elevated his boys to the only remaining full-time positions on the shrinking force, in part to keep a closer eye on them. Pinty and the other selectmen refused to promote from within, yet were unable to attract a suitable replacement at the salary offered, to a town with no budget for police uniforms. So the chief's position remained vacant, and into this vacuum of power had risen Bucky Pail, with his brother at his right hand.

They stopped to rest in the middle of the intersection of Main and Mill, standing the bloodied Indian right out in front of the station, below the flag. Stokes swapped his ball cap and sunglasses for the headdress of turkey feathers, and the rest of them amused themselves posing for pictures like jackasses.

Pinty saw parents turning their kids away from the vulgar effigy.

"Pinty," said Donny.

Pinty squeezed the handle of his walking stick and shook his head. "If I can take it," he said, "you can too."

Tracy Mithers looked at them, confused. Her mother signed something, her daughter refusing to translate it until Paula Mithers clapped and pointed angrily at Pinty and Donny.

Tracy could not look at either of them. "My mother says to say that . . . you are both a disgrace."

Pinty watched Donny's eyes go dead. Pinty tried to grab his arm again, but it was too much for Donny, seeing Pinty's honor suffer like that. He pulled away and started off the curb toward the jackasses, Pinty calling after him, "Donny," and then once again, as loud as he dared, *"Donald."*

If Donny had one weakness, it was him: it was Pinty. What he felt he owed the old man. But Pinty didn't mind playing possum, now that the plan was in action and there was finally some hope. The town had abided these overgrown punks for too long now. Pinty only hoped that Donny didn't let them push him too far too soon.

6
MADDOX

MADDOX WAS TUNNELED IN. Bucky stood a few steps away from the spectacle, eyeballing the parade crowd through his dark shades, the old musket in his hands. Maddox remembered something from a college survey course on twentieth-century history about all despots having in common an innate knack for symbolism.

Maddox still carried pressure on his elbow from Pinty's surprisingly strong grip as he went up to Bucky and said, "That's enough."

Bucky looked at him. Maddox was close enough to see his buzzard eyes through the tinted shades. Pure amusement. "You say something, rookie?"

Bucky's intimidation came less from his size—he was big enough, but no bigger than Maddox—than from his eyes. Carny eyes, Maddox thought, assessing you while his dirty hands ripped your ticket, a guy with nothing in his life except dark thoughts. As a sergeant, Bucky outranked him, Maddox being just an auxiliary patrolman with the minimum 120 hours of in-house training. But Maddox could not stop himself. He could not stand by and let Pinty suffer this indignity. "I said it's time to break it up. Move on."

Bucky's grin widened. He looked over at the others, including them in this, then checked back once more as though Maddox might be putting him on. "Hey, boys?" said Bucky, speaking through his grin. "Maddox here is shutting us down."

"You put me on parade security," Maddox said. "This is disturbing the peace. It's time to move along."

"Disturbing the peace?"

"You're scaring kids."

"*Scaring* kids?" said Bucky, gesturing at the bandaged statue with his musket. "This here's a history lesson." Bucky turned back in such a way that the long, thin barrel of the musket was directed right at Maddox's gut. "This pop gun right here is a genuine Indian killer."

Maddox grabbed the muzzle and shoved it backward so that the butt of the weapon jabbed Bucky in the ribs, then pointed the muzzle skyward.

Bucky's eyes flared a moment behind his glasses—as shocked by Maddox's impudence as he was by the speed of his reflexes—lips curling to reveal the savage lurking inside the grin.

Maddox saw how far he had overstepped then. Bucky shook his grinning head, barely able to contain himself, overwhelmed by this great gift. The chance to belittle and demean Maddox in public. To humble him in the crossroads of Black Falls.

The others spread out around him, Maddox having nowhere to go. His neck burned, not because he would lose this confrontation, but because he had allowed himself to be drawn into it in the first place. All the station house tensions came bubbling to the surface. He had crossed a line, and things would only get more difficult from here on in.

"If I got this straight," said Bucky, "you're saying if we don't move our Injun friend here in a timely and forthright manner, you gonna cuff us all and take us in?" His half-clever smile fell away. "All by yourself?"

Maddox could not back down, and anyway, he wanted this too, more than anyone. He went cap brim to cap brim with Bucky, ready to jeopardize everything just to throw down with these goons.

A shadow fell across him. Maddox heard the prodding of the walking stick on pavement, and his heart simultaneously rose and fell.

"Hot one today, isn't it, boys?" said Pinty, appearing at Maddox's right shoulder.

Behind Bucky, Eddie Pail eased back. Even Bucky's eyes flickered a little, the way a candle does when a door is opened.

Maddox said, still staring hard at Bucky, "This is nothing, Pinty."

"Good," said Pinty. "Because it just wouldn't do to have Black Falls' own sworn peacekeepers brawling in the center of town on its two-hundred-fiftieth birthday."

Bucky pulled off his sunglasses, trying to turn his deep-eyed stare on Pinty, but it got him nowhere. As an elder statesman, Pinty still wielded a bit of moral authority.

"Now how about showing a little respect for the town and for yourselves," said Pinty, crowbarring Maddox and Bucky apart with his walking stick, "and let's everyone go on his merry way."

Bucky backed off but his eyes would not let go of Maddox. His look said that someday Pinty wouldn't be around to bail Maddox out.

Maddox banked that look, and the feeling it left him with, then turned away, part of him charging up like a battery, filling with new resolve. The other part of him remained pissed off, at himself, at the town, and even, he realized, at Pinty. Not for intervening. He was pissed off at Pinty for sticking with this backward town, for being the devoted captain who had to go down with this flooding ship.

The parade was breaking up now, a sad affair, more funereal than celebratory. Maddox cared little for the future of the town, but he cared about Pinty, who, to his mind, *was* the town. The aging Greek, seventy-one now, was a physical contradiction: barrel-chested on top and slender on the bottom, his waist and legs too small for the rest of him, carrying his weight like a vest of old muscle. As chief of police and town selectman, he had all but ruled Black Falls for the past quarter century. A benevolent dictator, the kind of man who mattered as much to a place as the place mattered to him. The decay of the police department haunted Pinty, his life's second-greatest disappointment after the early death of his only son. A proud man, and tired, leaning heavily on his oak walking stick, Pinty's last great gambit was to right the course of the police department before it was too late, to take the poison out of the well before it wiped out the entire town.

With that in mind, the vacancy of the balcony at the corner of Main and Number 8 bothered Maddox like a premonition. "Scarecrow" was the nickname the cops had given to Sinclair, for his thin, unstuffed frame and his ever-present watchfulness over the center of town, looking down from his balcony like a mannequin of rags and straw. Maddox was turning away from the sight of it when he walked right into Ripsbaugh.

"Kane," said Maddox, startled backward.

"Went back for your deer this morning," Ripsbaugh said.

"Oh, right," said Maddox. He saw again the deer's head crack open beneath his boot. "Thanks."

"Wasn't much left. A hoof, patches of fur and hide. A chunk of leg. The rest was gone."

"Gone?"

"Coyotes. Must have gotten to it overnight. They're all over town this year. Got no fear. Keep chewing holes through the dump fence."

Maddox guessed that there was a Kane Ripsbaugh in every small town in the country. A man indivisible from the landscape, someone you see all the time but never really look at, who would fade away altogether were it not for the rake or shovel in his dirt-browned hands. A constant. A man everybody waves to and nobody knows.

Ripsbaugh stood at about Maddox's height, in a no-brand brown T-shirt, knee-length bleach-spotted beige shorts, and crusted gray work boots with wiry laces untied. His eyes looked less silvery in sunlight, more gray against his dark eyebrows, his mossy hair shaved short like a prisoner's, his hands mittlike and dark with work-toughened nails.

Maddox was also getting the familiar smell of shit, low-grade but pungent enough, that was part of Ripsbaugh's peculiar charm. In addition to running the town's highway department, Ripsbaugh also owned and operated Cold River Septic out of a garage next to his home.

Ripsbaugh nodded, lingering, as though he wanted to say something more. "Heard what you said to those others."

Maddox shrugged. "Just running off my mouth."

"Somebody had to."

"What good it will do."

"You need any help, anything, you know where I am. Town needs reviving."

"That it does, Kane. That it does." Maddox started away, then remembered something. "Hey. Last night when you were driving around, you didn't hear a gunshot, did you?"

"Before yours, you mean?"

Maddox nodded.

"No," said Ripsbaugh, thinking back. "Why?"

Maddox shook his head like it was no big deal. Inside he was frowning at the mystery. "No reason."

7
WANDA

WANDA WAS WEARING A TANK shirt, blue pastel. Used to fit her better, drooping too much under her arms now, giving the boys a piece of profile whenever she leaned the right way. The teasing wink of her cup crease. She looked down to see what else, and on her skinny hips were beige terry-cloth shorts with white racing stripes.

She thought she saw movement in one of his upstairs windows as she came to his driveway. She had wanted to surprise him. That was the whole point of walking all this way. Playing out different seduction scenarios on the walk over. She didn't know why she was fixated. It wasn't even *him*, probably, if she had to be honest. It was her *idea* of him.

The good cop. The incorruptible.

She turned in past the FOR SALE sign. The surface of his driveway was hot as a cookie sheet, so she tread the grass lane next to it, feeling slinky in her bare feet. She followed the flagstones past a big planter in front, where the face of his house angled toward the quiet street. It was pretty isolated, bordering a quarter acre of buggy, high-weed wetlands.

There he was, sitting on the front step. He had seen her coming from the window. She couldn't even sneak up on this guy.

She spread out *ta-da* hands. "Trick-or-treat."

Maddox said, "I think you're a couple of months early."

"This is how I do it. Start early, avoid the Halloween crowds." She liked what her mouth was saying. "Surprised?"

"You could say."

"*Pleasantly* surprised?"

"Surprised."

"What if I told you I'm here to open my heart to you? To bare my everlasting soul."

He had on a great-looking, soft green cotton tank shirt, hanging off his thick shoulders and chest. His shorts were knee-length, his calves hairy but not furry. He sat half in and half out of shadow, leaning back against one of the narrow pillars. Almost guarding his house from her. She felt powerful and feared, and it made her smile.

"You're drenched," he said.

"I looked a lot better when I started out."

"What's with the wristbands?"

She wore two big ones together on her left arm. No pain today, at least not right now. "It's a look," she said. She was proud of her skinny limbs. "I think I burned some new freckles into my shoulders." She moved the straps to check, giving him a little peek inside.

"Your feet okay?" he said.

She wiggled her toes. They were filthy, and worse inside the cracks. She saw a little blood around her left heel, nothing to get excited about. "I walked a long way," she said, working a smirk. "You should be flattered. I started out in these flip-flops, but the thong thing was cutting into my toe cleavage, killing me."

"Toe cleavage?"

"Don't pretend you don't know what that is. I passed this yard, and there was this little bike, pink with tassels? The kind I always wanted as a girl. Though maybe I shouldn't be telling this to a cop."

"You shouldn't be telling it to anyone. You stole a little girl's bicycle?"

"I borrowed it, who do you think I am? Not my fault if the chain snapped." She chewed on a cuticle, what was left of her fingernail. "I was going to bring it back."

"You walked barefoot all the way here from Bucky's house?"

She put her hand on her hip. "Didn't take long for *him* to come up. Jesus. Like talking to a guy who only wants to talk about your best friend or your sister or something. Except in this case, it's my *guy* he's obsessed with."

"You don't stay over at Bucky's?"

"You know I don't."

"I must have forgot."

"No, you didn't. You wanted to make your point that he doesn't treat me right."

"He's a private guy that way."

"And what's wrong with that?"

"I don't know. You think he has someone else?"

"He's a Black Falls cop. What do you think?"

"And that's fine with you."

"Maybe I got somebody else too." She tried to wink at him but she had never been very good at winking. "Hey, if I wanted to be married to someone, I'd be married, right? We have something different from that. Something deeper."

"I'll bet those are his words exactly."

"Like partners. Maybe he chases it on the side, but he can only catch so much. I know he doesn't bring it home with him. No one gets inside his place 'cept me. Why I captivate you so."

"What's he do up there on his mountain, he needs so much privacy?"

She moved to the short stone patio before the brick step. "Kiss me and I'll tell you everything you want to know."

Maddox smiled in that way he had, of appraising her, which made her frown and sent her back to working on her nail.

"You seem a little hyped up," he said. "You eat anything today?"

"I had a Popsicle."

"That's not food."

"Oh, sorry. See, the food stamp people got me and Daddy on this strict twenty-four-dollars-a-month diet." She tried out a wide, dirty grin. "You want to take me inside, *feed* me something?"

"I don't think so."

She scratched the itch on the back of her neck. "You are such a drag, you know that? It's just rude, not inviting me inside. Why you so hot for Bucky?"

"I'm not."

"So hot for him instead of me."

"Give me a break."

"So secretive all the time. Talk about privacy." She shifted posture, her bare knees rubbing. "You're playing me. You think I don't know it."

"Then that means that you're playing me."

"No. Because I don't play."

"You said you and Bucky are partners. Partners in what?"

"Partners in life."

"Uh-huh."

"You know, he was a new cop when I met him. Just like you. Used to cruise by me in his patrol car when I was walking home from school. Kept offering me rides, until I took him up on it." She smiled. "He liked it on the hood of his patrol car. He was into being a cop when it was new. What about you? You into it still?"

"I'm not that into it."

She looked him over. "You're into it, all right. What is it you do there all night at the station by yourself, anyway?"

"Fight crime."

She snickered. "You're a bad boy. You are. Act all good, but you're bad inside, I can see it. You do bad things."

That hit something in him. Something real. She watched his eyes narrow, and was surprised.

"Maybe your bedroom's air-conditioned," she said. "We could go talk in there."

"No."

"What are you so afraid of?" She took another step closer to him, her bare feet touching the smooth stone landing, just now starting to feel the day's journey in her soles. "You know you don't come around me just for the questions."

"No?"

"No. The way you look at me sometimes. Not now. Today you're being kind of a dick. But other times."

Maddox looked out at the overgrown marsh his house faced, the weeds humming with bugs. "I guess maybe you remind me of some-one."

She was shocked to get any water out of this stone. "All right. Now it comes out. Now we're getting somewhere. Not your mother, I hope."

"Are you kidding me?"

"First love? College sweetheart? Old girlfriend?"

"Just someone I knew."

"And she's dead now?"

He showed surprise at her insight. Even Wanda was a little impressed with herself.

"So come on, then," she said, moving closer still. His sneakers were flat on the landing, his bent legs bunching up his package in between. She reached out and touched his bare knee. "Let's start up the old air conditioner. Go for a spin on my pink bike. What do you say?"

Maddox stood, a head taller than she, so that her hand fell from his knee. "I have to get ready for work now."

"It's personal, this thing between you and Bucky. I can tell. So what better way to fuck him over?" She reached for his shorts over his thighs, wanting to run her hand up inside.

Maddox shook his head. "It's not like that."

"Of course it is. The ultimate get-back. You can't fuck him so you fuck the one he fucks. Believe me—he would jump all over your girl. If you had one."

Maddox's hand guided hers away from his shorts with a firm grip. "Maybe you don't realize what an ugly thing that is to say."

Wanda could only smile at the chill she felt, brought on by her discovery. "You *do* have a girl?"

Maddox reached out and pulled the sunglasses off her face. It was confusing because she had forgotten she was even wearing sunglasses, and so the change in light disoriented her. A pair she had borrowed from Bucky, too big for her face.

"Good Christ," said Maddox.

"Give those back."

"When was the last time you slept?"

She squinted, nearly blind, the day so bright. "Sleeping alone is so boring."

"Look at me."

She couldn't. Her eyes were stinging and watering over.

He handed back her glasses. She put them on and waited until she could see him good again. He was looking at her forearm. The sweatbands. He reached for her wrist, and she pulled back before he could touch it.

He didn't like that.

"You listen now," he said. "Don't ever come to my house again. But especially don't think you can hit up and then come by. That's not how I live here. You want me to bust you right now?"

"Oh, that would be good. Yeah, go ahead. Rookie cop busting his sergeant's girl."

"You want to talk, and I mean *talk,* you page me. You have the number. Otherwise you wait for me to get in touch with you. Understood?"

"Understood," she said back at him, with sixth-grade petulance. She took out some aggression swatting at a fly buzzing around her head. "So, what, am I even going to get a ride back home?"

He looked at her like she knew better.

"Hard-ass," she said. "Can I at least use your bathroom first?

I'm serious, the toilet's stopped up at my dad's. The plumbing quit—*I'm serious*. He dug a latrine outside last night. Don't make me pee in the woods. Pretty please? You can wait out here, where it's safe."

Maddox stepped aside. "Make it fast," he said.

She curtsied and flipped him off and walked up the steps past him.

8
TRACY

TRACY MITHERS SAW Donny Maddox out in front of his house, so she left her pickup in the driveway rather than use the remote garage door opener he had given her. She followed the flagstones to where he waited with his hands in his pockets, a tank shirt baring his arms, shorts baring his legs.

My man.

Seeing him at the parade that morning and not being able to talk to him was murder, and how the day had dragged on since. The hours she stole each week to be with him were her life now. The rest of the time was just waiting. She wanted to bound up to him and leap into his arms, but something about the way he was standing outside alone in the sun slowed her.

"What's wrong?" she said.

He shook his head, a strange look on his face, a tension. He glanced at his screen door. "Nothing's wrong," he said. "But I don't know if you'll agree."

"Okay," she said, still smiling but confused. "What does that mean?"

"Remember what I said to you when we first started this? That I would be straight with you? That I would never lie to you, no matter what?"

She remembered, all right. They had been in his bed. He had been studying her hand, fingers entwined with his. He had kissed the underside of her wrist, her beating pulse.

He said, "I promised you that, right?"

Now she was getting scared. "Yes."

His screen door opened and a woman stepped out, wiping wetness from her chin as though she had just slurped water from a sink tap.

A bomb went off. The planet cracked open with a tremendous, shuddering roar, and Tracy stood in a deep crater of earth now, the heated air buzzing around her with smoke and steam.

The woman saw Tracy and stopped. They recognized each other.

Oh my God.

Wanda Tedmond.

"Ha," said Wanda, stopping. "What do you know?" She looked at Donny with surprise that, by the time she looked back at Tracy, turned mocking. "Tracy Mithers, right? The llama girl."

Tracy stared at the skinny girl's filthy bare feet.

Wanda walked down the steps and across the stone landing to the grass. "I helped myself to some water, hope that was okay."

She was talking to Donny. Familiar with him.

Her toes were wide-spaced and short and ugly. The nails were unpainted and ground down. The dirt around the bottoms of her heels looked congealed with blood.

Wanda said to him, "You should have told me you were expecting someone."

Her collarbone stood out like a hanger on which her overwashed blue tank top hung, her bony legs rising into beige, Juniors-department Adidas shorts with white piping held up by no hips at all. She wore sweatbands on her forearms like she was a rapper, and a pair of men's sunglasses sat perched on the bridge of her nose, chrome-rimmed, wide and obnoxious on her underfed face.

Tracy looked at Maddox. He looked right back at her.

"Tomboy cutoffs," Wanda said, eyeing Tracy. She wasn't at all flummoxed by the awkwardness of their encounter. "The farm girl look. That works, huh? Once you scrub all that llama shit off your knees, I guess."

The artlessness of the insult stunned Tracy. They had no history

Tracy was aware of, good or bad, none at all. If she was exacting revenge, it was not at Tracy's expense: it was at Donny's. And that shocked Tracy even more.

"Anyways," said Wanda, "I wouldn't want to intrude. Just stopped by to say hi." She smiled at Donny and started away, passing a few steps wide of Tracy. "Bye."

Closer, the more hideous Wanda appeared to Tracy. Skinny verging on frail, her hair a sweaty, mustardy mess, making her look drowned. Her limp boobs were barely covered by the stringy tank; Tracy saw ribs pressing through its sides. And she had sores. Like pimples but without whiteheads on them. Scratch marks on her neck.

Say something.

"See you around," said Tracy. Not brilliant, but sort of cutting.

"Oh, definitely," said Wanda, with a quick little smile back at Tracy that said, *Game on, slut.*

Wanda walked away with her head angled down, knowing her skinny backside had an audience. She reached the FOR SALE sign and turned the corner.

No car. Barefoot, no shoes in her hands. No handbag, no pockets, even. Wanda Tedmond had walked all this way without any money or keys. *For what?*

Tracy waited many moments before turning back to Donny. She wanted to say something poised. Her heart was pounding in her ears.

"Well," she said. "That was a surprise."

Donny was nodding. "For me too."

"Really."

"Entirely."

"Hm," she said through tight lips, trying to keep from shaking. She kept swallowing, to calm herself, looking out toward the wetlands but not seeing anything.

Donny said, "She asked to use the bathroom."

"For what, to shoot up drugs in there?"

"What do you know about shooting drugs?"

"What do you know about having a girl like that inside your house?"

"You notice, I stayed outside."

"Because you knew I was coming."

She might have been yelling. It was a possibility. She stopped speaking for a little while because she did not want to seem hysterical. Her mother was the one who got hysterical.

Tracy felt the sun boring a hole into her. "I only wish you had told me you liked girls that *skinny*. Girls on a sperm-only diet."

Wow. The smile stretching her cheeks felt tight as a strap. The burning in her throat was acid left over from the taste of those words.

Donny retreated to his front step and sat down. His strategy was to try and wait her out.

Tracy said, "Isn't she with Bucky Pail already?"

"I believe so."

"So one Black Falls cop isn't enough for her? Does she want to take on all six at once?"

"This is how women talk about each other when the gloves come off?"

"When one is sniffing around my man? *You bet*."

She then had a wild thought that he was holding back a smile.

"Am I being ridiculous?" she said, her voice getting away from her again. "Do I look ridiculous? Do I look *hysterical*?"

"No. You look pissed, and you have every right."

"You're goddamn right about that, mister." *Mister?* She nodded like she had won the argument. "*Goddamn* right about that." She folded her arms and walked in a neat little circle. "So what are you going to tell me? This has something to do with work?"

"That's right."

"Her walking halfway across town barefoot to your house. On a Saturday afternoon. Uninvited?"

"Completely uninvited."

She was the cop now, checking his eyes for lies. Breaking down his alibi. "But you won't tell me why."

"I don't know why."

She stopped. "Come *on*."

"I did not invite her here. I don't know why she showed up."

Tracy threw her hands out at him. "How do you know her at all? You're a Black Falls cop. An auxiliary patrolman, part-time!" The pounding surged inside her again. "Fine. Then why do you *think* she came here, to you, today, this hour?"

"Honestly? For sex. And possibly air-conditioning."

Tracy kept staring. The thought was so repulsive to her, she needed to show him how much it hurt by baring her wound. "And what about me?" she said. "Is that what I come here for?"

He very wisely declined to answer that.

"She was inside your *house*," said Tracy. "That no-ass *trash*."

Tracy remembered when Wanda repeated eleventh grade and wound up in some of Tracy's study periods and gym class. How she was always being sent to the office. A hard girl with hashed-up hair and an underage, oversexed snarl, who made out with boys between classes, right there in the hallway. When Wanda dropped out for good halfway through the year, every single girl in Tracy's class sighed with relief.

"So she's poor," Tracy said. "And we're all supposed to feel sorry for her. But, God—I could *loan* her a bra if she needs one. I work. I might get my knees rough working around a barn, but I don't need to live off a man."

He nodded, infuriating her.

"And me, stupid me—I was coming here to apologize to *you*. For my mother this morning. For the way she lumped you in with the rest of the cops in town." She shook her head. "It's proof anyway that my mother doesn't know anything about us. No one did—until today. Until Wanda fucking Tedmond. But, whatever."

It was stupid. The afternoon was ruined, the day was ruined, everything was ruined. When Tracy got disappointed like this, she always thought of her mother, who was the queen of disappointment. She remembered her scowling at Donny that morning.

"What did Pinty mean? 'If I can take it, you can too'?"

"What?" Donny said.

"This morning. See, sometimes when I sign for my mother, people talk around me like I'm deaf too. To keep you from going after the Pails, he said, 'If I can take it, you can too.' Take what?"

"I can't really get into it."

"No, of course not. Because of how *critical* your part-time police work in Black Falls is. I'm sorry, Donny, but this is bullshit. It's *crap,* this whole thing. Skinny cop-sluts coming out of your house in the middle of the day? Your truth-only pledge, which lets you dodge all the questions you don't want to answer? That's so convenient for you."

"You have every right to be angry—"

"Stop agreeing with me!"

"I've been up front with you all along. I've said the whole time, once I sell this house—"

"You're leaving, good-bye. I know it. I'm shrill."

She had lost herself in this relationship, happily, purposefully, using it to escape from everything else in her life. Over these past few months she had felt herself growing in ways and at speeds beyond anything she had ever experienced.

Best of all, it was an affair. A beautiful secret. She had a *man.*

Now the fact that he had become so much in her life so fast scared her. He was the only good thing she had, and what would that mean once he went away?

She was pissed off, she was scared, and yet . . . she still wanted to believe him. "I don't understand," she said, "why everything has to be so undercover with you."

His patient look vanished then. Almost like she had offended him somehow.

But bitching at him wasn't going to get her anywhere. This much she had learned from her mother, from her parents' divorce.

"I can't do this right now," she said. It was only dinner they had planned, because he was working an overnight. But still: saying this took great courage. "I can't stay. Don't you see?"

"Stay," he said. "Stay and talk."

She shook her head. "I can't. I need to think, or something."

Huge and scary, walking away from him like that. She was punishing him, yes, but she was also, if he could see it, demanding respect. A drastic move, but not a deal breaker. Not a relationship ender.

She hoped.

As she drove off in her old Ford, gripping the steering wheel, this seemed like just a preview of coming attractions. How it was going to end between them for good. Which made Tracy realize, for the umpteenth time, just how far she had fallen for him.

9
HEAVEY

"I KEPT THE BOYS OUT of the pool today," said Heavey, standing over Maddox's shoulder. "I'll tell you, it wasn't easy."

"I appreciate it," said Maddox.

Maddox, in his cop shirt and cap, squatted over the impression in the dirt near the aboveground swimming pool. The rest of the back-yard was grass, but the boys had worn out a track between the small skateboard ramps and the pool ladder.

Heavey said, "It's a sneaker, right? Adult size."

Heavey could tell by the outline of the tread, the way it was bro-ken with notches. The center of the tread had not made an imprint. Heavey brought out his two pairs of sneakers, as well as Gayle's walk-ing shoes, to prove he wasn't crazy.

With the sun going down, Maddox brightened the impression with his flashlight beam. Marks before and after it indicated tracks from the treeline along the right side of the yard to the rear of the house. Heavey said, "Ground dried up a bit today with the heat."

"Muggy last night," said Maddox, eyeing the edge of the forest. "No AC in my patrol car. Your house air-conditioned?"

"Not centrally. We've got a unit in the bedroom window. I keep it on Economy and it cycles on and off. Does the job."

"It cycled on soon after you heard the shot?"

Heavey remembered now, how after going around checking on the boys and double-checking doors and windows, he had jumped when the box started up again in his bedroom. "In fact it did."

Maddox straightened and took in the yard in the dying light. Heavey tried to see what he saw, with a visitor's eyes. The alligator float drifting in the pool, the safety-netted trampoline, the T-ball stand, the swing set, the three matching electric cars.

"Guilty as charged," Heavey said.

"What's that?"

"Spoiling three boys. We tried not to, but I guess it's having all our kids in one shot. Treating them equally."

"I was just thinking how private it is here. The land between the homes."

"Summer leaves make it more so. Why?"

"Nothing's missing, right?"

"No, not a thing. The boys would know, believe me. If one doesn't have something that the other two have, it's Armageddon."

Heavey followed Maddox's eye back to the house. Three orange heads ducked below the sill of the upstairs den window. His boys loved to play spies.

Maddox moved toward the house alongside the approximate foot trail. Grass grew sparsely around the foundation, despite Heavey's repeated attempts at seeding—something about drainage, too much sand in the soil.

Maddox used his beam on the ground. Right outside the boys' bedroom, he illuminated what could have been the toe half of another imprint. As from someone standing on the balls of his feet.

Maddox sized up the window while Heavey, alarmed, watched his reflection in the glass. "All right if I . . . ?"

"Go ahead," said Heavey, and Maddox cupped his hand over his eyes, careful not to touch the window as he peered inside. Heavey explained, "We knocked down a wall to make one big room so all three boys could be together."

"Your boys sleep with a night-light?"

"A desk lamp, dimmed low."

Maddox kept looking. "And you're sure it was a woman you saw?"

"Yes. Back a couple of weeks ago now."

"If it was night, how did you know it was a woman? Could you see her face?"

"Here's what it was. I heard something outside, or maybe just felt something was wrong, one of those parental things. I came down to check on the boys, and as I open up the door, I can see something moving outside the window. Running away. I tripped over toys, getting to the window just in time to see her disappearing into the trees. Dressed all in black, thin, with long dark hair."

"A black dress?"

"No. More like a sweat suit or something."

"And sneakers."

"Apparently."

"But it could have been a man in a wig."

"Well—Jesus Christ."

"It couldn't have been?"

Heavey became flustered, unable even to consider it. "What I saw was a woman."

Maddox turned his flashlight beam at an angle to the window. He breathed onto the cooling glass, his warm breath revealing a few smudges and handprints. But all boy-sized.

"Neat trick," said Heavey.

Maddox turned and ran his beam over the yard to the forest, inside which it was already night. "This person ran into the trees. Where?"

Heavey showed him. Maddox skimmed his flashlight beam over the ground, but browned pine needles and last autumn's leaves obscured any footprints. "Boys play army in here," said Heavey. "I don't know if I'd build a house on the edge of a forest again. You have kids?"

Maddox shook his head, looking back at the house, then circling to the right, just inside the perimeter. He kept checking the house, maybe looking for a good view of it from the trees.

Heavey said, "Real sorry to hear about your mother. She had a fall?"

"She had been sick for a while. Her lungs. Medication made her unsteady."

"Stairs?"

"Bathroom floor."

"Most dangerous room in the house. I lost my mother two years ago this September, to viral pneumonia. I was the baby of the family. Your mother was insured?"

"Enough to cover the burial."

"Good for her. I tell you, most people around here, they've either forgotten or never learned how to plan for the future. They got no cushion in their lives. Living day to day."

Maddox found a good vantage point on the house, almost in line with the sneaker treads heading past the skateboard ramps. He scoured the ground with his flashlight beam, toeing at the soft forest floor. Heavey thought he saw something illuminated, white and small.

Maddox became very still, focusing his beam on this tiny object. Not as thick as a smoked-down cigarette butt, unless maybe it was the hand-rolled kind. It seemed important until, suddenly, with his hiking boot, Maddox scattered whatever it was back among the dead leaves, clicking off his light.

10
ZOO LADY

THE UPSTAIRS DOORBELL rang a fifth time, and Horton and Glynda scrambled back onto the front windowsill to scratch at the glass. Norman howled in despair from his pillow bed, unable to get up due to his leg splints. Felicia, the lamp-shade-collared beagle, fretted back and forth along the kitchen floor, *trot-trot-trot,* while Carlton, one of two skinny ex–racetrack greyhounds, sat up on the tea-rose-colored sofa and rhythmically sniffed the air. Belouis, a three-legged Canadian hairless, rolled onto his back on top of the refrigerator and caterwauled.

Penelope and Vernon would tear down her already shredded curtains unless somebody answered the front door. Miss Beverly shushed them to no avail, finally turning down Bill O'Reilly and shuffling through the living room to her door. She didn't realize she was barefoot until she was already out on the old black-and-white diamond tile of the entranceway, squeezing through with only two cats—Lucinda and Raoul—escaping.

She hated her damaged feet, her blunted toes and the perpetual bruising over the arch. The town knew her only as the Zoo Lady, foster mother to a menagerie of abandoned and rescued animals, but in her former life, she had been a dancer, and a great one. She had owned apartments in both Manhattan and Paris. She had hoofed on Broadway, and never in a chorus line. She had toured all of Europe, declined marriage proposals from four separate men, and once dined with a prince. She had danced for George Balanchine and with Gene Kelly. She had affairs with two movie stars, only one of which she regretted.

It was a policeman, and he had seen her there, and it was too late to go back inside for her shoes now, not with all the yipping and scratching at the door behind her. Impossible to keep a pair of slippers with all the gnawers in the house, which was why she stored her $750 orthopedic shoes in the refrigerator. A crazy-lady thing to do, she realized, but better that than allow them to become two very expensive chew toys.

If this young gentleman was the one who would someday break in and find her gone on to her final reward, he would also discover, along with the shoes, her last will sealed in plastic in the freezer. And her two-volume autobiography, neatly typed on four reams of rose-scented paper, light on scandal but heavy on a life of accrued knowledge, Part One in the meat drawer and Part Two in the crisper.

She had once read a newspaper story about an elderly shut-in found a week after her death, her hungry cats feasting upon her body. In fact, Miss Beverly thought that would be quite all right with her. She never had a little baby of her own to feed. She only hoped she tasted good enough.

She was not surprised to see a policeman at the door, nor foolish enough to ask why. She had considered herself fortunate, after a decade of declining health and ruinous investments, to find a landlord sympathetic to her animal ministry. Of course, Mr. Sinclair could little afford to complain, given that he had been compelled by law to disclose his probationary status as a convicted child molester to all prospective tenants. So the rent was low and her infirm pets tolerated.

She pulled open the front door just a few inches, so that no one would escape into the night.

No, she answered the policeman, she hadn't seen Mr. Sinclair at all today. Though she had heard his footsteps earlier, upstairs. But nothing for a few hours now.

He seemed angry, yet paid her the courtesy of politeness, which was not often the case anymore. People today felt justified in their anger and their right to broadcast it around.

He was handsome enough, in an American way. She could still notice these things. She hoped he would be the one who would eventually find her.

"No, no message," he said, stepping back for another look up at Mr. Sinclair's black-curtained windows. "I'll stop back some other time."

11
FROND

FROM THE OUTSIDE, the Gas-Gulp-’N-Go looked like a bait shack with two old-fashioned fuel pumps in front. Inside, it didn’t look much better. Nightcrawlers in Styrofoam cups of soil were stocked next to the butter and cream in the back coolers. The newly repealed Massachusetts blue laws meant that the liquor cabinet was no longer chained on church day. The Gulp was the only place in Black Falls where you could buy your milk, bread, newspaper, cigarettes, lottery, booze, and porn. A startling amount of porn, shrink-wrapped magazines and boxed VHS movies pasted with happy-face stickers to cover offending penetrations while leaving the rest of the image intact.

Randall Frond bumped the wire carousel as he passed it, the porn rack creaking guiltily. He was the only one in there, having just made it before the store’s nine o’clock closing. Frond had a cold. He had tried his usual homeopathic herbal remedies—eucalyptus oil, ginger root, yarrow leaf, and elm bark—but found he couldn’t sweat it away. So here he was, reduced to searching for off-the-shelf cold medicine, the taking of which went expressly against his New Age philosophy. But that’s how bad he was plugged up. The last time he’d swallowed a Sudafed, in college during finals week, he had the craziest dreams in his life. Something that messes with your brain chemistry like that can’t be any good for you. His girlfriend at the time saved his GPA by brewing him some cinnamon honey tea and feeding him echinacea and raw garlic.

And now, as he prepared to violate his closely held principles for the sake of his sinuses, what did he find before him but empty shelves. Plenty of liquid remedies, Robitussin and NyQuil, but no Sudafed, no Contac, nothing with enough punch to clean out the wad of wet cotton inside his head. Summer colds were the worst.

He brought a bag of Halls drops—their paltry 5.6 milligrams of menthol would have to do—to the front counter, where the owner of the Gulp, the man known as Big Bobby Loom, waited. Frond asked about the Sudafed and received a surly shrug.

Loom said, looking at him over the bag of cough suppressants, "You're the witch, right?"

It wasn't a term Frond cared to deny. Only in its modern connotations was it inaccurate. "That's right," said Frond.

Loom took his money and made change and said not another word.

Feeling worse now than when he had walked in, Frond exited through the swinging door. That's what he got for staying in a town this size; everybody knew everybody else's business.

He was almost at his Jeep when headlights pulled in off Main. Frond made out the light rack on the roof of the patrol car, and slowed near the ice chest, cornered. He wanted to avoid another costly go-round with the Pail brothers. Bogus speeding tickets had already wiped out his "Safe Driver" steps and raised his insurance rate three hundred dollars.

The cop parked right next to his car. Frond saw that it was the new hire, the one they called Maddox. He felt a dash of relief, but kept moving just the same, pulling open his unlocked door. He trusted none of them.

Frond had moved up here seven years ago. Sick of the pace and cost of living in the real world, and in an effort to renounce consumerism, he gave away his television and most of his possessions and retreated to a stone-and-timber house. He subsisted now on Internet sales of New Age paraphernalia and as an online broker—his 56K dial-up modem demanded Zen-like patience—for a consortium of potters and weavers in the hills of Mitchum County.

But the modern world didn't like losing even one consumer. That was the only way he could explain his recent turn of bad karma. One good deed had begat a chain of punishments and tiny agonies.

He was fishing his keys out of his shorts pocket when Maddox came around, asking, "Everything all right?"

He started up the engine. Something uneasy about this one. Not an evil vibe, as from the others, but a strange one. He struck Frond as a watcher, as a seeker, and Frond was usually right about people.

Maddox said, "You looked a little spooked when I pulled up."

"Did I?" said Frond, swiping at his nose. Fear worked as well as cayenne in loosening up the nasal passages. "No, just the bright head-lights."

"I thought it might be the sight of the patrol car. I heard you had some run-ins with other members of the department."

Harassment was the legal term for it. Intimidation was the purpose. Ever since he had passed Bucky Pail beating up a man in hand-cuffs by the side of the road. What did it matter that Dillon Sinclair, the sex offender, was the one getting smacked around? Frond did what any good citizen of the world would do: he filed a complaint with the county through the state police. Now he worried every time he left his house.

Maddox said, "If you feel that some members of the police force are overstepping their authority, you should come forward."

"I think I tried that, didn't I?" What was this? Using the new guy to get to him? "They want to punish me until I move, and they might just get their way. You're not so new that you can't know. I'm not the only one who's scared."

The swinging door slapped shut behind Maddox, Big Bobby Loom locking up for the night. He looked them over talking together, then turned and swayed toward his white Fairlane parked around the side.

Why was Frond bothering? When would he learn to keep his mouth closed around Black Falls cops? He shifted his Jeep into gear. "I'm no crusader. Not anymore. State police promised me they'd do something." He was pulling away. "I'm still waiting."

12
TRACY

T RACY COULDN'T SLEEP.

    She didn't want to call, but lying there in the dark wasn't getting her anywhere, thinking hard and not sleeping, so she picked up the phone. The green-backlit number pad was the only light in her room as she dialed three numbers.

"Nine-one-one. What's your emergency?"

"Yes, well . . . there's this guy I've been seeing for about four months, okay?"

"Ma'am?"

"Actually, four months, six days, twenty-two hours. Give or take a few minutes."

"Go ahead."

"Well, today I stopped by his house and I caught him with this total low-rent hoochie."

"You say a hoochie?"

"Big-time hoochie."

"Ma'am, this line is intended for emergencies only."

"This is an emergency, or it was—for me, anyway. There was an altercation, but it was mostly verbal. Actually, it was mostly me."

"Anyone hurt?"

"Not really, no. I tried to inflict some emotional damage, but as usual it totally backfired. So now I'm home all alone, stressing out that I embarrassed myself beyond repair."

"I'm sure that's not the case. I bet you behaved admirably well under the circumstances."

"I just wanted you to know. I'm not mad."

"Good."

"But I'm no pushover either. I'm no doormat."

"Okay."

"But leaving you that way, us parting the way we did . . . that hurt the most. That felt really shitty. I don't ever want to do that again, okay?"

"Okay."

"Okay. What are you doing now? I picture you sulking the night away."

"I'm reading. While I sulk."

She pushed herself up on her pillow. "That same war book?"

"Volume three. Marching toward Appomattox."

"Do you think it's weird that people have favorite wars?"

"I guess I do, yeah."

"I'd say Revolutionary War people are optimists. Birth of a nation and all that. Brightly colored uniforms, fireworks in the sky—right? World War Two people, they seem sort of downbeat. Drab and tough and dirty. We won, but at what cost? Realists. But Civil War people— I would say we are humanists. You know, brother against brother, a nation divided. People interested in people, in their fellow countrymen."

"And slow readers."

"That too. Did you bring lunch? Since we never actually ate, I thought maybe I could—"

"I did bring something, yeah."

She shook her head in the darkness of the room, pushing past his reluctance. "Well, do you want some company when you take your forty? A midnight lunch, like the first time—"

"I can't. Not tonight."

She lay very still in order that he wouldn't hear the pillow crunching or the mattress creaking or any other sounds of distress. "You have to be somewhere later?"

"I do."

"Okay," she said. She moved her head a little, just to clue him in. "And I'm not going to take that the wrong way. I'm not going to over-react."

"Good."

"I'm definitely not going to think you're meeting Wanda."

"You know I'm not."

"Of course I do." She let some silence play. "Of course."

"The badge and the gun, they mean something in a town full of nothing. To some people. That's all that is."

Not me, she thought. She wished he would take them both off, and for good. She pictured him there at the station with his book open on his lap, wondering why he bothered with her at all. "Is this humiliating call going to be saved forever on tape?"

"I switched off the recorder when the Sam Lake address came up."

"You're lucky she's so gross, you know. I mean—*lucky*."

"I do know it."

"I can tell by your voice, you're smiling."

"I can tell by yours, you're lying down. In bed?"

"I was worried you were going to try and hand me some bull-shit. Like that she was in trouble or something. Like you were 'help-ing' her."

"What are you wearing?"

"Uh-uh," she said. "No way."

"I can tell by your voice," he said, "you're smiling."

"Just tell me that all this sneaking around is really necessary."

"All this sneaking around is really necessary."

"I don't know how cops' wives do it. I really can't imagine."

"You can't?"

She couldn't believe he had just said that. "Don't play with me. Mr. 'I'll-never-lie-to-you.' Mr. 'I'll-be-brutally-honest-when-it's-time-to-break-your-heart.' "

Across the silence of the phone line, she broadcast her thoughts: *Ask me to go away with you. See how fast I can pack.*

Yet the shame of this secret desire, her guilty ambition, reddened her cheeks. She thought of the barn, the llamas sleeping under the summer moon, and everything she had to do after dawn. But especially her mother, in her bed in the room across the hall. How profoundly the deaf sleep.

13
CULLEN

"SUMMER MORNINGS," said Cullen. "The air, before it heats up? Nothing like it. A gift. This is the only time of year when I don't question what the hell are we doing still living here."

Maddox, taciturn Maddox, sat over his food across from Cullen in the red vinyl booth.

"Must be nice for you these days," said Cullen, pursuing him, "seeing the sun come up. I don't imagine that happened much in your previous incarnations."

Maddox picked apart his omelet with the precision of a laboratory scientist, exposing and extracting cubes of Canadian bacon, chunks of green pepper and mushroom, inspecting each before allowing them into his mouth. "Not really."

Cullen surveyed his own lumberjack special, which had seemed like such a good idea when he ordered it. Now he'd be knocked out all morning, bloated and yawning.

Cullen sponged up some blueberry syrup, washed it down with a gulp of coffee. He looked out the window of the pancake house, cars curling around the rotary and up the highway ramps. Rainfield was a mid-sized town of strip malls, fast food, and on-the-go convenience massed like plaque at the arterial interchange of a north-south interstate and an east-west route. Not much to look at, and even less to visit, but with its Best Buy, Kohl's, chain restaurants, and a six-screen movie theater, to the scratch towns of northern Mitchum County it was a metropolis. The region's Las Vegas.

Most people, when they hear the words "western Massachusetts," think of the rustic Berkshires, wine and cheese on the lawn at Tanglewood, or antiqueing in Stockbridge. But getting out to Norman Rockwell country from Boston means passing through Mitchum County first. It is the only county in Massachusetts without a city. The Cold River Valley is 725 square miles of natural isolation, rivers, hills, farmlands, and old New England. Less visible to the naked eye is the fact that, while per capita crime rates are generally low, domestic ills such as spousal and child abuse, child neglect, single-parent families, and unemployment run high. Towns that rank at the bottom in median income, yet near the top in lottery revenue. A well of desperation hidden deep in the valley, pain-filled voices that go unheard.

Cullen saw Rainfield as an open-air convenience store spread out over miles. A good deal of drug crime happened here, with the associated sordid living and dead-end behavior. This place made the town of Mitchum, the county seat where Cullen lived and worked as a prosecutor of narcotics crimes for the district attorney's office, look quaint and almost clean. The amounts seized in busts here were not large by national standards, nor was the level of drug violence statistically very high. But the devastation to families was the same if not worse.

Heroin came across from upstate New York, pot down from Canada. Cocaine was cheap these days, but currently on the ebb. What surprised Cullen most about what he saw was the effect that market forces had on drug trends. People don't become addicted to a particular drug, he had learned. They become addicted to doing drugs, period, and when conditions such as purity or availability or price change drastically, people will trade one poison for another. Simple as that. No brand loyalty exists when you're dopesick and looking to score.

It would be nice to get on top of things for a change. To be ahead of the curve. They had a real chance here to head off the Next Big Thing before it metastasized and reshaped the landscape.

Maddox wiped his mouth, again sweeping the restaurant with his eyes. Force of habit, Cullen guessed. Meeting with Maddox always put him on edge.

"My boy, Kyle," said Cullen, checking his watch and signaling the server for the check. "A soccer prodigy. Or so I'm told. Great moves, fast feet, everybody telling me, 'Hire a coach, you'll make it all back in scholarships. Groom him.' I'm like, groom him for what? It's *soccer.* Maybe the eighth or ninth most popular sport in the United States, behind Frisbee and probably bowling. Kids have been playing in leagues for two generations now, and it's catching on about as fast as the metric system. Watching him the other day, I figured out why. You know why?"

Maddox shrugged, barely putting forth the effort of humoring him.

"Because Americans don't trust a game where you can't use your hands. A sport that actually *forbids* use of the hands, people can't understand that. 'Pick up the damn ball and throw it in the frigging net!' But he's eight, what does he know? He loves it. So I put him in a camp for the summer. We'll see what happens."

Maddox pulled six jelly packets from the sugar caddy, stacking them and unstacking them like a casino dealer. In terms of exchanging information, these monthly get-togethers were strictly a formality and could have been transacted over the telephone. They met so that Cullen could evaluate Maddox in person. And, as usual, he found himself doing most of the talking.

"Six months now," said Cullen. "Here's the word, and it comes from on high. She believes we will be able to move on this. She *wants* to move on this, sooner rather than later."

"This an election year?"

"Hey—every year is an election year. But don't get on her for that. There's always that part of it, of everything, that's the job. But she is good, and by that I mean, she is a prosecutor. This is a big juicy piece of meat here. She wants to carve it up nice and thick."

"Okay." Maddox nodded, still scanning the joint. "Good."

"But it's not enough yet. The press'll gobble up any bloody thing she throws down for them, but for herself, and for the community at large, she's got expensive tastes. She wants to serve this up right."

"Fine by me."

"I know it's fine by you. It's been six months."

Maddox said, "You're thinking, Hey, it's a small town, make fast work of it. But it's just the opposite. Everybody knows everybody else. That said, things are starting to break open now. I thought I was going to have something for you this morning. Something of consequence."

Cullen waited. "But?"

"But he stood me up last night."

"Okay. What does that mean to you?"

"I don't know. Either of two things. Either something is up with him—or else he's ducking me. Which means that something else is up."

"Where can he go, right? Small town. He has to turn up."

Maddox shrugged, leaving it at that.

Cullen said, "They want me to revisit with you the hardware."

"Look," said Maddox, firm but not agitated. "It's not that I have anything against it. No one's frisking me or anything like that. It's just unnecessary. They don't discuss anything in front of me. This isn't like before, when I'm a party to illegal activity. I'm just a snoop here. But what I get, when I get it, will be better than words on a wire. It will be evidence, hard and fast."

"You're that sure."

"Why not?"

"I don't know. You think another thirty days?"

"I hope." He sat back, extending his arm over the top of the booth. "Don't think I'm enjoying myself here."

Cullen looked him over again. Maddox smelled confident, a big change from when they started. "What about you? They'll want to know I asked."

Maddox soured the way Kyle did when Cullen made a show of

touring the mowed lawn before paying out his allowance. His arm came back off the booth, his shoulders tight again. Tired of being checked up on all the time. "How am I, you mean?"

"How are you, I mean."

"How do I seem?"

"Tired. Frustrated. Impatient."

"That's about right," Maddox said, and then he was out of the booth, moving with surprising speed to the door.

14
VAL

HER DOORBELL NEVER RANG, but when it did, on this particular afternoon, the door opened back fifteen years.

"Donny," said Valerie Ripsbaugh, seeing him in the doorway with the haze of late-day heat behind him. She recognized him instantly, but not because he hadn't changed. There was more of him now, and in all the right places. As though the skinny boy she knew in high school had been ingested by this man.

With fifteen years rushing up on her, she looked down at herself. Red plaid pajama pants with a hole in the knee, flat-soled flip-flops, and a loose cranberry jersey. What he must have been thinking as he compared the Valerie Sinclair of yesteryear to the Val Ripsbaugh of today. She looked away, wishing he would too.

"Val," he said. "How have you been?"

Most people, she didn't care. She had let herself go a long time ago. But Donny Maddox, he was the one mirror she could not pass. In him she felt a sort of death. Though they had only been academic rivals, never boyfriend and girlfriend, Donny more than any other person had defined Val's high school years.

"If you're looking for Kane," she said, "he's gone." She glanced over at the fenced-in septic service garage adjacent to their yard, the reason why all the window fans in her house faced out.

"No," he said, "I came to talk to you."

Only then did it occur to her that something might have happened to Kane. She always thought of her husband as vulnerable to nothing and no one except her. "Is it Kane? Is everything okay?"

"Oh—yes." He reached up for his cap as though he had forgotten he was wearing the team uniform. Seeing him dressed as a local cop was so wrong. "Everything's fine."

Her reaction did not go quite as far as disappointment—she wasn't that callous—but it was something like readiness, a borderline eagerness, which was close enough. *I could sell the house. I could start over. I could be free.*

Donny had kept himself in shape. He had found balance in his life. A few years earlier he would have seen a slimmer Val Ripsbaugh. Always up and down with her. If she wasn't dieting, she was bingeing; if she wasn't exercising, she was sleeping twelve hours a day. She could never get any traction in the middle ground. Yet she never recognized this compulsive behavior for what it was until she was out of one rut and into another.

Donny said, "It's about your brother."

Val nodded, fighting that sinking feeling she got whenever Dill's name came up. "What's he done now?"

"Nothing. That I know of. He's just missing. We usually see him around the center of town, at least up on his porch. But no one has recently."

If Donny was coming inside, she'd have to stash the wineglass in the sink, cap the open jug on the kitchen counter. "He wouldn't come here. If that's what you're asking."

"No, no. Just if you've seen him, or heard anything from him."

"The police need to know where their sex offenders are."

Donny shrugged, allowing that that was the extent of it.

She stepped back, her hand still on the doorknob. "I can't believe it, Donny. I can't believe you're a . . . a *cop.*"

"I know."

"I can't believe you came *back.* You got out. You had a free ride to college. You were *gone.* On *my* scholarship."

She forced a smile to leaven her bitterness, but it didn't work.

In the year of their graduation from Cold River Regional High School, one full scholarship had been offered to the Black Falls senior with the highest cumulative grade point average. Because her tax-cheat father wouldn't open himself up to the scrutiny of a financial aid application, this blind scholarship had been her one and only hope. Val led the class academically until their final semester, when she was edged out by Donny, by exactly one-tenth of one percentage point. Just like that, her art career dreams went up in smoke.

"I heard about your mother," she said. "Sounded like it was awful at the end. I was very sorry. I always liked her." The Sinclairs and the Maddoxes had lived on the same street, Val having moved to Black Falls when she was seven. Single-parent kids, both of them—Val with her crooked father, Donny with his troubled mother—and Val used to fantasize about their parents marrying and Mrs. Maddox becoming her mother and protector. Even into high school, she was always on her best behavior around Donny's mom, on the off chance that, even if she couldn't find a way to fall in love with Val's father, maybe she would fall in love with Val. Maybe enough to want her as her own daughter. "But why have you stayed?"

"Just to sell her house and get her things settled." He smiled a smile that had no meaning behind it. "I'm kind of stuck here until then."

"You've got nothing else out there waiting for you? Where have you been all this time? What've you been doing? We heard rumors."

"Rumors?"

"Town talk, you know. After the way you left. All the promises you made, then broke. Me, I was laughing. I hope I would have had the guts to screw off like you did."

"What rumors?"

"Someone said you'd joined a band. Or that you were in banking or finance or something. Someone said they'd read somewhere that you'd founded one of those Internet companies and made a billion dollars."

He smiled and shook his head, relieved to change the subject. "No, nothing like that. Just bouncing around. What about you? You still draw?"

She huffed out a laugh at her long-ago artistic pretensions.

"What?" he said. "You were good."

"You know how they say that if you really want to make God laugh, tell him your plans? God had milk coming out of his nose every time I opened my mouth about art school."

Donny shook his head. "None of us are the people we hoped we would be. Probably nobody ever is. But you're happy, right?" He leaned back for a look at the house. "You have a home. A husband."

She flashed a quick, hard smile, preferable to flowing tears. She looked down at the thin wedding band cutting into her swollen finger. "So, I don't know where Dill is," she told him. "No idea."

"Okay," said Donny. "Hey, I'm sorry if I . . ."

She shook her head, wanting very much not to say anything she would regret. "I was happy for you, Donny. Really, I was. Crushed for myself. I mean, a B-plus instead of an A-minus, and poof, your future plans are no more. But at least, with you getting away . . . one dove got free, you know? If it couldn't be me. I just—I didn't ever think you'd waste it. But now, fifteen years later, you're here again. It's a little hard for me to see. So don't take this the wrong way, Donny. Please don't take this the wrong way. But I really wish you had never come back."

After closing the door, she stood with her hands trembling in a prayer pose against her nose and lips, then went to refill her glass of wine.

15
BUCKY

THEY CAME UP Old Red Road in the rescue truck, Bucky and Eddie, the box siren whirring out of the roof over their heads. Eddie slowed when he saw Maddox's blues skimming the dark trees, and eased in around the corner.

Twenty bucks extra they were paid each month, the Black Falls Volunteer Fire and Rescue, to keep their town pagers handy night and day. Seven more bucks per call, per hour, on top of that. Because of the overlap in certification training, the police force and fire and rescue were one and the same, the off-duty cops available as on-call firefighters.

Except rookie Maddox. He had not, and as far as Bucky was concerned, would never be invited to join.

Beyond the patrol car, a mustard gold Subaru wagon sat steaming. It had punched straight into a broad tree trunk, its hood mashed like a broken fist. The impact had brought a heavy limb down on the roof, and gasoline from the fuel line was puddling into the road, streaked green with antifreeze.

The pumper truck came up behind them and Eddie hopped out, him and Mort taking the ice ladder down off its hooks in order to flip open the side compartments and pull out the medical cases. Bucky dropped out of the passenger-side door wearing old painter's pants and a ribbed tank shirt, grinding his cigarette butt into the dirt shoulder and spitting into the trees. He reached for a fire extinguisher and a red ax and walked to the car as the other two jogged past him.

Maddox was at the Subaru, trying to talk to the driver and passenger inside. He stepped back as they arrived. "I called the ambulance," he said.

Best-case scenario—nighttime, no traffic tie-ups, drivers who didn't get lost more than once—it was a thirty-minute ambulance run from Rainfield into Black Falls. Leaving Bucky plenty of time.

He checked the hissing engine first, verifying that it was steam rising and not smoke. The windshield had shattered over the crumpled hood and the dash, so that when Bucky unclipped the small flashlight from his belt, its beam shone through an empty frame.

Both front air bags had deployed, hanging empty now, the driver and the passenger dusted in cornstarch from the bags, like mimes that had been in a car accident on their way to the circus. Oak leaves lay among the starch and chunks of glass.

The driver had flipped open the vanity mirror in his visor. His nose was busted, swollen and pulpy, but what bothered him was the glass. He was picking it out of his dusted skin with his fingertips, tenderly removing the shards and arranging them like a row of bloody diamonds on the dash over the radio.

Bucky knew his face but not his name. The passenger too. Wanda had pointed them out to him once. Foster kids, maybe fifteen or sixteen years old. Bucky kept his beam on them so they couldn't make him out, just in case. Glass sparkled in their scalps. He beamed the driver's eyes and the kid's pupils were eight-balled.

"Damn," said the kid, wincing, but never stopping his digging. "Gotta clean it out. They still coming?"

"Who?" said Bucky.

"Them that's chasing us."

Pure paranoia. Bucky watched the kid pluck a large fragment out of his cheek, a layer or two deep inside the dermis, yet show no sign of pain. All this while the one in the passenger seat whimpered softly,

mime tears streaking the powder on his cheeks from the corner of
each eye.

Christ, thought Bucky. It was something to see firsthand. Everything they said about this stuff. Exactly as advertised. No shit.

He felt a surge of omnipotence that was difficult to contain. He
pulled himself away, letting the others work as he backed off upwind
from the fuel spill and sparked another Winston Gold.

Eddie and Stokes readied a c-collar and tried to get the driver to
give up on the glass in his face. Ullard remained at the pumper, hanging on to the side mirror, still wearing sleep boxers and a zipped wind-
breaker, looking very happily shitfaced.

Maddox came up the road, Bucky speaking first to neutralize him.
"Two drunk kids joyriding in a stolen car."

"Drunk?" said Maddox. "You see that kid pulling glass out of his
face?"

"Saw a guy once in a car pinned under a fence, insisted he was still
inside his own garage. Wondered how I got in."

"You see their eyes?"

Bucky talked smoke at him. "Yeah, I saw their eyes. What are you,
a doctor? Snap some accident scene pictures and call in Ripsbaugh to
mop up. Then take off."

But Maddox didn't leave right away. He lingered, looking kind of
funny at Bucky, almost puzzled, like he was thinking something.
Smelling something.

"The fuck are you doing?" said Bucky, his voice raised loud enough
for the others to hear. He blew more smoke his way. "Are you fucking
sniffing on me, you queer motherfuck? The fuck is your problem?"

Maddox stood steadfast in the dissipating haze, resetting himself.
"I have a problem?"

"You do. I am your problem. Remember that."

A school-yard stare, but nothing more. Never anything more,
thought Bucky, Maddox always holding himself back. The brain
inside was always working—but on what?

"Look at you here, pussyfooting around," said Bucky. "Fucking college boy playing cop. You know what I think? I think you ought to be real careful on these shit-shift overnights. Accidents do happen."

"That right?"

"That's fucking right. Like that deer that hit you—you just never know. You're out here all on your own. Long way from civilization. Think about who your lifeline is. Ain't no ambulance." Bucky peeled off a grin. "It's us. It's me. You think about that sometime."

Bucky flicked his cigarette butt at Maddox's boots and walked back to the wreck, where both boys were now out and being strapped to backboards. "Fucking homo," Bucky said to the others. He tossed a look back at Maddox and yelled, "Pictures, camera, snap-snap, let's go!" and stared him back to his patrol car.

"Fucking spook," said Bucky, turning back to the strapped-down boys at his feet. He kneeled and went through their pockets quickly, finding nothing, no IDs. He looked into their faces and would have said something, would have warned them against talking, but their eyes were so far gone with shock and dope that any threat would have been wasted.

He leaned into the car and studied the seat with his flashlight beam, then cracked open the glove and emptied the contents onto the floor. Two small plastic zippered envelopes slid out. Bucky reached in and pocketed them quick, making sure there weren't any more.

Maddox came up with the Polaroid as Bucky stepped back. Bucky watched him snap his pictures, making him feel his presence. Goading him into saying something, making a move. But Maddox worked silently until the ambulance arrived. Bucky caught up with one of the EMTs after they had loaded in the boys. He showed the guy his cop badge.

The EMT said, "It'll be Rainfield Good Samaritan."

"We found a bottle of vanilla schnapps in the backseat there," lied Bucky. "Pretty cut-and-dried."

"Vanilla?" snorted the EMT, not so long out of his teens himself. "Any flavor they don't make that mouthwash in?"

"Kids like their poison sweet. No IDs yet, but we'll track down the parents and phone in the particulars."

"You got it. Have a good one."

Bucky tucked his badge away. "I'll sure try."

16
RIPSBAUGH

RIPSBAUGH PULLED UP on the scene just as Stoddard's mechanic was driving off with the wreck. It looked bad but not fatal. The wound in the tree trunk oozed sap, but it too would survive, though with a good scar.

Maddox stood at his patrol car, arms folded, apart from the layabouts near the pumper and the rescue truck farther up the road. Ripsbaugh pulled around the road flares and angled in next to Maddox's car, silencing the engine and stepping out of the cab. He walked to the back of his truck, his untied bootlaces flicking at his heels.

"Late call," said Maddox, coming over.

Ripsbaugh dropped the rear door. "Usually is."

"Couple of kids, nothing too serious." Maddox glanced at the other cops. "Some glass in the road, along with the fuel."

Ripsbaugh dragged out an open sack of sawdust. He lugged it over and emptied it onto the gasoline spill, then hauled out two buckets of cat litter and shook them on top of that. The blade of his long-handled shovel scraped the pickup bed as he slid it out.

The gas-soaked gravel scooped up like cornmeal and he shoveled it back into the plastic buckets. He kept his head down, working steadily but without haste, as was his manner. He remembered the last car accident he had to clean up—Ibbits, the escaped prisoner—and how Bucky had watched over him as though afraid Ripsbaugh would steal something from the burned wreck. This time Bucky was relaxed, all of them loitering by the pumper, prolonging the accident call into an extra hour's pay.

Ripsbaugh pretended not to notice them, in the same way he generally pretended not to notice anyone, work being a cloak of invisibility he pulled over himself. Ullard was drunk as usual, nodding off against the front tire, and Stokes drew a laugh by kicking him over. Bucky took a drag off a stubby cigarette and, with his patented Pail grin, pretended to launch the lit butt at Ripsbaugh and the fuel-sodden sand.

The others snickered hard. Ripsbaugh continued scraping his shovel like he hadn't noticed.

"Hey, Buck," said Eddie, sitting on the rear bumper of the rescue truck, looking to impress his younger brother. "Remember that high school janitor? The one with the crazy walleye?"

Bucky said, "The one I pulled the firecracker stunt on."

"Every time some freshman girl coughed up her macaroni, he'd come in wheeling his bucket of slosh, sprinkle that odor-eating powder on the mess, and mop it up. Frigging thirty years he was there, mopping up kiddie spew once a week. What a life."

Bucky said, "Seems to me that black folk, when they mop up, usually whistle a happy tune."

The others laughed aggressively, Eddie harder than anyone. "Hey, Kane," Eddie said, emboldened. "Know any tunes to pass the time?"

Ripsbaugh slowed the rhythm of his road scraping to a stop. With both hands resting comfortably on the handle of the shovel, he stood there, looking at them all. Nothing threatening in his manner. Nothing in his face. Just him leaning on his shovel, standing, staring.

Their chuckling petered out, the sneer draining from their smiles, faces going soft and empty. All except Bucky, who kept up his tomcat grin. He didn't back down, but he didn't say anything else either.

Ripsbaugh finished his shoveling and began hauling the heavy buckets back to his truck. Maddox was there and helped him load them in one at a time, the old truck's springy suspension dipping a bit under the weight. Ripsbaugh pulled out a broom and a large paper bag and returned to the roadside by the gouged oak, sweeping up chunks of windshield.

Maddox followed. The cops were packing to leave, trying to rouse Ullard. Maddox said, "Val tell you I stopped by earlier?"

Ripsbaugh said, without looking up or breaking pace, "She did."

"Seemed like I might have upset her. I hope not."

"She upsets easily these days."

"I was looking for Dill."

"She said that. Building up probable cause, I suppose."

Maddox paused. "Building up what?"

Ripsbaugh kept right on sweeping. "I figure you want to get inside his place. Legally, you can't just walk in. Even a sex offender's got rights. So you establish a threshold of suspicion. That's how you build it."

Maddox was interested. "Go on."

"There was a case like this on Court TV a month or so back. You have to get a family member to say that he's missed an appointment, or that someone's worried about his health. Or a neighbor to say he hasn't been cutting his lawn. Make it a public safety issue. That's your in."

"I see," said Maddox. "Probable cause."

"I figured maybe that was what you were going for."

"You a crime buff?"

"I watch all those shows."

The pumper and the rescue truck engines started, backing up beeping into the road, Maddox following the vehicles with his eyes until they pulled away. "Maybe you should have been made cop here, not me."

Ripsbaugh regripped the handle of the broom and swept up the last of the shattered glass, now whistling a slow tune.

17
MADDOX

O N THE MORNING OF Donald Christopher Maddox's second
birthday, February 4, 1974, Sergeant Pintopolumanos was
patrolling the town with Officer Reginald Maddox. Black Falls'
finest rode in pairs back then, as with the logging industry still largely
unregulated and the paper mill in full operation, the department was
twenty men strong and still growing. Maddox's father had come late
to police work, having struggled for seven years at a career selling pre-
fabricated office dividers: cork and wood partitions for the precubicle
age. The last sale he made was to the Black Falls PD. During a tour
of the premises, Sergeant Pinty picked up on the salesman's interest
in police work and invited him to apply for a position. Maddox's
mother, newly pregnant at the time, was won over by the bucolic setting of northern Mitchum County, and three months later the Maddoxes moved from a tiny apartment in the Boston neighborhood of
Readville to a three-bedroom house in Black Falls.

At a little after ten on that February morning, Pintopolumanos and
Maddox came upon a white Cadillac parked under a thin sheet of
snow just off the shoulder at the eastern end of Main Street, less than
one hundred yards from where the road crossed into neighboring
Brattle. Snoring in the driver's seat was a man named Jack Metters, a
lower-echelon hoodlum from East Boston transporting a trunkful of
life sentences in the form of two dozen stolen army machine guns.

Metters awoke to Officer Maddox's window knock, emerging

from his Caddy with a yawn and a smile. He asked the name of the town he was in, and before Maddox's father could even answer, Metters fired a .38 Special five times with his right hand deep in the pocket of his pea jacket, dropping both policemen into the day-old snow.

Metters shed his burning coat, climbed back into his car, and continued on toward Boston, meeting his end less than one hour later in a roadblock shootout with state police.

Officer Maddox alligator-crawled back to his patrol car with two holes in his chest and one in his thigh, and died talking into the dash radio.

Pinty dragged himself off the road, where responding officers found him sitting against a young oak on a blanket of red snow, reporting no pain, only a low-voltage tingling in his toes.

Two rounds had shattered Pinty's hips. The doctors who performed his surgeries told him he would never walk again. Pinty sought a second opinion—his own—and in the summer of 1975 returned to the same tree he had been found under, stepping from the car under his own power and chopping down that young oak with an ax. He milled the wood himself, fashioning his walking stick and topping it with a smooth, silver English grip ordered from a catalog.

Looking at the walking stick now, the nub of it tapping against the toe of Pinty's boot as he sat deep in a big-armed, mission-style chair, Maddox was reminded of Pinty's determination, of the man's strength and pride. The police department was his life's work, as was, by extension, Black Falls itself, and the prospect of bequeathing his legacy to a band of brigands was eating him up inside.

"Cancers," Pinty said, after Maddox's recap. "Got to carve them out with a knife. Cut them right out of our own goddamn belly."

Maddox sat facing him on a skirted, powder blue sofa. Mrs. Pinty's China dolls smiled from their display shelves in the formal living room, the collection untouched since her death. Maddox had stopped by after his shift, early enough to find Pinty with his breakfast napkin still tucked inside his collar, but not so early that he didn't have his hairpiece in place. Pinty's modest fluff of vanity was a decade old now, a shade or two darker than his existing silver fringe.

Pinty was in the process of converting his house for first-floor living. Maddox saw the folded wheelchair hidden behind the sofa.

"Ever heard the term 'formication'?"

Pinty scowled. He was not in a learning mood. "That's when a man and a woman . . ."

Maddox smiled. "It's the sensation of insects creeping beneath your skin."

"That's something they need a name for?"

"Causes you to pick at your own flesh. People get obsessed, they wind up tearing apart their face, their arms."

"It was probably just the shock of the crash."

"That's what Bucky said."

Pinty didn't like that, jabbing at the rug with the rubber nub and twisting the handle, as though screwing the cane into the floor.

"Look," Maddox said. "I know you don't want to believe it."

Pinty gripped the fat arm of his chair, Maddox knowing better than to help him get to his feet. Stiff from sitting too long, Pinty hobbled over to the China dolls, as though presenting himself before their glass-eyed innocence. "So, this guff about the schnapps?"

"Cover story. Kids drunk, and now dazed from the crash. He doesn't want them drug tested."

Pinty sagged a bit before the display. "If you're right about all this, Donny . . ."

"It's not about me being right. It's about Bucky going down." Maddox frowned, remembering Bucky's attempt at intimidation at the accident scene, then summarizing the exchange for Pinty. "He basically outlined the Ibbits crash scenario to me."

In October of the previous year, a man living out of a 1989 Ford Escort had died in a fiery, one-car crash way up in the hills above town. By the time the Rainfield Good Samaritan ambulance arrived to take over for Black Falls Fire and Rescue, the blaze had long since burned through the Escort, its driver, and all his belongings.

The wrecking company recovered enough of the VIN number to trace the car back to a California fugitive named Hugo Ibbits, which occasioned a visit to Black Falls from a U.S. Marshal. It turned out that Ibbits was a former chiropractor who, six months before his death, skipped out of Fresno while awaiting trial on malpractice and insurance fraud charges. He had been a prominent player in a complex automobile insurance scam set up to finance the mass production of crystal methamphetamine, of which the ex–Dr. Ibbits was an addict.

After some initial confusion over the exact time line, the marshal was informed that Ibbits had not been held in the Black Falls lockup on a vagrancy charge over the long Columbus Day weekend, as was initially thought, but was released following a traffic stop late Friday afternoon. Witnesses who had claimed to see Bucky Pail handcuff and arrest the driver of a beat-up Ford Escort outside the Falls Diner three days before the late-Monday-night crash later changed their stories. Once the fugitive's remains were proven conclusively to be Ibbits's, the matter was considered closed.

Maddox said, "And another thing. I don't know where Bucky was when his beeper went off tonight. But when I got up close to him, there was this smell."

"Yeah?" grumbled Pinty. "Like corruption?"

"Like ammonia. Or cat piss. Same smell I got when the Zoo Lady pulled open the front door of Sinclair's building."

Pinty turned to him. "You're saying?"

"Well, I finally got a call back this morning from the probation office. Sinclair's caseworker is away on vacation for two weeks. That's why we haven't heard anything about him missing his court-ordered group sessions." Maddox briefly considered telling Pinty about the footprints in Heavey's backyard, the hand-rolled cigarette he had found in the trees. He decided Pinty was red-faced enough as it was. "Zoo Lady hasn't seen him. Says she heard him upstairs. But then again . . ."

"Then again she's the goddamn Zoo Lady."

"The woman sings to her dogs to help them urinate in the street. And she's one of the least crazy people in town."

Pinty discovered his breakfast napkin and pulled it from the neck of his loose-collared, Cuban-style shirt. "You think they got onto him somehow? Maybe decided to finish what they started before that kook Frond got in their way?"

Maddox scowled at the mental image of that fidgety freak Sinclair, reminded once again that the future of the town and Pinty's legacy rode on that skinny pervert's shoulders.

18
FROND

NOISES BROUGHT HIM BACK. Like a knuckle tap-tap-tapping on his consciousness. Randall Frond's eyes fluttered open, only to have his forehead, brow, and lids slam down immediately again like a crash gate.

A smashing headache. He was hurt. He didn't know how, yet—maybe badly—but he was not paralyzed.

He was restrained.

He heard the protest of the old mattress as he moved. He was tied up, facedown, on the bed in his spare room.

Okay. He was being robbed.

He had maybe forty dollars in cash in the kitchen downstairs. No television. No consumer electronics, other than his computer. Nothing thieves *want*.

His arms were pulled behind him, wrists bound by something cutting like wire or twine, also his ankles. He tried to twiddle his fingers, to see if he could get loose, but without circulation they were dead.

In T-shirt and boxers, he had just come out of the bathroom. He was taking quick little showers three times a day to keep the humidity from driving him mad—he owned only one window fan, no air conditioner—but it was a losing battle. Sweat popped from his pores as soon as he toweled off, which was when he had heard the loose board on the stairs. The third step from the top: he knew exactly where it was. Artists would occasionally drop by for him to take pictures of their wares, which he fronted for them on eBay, but unlike most others in town, Frond locked his doors. A real-world habit he had been unable to shake. He'd said, "Hello?" and stepped into the hallway with a stick of deodorant in his hand.

Rummaging. He heard that now. Near, on the other side of the wall. The bathroom? What were they looking for in there?

Water ran through the pipes. You could hear it wash all the way down into the basement. *Creak, creak*—the sound of the wooden towel rack.

Burglars who washed their hands?

He shut his eyes. He tried to journey to another place. He worried about freeing himself after they were gone. It could be days until someone else came by.

And what then? What could he do about this robbery? Call his friends at the police station?

What happened when the thieves didn't find anything worth taking? What if they were messed up on drugs or something? What if they came back in here pissed off and wild? All they needed was one of these pillows. Hold it over his head, and in a minute or two he would be on to the next life. He was utterly vulnerable.

Panic rising, he started rocking himself. He wasn't even aware at first, but then he began to rock in earnest, desperate to get his face off this soft comforter. His arms were numb and aching at the same time, almost like phantom limbs, as he tried to get some back-and-forth momentum.

He got too much. He rolled onto his arms and his tied-back feet, arching his belly, then tumbled off the bed, landing hard on his side with an *"Ooof!"* that knocked the wind out of him.

He was sucking for breath when he realized the rummaging had stopped.

Footsteps now. Leaving the bathroom, coming around through the hallway.

Oh God.

He regained his breath with a great and awful groan, lying there facing the underside of the bed, where his fireproof safe was.

The footsteps were in the room now. He could feel their weight on the floor. They were going to be pissed off. They were going to break his arms.

"I'm sorry," Frond said. "I fell. I just fell. I'm sorry. Take anything you want."

Silence. Maybe it was better not to hear the intruder's voice. Good that he was facing away from the door.

"I know it's not much. I don't have much. Some cash in the creamer in the downstairs cupboard. I gave away everything when I moved up here."

Waiting.

Nothing.

But in the awful silence, huge in the room, like an enormous bell without a clapper—something about the intruder's malevolent presence, his barely heard breathing, gave Frond a sudden, terrible insight.

"Bucky Pail?" he said.

The footsteps moved. Coming toward him. Whispering on the maple floor, sneakers.

"Wait. Listen, Bucky. You wanted me out of town—I'll go. Now. I swear, I'll leave tonight. Not a word to anyone, I'll just go—"

Hands seized his bent leg, smooth-fingered, almost without texture, dragging him from the bed.

"I promise," Frond pleaded. "I'll never tell anyone."

His sweaty flesh squeaked against the floor varnish, creating a friction burn, until he bumped up over the raised threshold of the doorway onto the rough carpeting of the upstairs hall. The strange hands were dragging him to the top of the stairs.

"*Wait! Please*—I don't know anything, I tell you. Listen to me. The state police. They said they were going to do something. They promised me, they said they were going to send someone."

The dragging stopped. Frond was on his belly, the hands moving to his arms now. He was staring down the curving wooden stairs.

"But they never did! Don't you see? They did nothing. It all came to nothing, and I . . . I was wrong. It was a stupid, stupid thing to do. Just please let me go, and I promise I'll never say—*No!*"

The stairs upended, rushing at him, tumbling, pummeling. Unable to protect his head or his neck or any part of him, he fell like a screaming human football, the blows coming faster and faster until they stopped.

Frond faced the bottom step. He tasted blood and rug and his neck was wrenched, his breath groaning through it.

Footsteps again. Coming down.

Frond had a fun-house angle on the curved staircase and the man descending them. Black sneakers. Black pants, black shirt. Black hair, wild and long.

But his face. Mashed and deformed, nearly inhuman—yet, somehow, horribly familiar.

Frond tried to scream as freakishly smooth hands reached for his head.

PART II
OVERKILL

19
TRACY

SHE WAS GREEDY FOR HIM. The rum and the foreplay made Tracy greedy, and she had been naked so long she was beyond willing, beyond desire, she wanted more more more now now now. She wanted it all at once. Everything. Right now.

She gripped his sides, pulling him closer to her and pushing him away at the same time. A fight she wanted to lose. Wanted so desperately to lose.

She bit down on his shoulder, but still he did not stop. He did not seem to mind it at all, so she bit down again and sucked on the hard ropy muscle until his hand reached for her neck. He forced back her open mouth, his fingers remaining at her jaw.

She swallowed so that he would feel her throat working under his hand. Feel her vulnerability, her trust. She gave him her throat as she gave herself to him, willingly. But still he refused to remove his tongue from her nipple.

Her bare heels dug at the mattress. His other hand teased the insides of her thighs and she grabbed it and pushed it where it needed to go. For a moment he obeyed her, and her hips jolted to the touch. Then his hand slid back along her leg. She tugged again at his wrist, and he lingered longer this time, but only enough to disappoint.

That hand tugged on hers. He wanted her to do it. Guiding the pads of her own fingers to her trimmed hair.

What he had wanted all along.

Her to do it herself.

She did, and finally he stopped at her breast. He watched.

Closing her eyes was a concession to the pretense that pure momentary ecstasy guided her fingers in their firm, circling touch—not years of shameful practice.

She reached for him, and he was so hard, and she was so proud, guiding him in, lifting her hips to meet and take him.

She held tight. She held on so tight. She was leaving her body, she was going off to that place.

That place.

Right there.

That place that place that fucking place . . .

He pulled out as he came, and she held him to her until he sagged. He lay at her side, breathing hard, and she looked down at his puddle in the bowl her belly made, dipping her fingers to feel the honeyness of him.

Him and the future of him. All his secrets.

Could it be her future?

His breathing evened out as he lay beside her. She knew she didn't want anyone else, ever. But what he wanted, she still did not know.

A COLD NIGHT in the dark month of February.

Tracy had gone out driving, her only getaway from the monotony of the farm, playing CDs in a portable player hooked up through the cassette slot in her truck, singing along when the mood struck or else just letting the music take her away.

The blue lights behind her brought her back fast. A woman knew not to get out of her car for a Black Falls cop. Tracy was in the hills a long way from the center of town.

She pulled over, watching the cop's shadow come out of the headlights. She rolled her window down just a crack. He shined his flashlight inside the car.

She didn't know him. She had heard that there was a new one in town.

"You follow me," he told her, through the window, then returned to his car.

She tailed him back to the center of town, to the police station driveway. She waited inside her car while he took her license and registration and ran them through the computer inside.

He returned and fed her identification back to her through the sliver of open window, along with a speeding ticket for $115.

Tracy was out of her truck in a flash.

"A hundred and fifteen dollars!" she said. "Do you know how much it costs to feed a llama?"

He stopped halfway back to his car, turning in surprise. "No," he said. "I don't."

"*This,*" she said, shaking the ticket, "is why you Black Falls cops have a bad name." On that, she turned, stomping back into her truck.

"*Hey!*"

The anger in his voice startled her. She turned to see the steam of the word dissipating around his head.

"Consider that the price of good advice," he said. "Don't go out driving around town alone. Especially at night. You might find yourself at the mercy of a different cop."

Something—the dreariness of the month, or the liberating spirit of the drive, or the warmth of her anger—kept her going. This outburst wasn't anything like her. "You can't just come into town, put on a stupid T-shirt, and start writing out tickets!"

Then she drove off fast, letting him watch her speed away.

The next day, still hot, she returned to the station to complain. Bucky Pail was at the front counter, shaking his head while she detailed her encounter with the overzealous new patrolman. "Let me see that," he said, taking the ticket from her, looking it over. "Sure, we can take care of this for you. Won't take more than a couple of minutes. Why don't you just come on around in back here . . ."

She had started to go with him. That was the scariest part. She actually walked to the end of the counter, ready to accompany him to the back. Because he was a policeman, and because he was offering to help.

She stopped, looking at his grinning eyes, his crooked thumb rubbing against the speeding ticket in his hand.

Shocked by her own gullibility as much as his leering behavior, she turned and walked fast out of the station.

Don Maddox's next shift was two nights later. Tracy made sure it was him before pulling into the station parking lot just after eleven. "You were right," she said.

She told him what had happened, or almost happened.

"What were you doing driving around out there, anyway?" he said.

"Just driving." She shrugged. "Getting away from this place without actually getting away. Trying to sort out my life."

"By singing along with the Foo Fighters?"

She smiled. He had a good memory. "Why not?" she said. "You like the Foo?"

He shrugged. "I likes me some Foo."

He said it just like that. The last thing she had expected to do that night was laugh.

"You could do better?" she said. "At sorting out a life?"

"Someone else's, or my own?"

"Someone else's."

She remembered the way he watched her smile. The way he had tried to be cool, deliberate and deliberating, with his shrug and a quick glance back at the station. "I'm going to be taking my forty in about a half hour."

"Is that really such a good idea?" she said. "Drinking a forty-ounce malt liquor on the job?"

"Radio code," he said. "For my midnight lunch."

They sat in the front seat of his patrol car, parked at the base of the twin waterfalls, splitting his tuna sandwich and watching the cascades spill out from beneath great caps of white ice.

* * *

SHE TURNED OVER beneath the cooled sheet, stretching a little, the muscles in her legs still pleasantly sore. This tussling between them, the struggle that manifested itself during sex, was like a play that mysteriously exposed the true hearts of its actors, revealing the tension in his, and the suspense in hers.

She couldn't feel him with her knee, and, opening her eyes, found him sitting at the foot of the bed. She watched him there, his broad, bare back, his face turned toward the window where the air conditioner blew its red ribbon. All new to her, this relationship thing. She was trying hard not to see every little mood change of his in terms of their success or demise. "Where are you?"

He looked back at her, not all the way. "Thinking about my mother," he said. "Living alone here. Dying alone. How I should have been with her."

They were on the new double bed in his old bedroom. The queen bed in the master bedroom across the hall was stripped to the mattress and box spring, as though his mother's body had been taken away just that morning.

The caffeine from the rum and Coke kept the alcohol pumping through him, the closest thing she had to a truth serum. This empty hour after sex was the only time he was vulnerable. She was learning how to navigate him. Asking the obvious next question—*Why weren't you with her?*—would have shut him right down. Besides, these misgivings about his mother's death were one reason he kept dragging his feet about selling her house. Which was fine with Tracy. Anything to keep him in Black Falls longer. Anything to give her more time.

She sat up with the sheet. "How did you get out in the first place?"

"Ah," he said, "that's a fun story." He turned down the air conditioner, lowering the volume of the rattling windowpane, then came back to lie down beside her. "The mill closed while I was in high school. Someone realized that Black Falls was suffering this 'brain drain,' meaning that everyone who *could* get out of town—the smarter kids, the motivated ones—was leaving and never coming back. Why the town wasn't getting anywhere. So to break the cycle, they came up with a plan. The Black Falls high school student graduating that next year with the highest grade point average would receive a full scholarship to a Massachusetts state university—with only one catch. It was a doozy. The recipient had to promise to return to Black Falls after graduation and work and live in the town for a minimum of five years. Like Black Falls ROTC, in a way. Not legally binding, but for a son or daughter of the town, a pledge." He was on his back, telling this story to the ceiling. "So they ran bake sales and bottle drives, they had pancake breakfasts and raffles, got sponsors, anything they could do to raise money. Pinty got behind it, figuring the town needed something to rally around as a ray-of-hope project in that first post-mill year. My mother didn't have much money, so this was my only real shot at affording school. And I busted my ass. And won it. I was the first, and, it turned out, only 'Black Falls Scholar.' Went to UMass Amherst, the honors program there, did my four years, graduated . . . and then never came back."

"No."

"Yep."

"Oh my."

"I jumped bail, basically. Sounds terrible, but honestly, I didn't plan it. Just that, when the time came, I couldn't bear to go back."

"But—your mother."

"I know." He nodded. "I know. She said no one ever gave her a hard time about it. It had been four years since I'd won—people forget. Besides, things were getting worse fast, and the town had enough to worry about. Letting Pinty down was the worst part. How I did that to him, I still don't know."

"Obviously, he forgives you. I mean, just the way you two were standing together at the parade. You're like the son he never had."

"Yeah, well." Donny shifted on the bed. "Actually, Pinty did have a son."

"He did?"

"You know at the diner, that one big wall with all the crap about the town?"

"Sure. Maps, old postcards, photographs."

"There's a portrait of an Army Ranger in uniform?"

"That's Pinty's son?"

"Gregory."

"Really? Was it Vietnam?"

"No. Yes—he fought in Vietnam. But he died after coming back. On a foam mattress in a friend's basement in Montague. With a needle in his arm."

She covered her open mouth. "Pinty's *son?*"

"So, with my father having been his partner, Pinty watched out for me growing up. My mother couldn't always hold everything together, so he helped me. Wanted big things for me." Donny laughed once through his nose. "Yeah. I'm a model son."

He was off the bed fast, turning the air-conditioning back up, standing before the blowing vent. It surprised her, hearing him talk like this. "You couldn't have stayed with her forever."

"No? Probably not. But where does the debt end?"

"I don't know. But if you ever figure it out, please tell me. I'm still paying. Every single day." It never occurred to Tracy that they had this in common: single-parent mothers. "I mean, she's deaf, okay? But she's totally self-sufficient, she can do everything for herself. Except run the farm single-handedly. Now, could she hire help? Of course she could. But she would much rather guilt me into staying. The truth is, she's afraid of being alone. Do you know she doesn't even ask where I go these nights? 'A friend's house' is all I tell her. Never once has she pressed. She knows damn well by now it's a guy. That her only daughter is 'running around.'" She smiled. "But to force the issue might piss me off, and give me that nudge I need to go away. My mother lives basically in fear of me, the most unhealthy relationship possible. I mean—can you imagine if I ever came right out and told her I was sleeping with a Black Falls cop?"

Donny said, "All the more reason not to."

"I guess." She rolled over onto her hip, turning more toward him. "Are there other reasons? Myself, I wouldn't mind holding hands in public, even just once."

"Because it's best."

"Best . . . for you? I don't see how it's best for me."

"This is a small town. The other cops don't like me much."

"Well, that's dramatic," she said. "I mean, I kind of liked sneaking around at first. It's getting a little old now. Sometimes it seems like this way just makes it easier for you to break it off with me when the time comes."

He checked her, maybe looking for a smile. She didn't have one for him.

"You never wanted to get mixed up with a local girl," she said. "Did you. You're so afraid of getting trapped here. Of winding up like everyone else."

She watched him brood on that, and noticed that he didn't tell her she was mistaken. "This arrangement is unfair to you," he said. "I know that. But I've been up front—"

"Please. Don't."

"I know you don't want to hear it, but I have been crystal clear, exactly so that there are no illusions. I am just passing through here."

"Donny—"

"I'm not doing this to be cruel. This is because I don't want to hurt you."

"Just stop, please. You have to not talk like that. Not after I just cleaned you off me with tissues."

Sometimes he looked angry when he was only thinking.

"Please," she said. "Just lie down next to me and shut up now. Please."

And he did. The room was quiet except for the air conditioner rattling the window. She lay on her side behind him, sad now, and sad about feeling sad.

After a while he laid his hand over her hip, and she didn't move away. She never slept, and he didn't seem to either.

She climbed into her truck before dawn, activating the garage door opener he had given her, the one thing of his she got to carry around. One day she was going to show up and open the door and the house was going to be empty, and him gone.

Implacable men. Every misfortune Tracy's mother had suffered over the past twelve years, she blamed on Tracy's father and his leaving them.

Her mother had to be proven wrong. *Had* to be.

She turned past the FOR SALE sign onto the street. Tracy's eyes remained damp the whole way home—not because things were bad between them, but because things were so good, and could be great, and still he was going to walk away. She drove on under the first candle of sky light like the dazed victim of an automobile accident that had yet to occur.

20
FRANKIE

THE DOORBELL KEPT ringing in the apartment, insistently, like the thumb pressing on the button was jabbing into Frankie's own temple. They weren't going away. Why didn't the Zoo Lady answer?

Maybe it was Dill at the door. Maybe he had lost his key.

A pretty hopeless hope, but you'll grab at almost anything if you wait long enough for someone.

Frankie went into the bedroom. The old floors were creaky and he tried to go softly heel-toe. The dogs howled downstairs like it was the moon itself ringing the bell. He heard them scratching at the walls.

Frankie went up alongside the black curtain over the left window. He peeked out, but couldn't see the door from this second-floor window because of the balcony.

It was twilight at the intersection of Main and Number 8. He looked for a car or something. Maybe Dill's bike.

The bell finally stopped, the silence loud, and then the caller backed out from the doorway into the street. Frankie saw the black cap and the white jersey with the blue word on it. A Black Falls cop checking the windows. Frankie froze. The curtain shifted ever so slightly, and he realized that this particular window was open a crack.

The cop was still looking. Frankie saw that he was trying to figure out a way to climb up and get inside.

Frankie backed away fast. Too fast.

"Hey!"

The cop's eyes had jumped. He was yelling now.

"Hey!"

Frankie heard boots on the stoop and the doorbell ringing again. Frankie swiped at his nose, pinched it hard. The cop was pounding on the door.

Frankie, knowing he had been made, opened the door to the downstairs. The cat stink rose up at him as he started down, arguing with himself all the way. He remembered things Dill had said about the cops in town. He almost turned back upstairs. The cop was bellowing, "Open up, Sinclair!" It was kind of a Three Little Pigs moment. He had a forceful voice that threatened to blow the house down.

At the first-floor landing, Frankie threw the lock and pulled back on the door—and the cop pushed right inside, backing Frankie hard against the handrail post at the bottom of the stairs.

"Who the hell are you?" said the cop. He had been expecting Dill.

"Frankie. Frankie Sculp."

This cop wasn't one of the brothers, the ones with the cave eyes. "Sinclair," he said, gripping Frankie's shirt as he looked up the stairs. "Where is he?"

"I don't know."

"You don't know. He's not here?"

"I thought—maybe you were him."

"What are you doing here? How'd you get in? You break in?"

"No." Frankie was fishing around inside the pocket of his cargo shorts for the key when, all of a sudden, the cop clamped a hand around Frankie's neck, gripping his forearm.

Frankie stared, eyes bulging. He tried to gulp but the cop's hand choked it.

"Slowly," said the cop.

The guy was pissed. Frankie blinked a couple of times, pleadingly, in lieu of speech, until the cop let up on his throat and then his arm.

Frankie brought out Dill's apartment key dangling at the end of a green sneaker lace.

The cop yanked it out of his hand. "He gave you this?"

Frankie swallowed hard, little tears popping out. He nodded.

"I'm around this corner a lot," said the cop. "How come I don't see you going in and out?"

Frankie shook his head. He shrugged.

"How long you been here today?"

"Dill lets me stay," Frankie said.

"Overnight?"

"Not usually."

"But sometimes. I want to know about recently."

"The past few days."

"Past few days. How many?"

"A week. I been waiting for him."

"You're saying you haven't seen Sinclair in a week."

Frankie nodded.

"How old are you, Frankie Sculp?"

"Sixteen."

"Where do you live?"

"With the Ansons. Over on Mill."

"Ansons? You a foster kid?"

Frankie shrug-nodded, feeling like he had been made to admit something.

"They know you're out here, where you are?"

"They know I'm out."

"At the apartment of a sex offender, they know that part of it?"

"I guess, not really."

Not that they would even care. The Ansons were a lot more interested in getting blitzed on their state stipend than feeding their foster kids.

"What do you come here for?"

"I just hang."

"What's here for you? Sinclair is your . . ."

"He's my friend."

"Your friend. That's great. You admire him? Want to be like him?"

"I don't know."

"How is it you 'hang'? What does that mean?"

"You know. Video games and stuff. He teaches me magic tricks sometimes."

"So what's he done now? Made himself disappear?"

"I don't know."

The cop was making a face, but it might have been the pet stink getting to him from the Zoo Lady's door. "Let's take a look upstairs."

Frankie went up ahead of him. The floor of the left-right hallway at the top was crowded with magic stuff, stacks of books and video dubs, poster tubes.

The cop looked both ways. "And you're sure he's not here now?"

"Sure I'm sure."

"But absolutely positive."

Frankie nodded.

"You two didn't have a quarrel recently, anything like that?"

Frankie tried to find the meaning behind the question. "A quarrel?"

"A spat. A fight, an argument. I'm not going to find him in bags or something, chopped up?"

Frankie didn't answer that. This cop was crazy.

"Okay," the cop said. "Come on."

Frankie followed him down the right end of the hall, past the door to the balcony, turning left into the living room. The cop's eyes went from the scarlet velvet wallpaper to the ruby loveseat to the old costume trunk set out as a coffee table. The Xbox console was hooked up to a small TV, where two ultimate fighters were frozen in midkick. Magic equipment and props were stacked up high behind the bar to the left: a silver-curtained disappearing booth, a levitating board, a card-dealing cart, juggling pins, Houdini-style chains and padlocks. At the opposite doorway stood a winking circus strongman, a seven-foot plaster dummy wearing only a loincloth and a handlebar mustache, a magician's top hat on his chipped bald head.

The cop continued, sticking his head in the bathroom, then entering the kitchen, keeping tabs on Frankie as he went. He eyed the old refrigerator and the huge ancient stove that doubled as a room heater in winter. The dirty dishes in the sink. "These dishes all yours?"

"Some."

"Some were left in there?"

"I guess. Yeah."

The cop whipped back the black theater curtain that dressed the pantry doorway, revealing Dill's computers, the multiple drives he had networked together, green "busy" lights winking. The screen saver showed fireworks exploding.

"You ever use this?" asked the cop.

"Sometimes," said Frankie. "He lets me."

The cop didn't touch it, stepping back out and walking along the other hallway, past the bookcase into Dill's front bedroom. He waded through the clothes and other junk strewn on the floor around the unmade bed. He turned his head to read the name on a credit card next to the tin of shoe polish on top of the bureau, but didn't pick it up. The closet door was ajar and he opened it the rest of the way with his hiking shoe, and Frankie realized that this cop didn't want to touch anything with his hands. Something bad was going on.

The cop leaned close to the headboard, eyeing a black wig hanging from the post. "What's this?"

"His makeup and things. He keeps all sorts. Theatrical makeup."

"You've been sleeping here?"

Frankie shook his head. "The sofa out there. Where the TV is."

The cop backed him into the hall, finishing his circuit of the place, returning to the door at the top of the stairs. He got up in Frankie's face there. "You're saying you have no idea where he is. None whatsoever."

"*No,*" Frankie said.

"If he was going somewhere, a trip or something, he would have told you?"

"A trip?"

"Would he have told you?"

"Yeah. He would have."

"And there's no sign of him having packed anything?"

"Packed? No."

"No signs of any struggle you might have straightened up."

"A struggle?"

"Chairs knocked over. Things broken. Like that."

Frankie shook his head.

The cop thought it over. "You seen a pager in here?"

"A pager?"

"A pager." The cop pulled one out of his back pocket, showed it to Frankie. A nice one, almost like a phone, with a screen for text messaging. "Like this?"

Frankie thought that was weird, but shook his head.

As the cop put away his pager, the ashtray caught his eye. A glass-bowled one on a gold stand that Dill said a theater usher had given him once. Its vermillion sand was studded with Dill's cigarette butts. The cop said, "You smoke these hand-rolled things too?"

"No."

"Know anybody else who does?"

"Just Dill."

The cop took a better look at Frankie then. Studying his eyes. Frankie looked away.

The cop said, "What *do* you smoke, then?"

"Smoke?" Frankie said. He shook his head.

"You got a cold or something? Your nose."

"Yeah. I think I do."

"Maybe it's a case of scurvy. Not getting enough vitamin C. You look like a kid who just walked off a pirate ship."

"What do you want from me?"

"I want you to listen up. Sinclair is *twice* your age, all right? You know his story?"

Frankie shook his head.

"You want to?"

Frankie shook his head harder.

"The way he got into trouble was giving kids magic lessons. What do you do for him here? What do you bring him?"

"I told you, we hang—"

"You think I can't look at you and just tell? And just *know*? It's in your skin, Frankie Sculp, it's in your eyes. That yellow bleached shit you call hair. Turn around. Smell the wall."

Frankie did, bumping up against it as the cop frisked him.

"You think of yourself as a dealer, huh? Real big-time, right? Sinclair your drug buddy?" The cop's hands picked his pockets. "If I find a needle you don't warn me about, I'm going to drive it into the back of your skull."

Frankie wasn't holding. It was a habit of his to stash his stash rather than walk it around. Right then it was under the top hat on the plaster strongman's head.

The cop turned him back around and got in his face. "I don't know what you're looking for here. If it's love or friendship or a father figure . . . I don't even know if you know. But get this. Whatever you're looking for, Dill Sinclair isn't it. I can guarantee you that. Find a new friend, and stop peddling this shit before it starts peddling you." He smacked him in the chest for emphasis. "If it hasn't already."

Frankie felt that same old icy shiver up his back. This cop pushing him around, making decisions for him, everyone making decisions for him, social workers, counselors, guardians. Strangers telling him what's best, deciding his life for him as they shuttled him from family to family, from school to school. And look at how great it had all turned out for him. Here he was stuck in Black Falls, Massachusetts. The asshole of the earth.

In fourteen months he would turn eighteen and age out of the foster-care system. Then he would be free.

"You cops are out to get him," Frankie said.

The cop cocked his head. "I'm looking for him. Is that the same thing?"

"He's going to get you. That's what he said." It was stupid to betray Dill's confidence like this, but Frankie couldn't help it. He had nothing else to throw back at this cop except his own empty hurt, wanting to scare somebody else for a change. "He knows a way, he said. All the cops. He's going to turn this shit-fucking town upside down."

He waited for the shove, the slap, the knee. Instead he got a hard stare, and strange words of caution. "That's something you should maybe keep to yourself, don't you think?"

Frankie stared. This cop didn't believe him? Or was this something else entirely? "Am I getting the key back?"

"All you're getting is a pass out of here, right now, and that means never come back. I want that understood. I want you crystal clear on that."

"Fuck you."

The cop shook his head. "No, man. No way. You want me to step on you. That's what you're used to. All you know is getting bounced around. And that's why I'm not going to do you that way. Why I'm not throwing you down these stairs right now. You think you're young enough to mess around with your life like this, like you're putting one over on the rest of the world? The world doesn't care, Frankie. The world welcomes statistics. But I'm not going to waste a speech on you. All you want is the back of someone's hand so you can go deeper into your sulk. You're leaving here now. And never coming back."

"I have to get my stuff—"

He started toward the living room, where his stash was, but the cop pushed him back against the wall, staring hard into his eyes like he knew.

Out on the street, walking away fast, tears pressured Frankie's eyes but would not fall.

Dill. Don't leave me alone in this town.

He looked back at the corner building. He saw a man standing on the darkened balcony, and his mind stuttered a moment, telling him it was Dill.

It wasn't. Just the cop. Watching Frankie go—but standing with his head turned. Utterly still and aware. As though listening to something.

Frankie heard the sounds then, distant, way up in the hills.

Sirens.

21
EDDIE

IT WAS A STRANGE-LOOKING house that got stranger the longer Eddie Pail worked around it. The front was constructed out of thick timber while the high wall on one side and the low wall on the other were built with river stones like ostrich eggs set in mortar.

Eddie had the long pole and was trying to break one of the top windows from the side lawn, but couldn't get enough force behind it. So he found some fist-sized rocks and started throwing. The third one cracked right through. He resumed with the pole, smashing out the rest of the glass, his hole venting black billows of smoke and wavy heat.

The pumper truck was parked up on the lawn, its hose splashing the exterior, the heated stones hissing as water became steam. The house smoked and dripped like something cooking and melting at the same time.

They yelled back and forth across the lawn, Mort and Stokes wrangling the water-plumped hose and aiming its stream into the high window. Smoke alarms squealed inside and occasionally there was a heat-crack of supporting timber, as fierce as a thunderclap of warning.

With the hot night and the angry blaze and them suffering inside their bunkers and helmets, Eddie was earning his pay on this call, every cent. At one point the pumper ran dry and Mort and Ullard had to drive over to the fire pond on Sundown to reload. The nearest neighbors appeared with drinking water for them, looking up at the smoke in awe.

The pumper returned but the vent did its job, just as training said it would. The smoke out of the upstairs window was starting to fade, the blaze dying out, and Bucky and Mort strapped on masks and tanks and went in through the front door with a hatchet and a pike pole. Eddie and Stokes kept the roof wet and cool, the smoke alarms crying even louder now that the air around the house had stopped whipping.

They came out minutes later, jackets damp and pitchy. Bucky shrugged off his tank and pulled back his helmet, mask, and neck guard, squinting from the heat. He sat on the grass and shed his heavy yellow gloves and dug in the pockets underneath his bunkers, coming out with a cigarette and lighting it up with fish white hands. He smoked deeply, the oxygen mask outline drawn on his face in black sweat.

"Ding-dong," said Bucky.

"What's that?" said Eddie.

"The witch is dead."

Eddie looked at the stinking house. "This is Frond's place?"

Ponytailed Frond with his socks and sandals. The photographer's vest he always wore, those empty little film loops.

Bucky said, "There's some other weird shit in there."

"Like what?"

"Weird witch shit."

Maddox appeared, standing beneath a crooked branch of the only tree in the yard. Bucky was right. Always watching them.

"Was he in bed?" Eddie asked.

"On the floor downstairs. Burned to a crisp."

"On the floor?" Eddie pictured the guy curled up and burning. He shuddered. Frond was in his forties, an able guy. "Why hadn't he gotten out—"

"How the hell would I know?" said Bucky.

Bucky's tone reminded Eddie that Frond was the snitch who had reported Bucky and Mort's traffic-stop beating of Sinclair to the state police. He watched his brother smoking into the air, leaning back on the grass with one hand, then stubbing out his butt and getting to his feet.

"Strap on Mort's tank," Bucky said to Eddie.

"What for?" Eddie looked up at the still-smoking house. "There could still be some hot spots."

"Just put on the damn tank."

Eddie's lip curled, but he did as he was told. He got Mort's tank up onto his shoulders and was wiping out the sooty mask with his glove when Maddox moved in front of them, setting up between them and the ax-chopped door.

"You can't go back inside," Maddox said.

Bucky's shoulders fell, tired and pissed. "Maddox, get the fuck out of our way."

Bucky started forward, his rubber boots splashing the oversoaked grass, but Maddox stood his ground. "You're just firefighters here. I'm the cop. Inside there is an unattended death."

"*Unattended death?*" said Bucky, mocking the proper terminology.

"This is a potential crime scene. We need a doctor here to certify."

"Maddox," said Eddie, more annoyed than protesting, "the witch fell down carrying a candle or something."

"Then waiting won't hurt."

Bucky was smiling and shaking his head in that happy, pissed-off way of his. "Maddox, Maddox, Maddox." He picked up the fire ax, weighing it in his hand. "We can go around you, over you, or through you. Your choice."

"Stand down, Bucky."

Bucky said, "I am going to enjoy this."

He took a step toward the door, and Maddox's hand went to his holster.

Bucky stopped short, as though he'd been flat-handed. "Are you *shitting* me?" he said, gleeful, then continuing forward.

"*Buck,*" said Eddie, sharp enough to halt him.

Eddie nodded to the neighbors in their robes watching from the lawn, and to the firebugs milling in the driveway, roused by sirens and sky-smoke. Witnesses.

Bucky turned back to face Maddox. But he stayed where he was. Eddie had vented his brother's anger just like the heat of that house fire. Next time Maddox might not be so lucky.

22
DR. BOLT

Dr. Gary Bolt stepped out of his Honda Prelude in the short driveway. The foul air reeked of things not meant to be burned, smoke detector alarms squealing out of the black-windowed house. Steam rising into the slanting light of the morning sun.

Two soot-blackened firemen sat on the front bumper of their truck. "How's the rice-burner running, doc?" they called to him.

Dr. Bolt put up a quick smile and slid his hand nervously into the pocket of his white coat. *Just keep moving. Get this over with.*

There was Bucky Pail, mashing a lit cigarette against a tree trunk. He came forward in his fireman's outfit, bunkers under a T-shirt. It made him look thicker than he did in his patrolman's uniform: the "camp counselor with a gun" look, as Dr. Bolt often thought of it. There was a cop here too, stepping away from the front of the house.

Dr. Bolt shoved his other trembling hand into his coat pocket. "Here I am," said Dr. Bolt to Bucky, gamely.

Dr. Bolt knew the cop's name as Maddox. Maddox looked him over and turned to Bucky. "The vet?" he said.

Bucky said, "Medical doctor, it's enough."

Dr. Bolt played at being jolly. "Now there's a ringing endorsement!"

"You can certify a death?" said Maddox.

Dr. Bolt shrugged, making wings of the flaps of his coat. "I can tell you if a man is alive or not."

"All we need," said Bucky, rushing this along. "Let's do this, doc."

They started over the spongy grass. "It's safe to enter?"

"Should be."

"Should be," said Dr. Bolt. He felt something squishy in his pocket, remembered his latex gloves. "I brought these." He distributed pairs. "Might help."

Maddox didn't take his pair right away, perhaps noticing Dr. Bolt's shaking hands.

The sedative he had taken was failing him. *Get through this. Do not get caught between these two. And do not piss off Bucky Pail.*

"Shall we?" said Dr. Bolt.

Bucky pushed in through the broken door. The front hallway was wet and hazy, and they stepped over puddles to a living room, its walls blistered and blackened almost to the ceiling. Morning sunlight streaming in through a smashed window created an almost churchlike atmosphere, and, in the soot-darkened room, an eerie sense of night-day. Parts of the wall and floor still offered steam, and everything reeked of carbon reversion.

Against the high wall stood a wide stone hearth licked black by flame. A few objects atop the broad mantle had survived the blaze. A pair of ornate silver candlesticks coated with melted red wax. A porcelain skull with a hollowed space as for burning incense. A chalice carved with a distorted crescent moon and star. A cracked rod of glass. A smoky crystal prism.

Dr. Bolt said, "Interesting."

Bucky led them to an open, burned-out doorway. A small office inside, a burnt lump that used to be a computer monitor set before a heat-warped ergonomic chair, now a modern-art installation. All that was once paper was now ash; all that was wood was now black; all that was metal was now melted. The room remained suffocatingly hot, the carbon odor mixing with sulfur and something like a meat smell, the air growing oppressive.

The corpse lay behind the chair, glistening black and crisp. Dr. Bolt's first instinct was to turn away, which he did, his fist covering his mouth until he regained his composure. The body's elbows and knees were drawn in almost to a fetal position, its tongue swollen between charred lips, its one visible eyelid puffed out like a venous, black egg. The contents of the midsection were exposed where they had cooked into the floor.

"Uhh," said Dr. Bolt, suppressing a sudden burp, his stomach rising into his throat. "Well—*ug-huh*—yes, I'd say he's deceased, all right." He cleared his throat again and almost lost it.

"Okay, then," said Bucky, ready to leave.

"His arms are broken," said Maddox.

Bucky squinted. Dr. Bolt didn't know how to read these two.

"Well," said Dr. Bolt, stepping wide around the body. "I do have some experience with barn fires." If only he knew what Bucky wanted from him here. "Extreme heat does do—*brr-hmm*—surprising things." He fumbled for the fat end of his necktie and pinched it over his nose. "The stomach eruption. Looks like a disemboweling, but the intestinal gases, when superheated, can rupture the stomach wall. Heat can also fracture bones."

"What about his eyes?" said Eddie, from the doorway.

"Well, every fluid has its boiling point," said Dr. Bolt, swallowing down more acid. "The muscles contract due to simple water evaporation. Why he appears so balled up here."

Bucky said, "Fine. You can write us up something?"

"Hold on," said Maddox. "We still have to identify the body."

"Identify?" said Bucky. "It's Frond's house. Guy lived alone." Then impatience got the better of him. "Fine, let's flip him over, see his face." Bucky fingered down the webbing of his latex gloves, kneeling at the corpse's feet. "Eddie, get the other end."

Eddie Pail came forward slowly, eyeing the job, crouching reluctantly and placing his hands near where the shoulder had burned into the floor.

"I don't know about moving him—" began Dr. Bolt.

"On three," snapped Bucky. "One, two—*heave*."

Later, after Dr. Bolt had finished disgorging his breakfast omelet onto the front lawn, he decided it wasn't the site of the reddened flesh stuck to the floorboards like dry meat on a nonstick grill that made him run from the house. Nor was it the underside of the skull, where it was stove into the brainpan.

No. It was the cracked chunks of black bone that came rolling out of the corpse's mouth. The shattered teeth tumbling forth like rotted dice from Death's own cup.

23
HESS

Trooper Leo Hess of the Mitchum County State Police Detective Unit yawned gustily, chewing the yawn on its way out. "This everybody?"

Pail, the local sergeant, nodded. Six men stood inside the station entrance, all in shorts and matching jerseys and black ball caps, looking more like a police softball team than working cops. The old building they were in resembled a humble chamber of commerce center more than a police station, with its screen door and porch, the unglassed front counter, two no-tech key-lock holding cells in back. Coming from the burned house in the hills, Hess had passed sagging shacks surrounded by gutted cars on cinder blocks, trailers nursing off silver tanks of propane, swayback barns and tarp-covered snowmobiles. Pockets of beauty amid acres of neglect. He rolled right through the center of town before realizing it *was* the center of town.

These guys just seemed confused. This was like coming out to some desert post to find the local army living off camel meat, too heat-silly to understand that the campaign had ended months ago. Hess was usually luckier than this. Murders were rare out in the sticks.

But whatever. He'd bump up his clearance rate, then head on back to Dodge. In and out in forty-eight hours. Leo the Lion was ready to roar.

"So, Sergeant Pail," he said. Bucky was a hayseed name. "Who did this?"

Pail's eyes were too deep-set to offer much. "How the hell would I know?"

Hess looked the others over. "I always ask," he said. "A town this size, local law usually knows what's going on. No suspects? No theories?"

The only one who moved was Maddox, the one they had waited for. The overnight patrolman whom Hess had told to come in early, so that he could address them all together. Maddox stood straighter in back, for a better look at Pail.

"Okay, then," said Hess. "Who called in the fire originally?"

"No one," said the other Pail, the taller, blond one. Brothers in the same police department: never a good thing.

"Who scrambled you, then?"

The one named Ullard said, "Bucky sent out a page."

Hess turned back to the small-eyed Pail, waiting.

"I saw black smoke in the sky," said Bucky. "They teach you that in the certification courses. Usually means a fire."

Hess crossed his big arms, keeping up his genial smile. "Looks like the fire had multiple points of origin. Anyone know what that means?"

Ullard said, "It started in different places?"

"Wow," said Hess, taking a moment to marvel. "It means the fire was set. Arson squad found these little—they looked like smoked-down cigars to me, turns out they're flares. Road flares and good old-fashioned unleaded gasoline. No frills. Somebody tried to burn down the house in a half-assed murder scene cover-up."

Now he had their attention.

"I say half-assed because only half the house burned, giving us plenty to work with—file that under 'Good.' Being almost twenty-four hours out now, that's a daylong head start for the assailant. But we can make up some of that time once we hear from our eyewitness."

Now came confused looks back and forth.

Eddie Pail was the first to take the bait. "Eyewitness?"

"The corpse," said Hess. "The vic. The presumed Mr. Frond. Dead men make the best witnesses. Why? Because they can't lie. They got no stake in this thing other than absolute truth. Same as me."

Two officers from Crime Scene Services—badgeless, casual in jeans and jerseys except for their latex gloves—opened the screen door to get Hess's attention. One held a small brush that looked like an archaeologist's tool, the other a rolled-up paper bag marked "Evidence" in red.

Hess gave them a hard look that only they could have construed as anger, and they backed out fast. Hess was not to be interrupted during his get-to-know-me spiel. He had to motivate these good old boys to work for him.

"Criminalists, huh?" said Hess, leaning forward as though taking them into his confidence. "Spook the shit out of me. Tiptoeing around with their brushes and lasers. Tweezing things, rolling them up in these little forensic doggy bags. Everything's an experiment with them. Guys haunt my *dreams*. Wouldn't amaze me in the least if the skinny one there was carrying his own shit in that paper bag. Probably huddled together in the mobile lab out there right now, happily picking through it. 'Joe, when did I eat corn?'"

Snickers from most of them. Hess twisted his thick gold wedding band as though screwing it onto his finger. He was working these yokels good. Be selling them time-shares in Puerto Rico next.

"But they're the ones making the cases these days. The kids who paid attention in chemistry class, who sat there and memorized the elements chart—they solve the crimes now. Me? I'm more like the coach. Used to be first-string quarterback, now I'm drawing up Xs and Os. If it's a promotion, I don't know. Bill Belichick. That's me now."

Two trouble spots identified. Bucky Pail, the shorter brother, wasn't lapping it up with the rest. A definite nail in the road going forward. And Maddox, the one lurking in back, almost hiding there, was another question mark. He chuckled like the others, but without sincerity. Could be he was just the black sheep of the bunch.

"Right, so, I'm a guy who likes to keep local law involved. Let's kick this thing around a little, shall we?" Hess had learned to use his eyebrows, raising them high like expectations, inviting candor, demanding truth. "A witch, huh? What do we make of that?"

Some shaken heads, no one committing to anything.

"Safe to say this is no random crime. There's no transient population here. Anybody passing through Black Falls—no offense—there's not a lot to stop for. So we can pretty much assume the witch knew his assailant. Is it a sex crime? Maybe."

"Sex crime?" said Eddie Pail, shaping up to be an easy mark.

"Why not? Looked like the guy had been in his underwear. I mean, if he's got obvious enemies, fine, we'll look at them. But I'm just as happy to start off with his friends."

He watched them process that.

"Guy'd been beaten up, and I mean *severely*. Busted to pieces. Just to let you know we're not playing here. House was also gone over pretty good. Our killer spent some quality time in there. And why not? No neighbors nearby, nobody to hear anything. Who here's working the note?"

Again they looked around. "What note?" said a big bag of shoulders, Mort Lees.

"The notification," said Hess. "Frond's next of kin."

Shrugs. Hadn't occurred to anyone. Eddie Pail looked at his brother, Bucky, who kept on looking straight at Hess.

"So," said Hess. "Anything else anybody wants to add?"

Bucky Pail said, "Maybe."

Hess nodded. "Go for it."

"We got a missing sex offender."

"Okay."

"You said sex crime."

"I sure did. What you got?"

"Scarecrow, we call him. Real name's Dillon Sinclair."

"Missing how long?"

"More than a week now, I guess."

Bucky Pail stepped past Hess and around the front counter to the beginning of the hallway behind. Pushpinned onto the corkboard outside a door labeled REPORTS ROOM were badly photocopied registration sheets featuring mugs and vitals of nine Level 2 and Level 3 sex offenders stacked three by three. Bucky fingered the one in the center, a small-headed guy with a firing-squad expression.

Hess skimmed the bio. "Kid-toucher," he said. "Girls or boys?"

"Boys."

"He's Level Two," said another voice. Hess was surprised to hear from Maddox now, still in back of the others. "Nonviolent."

Hess nodded, taking the opportunity to drill Maddox with a stare, then turned back to Bucky Pail. What were these two trying to tell him?

Hess pointed to the SO's picture. "What's with the eyebrows?"

"He shaves them off," said Bucky Pail. "Guy's a full-time freak."

In the photo, Sinclair had been posed against the wall opposite where Hess was now, unsmiling, borderline scared, the missing facial hair making him look alien and terminally ill. Probably was the look he was going for.

"All right, gentlemen," said Hess, looking to wind this up. "Look, maybe you don't want us here, and maybe we don't even want to be here. A blind date is what it is, and I've been on some pretty rough ones. Let me do my job, and I'll let you do yours, so long as you understand that, when the time comes to dance, I'll be the one leading. If you're good with that, then I'm good with you. We good?"

Unenthusiastic nods. A troop of sad sacks and misfits. Hess had a fun forty-eight hours ahead of him.

24
WANDA

SHE DREAMED AGAIN that she was dead and floating through town. Landing in different places, people stopping and staring as she walked up to them, awaiting her caress. She touched them over their hearts and some fell dead limp right away, as if she were one of those revival faith healers on TV. Others shivered at the contact, jolted by the release of their souls from their bodies, and then joined the small mob following her. When she came to Bucky, he was standing outside his backyard trailer, the one that stunk so bad, whose curtained windows and padlocked door glowed wild white from within. She reached for him but froze in midembrace. It was his eyes. Empty black sockets. She looked at her hand, and it was black now with all the death she had brought to people. Her nails were rotted and peeling off, knuckles shriveled to the bone. She pulled it back in shame, and Bucky turned away, leaving her to walk on alone.

"Wanda. Wake up. Wanda!"

Something peeled back her eyelid. Her vision was blurred. Donny Maddox called her name.

You came to beg me to spare you, she tried to say, though her lips wouldn't move the words right.

The bed shaking now, an earthquake. Ride it out. What the fuck.

The massive thumb opened her eye again. Like looking up through a deep hole in the ground. "Wake up."

"I'm dead," she sneered, and tried to roll over, but the bed wouldn't let her.

"You're burning up." The covers were peeled back like foil off a TV dinner. "You're wearing sweats?"

"Freezing," she said, grabbing after the sheets. "How'd you get in here?"

He was dream Donny, trying to reach her in a dream within a dream. He was that clever. "Listen," he said. "It's important. I need to know. Bucky ever talk about Frond?"

"I couldn't touch him," she said. "My black hand."

Shaking again, her head getting tossed. "Frond," Donny said, full into her face.

"No," she answered.

"Bucky never talks about him?"

"Are you really in my bedroom?"

His hands came off her shoulders and she wriggled back into comfort.

Noises kept her from sinking down for good. She opened an eye and saw Donny's back to her, leaning over her nightstand, the drawer open. "Going through my stuff?"

"You're dreaming," he told her.

"If I'm dreaming then get in here and fuck my ass."

When nothing happened, her eyes fell shut again, tiny black hands pulling her down.

25
PINTY

DONNY MADE HIM turn out the light over the front steps. He kept checking the road. "This escalates everything."

Pinty gripped the doorknob in order to take pressure off his hips, switching weight from one leg to the other. His right foot had been numb all day, almost causing a fall. He'd had a dizzy spell earlier, so he was trying to take it easy. "Work it to your advantage."

"It just doesn't make any *sense*."

"Why not? It's revenge. Frond reported him."

"But why now? Why bring the state police here? It's too dangerous a distraction. Staying under the radar, that's Bucky's only plan."

"Then?"

"I don't know." Donny pulled his cap off and ruffled his hair. "I can't think."

"Severely beaten, you say?"

"And now I've got this state trooper. A buzz-cut guy, a weight lifter, right? Something to prove. Looking for some ass to kick."

"Maybe he'll come and go."

"And what if he doesn't? What if Bucky has to shut everything down for a couple of weeks? Then what?"

"Donny." Pinty leaned on the doorknob, needing to sit down. "Relax."

"*Frond,*" said Donny, like he couldn't get it through his head. "The timing of it makes no sense."

Donny's patrol car squawked in the driveway. An unfamiliar voice came over the police radio band.

It was a state trooper, summoning Patrolman Maddox back to the station.

Donny stared at Pinty, a look of resignation on his face. "Here it comes," he said, pulling his cap back on his head.

26
HESS

"FRIGGIN' DIAL-UP," Hess was telling the Mitchum barracks dispatch. "Goddamn stagecoach technology. Three phone jacks the entire place. Radio reception's for shit, units are R-1 all over town. And my Nextel two-way, that would be like voodoo science here. Bringing fire to the aborigines. So this is the number. The non-emergency line. Requisition me some bear repellent and a telegraph machine. Right."

Hess hung up and reached for his water bottle, chugged. The screen door whined and Patrolman Maddox, in the uniform jersey and ball cap, walked in looking like a guy assigned to beach patrol a hundred miles from shore. Decent build on him, but no rip. Five months this rookie had been on the job, without academy training or state certification. As much a cop as Hess was king of Tunisia.

"Sorry to haul you back in," said Hess, not really sorry at all. "You're new on the job, huh?"

"Yeah, just part-time."

"Holding down the fort on overnights?"

"Basically."

"Got aspirations, or is this what works for you now?"

"This works now."

"Really? Surprises me. Most guys get a taste of cop, they can't think of doing anything else."

"My father was a patrolman here, long time ago."

"Walking a mile in his shoes, huh? Making a little peace with the old man?"

"I guess."

"Makes sense. So you're from this town?"

"Originally, yeah."

"Moved away? And actually came back?"

"Hard to believe, huh?"

Maddox was giving him nothing. Maybe he had nothing to give. "You knew this Frond?"

"By sight. He stood out a little."

"Been to his Web page? His online store?"

"No."

"I have had that pleasure. Crystals, quartz stones. All kinds of New Age crap. Healing metals. Wind chimes. Pottery."

"I knew he brokered sales for some of the artists living in the hills."

"My interview list is filling up with fruitcakes. Guy claimed to be a Druid."

"Uh-huh."

"An ovate, a diviner, an interpreter of Druid mysteries. Yeah. Too much Led Zep in high school. Know what an athame is?"

"A what?"

"Exactly. It's a ceremonial dagger. Pictured on his site. Ivory-handled with a double-edged blade. He put up images of all his toys, these candlesticks, some prism thing, a 'thurible,' which I learned is an incense burner—his was in the shape of a skull. We recovered all these things from the mantle over his fireplace, but not the dagger. I know you were first on scene when they went inside. You see this athame there?"

Maddox thought before answering. The guy was careful, Hess noticed. He wasn't overeager to work with the big boys, and he wasn't intimidated either. "No."

"You seem sure."

"I wasn't looking for it, but I'm pretty sure."

"It's the only thing missing. Not worth much money."

Maddox shrugged.

"How many more witches you got up here?"

Maddox smiled. "That I know of?"

"Cult activity is what I'm getting at."

"No. Nothing I'm aware of."

Hess nodded. "Other thing I'm hearing is that Frond had issues with some of the cops. I don't have the full story, but I know he broke up a traffic stop or some such where a suspect was being beaten—that suspect being your missing sex offender."

"Yeah. That was before my time."

Hess waited, watching him. Realized he was treating this guy like a suspect. Outside the front windows he saw two sleds pull into the driveway—blue-on-blue state police cruisers—escorting an old orange pickup truck carrying something under a tarp in the bed.

"This is us," said Hess, pushing out the screen door ahead of Maddox. A police station with a front porch: this was a first. Three stone steps led to the driveway.

The town DPW guy got out of his pickup, a broad-backed cluck with a close-shaved head who, with his build and facial expression, wouldn't have looked out of place in a prison yard. He wiped his dirty hands on the hips of his dirty shorts. "Don," the guy said, to Maddox.

"Here's what I need," Hess told Maddox. "We found an old safe in the house, under an upstairs bed. Your public works man here was good enough to haul it out for us—your name again?"

The guy mumbled it. He was as slow-moving as the rest, maybe even slower. Cement in the veins. The cruiser lights bothered him, making him squint.

"I could wait for morning and ship this box back to civilization, but that would cost me at least another half day and I don't want that. I need a machinist in town—or a safecracker, if you got one—but more likely somebody who can drill through this thing and pop it open. Mr. Ripsbaugh here suggested a name, and, given the late

hour, I wanted you to come along as a familiar face, to make introductions."

Maddox looked at Ripsbaugh.

"Kitner," Ripsbaugh said.

Maddox mulled over the name, looking surprised. He turned to
Hess. "Okay," he said. "But there's something you need to know
about Kitner first."

27
KITNER

THE KNOCKING WAS going to wake up Ma. In sleep shorts, Steve Kitner pulled the door open, first a little, then wider, seeing headlights in the dirt lot.

One of the local cops was standing on his top step. Behind him were real state police cruisers.

"Aw, shit," said Kitner, a wave of depression overcoming him like rigor mortis. "Look, I'm clean, man. Whatever. I'm innocent. This is bullshit."

The cop said, "It's nothing like that, Kitner."

He knew this day was coming—*knew* it. Knock on his door and take him away. That shoved-up-against-the-wall feeling again. "I'm registered like I'm supposed to be. I'm a citizen now."

The cop showed him an open palm. "Listen to me."

Kitner didn't hear single words, only the general idea: the staties wanted a favor from him.

It seemed almost like a trap, though they had nothing to trap him for. He hadn't done anything wrong. They were only making him feel like he had.

A favor seemed like a good idea. "Shit, yeah, I'll help you out, why not."

He pushed through the aluminum door, reminded he was barefoot by the rocky driveway. He wore only saggy boxers and a string tank, but who cared.

Unless there were female troopers here.

He hoped Ma wouldn't wake up, see the cars, have a conniption. Wouldn't be bad later to tell her how he helped out cops. How he was being so good.

He walked inside the garage-turned-shop at the outside of the road curve, under the unlit sign reading KITNER TOOL & DIE. He hit the red stopper and the power started up, the shop blinking to life. He found a pair of the old man's safety boots and lifted his leather apron off its peg.

Two tall troopers lugged in an old safe dusty with fingerprint powder. Kitner pointed to the larger drill press and they thunked it down there and stretched their backs.

A plainclothesman with cobra arms came in, said nothing. The hard-ass act. Then the local cop and that guy Ripsbaugh, the town roadworker.

No women.

The safe, she was a beauty. Short and stout, maybe two and a half cubic feet of volume, a black dial with ivory numbers over a small silver handle.

"Pretty box," said Kitner, stroking his tonguelike goatee. "Turn her upside down. Bottom's usually the softest." *Just like a woman,* he almost added, but thought better, thanks to his conditioning. He smiled as the troopers did his bidding.

Nineteen eighty-eight was the last time he had shared a room with this much law. From the way the plainclothes guy eyeballed him, Kitner figured they all knew about his Merrimack County prior. How he had gotten loaded on blackberry brandy and amphetamines one night during a freak snowstorm and how, driving around looking to score more dope, he had happened upon a female motorist stuck in a snowbank and how, after offering to help dig her out, he had strangled her unconscious instead and raped her in the backseat. They found him sleeping there later, on the nod, so the guilty plea was his best bet. He pled and did his time. Prison wasn't bad because he had been in the army, if briefly. Afterward, he tried to make it elsewhere, but the

Level 3 label meant "most likely to reoffend," so he couldn't hold a job or an apartment anywhere without people smashing in his windows and calling him up in the middle of the night and threatening to slice off and feed him his own dick. So when his dad died he resettled up here and took over the old man's shop. Not like he had a long list of options.

It was better here, like a self-imposed exile. Not being able to afford a car removed a lot of temptation. Sometimes, maybe once a month, he felt the change in his metabolism, that old sweet tooth starting to tingle. Sometimes, when he looked around at the old man's shop with its dingy floors and power machinery, he saw a dungeon in waiting. Sometimes he thought about what it would be like to work on people here instead of metal. Building a person, a woman, to his own specifications, so he wouldn't have to worry about breaking laws ever again. If he had all the money in the world he would build himself a harem of women and be real good to them.

He pulled on rubber-strapped goggles and went to work. He screwed open the chuck and inserted an old drill bit shank, one he could afford to dull or even snap, closing the three jaws tight around it. He pedaled the power and turned the drill rpm to 300 and wheeled the lever down for its first bite. The box screamed, again and again, and he kept at it, spraying sparks and hot filings. Old steel and many layers thick. It was nice to let himself go. The casing resisted so he reset the bit for another assault, and with a few whining thrusts finally pushed through. He drove again and again at the casing, wailing on it, widening his bore to spread the gap. So absorbed was he that he didn't even notice when Ripsbaugh exited the shop. Finally, by adjusting and readjusting his aim, he joined all the various holes, having chewed open a gash large enough to admit a man's hand.

He offered to keep going but the plainclothesman stopped him, shining a light down inside and then handing Kitner a pair of latex gloves. Kitner tested the hot wound, then reached inside, getting his fist in almost to the elbow. He felt around the cavity and pulled out a manila envelope.

The plainclothesman took it from him. Kitner saw the local cop looking on from the open front door.

"Tax returns," said the plainclothesman, inspecting the contents. "Canceled checks." He scanned a signed document with disgust. "Fucking health care proxy. Nothing."

"There's a drawer in the top," Kitner told him, so helpful. "On the bottom now. Feels thin, if you want me to get in there."

He did. Kitner twisted a longer bit into the chuck, working deeper into the existing hole. The safe gave up the drawer with almost no resistance. The plainclothesman handed Kitner his flashlight and a second pair of latex gloves.

The guy was getting impatient. "Is it a dagger?" he asked.

Kitner noticed that the local cop had moved inside the doors now. Kitner got his arm all the way in, pulling out a short stack of small, cream-colored envelopes tied together with a cherry red ribbon. Plainclothes held out his own gloved hands and Kitner served him the packet like a fancy slice of cake. Plainclothes lifted the letters to his nose—the perfume had a vanilla smell—then pulled at the tie, the bow knot yielding and falling limp, the envelopes undressed.

Kitner watched him open the top one, pulling out thread-flecked stationery folded into thirds. The handwriting was small and neat in red ink. Two sheets, though the handwriting on the second one ended halfway down. Below it were two pencil drawings that made Kitner go up on his toes, trying to see better over Plainclothes's shoulder.

The first sketch was of a woman's nude torso. One breast hung free, the other one cupped in her hand, mashed and raised in offering.

The second one below it showed the same woman but from shoulders to knees. She sat legs open, her right hand covering her pussy except for her middle finger, stuck deep inside.

Plainclothes pulled the letter to his chest like he was hiding a poker hand, and Kitner came down off his toes, wondering if maybe he had made a noise or something. The guy moved away, taking the rest of the envelopes with him.

Plainclothes summoned the local cop with a flick of his finger and showed him the first letter, including the drawings.

"'Love always, V,'" said the plainclothes cop, pointing out the signature. "Any ideas?"

The local cop's eyes clouded, and not because of the dirty pictures. He knew, all right. It cheered Kitner, a little, to think of somebody else eating trouble for a change.

28
MADDOX

MADDOX WAITED OUTSIDE the station, on the sidewalk at the end of the grassy slope, staying near the action while maintaining enough distance between himself and the state troopers. It was just after eight and his shift was over—Stokes and Ullard had already driven their patrol cars past him into the driveway—but Maddox lingered, pretending he was enjoying the morning heat and had nowhere better to go. Above him, the great flag rustled like a horse too lathered to lift its own head.

Stokes and red-eyed Ullard came out to see him. "They closed off rooms in there," Stokes said. "What's up? They get someone?"

Maddox pretended not to know who it was, liking how, when Bucky wasn't around, the other cops could be civil if they wanted something from him.

Three kids came biking across the iron bridge, two on banana-seat bikes and one on a taller ten-speed, turning past the station. The ten-speed was an old Schwinn, black with black electrical tape wound around the handlebars.

Maddox recognized the bike. He yelled, "Hey!" and took off suddenly down Main Street after them.

After a few more yells, they slowed for him, letting him come jogging up. They were scuzzy mill-house locals, still growing into themselves at thirteen. Maddox grabbed the arm of the kid on the ten-speed to hold him where he was.

On the down tube of the triangle frame, the letter *g* had been added in Wite-Out to the brand name, to read, Austin Powers–style, "Schwinng."

Dillon Sinclair's bike. With his driver's license suspended, this bicycle had been Sinclair's only legal mode of transportation, taking him back and forth to the Gulp.

"I found it," said the kid, in answer to Maddox's question. He looked malnourished, maladapted, probably just about mal-everything.

"Found it where?"

"Woods."

"Be a little more specific."

"Toad Bridge. That little bridge off Edge Road. We was catching bullfrogs." He glanced at his homeys for backup. "It was right there in the trees."

A low one-lane bridge crossing a creek. Edge Road was where Heavey lived. "And you just helped yourself."

"If somebody else was throwing it away? Yeah."

Maddox kept at him, his friends too, trying to shake something else out of them, but the story held up. Maddox took names and told the kid he was impounding the bike and let them all go with a warning.

He walked the bike back up the sidewalk along Main, trying to figure out what Sinclair's ride was doing hidden or thrown down by the side of the bridge. He walked it around to the dirt lot behind the station, wondering where to park it while he figured things out. A voice from the back steps called to him.

"You Maddox?"

Maddox looked up at the trooper leaning out of the back door in his regulation summer duty uniform: wide-brimmed Mountie hat, straight-leg slacks, combat boots, a badge over the two pens in his left chest pocket, a small ceremonial silver whistle buttoned over the right.

"Yeah," said Maddox.

"Trooper Hess to have a word with you."

Maddox leaned the bike against the wooden slat fence behind the extra patrol car and followed the trooper inside to the old chief's office.

Hess stood behind the empty desk scratching at the buzzed back of his neck. He wore a ribbed rayon shirt tucked into wrinkle-guard dress pants with a braided brown belt: conservative and professional, with a hint of the sportsman. His chest was jacked, but it was the arms that impressed, maybe a little too much. He had invested a lot of gym hours in those biceps. Like a woman with a big chest, they were his defining feature.

Maddox remembered his first look at the guy as he emerged from his unmarked to eyeball the station, Hess's expression saying, *They got me off the lat machine for this?*

"So," Hess said, dropping his hands into his pleated pockets and letting them run around in there. "What's your take?"

"On Valerie Ripsbaugh?"

"We already know our doer isn't a woman. He's a man, right-handed, medium height, between five eight and six foot. Size ten and a half sneaker."

This was Hess showing off, as with his arms. He liked to dazzle. Maddox said, "Okay."

"Talk to me about the husband. Struck me as a little slow on the uptake."

"Inward, maybe. He's a town guy. His entire world's about this small."

"Any trouble from him you know of?"

"Less than none. He's the town caretaker. Looks after this place like it's his dying father."

Hess nodded, arms crossed tight. "He's not answering his radio, and we already tried his pager. Any idea where we can find him this time of day?"

"You're bringing him in?"

Hess nodded, all confidence. "Yeah, we're bringing him in."

Maddox still could not believe it. He had thought nothing of Ripsbaugh leaving Kitner's shop early, muttering good-bye as he moved through the door. "I don't know. The dump, maybe."

"You're shocked."

"I'm surprised, yeah. Ripsbaugh. Tearing someone apart like that. Doesn't make sense."

"Overkill. Know what that means? That it was very, very personal. A revenge killing. You ever been married?"

"No."

"There's nothing shocking about it. Especially with the quiet ones. Like yourself." Hess smiled, feeling magnanimous. "You're headed home? Do us a favor and drop Mrs. Ripsbaugh at her house. She's free to go."

VAL STARED AT THE floor of Maddox's patrol car, sitting lumpily next to him, sinking into herself and her baggy clothes. She had always had what Maddox's mother called "natural mascara," a darkness tracing the wing-shaped contours of her eyes, different from the bruised quality of her lids. In high school it had been the hallmark of Val's small-town exoticism.

Now it looked as though that mascara was starting to run. Maddox leaned on the gas pedal, the station receding on their right. He wanted to get her home fast. Because he was uncomfortable, and because he wanted to deliver this news to Pinty.

"Can you smell it on me?" she said.

"Smell what?" said Maddox.

She plucked at the skin on the back of her left hand, pinching herself. "The shit. I scrub myself raw, but the stink from his septic business—it's in my skin now. It's in my hair. Part of me. I can't get it out." Twisting at the back of her hand now, squeezing her flesh white.

"Val," said Maddox, passing her brother's place at the corner of Number 8 Road. "Things could still work out. Nothing's settled yet."

"Look at me, Donny. Look what I've become." She raised her

hands as though something warm and sticky had spilled in her lap. "*Look* at me."

She was weeping, and Maddox didn't know what to do. He wanted to get her home, but she was choking on her sobs, dissolving in the seat next to him, and he couldn't drive. He turned in fast at the Gulp, parking among the losing scratch tickets in back.

She cried hard into her hands, then pulled them away, reading something in the wetness on her palms. "He saved the letters," she said. "He *did* care, I knew he did. It *meant* something." Her hands closed into fists, and she turned to Maddox with sudden sobriety. "He helped me. When I met him, I was at my heaviest. The backaches— I was miserable. He turned it all around. He changed me, he *delivered* me. And, he was erudite. We talked. Really talked—about nature, about the stars. He knew so much. He had lived in California. He wanted me to go away with him. Everything he said to me was ice cream. I felt so good with him. I felt special."

That last word twisted in Maddox's side. He thought back to the Val Sinclair he had known in school: not beautiful, exactly, but different, mysterious somehow, with burgundy lips and licorice black hair and a hint of foreign blood in her winged eyes. Now the fullness of her face, the tired tangle of her hair, the coarse oatmeal texture of her skin—it was as though the town had exacted its revenge by blunting her features over time, like the Cold River's current dulling its bed stones.

How shocked he had been, returning home from college that first summer, to learn that Valerie Sinclair had become Mrs. Kane Ripsbaugh. A girl who had once spoken of nothing other than her desire to escape Black Falls. Her marrying the town caretaker, a man twenty years her senior, had hit Maddox with the force of a classmate's suicide. It made no sense. It never occurred to him at the time how bad her home life must have been—any family that could have produced Dill Sinclair . . . .

Val was really pinching the skin on the back of her hand now,

twisting it like the key to a windup toy. "Did they . . . ?" she said, looking first at Maddox, then down to the floorboard again. "Did you see
the letters?"

"I saw one."

"Some of them," she said, "they were personal, maybe a little . . ."

Her humiliation was nearly complete, and for Maddox, almost
unbearable. "Yeah," he said.

A smile of intense pain. Her palms came up to blind her eyes. "He
made me *feel* something," she said, trying to explain. "Something I
hadn't felt in a long time . . ."

She crumpled again, shuddering and crying there next to him.
Maddox was searching for something—anything—to say when she
turned toward him and began sobbing hard into his shoulder. He held
her lightly as her chest heaved against him with bucking gasps, and
he began to worry that someone from the store would come around
back and mistake this clinch for something more than it was.

So concerned was he that he misconstrued her nuzzling sniffles for
progress, an indication that she was settling down. It was several more
moments before he realized she was in fact nibbling at his neck with
light, wet tastes of his skin just above his collar, her kisses rising up to
the jawline beneath his ear.

Stunned by her sudden and inappropriate affection, he let it go
many more seconds than he otherwise would have before abruptly
pulling away.

She stayed where she was, on her side of the front seat, not
ashamed or embarrassed, cheeks glistening with mashed tears, eye-
lashes damp and shiny black. "I think he did it."

"What?" Maddox said.

She stared into the middle ground between them, as though coming to terms with this herself.

Maddox, still mystified by the kissing, felt something else now,
something like danger. He had a sense that marriages generated their
own peculiar force field, some more powerful than others. Especially

the less likely unions. The warped vibrations of this one were warning him to keep away.

"You need to get home," he said, throwing the car into drive and
making for the road.

A STATE POLICE CRUISER pulled up across the street from Ripsbaugh's driveway as Maddox drove off after dropping off Val. It was
only a matter of time before they picked him up, and Maddox felt a
pang of sympathy for the hunted man.

Ripsbaugh the loner. Ripsbaugh the vengeful. Ripsbaugh the
cuckold.

His tires crunched onto Pinty's white-rock driveway and he got
out and ducked underneath Mrs. Pinty's arbor, the woven ivy making him think of Pinty's hairpiece and the Vitalis he insisted on
sprinkling over it, more fragrant than anything in these hedges. The
front door was unlocked as usual, and he entered into the middle
landing, calling Pinty's name. He went downstairs to where Pinty
had moved his bed, then checked the newly converted kitchen and
found Pinty's walking stick leaned up against the end of the counter.
Through the sliding glass doors he saw the wheelchair out on the
brick patio beneath the raised deck, and Pinty lying on his side next
to it.

Maddox threw open the door. Pinty was not moving and Maddox's eyes did not know what to take in first. The gray pallor of Pinty's
face. His fists clenched and drawn to his chest as though pulling back
on reins. A spray of pallid yellow vomit on the brick, already visited
by ants.

Maddox rolled Pinty onto his back. Pinty's eyes were closed and for
a moment Maddox could not remember any of his training. He got
that same suffocating feeling as when he thought about his mother
dying alone.

A-B-C. Airway, Breathing, Circulation.

He put his ear to Pinty's nose and felt warm breath push faintly against it. He jabbed two fingers into the soft flesh beneath the ridge of Pinty's jawbone, locating a pressure point, the pulse slow yet persistent. He raised Pinty's neck in order to tilt up his head, and heard a gurgle.

Inside he found the phone and punched in 911. He got a state trooper at the station and instructed him to skip the ambulance call and instead order a medical helicopter.

When Bucky Pail and Keith Ullard and Bart Stokes arrived anyway, carrying equipment cases from their rescue truck and accompanied by Eddie Pail and Mort Lees in POLICE shirts, Maddox stood firm. "Stay away," he warned them.

"Maddox," scolded Eddie, bullheadedly trying to get around him to Pinty.

Maddox kicked the wheelchair into their way. "You don't touch him."

"Get away, Maddox," said Bucky.

Bucky knelt down to unclasp his blue tackle box of medical supplies. Maddox kicked it over.

Bucky stood, whipping his cigarette into the grass. The five of them fanned out around Maddox on the bricks. Maddox warned them again to keep away, and Mort Lees charged him from the side.

It seemed stupid later, everything coming to a head there with Pinty lying unconscious on the ground. But this brawl had been months in the making. Maddox blamed them for Pinty's sudden decline, and unloaded his anger onto them as they unloaded theirs onto him. Maddox tried to single out Bucky for some special vengeance, but, true to form, Bucky remained out on the periphery of the fray, jumping in only when he had a clear punch.

Yet Maddox held his own, never letting them pin him down. It was the arriving troopers following up on the 911 call who broke it up. The medical helicopter set down in Pinty's backyard soon after, flight nurses climbing out wearing helmets.

Maddox rode with him to the hospital, gripping Pinty's hand in the sideways sunlight as Black Falls shrunk away below them.

Pinty was wheeled off after they landed. Maddox declined an ER trip for his face, and was instead escorted to a windowless room where, left alone, he paced among cloth-covered chairs with small boxes of half-sized tissues poised on each wooden arm. Pale ocean watercolors hung on the walls—lonely boats, empty docks, muted sunsets—and Maddox realized they had installed him in the grief room.

29
CULLEN

CULLEN LOOKED AT THE ring cuts on Maddox's cheeks and fore-head, the abrasion on his neck, and the bruise under his left eye, not quite black but definitely blue.

"Fighting your fellow peace officers," said Cullen. "That's good strategy."

Maddox mock-smiled, raising his eyebrows. "Yup."

"Making friends all over the place. About ready to pack it in, then?"

Maddox didn't dignify that. He looked at the blank screen of the television set he had switched off as soon as they had stepped inside the empty waiting area.

"Good," said Cullen, wanting to come off motivational rather than bitchy. "May I ask what your thinking was there?"

"My thinking was, I'm going to kick these sons of bitches' asses for what they've done to him."

Cullen nodded. Maddox had plenty more fight in him, which was a good thing, if properly channeled. Cullen noticed that, though Maddox had not left the hospital since bringing in the old man, the gray T-shirt he wore was fresh and not speckled with blood. Maddox had somebody bringing him things.

Cullen loosened his tie and flopped it out straight over his belly, glancing out the window of Rainfield Good Samaritan. Every win-dow he had ever stood at or sat by in Rainfield looked out at some segment of the interstate or one of the gas station islands that fed it. "Okay. *I* have to kick some ass here now. This is supposed to be your rehab assignment."

Maddox frowned and sat back, inspecting the tender parts of his discolored knuckles.

"You were frustrated," said Cullen. "You thought you had them on the murdered snitch. You wanted them for it. Turns out, the snitch got pushed over by someone else."

"I don't know that for sure."

"Then allow me to convince you. Crime Scene Services got clever working over the witch's house. They figured the killer had spent some time there, so they keyed in on a couple of things. One was the fact that the towel rack in the upstairs bathroom was empty. Maybe the towels were used to wipe up or clean off something, maybe even the assailant himself. Luckily, this was on the side of the house that didn't burn so bad. First thing they scored were footwear impressions from the wet bath mat."

"Size ten and a half sneakers," said Maddox. "Hess already dangled that detail."

"Then they found that the sink—faucet, cabinet, vanity, whole thing—had been wiped down, scrubbed clean. Again—a good spot for cleaning something off, maybe washing up. A defensive wound, perhaps. So they went down into the plumbing. The pipes under-neath the sink. Pulled the drain traps, and there was blood."

"Blood?" said Maddox. "Heat from the fire didn't cook it?"

"Not all. Blood type immediately excluded the victim, Frond. While all this was going on, they turned up that safe under a bed upstairs. The letters."

"Right."

"Her husband, the roads guy, admits to knowing about his wife and the witch. Guy's alibi is soft, very uncorroborated. But the criti-cal thing is this gash on his arm."

Maddox looked at him now.

"Yeah," said Cullen. "Snagged it on a fence post, he said, but it fits

just fine as a defensive wound. Typical overhelpful type, this guy, Ripsbaugh. Hess asked him for theories about who could have done this,
and how. You know that old routine, 'If you didn't do it, tell me how
someone else could have.' I saw only five minutes of the tape, but it's
pretty pathetic, this guy holding forth with his theories."

"He's a cop buff."

"I know. They found all these true crime paperbacks in his house,
and forensics shows on tape. Criminal genius of the armchair variety.
Until Hess offered him straight out—'Hey, let me exclude you: volunteer a DNA sample.' That's when the guy started to stumble,
started shutting down. Knew enough about DNA to want nothing to
do with it, I guess. He refused outright. So Hess went prob cause,
subpoenaed a cheek swab—which they got—and now it's a wait for
the results."

Maddox rubbed his raw knuckles. "He's locked up?"

"No need. Not until the DNA comes back. Guy's not exactly a
flight risk, right? He's being tailed twenty-four/seven, see if he
cracks."

"So this is going to go on for a while."

"Actually, not so. A colleague in my office says Hess called in a chit
at the lab in Sudbury. He's gotten somebody to cut through the back-
log for him, push him to the top of the list. Apparently, Hess doesn't
like this Ripsbaugh. Either that or he wants out of Black Falls even
faster than you do."

"Hess," said Maddox. A look of disdain.

"'Leo the Lion,' they call him. King of the Jungle."

"There was somebody else from the DA's office at the station."

Cullen shrugged. "Probably a clerk helping to write up affidavits,
that's all. No one knows you, or about you. How you want it, right?"

"How it has to be. How it is."

"Fine line, my friend. A dangerous game."

"You want dangerous? With Pinty gone, I'm all alone in town now.
Unprotected."

"So go to Hess. Come out to him. What's the harm?"

"Not how it's done."

Cullen dismissed that. "You just don't like him."

Maddox sat forward. "If something does happen to me, anything, an accident, if I die choking on my food, you fall on the town like the U.S. Marines." Maddox waited for Cullen to agree to that, then sat back again. "Ripsbaugh have a lawyer yet?"

"Hess actually advised him to get one after the DNA swab."

"And?"

"Ripsbaugh said only guilty people need lawyers."

Maddox shook his head. "Jesus."

"Comical, how wrong he's going. Getting away with murder looks so easy on TV. Motive and opportunity—sure, that's all circumstantial. But not blood evidence. And this isn't mere DNA, mind you. Actual *blood*."

"No latents?"

"Guy watches TV, are you kidding? Children pocketing bubble gum at the corner store wear gloves now. CSS found traces of talcum at the witch's house, so they're thinking latex."

Maddox shook his head grimly.

Cullen went on. "As to Hess. You want to 'don't ask, don't tell' him? Maybe that's okay for now. But. You cannot withhold evidentiary material or mislead him in any way. We're already walking the tightrope with this. *Don't* cost the county money. That's the golden rule."

Maddox nodded. That satisfied both their pro forma obligations.

A pretty nurse with a thin, well-bred nose poked her head in, smiling at Maddox. "You can go back in now."

Cullen thought how they must love Maddox here. Heart-on-his-sleeve moody, devoted to a dying old man, and all nicked and banged up himself. Like a teddy bear tossed from a moving car.

Two doors down the curved hallway, they entered the warm, white hospital room. Cullen had met Pinty only once, six months ago, at the start of all this, and the man whose hand he shook then resembled not at all the sleeping ghost he visited now. His lips were slack around the tube in his mouth, flesh sagging off his proud jaw. The large head-board looked like an uncarved headstone, and Maddox, standing at the foot of the bed, an early mourner. The old man's hairpiece, Cullen guessed, was in a plastic bag inside the nightstand drawer. No such thing as dignity in death. Not that Cullen ever saw.

Maddox said, looking down at the old man, "Blood clots broke loose from his legs. Lodged in his brain and possibly his heart. He had a series of small strokes, but they won't know the damage until he regains consciousness. 'Until and unless,' they say."

"You blame the stress?"

"I do."

Cullen dropped into the padded chair that flattened out into Mad-dox's night bed. A yellow plastic tray held his uneaten lunch. Maddox must have told them he was family. That was his cover here.

"I could get those guys right this minute if I wanted," Maddox said. "Multiple counts of harassment, excessive use of force, abuse of power. All sorts of bullshit they could worm their way around in court with lawyers stalling and all that. No. When I get them, they're going to know they've been gotten." He looked down at the old man. "I'll cut them so deep, everything's going to come pouring out."

Maddox was vengeful now. Triple the motivation.

Cullen chewed his lip thoughtfully. "Just one more question, then."

Maddox didn't look up. "What's that?"

"Where the hell is Sinclair?"

30
TRACY

DONNY SAT NEXT TO HER in her old Ford pickup. He was quiet most of the way, but not silent, not morose. More anxious than anything. She guessed that it was his having just left Pinty for the first time. If anything happened to Pinty while he was gone, it would be like his mother all over again.

The week's groceries she had bought for her mother as an excuse for this midday excursion to Rainfield knocked around in plastic bags behind the seat. They passed a slumping barn with a faded HAY FOR SALE sign leaning against a decaying tractor set out as yard art. Back in Black Falls, they picked up the Cold River running along Main. Across the street from the mailbox reading RIPSBAUGH was a state police cruiser.

"Kind of creepy," Tracy said, "having them in town. A little like an occupation." She watched the whip-antennaed cruiser shrinking in her rearview mirror. "They've been following him everywhere. The one time I saw them, heading up toward the highway department garage, it was like a little parade."

"How's he handling it?"

"He was driving straight along like he wasn't even aware. Maybe he isn't."

They passed the Falls Diner and the Gas-Gulp-'N-Go, the crumbling mill houses coming into view.

Tracy said, "I heard they found a sex video of his wife and Mr. Frond."

The phrase "sex video" roused him a bit. "No," he said, sitting up, watching Number 8 Road go past. "They were just love letters. High school–type stuff. But with drawings."

"Drawings?"

"She was a good artist in school. Still is, by the look of it."

"Dirty stuff?"

"Or erotic, depending on your point of view."

"Dirty," she said, hoping to cheer him up. "Drawings make more sense to me, anyway." She had imagined an Internet-type video of an older, ponytailed guy and a heavy woman doing it. Ick. "In drawings you can make yourself thinner."

They passed another state police cruiser parked outside the police station and didn't talk again until she pulled into Pinty's white-stone driveway, behind Donny's patrol car. "Thanks," he said. "For the ride, for bringing me my stuff, for everything."

"Wish I could stay with you. But I have to get back, finish up for the day."

He took his leather toiletry bag, the one she had packed for him. How strange it had felt, being inside his house alone. Walking room to room, poking around his bathroom things. He said, "I'm heading in to work soon, anyway."

She touched the cut just under his sideburn, now healed to a nick. "Good luck there."

He nodded. "I don't even know if I can still call myself a policeman here without Pinty to back me up."

"Please be careful."

He kissed her once, lightly, and she pulled him closer for a real one, kissing him longer and better. She rubbed his arm. "I know how much Pinty meant to you," she said, then realized she had spoken in the past tense. "*Means* to you, sorry."

"He's made fools out of doctors before," said Donny. "He'll be home again."

Tracy smiled and nodded, admiring his stubborn faith though she did not share it. "I know he's all you have."

31

HESS

ALPABLE EXCITEMENT among the uniforms, the duty troopers
all extra-alert and garrulous, gobbling up oxygen inside the station; the hunting party anticipating the kill.

What Hess would remember most about this sour-smelling place
was the sheer amount of crank mags stored up in the break room. A
mountain of the stuff, had to be a record for a force this tiny. One time
he'd had the occasion to visit a firehouse in a midsized town that was
using an anatomically correct female mannequin for training exercises
as well as other, less official pursuits. That squad was eventually dis-
banded and reassigned after word got out that they had invited a local
stripper to dance on the fire pole during a shift change. Not that Hess
had any moral objections to this stuff, but good Christ, there was a
time and, more to the point, a place.

Maddox entered the break room looking to store his nylon lunch
sack in the fridge. He seemed a little pale to Hess, maybe from worry,
like he had lost some weight in the days he had taken off to sit with
his friend in the hospital.

Bucky Pail came in on Maddox's heels, grinning like his shirt was
on fire and he liked the burn. Until he saw Hess, whose presence was
a bucket of cold water. The action on his face flattened out, all that
Maddox saw when he turned.

Pail still had the scrape bloom on his cheek, like he had gotten
grazed with a boot tread. Maddox's abrasions were far less worse than

Hess had been led to believe, and in a strange way it reassured him to know that Maddox hadn't gotten his ass kicked by these hillbillies.

"Some police department," said Hess. "I'm almost sorry to leave it. Almost."

Maddox ignored Hess, looking at Pail. Waiting.

When Hess didn't make any move to exit the room, Pail's grin got hot. "Later," he said to Maddox, with lots of tongue on the *L*, then turned and went out.

"Five against one," Hess said to Maddox. "You did all right for yourself. Seems like it's not over yet."

"Not by a long shot," said Maddox.

"You timed your return right. We're just about to arrest your highway department man for murder."

A trooper ducked in, hooking his thumb back toward the hall. "DiBenedicto's on the line."

"Here we go," announced Hess, rolling his shoulders as he went into the hallway.

Joe Bryson, Hess's training partner who had come from the Mitchum barracks to watch him mop up this case, closed the door inside the old chief's office. Hess punched the button on the telephone. "Jimmy D., you're on speaker. How we look?"

"Leo," came Jimmy DiBenedicto's voice, "we have exact matches in eight combinations—"

"Gimme the odds first, Jimbo. The stats that I love. This guy is one in how many hundreds of millions?"

"I haven't had a chance to do the math yet, Leo. But two of the matches are extremely rare, so it's a lock. Listen—who else you got there?"

"Couple of good people, Jimmy." Hess shifted balance, looking at Bryson, the county attorney in short sleeves, Fogarty, and the other guy from CSS. He reasserted himself. "Everybody who should be here is here, Jimmy. It's fine. Go ahead."

"Leo," came the filtered voice. "Maybe you want to pick up."

Hess cocked his head. Eyeing the phone from a different angle.

"No, Jimmy, I'm sure I don't want to pick up. You said you had an exact match on the autorads."

"I carried this thing across the hall myself, Leo. It's one to one. Only not with the swab you submitted. It's a rad out of the convicted felon database."

"The CODIS?"

Hess did pick up the handset then. Like the world's lightest dumb-bell.

Hess did not hang up after the conversation. He snapped the handset in half instead. He stood there a moment with the cracked plastic and exposed wire in his hands, then dispatched Bryson to bring him Pail and Maddox.

They appeared before his desk. Maddox saw the busted phone on the blotter and knew immediately that something was up.

Hess made them wait, burning off a little more anger at their expense, making them suffer for his aggravation. This ass-crack town, this fucking bitch of a case. And these two banged-up playground cops. *What did I do to deserve this?*

"This missing sex offender," said Hess.

Now Maddox looked confused. Pail said, "Scarecrow?"

Hess scowled at this room he was going to be stuck in a little while longer. "I need to know everything about him there is to know."

Part III
SCARECROW

32
HESS

B RYSON WAS ONLY a few weeks out of uniform, but Hess had detected a change in him since the DNA rads came back. Used to be Bryson would ape Hess. Hess would turn around with his arms crossed and find Bryson standing there, arms crossed. Hess would walk in chewing one of the spearmint toothpicks he kept in the ashtray of his car, and a day or two later Bryson would be switching a pick from one corner of his mouth to the other like it was something he'd been doing all his life. Bryson had started working out more, Hess noticed, and shaping his hair flatter on top, and talking about church. Like Hess's boys, Bryson was learning by imitation, paying out respect in the form of flattery.

But now, ever since the DNA flop, Hess noticed Bryson standing back from him a bit. Tossing out questions where before he was content to listen and let Hess speak. Pointing out things to the CSS guys without routing it through Hess first.

Hess wasn't overly sensitive, but he *was* observant; that was what made him, working out of the smallest barracks with the least resources at hand, the trooper with the highest clearance rate of any other DU investigator statewide. Getting this understudy heat from Bryson was the capper on a bad stretch of slow-motion progress. Hess needed to turn this ship around, and fast. Not just for his batting average but for himself. Someday his boys were going to look at their dad and see not a Superman but a guy who was simply doing his best. He could accept that from his boys, but not from Bryson, not just yet.

CSS wouldn't allow the windows to be opened as they went about their glove-and-bag dissection of the sex offender's crib. What struck Hess most about Sinclair's black-curtained place were the contents of the guy's kitchen cabinets: Devil Dogs, Beefaroni, snack-pack puddings, Kool-Aid mix, and boxes and boxes of cereal, from Apple Jacks to Quisp. The ultimate pantry as imagined by a ten-year-old boy.

Hess was encouraged by the black wig they had found hanging scalplike on Sinclair's bedpost. It was human hair, more expensive than an acrylic wig and much more realistic in wear and feel. CSS had recovered eleven different hair follicles from inside Frond's bathroom, stairs, and second-floor hallway, all black, all of similar length, but varying in ethnicity: two Caucasian, two Negroid, and seven Mongoloid or Asian. Turned out, Hess learned, that dozens of different donors—including cadavers—are used to make one human-hair wig.

So, no match on the hair, but the dots were there to connect. Sinclair's credit card showed he had laid out eight bills for a new wig in March, this one an inch longer than the one found hanging on his bed—the length matching the hairs recovered from Frond's.

The wig was good and the blood was better, but what Hess needed now was to establish some before-murder connection between Sinclair and Frond. Not for motive. Motive can cloud a case as much as clarify it, especially in court. Defense attorneys can have a field day with motive. Hess himself had a legally compelling motive to do away with a dozen people who had wronged him over the years. In order to feed the DA a solid conviction, he needed to link Sinclair to Frond in life, not just in death.

To that end, Hess was pulling books from Sinclair's collection on the occult. Working the Magician and the Witch angle. It had potential, considering the missing athame. He was in the side hallway flipping through a book of voodoo recipes when a CSS criminalist entered the kitchen with Maddox in tow.

Turned out Maddox—surprise, surprise—had been inside Sinclair's place before. They were taking him through again to ascertain what surfaces he had touched—he claimed none—or what if anything appeared missing or moved.

Bottom line: Something about Maddox rubbed Hess the wrong way. Something about him Hess did not like. Did not like or did not trust. Beyond the sense that the feeling was quite mutual. It was there in the way Maddox watched the criminalists and computer techs going about their work. Nothing in his interest said "part-time cop." There was no outsider awe, only compulsive vigilance.

In other words, he did not strike Hess as a man blown back into this town by circumstance. More like a man with a knack for moving with the eye of a storm.

Hess let them finish—waited until they asked him about the empty docking station wired to Sinclair's PC, the camera to which also appeared to be missing—before catching up with him outside on the chipped sidewalk near the CSS van.

Maddox eyed the modest crowd gathered across the intersection, mothers with their arms tight around their children. Hess said, "They don't like it."

Maddox turned, didn't startle. "What's to like?"

"Sex offender accused of murder. That's a real-life monster in your neighborhood."

Maddox nodded, knowing that Hess had a point, and waiting for him to get to it.

"I gotta hand it to you, Maddox. You don't seem fazed."

"Fazed?"

"Dealing with real police. On a real crime, a murder. You don't seem too impressed with us, and you don't seem annoyed by our presence, and those are the two small-town-cop responses we usually get. Envy or resentment."

He shrugged. "I'm part-time. A spectator."

Hess reminded himself that this "spectator" was the first to get inside Sinclair's apartment after he went missing. Had turned up

Sinclair's bike before anyone even knew it was gone. A good bit of diligence from a man with no career to make, just a guy passing through town.

"See," said Hess, "that doesn't do it for me. This isn't the sort of thing you stumble into, police work. A job you do awhile before moving on to the next thing. People burn out all the time, but rarely do they walk out. No small-town cop I ever met didn't dream of the big time."

Maddox shrugged again. "Now you met him."

"I had this therapist one time. I was in a crisis-incident thing, a shooting; they make you do an exit interview and mandatory counseling. It's paid time, you sit, you chat." Hess letting Maddox know he didn't buy into it much. "But this one thing she told me stuck. It was that guys drawn to police work are really only sublimating antisocial or violent impulses. Policing the impulsive, aggressive parts of themselves, and at the same time allowing them an outlet. In her words. Make sense to you?"

"I guess."

"Makes sense to me. Over the years I've seen it prove out. Guys don't become cops to help old ladies cross the street. They don't come in looking to 'do good.' They come in looking to stop bad. They come in looking to impose order. It's the uniform they join for, dressing themselves up in the law and wearing it around so everyone can see: Me, good guy. Me, not bad."

Maddox pulled at his sweat-spotted POLICE jersey. "I didn't join for the uniform."

"No, I guess you didn't. You said your father was on the job once upon a time. I'm assuming that's how you got hired on, second-generation?"

"Pretty much."

"Sinclair's father was a cop."

"For a couple of years. He was a builder after that."

"Had a falling-out with the force. Now, kids of cops, that's a whole 'nother thing. Lots of second-generation cops among them—

myself included. Plenty of screwups too, though, like Sinclair. And some of both. Like these Pail brothers. Those are the ones to watch out for."

"You think?" said Maddox.

Hess smiled at the way Maddox parried. "You know something else I figured out? With you filling up your own patrol car here, and the price of a gallon of gas being what it is these days? I figure working as a cop in Black Falls is actually *costing* you. Which shows extraordinary dedication. For someone just marking time. I mean, I consider myself a good cop. But even I have to get paid every two weeks, you know? Gotta get that take-home. Or are there some incentives to being a Black Falls cop that I don't know about?"

Maddox tapped his brim. "There's these swell caps."

"So how was it you happened to wind up inside Sinclair's apartment that first time?"

"I told you. I was driving past and saw movement in the window. He's a registered SO who hadn't been seen in a while, so I pulled over, knocked on the door. The kid answered and let me up."

"The kid. This Frankie Sculp, right?"

"That's right."

"Foster kid, been staying here. Didn't know where Sinclair was."

"Correct."

Hess nodded. "But you knew Sinclair from before, right?"

"You mean as kids? We lived on the same street, on opposite ends. But I didn't *know him* know him. That was a long time ago."

"You two didn't pal around the neighborhood?"

"He was two grades older than me."

"His sister was your age."

Maddox nodded slowly. Getting it now. Maddox said, "You know a lot."

"I keep my ears open," said Hess. "So she has an affair with a guy, who her brother then kills."

Maddox said, "You've interviewed her again, I assume. They weren't close. I doubt she's even spoken to him since he got out of prison."

"Still, the Sinclair connection is a pretty strong link. Would you contest that?"

"It's a link," agreed Maddox. "But not a strong one."

"In your professional opinion."

Maddox shrugged. "You asked."

"Maybe Sinclair and Frond had something else going. His books here, he's got a lot of occult stuff. Frond with his New Age whatever, it's a common area of interest. Maybe they connected after Frond dropped dime on Pail for beating up Sinclair at that traffic stop. Bonded, you know? Banded together to curse the police department, or what have you. Some sort of cult thing."

"A black mass or something."

"Or something, yeah. See, I don't chuckle about it myself, because this stupid shit, it's happened before. Retarded backwoods rituals where someone gets overzealous, goes too far. People can lose their bearings in these remote towns. Lose control."

Maddox said nothing, waiting. Hess was doing most of the talking, but sometimes that worked. Sometimes that drew them out.

"This 'Scarecrow' took a lot of abuse in this town, sounds like. Maybe he'd finally had enough. Maybe Frond let slip that he had some money stashed around his place, and maybe Sinclair was thinking about skipping town and decided he'd get a lot further with cash in hand. Maybe Frond came home and found him ransacking his place, and Sinclair panicked."

"All 'maybe's."

"Well, I'm doing what I can. I've got a suspect in a murder case who's up and disappeared. Completely vanished—I don't know where, I don't know how. Left behind practically everything, including a closet full of clothes, luggage, cash in a bank account which remains untouched, and the only credit card to his name is the Discover card on his bedroom bureau. Took his bicycle, maybe, but didn't get very far on it. Everything else, he left behind. Including a little blood at the scene of the crime, the imprint of a size ten and a half Chuck Taylor tread, and various black follicles from a wig of human hair. But wait. Hold on. One other thing he didn't leave behind. One thing for me to focus on. The missing piece, right? The thing that doesn't fit. You know what I'm talking about?"

Maddox shook his head, passably curious.

"Sinclair's digital camera. That empty docking station hooked up to his computer in there. Purchased in early May over the Internet, with said Discover card—camera, hot dock, and media card. Sinclair fooled around with it a bit, took some test shots in his apartment. We know this because he installed the viewing software and uploaded a few date-coded images into his computer. But after that? Nothing. Nothing at all in the two months leading up to his disappearance and Frond's murder. Meaning, to my mind, there's a pretty good chance this camera's got some pictures sitting in its memory card. Pictures that maybe even could give us a line on where he is now. You said the docking station was empty when you were inside his place the first time. It's a small camera, by the way. Pocket-sized."

Maddox said, "Are you accusing me of something?"

"Look, you're stuck here in the middle of nowhere. Free reign on your night shifts, nobody watching. No chief or shift sergeant crawling up your ass. You're not making any money. And nobody has a crystal ball—nobody knows how one little act, an impulse, a spur-of-the-moment decision, is going to affect everything else down the road. Hell, you might even regret it, but can't see how to make it right. I'm saying, so long as I get that media card back intact? No harm, no foul."

Maddox worked hard to keep his cool. A tough read, this guy. "Why don't you ask the kid who was staying here where the camera is?"

"I'd like to," said Hess. "I'd like to very much."

Maddox waited. "And?"

"We checked with the Ansons, his foster parents. They haven't seen him in days."

"The Ansons aren't known as the most diligent guardians," Maddox said. Then he thought about it. "Wait a minute. Are you saying he's missing?"

"That's what I'm saying."

For the first time since he'd met him, Hess saw Maddox look surprised.

33
BUCKY

Bucky was waiting with Eddie and Mort Lees when Maddox came out the back door. Maddox hesitated, and thought Bucky didn't see it, then continued down the steps toward his patrol car.

Bucky moved out in front of the others, touching his own abraded cheek as though it were wet with paint. "Thought only girls kicked."

Maddox said, "All I could manage with you letting your boys here do the real fighting."

Bucky grinned. "I'm gonna miss you, Maddox."

"Oh? I'm going somewhere?"

"You getting along good with the troopers? Hanging out at Scarecrow's apartment there? You seem to be their boy now."

"Yeah," said Maddox, keeping an eye on the others. "They're a fun bunch."

"Uptight shits," said Bucky. "Their whistles and faggoty-ass boots. The fucking gay Gestapo, marching in here." He nodded at the station. "Putting us out of our own house like cats."

Eddie chimed in. "Mountie assholes."

Bucky said, "Scarecrow needs to be caught? So put me on it. I've tangled with him before."

Maddox said, "Slapping around a guy in handcuffs isn't exactly tangling."

Bucky grinned harder, enjoying this. Maddox couldn't touch him anymore. "You think Frond wishes he'd kept his big mouth shut now?

Trying to turn *me* in? They say karma's a bitch—but *man*. That same piece of shit he was defending coming back and killing his ass? So funny it's almost sad."

Maddox said, "Sinclair would be in prison right now if your *tangling* hadn't gotten him out of that drunk driving conviction. If you hadn't messed up the arrest."

Bucky was having a hard time keeping victory from bursting out of him. "I really am gonna miss you, Maddox."

"Is that right?"

Bucky stepped closer. "How's it feel? No Pinty here to bail you out anymore. Nobody to run to. What's it like, being all alone?"

"Pinty's coming back."

"That's not what I heard. Not what I saw there out on his back patio. Reality is, the old man's time has come and gone. And so has his pet cop's. Once Pinty kicks, you can consider yourself unemployed."

Maddox said, "You're not police chief yet."

"But I will be. That's the beauty of it. With no Pinty to hold me back anymore? I might even run for his seat on the board of selectmen when it opens up." Bucky looked to the others for enthusiasm. "Be the new Pinty in town."

They were all smiles. Maddox was pretending hard that Bucky wasn't getting under his skin, but the truth was so obvious, and so good.

The rear screen door squealed. A plainclothes trooper looked out. "Maddox? The K-9 units are here. Hess wants you over at the bridge."

Maddox thumbed back at his patrol car. "I was on my way home."

The trooper said, "You're the one who found the bike. Hess wants you there." He turned and went back inside, the door whacking shut.

Maddox cursed under his breath. That surprised Bucky. So Maddox wasn't sucking up to them after all. He was their lackey. This gave Bucky another quiet thrill.

"K-9?" he said, almost laughing before he could get it out. "I guess somebody's got to scoop up all that dog shit."

That broke up the others.

"Put that paper diploma of yours to good use," said Bucky, another kick in the shins.

But Maddox didn't sulk. Instead, he came up eye to eye, his voice dropping so that only Bucky could hear him. "Your day is coming."

Bucky tried hard to keep up his mirth. Maddox's eyes were eager and hard, like he had more to say but preferred to sit on his information like a fucking hen on a warm egg.

Bluffing. All bullshit. Maddox knew nothing. Smug fuck.

Bucky burned so hot that he had to remind himself that he was in fact winning here. That everything, from Frond being murdered to Pinty going down, was falling his way. Like a giant hand clearing a path for him. Everything meant to be. All he had to do was sit back, and Maddox would be next. Then absolutely nothing would stand in his way.

Maddox turned and walked to the stairs, Bucky resurrecting his grin for the others. "I'm gonna miss him," Bucky said. "I truly am."

34
MADDOX

MADDOX DROVE FAST, setting aside his disgust for Pail in order to focus on the missing Frankie Sculp. That sullen kid with the dyed-gold hair. His hungry eyes and shoved-in face, as though the doctor had flat-handed him at birth. His face rippled with acne, his skin the color and consistency of a peeled-apart peanut butter and jelly sandwich.

"He knows a way, he said. All the cops. He's going to turn this shit-fucking town upside down."

Maddox shouldn't have let him go. Shouldn't have tossed him back for fear of scaring away the bigger fish . . .

But then again, it hardly mattered what Maddox or anyone else did. Truth was, Frankie had the mark on him. Maddox had seen it before. The kid had been bred to cut a path to his own self-destruction. Maddox only hoped he had not arrived there yet. Maddox would have to start looking for Frankie himself, though with Pinty being in the hospital, and Hess yanking his leash, his walking-around time was severely limited.

He passed the red STATE FARM INSURANCE AGENT sign at the end of Walt Heavey's driveway, thinking of the hand-rolled cigarette butt he had found there, frowning again at the thought of Sinclair lurking around Heavey's house. That weak-minded fool. Why, of all people, would he kill Frond? The one guy who had intervened on his behalf with Bucky's abuse? Even if Sinclair had somehow found out about

Frond sleeping with his sister—Sinclair had no stake in that. He and Val were brother and sister in name only.

Maddox neared the one-lane bridge that marked the paved end of Edge Road and the beginning of a tagged-on half mile of dirt and rock. He pulled over behind an unmarked cruiser and walked to the gravel turnout just before the short, rusted span that bore no name. The three rat-tailed boys who had called it "Toad Bridge" stood below, on the hard bank of the dribbling, heat-strangled brook, showing state police Crime Scene Services technicians where they had discovered Sinclair's bicycle.

Walt Heavey was also present, having walked down from his house. He was testifying in front of Hess, who stood back off the road in the shade, spraying his big arms with bug repellent. "I'm telling you, there is something going on in these woods."

"This woman at your boys' window," said Hess, arms glistening sleeve to wrist. "She had long black hair. How long?"

"Below the shoulder."

Hess was working the wig angle. Sinclair had been known to wear that thing out on his balcony after dusk, overlooking the center of town. He asked Heavey, "Ever hear anything in the woods at night like music, or chanting?"

Heavey gave this serious thought. "No, sir. But you are looking at a man in the insurance game fourteen years now, as level as they come. And I am telling you, there is something going on in these woods."

Hess thanked him and Heavey went away satisfied. Hess handed the aerosol can back to Bryson and turned to Maddox. "He said something about you shooting a deer the same night he heard his gunshot?"

"Back up the road by the falls."

Hess smoothed a goatee that was not there and said no more. His sandy hair was thinned back from his forehead, showing a lot of scalp. Premature hair loss was a common trait among hard-core weight trainers, especially those who had relied on supplements in the past.

Handlers led two lean German shepherds out of a K-9 van on long leather leashes, sitting them at attention about ten meters back from the bridge. Hess admired the dogs' muscular obedience, until something farther back along the road put a shadow of anger across his face.

Maddox turned and saw the orange highway department pickup parked back at the turn. Ripsbaugh was unloading an armful of traffic cones.

Hess summoned a uniformed trooper to his side, his voice quiet but forceful. "I want him out of here."

Maddox stepped up before the trooper started off. "I'll do it," he said.

Hess looked at Maddox, wondering why he would bother, then permitted it with a flick of his wrist.

Maddox walked back past the cars lining the baking road to where Ripsbaugh was setting down his cones. "Kane," Maddox said.

Ripsbaugh straightened, Maddox getting a sense of the strength inside his saggy pants and silent attitude, years of steady labor bound up in muscle. "Don."

"Hey, uh . . ." He nodded back at Hess. "They want you to leave. They don't want you around."

Ripsbaugh stared. "I'm closing off the road. This turn here—"

"I know. I know. I'm just telling you what they said."

Ripsbaugh looked toward the turnout at the bridge. Hess was ignoring him, talking to someone else. Ripsbaugh was usually hard to read, but here the insult was plain.

Twelve hours after the DNA results had come back, Ripsbaugh's state police shadow simply disappeared. No apology to Ripsbaugh, no explanation. Because Ripsbaugh was never officially charged, he didn't have to be officially cleared. So add to the taint of cuckoldry a cloud of suspicion still lingering over Ripsbaugh's head.

Maddox said, "Leave the cones with me. I'll pick them up when they're through here, run them on back to you."

Ripsbaugh slowly set down the cones. He was the kind of man

who knew little of life other than the satisfaction of hard work. Take away his work and you leave him with nothing.

Maddox returned to the bridge. They had brought the boys up from the brook and sent down the dogs, handlers walking them back and forth over the cracked mud bank. The dogs sniffed and prodded aggressively, turning up zilch. Then CSS guys tossed down paper bags for the handlers to rip open underneath the dogs' noses, one containing a black T-shirt, the other a ratty pair of black crew-length socks. Clothes from Sinclair's apartment. The handlers snapped commands in German, and the dogs dutifully explored the site a second time. One of them seemed to scent something, but was unable to follow it.

The handlers then led them in wider, concentric circles. Maddox slapped at bugs while Hess remained a portrait of serenity, watching the police dogs working below for him.

As they moved to the Borderlands side of the short bridge, the handlers regripped leashes, winding the taut straps around their wrists as the dogs started to pull. A handler called up to say that they were "indicating," and a CSS guy moved sideways down the short embankment carrying an oversized pair of tweezers and a paper evidence bag. What he found on the top curve of the bank he held up for Hess to see.

Maddox wasn't sure. But he thought it might be the flattened butt of a hand-rolled cigarette.

You weak-minded fool.

The dogs led their handlers farther into the trees, skirting the dry, snaking bank of the brook. Hess and Bryson made their way down to follow, as did Maddox after a moment, tagging along unnoticed.

The dogs abruptly left the brook for the trees, straining against their leashes and pawing through the litter of the forest floor, scrambling over lumpy roots, following a trail. Maddox tried to envision it as he moved. Sinclair ditching his bike by the bridge. Hiking through the forest along this very route. Hiking or running? Could he have been chased?

The midnight gunshot Heavey had heard. Could Sinclair have

found his way through these woods after dark, even with a flashlight? What was he doing biking out here in the first place?

The dogs' barking picked up, and Maddox saw sunlight ahead, a clearing in the trees. The old fire road. Hard-packed and baking in the heat.

The dogs stopped, snarling, pawing madly at the shoulder of the road. Uncanny, the canine sense of smell. Nearly psychic in its ability.

The handlers promenaded the animals around a small perimeter, but to no avail. The dogs strained to get back toward the shoulder. The trail had ended.

The handlers released them from command and their leashes, the dogs jumping back and forth among the dead leaves and pine needles, digging at the ground, agitated and whimpering. They were indicating something, and suffering for their inability to communicate just what it was.

Hess stepped past them out into the middle of the road. He looked west where it curved, disappearing into the treeline. "Where's this go?"

No one else answered, and Maddox realized he was being addressed. "Access road. Runs the length of the forest, from the trailheads on the northeast side of town out to Aylesbury, I think. Near the state border. Ungated at either end."

Hess looked the other way, back toward Black Falls. "Who drives it?"

"No one. Unless you're looking to wreck your suspension. Teenagers run it on a dare sometimes."

"Teenagers?"

"'Hell Road,' they call it. Every year, every graduating class. Rite of passage. The old haunted-forest thing."

"What's the legend?"

"Pequoig Indian spirits seeking revenge for a massacre out at the falls. That's the classic version. Others say there was a boy who got lost out here and froze to death around the turn of the last century. People claim to hear him crying and calling out for help after the first snow."

Hess nodded. "Nothing else?"

"You could probably find somebody who would talk up midnight masses and devil worship."

Hess didn't like the way Maddox phrased that. He passed another silent judgment on Maddox, then looked away, ignoring him. "Hell Road," he said to Bryson.

Bryson shielded his eyes from the high sun. "A midnight stroll through the forest seems unlikely, though stranger things have happened. And that gunshot report, it's still a big 'if' in my book. But the dogs place him here, no question. He could have met someone." Bryson mimed his theory, intrigued by the possibility. "Shot them, took their car. Because he needed wheels, because he knew he was blowing town. He went after Frond maybe for some traveling cash."

Hess said, "Forty dollars was still tucked inside the kitchen creamer."

"So he failed."

"Then what's he doing for money? No ATM hits, no pings out in the real world."

"Hiding. A wanted man."

Hess closed one eye. "Okay, but if he had a gun, why didn't he shoot Frond? Why tear him up like that?"

Bryson sputtered, out of gas.

Hess said, "What if he didn't go anywhere at all?"

Bryson squinted. To Maddox, it seemed like Hess had left Bryson twisting. Like he had allowed him to fail here.

Hess said, "Maybe he was only trying to look disappeared. Maybe he walked out here, turned around, walked right back. Left the bike where he had dumped it, waded through stream water back toward town." Hess chewed the inside of his cheek, watching the confounded dogs. "We know he was inside the witch's house for some amount of time. Days, maybe."

Bryson said, "You're saying Sinclair's still nearby?"

"We've got alerts out there. A guy with shaved eyebrows, that's tough to miss."

Bryson scanned the trees they had just walked out of. "Okay. Then where's he hiding now?"

While Maddox was distracted by this back-and-forth, one of the unleashed dogs had cut back around its handler toward him. Maddox stiffened, the dog nudging his shin, starting a low-grade growl.

The handler heeled the dog with a German command, and it sat at eager attention, eyes fixed on Maddox, lips back and baring its teeth.

Maddox explained, "I was inside the apartment earlier."

The handler said nothing. He took up the leash, wound it tightly around his hand, and eased the hungry dog away.

Maddox saw Hess standing closer to the shoulder now, watching him, his big arms pretzeled.

35
RIPSBAUGH

IPSBAUGH RIMMED THE fire pit in the Bobcat, dozing dirt onto the smoldering ash. Cinders lifted off in a huff of protest, flakes of leaf and yard bag flaring orange before dying black and drifting down like hell snow. Smoke rose from the pit, gray and thin.

The heat off the crater made things wavy, but the white jersey immediately attracted Ripsbaugh's eye, as will any clean thing in a dump. Maddox coming toward him between lanes of landfill. Ripsbaugh made another smothering pass, covering up the carcass of a pillaging coyote he had snared with an illegal leg trap.

"Saw the smoke," said Maddox, talking over the Bobcat engine. "I dropped the cones in the back of your truck."

Ripsbaugh nodded and motioned Maddox aboard. Maddox gripped the outside of the cage as Ripsbaugh drove back up the rise to the equipment shack. Maddox stepped off as Ripsbaugh killed the ignition and climbed out, plucking his T-shirt away from his sweat-soaked sides. He swiped at his brow with his back-pocket rag, admiring the soot that rubbed off.

Maddox's face and nose looked pinched, but to Ripsbaugh the stench of sun-baked garbage was second nature. Maddox said, "How do you stand burning in this heat?"

"Piles up otherwise. It don't stop for summer." He popped open the Igloo cooler just inside the door, offering Maddox a Coors, which he declined. "I earned this one," said Ripsbaugh, cracking it open, exploding a spray of mist and a lazy spill of foam.

He drank down half, wincing under the high sun, then caught sight of a wing flapping over the top of a dirt hillock across the lane. He handed Maddox his beer and reached back inside the shed for his spade, mounting the rise in four long strides, blade raised.

Two massive turkey vultures spread their wings, lifting off slowly away from him, hauling their ugly bodies into the hot, heavy air.

Their meal was a dead possum, which Ripsbaugh scooped and flung down the other side. Maddox eyed the blood smear on the spade as Ripsbaugh returned, taking his beer, drinking another lick and starting up the dusty road toward the front gate. "They find anything?"

"Dogs scented a trail. Led out to the fire road through the Borderlands. Ended there."

"It's Dill they're looking at?"

Maddox nodded. "What do you think?"

"I'm wondering who's next if he doesn't work out for them." They walked a few more steps in silence. "It's not what they done to me so much. The letters they found, the cut on my arm—I understand these things. But give me a fair shake. This guy Hess, the way he went about it. How he had it all decided. Sawed off my leg without waiting for the cancer test to come back first."

"It's not right, how they treated you."

"I can take it. Being that I knew I was innocent, that made it all just strange. But what it did to Val. What it put her through. Once they come in that door, once they get inside your house, everything you ever said or did can and will be used against you. It was open season. And Val, she's not that strong. She's sick to death about anyone knowing her business, never mind the whole town."

"You could sue."

Ripsbaugh shook his head. "Not put her through that again."

Maddox looked at him. "You're a good man, Kane."

"Naw," he said, taking another pull on the can, then crushing it in his fist, tossing it near the door of the recycling shed. "No such thing."

He felt Maddox looking him over, as though Maddox had decided something. "You said something to me once about wanting to help. If I were to ask you for a favor, even if it didn't seem to make sense at the time, could you do it anyway, without saying anything to anyone else?"

Ripsbaugh hesitated with his hand on the gate latch. An unforeseen result of his persecution by Hess and the state police was that he had apparently gained some measure of Maddox's trust.

Ripsbaugh asked him, point-blank, "Were you a cop before all this?"

Maddox's face showed nothing as he stepped through the gate. "I'll be in touch."

36
TRACY

AFTER DR. BOLT HAD to leave in such a hurry, Tracy sat with Rosalie in the first stall. The old cowshed closest to the house was where she and her mother stabled late-term pregnant llamas and their newborn crias. Dr. Bolt's best estimate for Rosalie was two to three weeks, but given the llama's gestation of nearly twelve months, she could deliver at any time. Restlessness and fidgeting would be the first signs of early labor.

Tracy sat on a stool in the open stall doorway, eating a tuna fish sandwich for dinner and watching the contented mother-to-be sitting on her hay bed. Rosalie's brown cameloid face looked anything but restless. Tracy marveled at how peaceful and serene she appeared, her high neck so straight and proud. How fulfilled.

Living on a farm, Tracy came up against the reality of biology every day, in such a way that it was impossible not to dwell on her own animal nature. She thought about the tiny pouch of eggs she had been assigned at birth. A humble legacy dwindling month by month. She was still young enough that she shouldn't worry, but Mithers women were known for their frugality, and squandering a precious commodity such as that was like heating an unused room or listening to a leaky faucet drip, drip, drip.

Tracy had received "the Talk" in sign language. Never before or since had her mother seemed more deaf than at that moment. In need of a convenient visual aid, she had taken Tracy to see the giant gumball machine outside Wal-Mart on their monthly visit to Rainfield for supplies.

What would it feel like, she wondered, once that quarter was dropped into the slot? The bright pink ball spiraling down to click against her brass door.

She ignored the horn the first time. It honked twice more in succession, like a signal, and she put down her sandwich on its wax paper and closed Rosalie's stall door and went down the wood ramp. Her shadow stretched long across the chewed grass in the peachy, late-day light. Half hidden behind a handful of birches sprung up along the western fence was a parked car. A police car.

She ducked past the kitchen window in case her mother was there, then cut through the gate and ran along the fence. She tried livening up her hair with her fingers as she went, turning the corner and seeing Donny out of the car, waiting for her in the shade.

These days, it never even occurred to her to play hard to get. She ran up and kissed him and held him and rubbed his stubbled cheek. When he smiled, she kissed him again.

"Tuna fish," he said.

She covered her mouth fast. "Sorry!"

He shook his head, kissing the knuckles over her lips.

"This is a surprise," she said, holding him hard. "You look tired."

He glanced through the peeling white tree trunks at the house. "I only have a minute. Wanted to make sure you knew not to call me at the station."

"Okay."

"Too crazy there. I'm never alone anymore. Page me if you need to get in touch."

"I will, I will. How's Pinty?"

Donny shrugged. "He mumbled in his sleep. I tried to convince the doctor that was a good sign."

She put her ear against his chest, not to listen but to get as close to him as possible. "So much going on," she said. "So many things at once."

"Tell me about it."

"And now Dillon Sinclair—my God. We locked the doors last night."

"I think everyone did."

She pulled back just enough to look up at him, feeling something in his manner. "What?"

"The guy doesn't have a single violent episode in his past. Four years of prison—nothing."

"I don't know anything about him."

"He was a magician," said Donny, "some local junior champion or like that. He dropped out of high school senior year and supposedly went to Boston, worked as a street performer in the subways for a while, hustling money. He was essentially homeless when they tracked him down after his father died. He had been left some properties in the center of town. But Sinclair didn't want to come back, so instead he used the rental income to relocate to Rainfield, where he started giving kids magic lessons in the back room of a music shop."

"Oh, no," said Tracy.

"Five kids came forward. He was convicted on only a single count."

"Don't tell me any more."

"I grew up on the same street as him. He was weird even then. He came over once or twice to play, right after they moved in, but it never worked. He stole my mother's cigarettes. I remember she tracked him down to a tree house behind their backyard. A nine-year-old, smoking. She didn't let me play with him anymore after that."

"Thank you, Mrs. Maddox."

"The guy's an authentic freak, but . . ."

"Are you saying you don't think it's him?"

He shrugged and looked down at her. "What do I know?"

She slipped her arms back under his. "That you miss me?"

"Yes," he said, and they kissed again. She pushed his hair back from his ears. She was constantly touching his face, forever making him real, admiring this trophy she was amazed to have won.

He looked through the trees. "Your mother," he said.

Tracy turned. There she was, outside the cowshed with her apron on. Yes—her mother still wore an apron while cooking. She also wore a whistle in case she needed to summon Tracy, though she rarely needed to use it, Tracy being so obedient.

Tracy's anger toward her was unreasonable and an utter waste of time, so she squashed it, channeling all her energies into one more kiss. "You call me," she told him.

Tracy's mother had the whistle in her hand when Tracy came around the side of the house. Her worry fell away. *Where'd you go?*

Nowhere. Tracy moved her hands casually. *Why?*

Her mother glanced back near the tree grove—not right at it, but in that general direction—and Tracy reminded herself that her mother was deaf but not blind.

37
DR. BOLT

DR. GARY BOLT UNTANGLED himself from the seatbelt of his Honda Prelude and rushed up the walkway, past his closed-for-the-day veterinary practice to the front door of his adjoining house.

The door was locked. Dr. Bolt knocked. He knocked again, harder. He stepped back to check the picture window that fronted the living room. The heavy gold curtains were closed, swaying.

Dr. Bolt moved to the seam of the door, speaking into it. "Frankie."

The voice came hissing from inside. "Who's with you? Are they with you?"

Dr. Bolt checked the street for onlookers. Not because of Frankie's paranoia, but because of his own. Dr. Bolt had neighbors. He was an aging bachelor whispering through his own front door.

Dr. Bolt said, "Please, let me in."

"They've been trading off cars. Passing every seven or eight minutes."

"Frankie." Dr. Bolt remained heroically patient. He put on his doctor's voice. He employed reason. "You interrupted me with a patient. You said it was an emergency."

"They're coming after me. I know too much."

Prior to this week, Dr. Bolt had known almost nothing of Frankie Sculp, not even his name. Only that, every few days, the boy crossed the farm fields to Dr. Bolt's back kennel to retrieve the little packages left there by a young lady named Wanda. Yes, Dr. Bolt knew what was in those little packages. The same drugs Frankie had been snorting off the webbing between his thumb and forefinger every few hours since he had appeared on Dr. Bolt's doorstep six days ago, saying he was scared, in trouble, and had no place else to go.

At the time, Dr. Bolt could hardly contain his excitement, nor believe his extraordinary good fortune. For he was at his very best helping strays.

Now here he was, one week later, standing out on his own welcome mat, begging Frankie to let him in.

"Frankie," he said. "I am alone. Please. Open this door."

"I checked your phones. For bugs."

Dr. Bolt did not understand. "You're seeing bugs now?"

"Police bugs! Surveillance! I checked every appliance."

"*Every* appliance? How did you—"

"And I opened up all the light switches and plug outlets. Anything near a power source. It's for your sake too."

Dr. Bolt closed his eyes, swooning a bit at the thought of the destruction awaiting him behind this door. "Frankie. This is known as clinical paranoia. You have not slept in a week—"

"Here they come again!"

Dr. Bolt heard a table—it would be the high credenza, the one standing beneath the picture window, that had been his mother's—fall, and then glass—yes, the frame holding his grandmother's engagement portrait, an antique, irreplaceable—smash and tinkle.

He whipped toward the street. A white sedan approached.

"Don't let them in, doc!" came Frankie's voice behind the window. "They'll kill you to get to me!"

The automobile rolled past, and Dr. Bolt recognized Mrs. Poulin leaning over the wheel. She brought her cockatoo in to get his wings clipped every three months. The bird's name was Hamilton. Mrs. Poulin waved.

Dr. Bolt stood there holding up his flat hand.

"What are you doing?" said Frankie. "Are you signaling them? *You're signaling them!*"

Dr. Bolt put down his shaking hand. Earlier in the day, one of his best customers, the kind of woman who could single-handedly keep his practice afloat for an entire year, who some in town unkindly referred to as the Zoo Lady, had asked him why he had left his stereo playing so loudly to an empty house.

And just now, Tracy Mithers, from the llama farm on Sam Lake, showed such concern for him as he threw together his bag and begged off in evident distress, pager in hand.

He was going to lose everything.

What Frankie did not know—and could not ever know, for it would only explode his already flaming paranoia—was that Dr. Bolt already had a legitimate reason to fear the Black Falls police. And by Black Falls police, he meant specifically Bucky Pail.

"Frankie. You paged me, do you remember? You said you needed me, you needed my help. I am here now. Let me come inside. Let me help you."

The curtain rippled again. He heard breathing on the other side of the door.

"Please," said Dr. Bolt.

The lock turned. The door was pulled open a few inches.

Frankie stood behind it, a steak knife in his hand, its tip bloodied.

His hunted eyes searched the street and yard, and then, settling on Dr. Bolt's kindly country-doctor face, the stress lines around them slackened. For a moment Frankie was just a teenager again, possessed of the neediness and confusion that marked his age.

He pulled the door open wider, and Dr. Bolt saw that Frankie had been using the knife tip to pick at the sores on his face.

"Help me," Frankie said.

He was an ugly boy, yet there was something beautiful in the pain of his ugliness, something angelic and touching. His vulnerability was exquisite. A mutt with a sad limp and a mangy coat. Wanting only to lay his head in the lap of an owner who would not mistreat him.

Dr. Bolt had always assumed that the predator-prey relationship came down to the simplicity of strength versus weakness. But it was so much more symbiotic than that. He saw it now as a negotiation of vulnerabilities. The very same vulnerability that made Dr. Bolt easy prey for a blackmailer like Bucky Pail—specifically, Dr. Bolt's affinity for the attentions of much younger men—was what compelled Dr. Bolt to exert his advantage over Frankie Sculp. In other words, the strong were just as vulnerable to the weak. There was no one without the other.

Inside, he found his living room dismantled. Completely destroyed. A shambles. What a damn fool he was. Much too old for these ups and downs.

But this was what a life without love did to you. It put you at risk. To the temptations of a mercurial teenager, and to a dark manipulator like Bucky Pail.

Dr. Bolt allowed the frail, weeping boy into his arms and helped him down the hallway to the bathroom, to dress his self-inflicted wounds.

38
CULLEN

CULLEN STOOD A COUPLE of careful feet away from his backyard swimming pool, still wearing his dress shirt and pants from the office. He maintained the pool from the beginning of June through the end of August, keeping it skimmed, pH-balanced, and algae-free for his wife and two sons and their daily summer guests, even though Cullen himself did not know how to swim. Witnessing the childhood drowning death of his older sister had left him with a pathological fear of immersion. Once every year or two, on a warm night and with his wife close at his side, he would sit at the edge of the shallow end for a few minutes and dip in his bare legs up to his shins, stirring the water he cleaned so diligently all season. His wife had grown up with a pool and thought it important that the boys not suffer for their father's phobia. So he had taken upon himself its care and feeding as a way of managing his fear, of localizing the source of his dread, trapping it here in his backyard, as one might take on the care and feeding of a chained dragon.

Why he had so much respect for Maddox, he supposed. Someone who could wade in over his head, swim around, touch bottom and resurface time and time again. Someone who could go under and hold his breath there for so long.

The crescent moon, silver as a scythe, grinned at him from the surface of the still and silent water. Cullen's sister's name had been Emily, and when she ran her hair had flown off her shoulders like golden wings. He had adored her.

A light came on in the second floor of the house. The shadow of his wife, whose name also happened to be Emily, passed the window of the upstairs bathroom. Rubbing in hand cream, getting ready for bed, her nightly routine.

Cullen stepped farther back from the edge, returning his attention to Maddox on the cordless. "You heard about the cadet class?"

Maddox said, "What?"

"A trainee class from New Braintree is being bused your way first thing in the morning. One hundred and something recruits for a field search of the state forest."

"The Borderlands?"

"I guess they had some K-9s indicate."

They were disconnected briefly, and a recording asked Maddox to please deposit seventy-five more cents.

Cullen said, "Where are you calling from?"

"A pay phone outside the gas station here." Tones sounded as Maddox's coins fell. "My point is, the guy's hitting on this cult stuff, which is bullshit. He's floundering. Desperate."

"See, Hess bet the house on the ditchdigger and his blood DNA, and lost. He thought he had a quick arrest to pad his clearance stats, told his sergeant it was a done deal, and now here he is, still working the same folder. Burning up manpower and money. Frankly, he got lucky with the sex offender angle, buying him a few more days. Because the DA won't be seen as soft on pedophiles. But he's got a very small window of time left to find Sinclair, and the sill's slamming down hard on his fingers."

"I think he's in deeper shit than he knows."

"You don't see Sinclair for this, but you're the only one. Hess is on the right track here. He's got blood, he's got hair—even if it is wig hair—he's got treads from the brand of sneaker the suspect was known to wear. He's got fibers from the offender's apartment—"

"He's got what?"

"Fibers matching a living room rug. As well as a few skin cells he likes for Sinclair, that he's still waiting on tests for. See? All your dancing around him is bullshit and counterproductive. Just come out to him. Our thing is dead and all but buried."

"No way. Not yet."

"If it's Sinclair—and, plainly, it is—then we've already lost. The case is nothing. It was thin to begin with, relying on the word of a convicted sex offender. But a convicted sex offender who's also a killer? Find a DA in this country, in this *world,* who would bring that case."

"It's not over, Cullen."

"You don't want it to be over, and neither do I. And stubbornness is a good trait, and as a lawyer I respect it. But I like common sense too. I know you're tight with Chief Pinto-I-can-never-pronounce-the-name. You two obviously go way back."

"Pinty."

"He's a good man."

"Cullen. It's more than that."

"Nobody likes to lose. Everybody wants to be the hero. But when you're down five runs in the ninth, one swing of the bat won't win it for you. You play small ball, keep the inning alive."

A pause. "Okay."

Cullen frowned at the moon smiling at him from the water. "But you're still gonna get up there and take your swing."

"I'm finishing this job."

"We're in the shit enough as it is. If Sinclair is found to have ben-efited from a deal with the DA's office before committing a capital crime—"

"Benefited how? The assault charges against Bucky Pail were a get-out-of-jail against his DUI."

"He got leniency for agreeing to assist this investigation, and you know that. On *my* recommendation. The five-year driver's license sus-pension was a slap on the wrist. We could have sent him to prison and let him file his suit from there. Anyway, you know it's a game of appearances, not actual facts. My boss needs to get elected again. Should she decide to run."

"Cullen, there's only one reason a forty-year-old lawyer goes back into the public sector as an assistant DA. You have political ambition yourself."

"What of it?"

"You need this as much as I do."

"I need to avoid embarrassments is what I need."

"You check on Sinclair's pager for me?"

Cullen sighed, which was another thing he caught himself doing more and more as he got older. "You're sure it hasn't turned up?"

"Not in the search of his place, I know that."

"It's still functioning, so far as we can tell." Cullen's hand found something in his pocket, a bottle cap, from the Bud Light he'd opened after getting home. He felt it in his palm, a tiny crown. "Still receiving pages, or able to. If it has a battery in it, and all that. What if they find it in the forest?"

"Christ."

"Those things save old messages? They can identify you through that?"

"Give me a little credit," said Maddox, "not to have signed off pages with my full name and birth date. I was always discreet. But the billing, I assume it goes right back to your office."

"Then the jig is up, and you flip over all your cards anyway."

"Sinclair still has the pager with him."

"Well, then, he's ignoring you. And why not? He's a killer, Maddox. Why does he want to hear from a cop?"

Silence expressed Maddox's dissent.

Cullen said, "Okay, fine, so how are you going forward from here?"

"Still trying to track down that kid who was inside Sinclair's place. And Wanda, I'm going to lean on her. I cooked up an excuse to go over to her house tomorrow. Enlisted Ripsbaugh's help with that one."

"The ditchdigger?" said Cullen, surprised. "You really do have it in for Hess, don't you."

Cullen stood there by the pool after he hung up, flipping the bottle cap in his hand. A water bug or some such insect swam across the moon crescent, rippling the black surface, and Cullen switched on the overnight filter, what he had come out here to do. The jets voided their air bubbles, the skimmers circulating water.

Maddox was turning crusader. Pulling the plug on him was going to be difficult, if not impossible. Cullen wondered how much further he could let this go.

39
MADDOX

THE MAN KNOWN AS "Bathrobe Bill" Tedmond said, "I don't know where Wanda is. She don't come and go regular. Don't keep hours. Phone rings and she's gone."

Wanda's father sat in a deep, itchy-looking armchair beside a tray table containing a gnawed pencil, an open wire-bound notebook listing expenses versus income, a smattering of bills and notices, and a once-white Slimline telephone stained smoker's-tooth yellow. The bathrobe was saddle brown terry cloth with a faux-silk shawl collar, and whenever Bill left the house, which was almost never, pants and slipper shoes underneath completed the ensemble. A window fan stirred hot air that fluttered the peeling green paper on the walls, sloughing off its backing glue like the lining of an ulcerated stomach. The laughing television had been placed in the center of the room, with everything else, Bathrobe Bill included, arranged around it.

No need for Maddox to hide his disappointment, Bathrobe Bill's eyes having yet to leave *Live with Regis and Kelly*. "When would you say you saw her last?"

"Time, I'm no good with. Yesterday, maybe. She sleeps a lot when she's here, and why not? Sleeping's free."

For sixteen years, Bill Tedmond drove long-haul: on the road for eight days, home for two. But his divorce from Wanda's mother triggered a decade-long depression, rendering him unable to work, though the state denied his disability claim. His rig remained parked outside under trees, its once-proud chrome caked with seasons of pollen and bird shit, plants and weeds growing out of the leaves composting on its roof. He was a recluse now, Black Falls' dirt-poor version of Howard Hughes, spending his days in front of a snowy television, keeping a careful tally of all the money he did not have.

"Well," said Maddox, moving this along, Bathrobe Bill like a black hole sucking up all health and ambition, "she mentioned you were having trouble with your plumbing."

"That's right enough. Hope she also mentioned I'd have even more trouble paying to fix it."

"I've got someone with me who will get things flowing again, no problem."

Bathrobe Bill nodded, still facing the TV. "I'll hang in here until you're done."

Maddox went to Ripsbaugh in the back hallway. Ripsbaugh wore a sweat-darkened T-shirt, overwashed shorts, and his usual boots with the peeling leather collars and worn-down toes. He sat before the "video diagnostics system" contraption Maddox had helped him wheel in. The unit's motor hummed as a mechanized spindle payed out red cable with a thinner silver wire spiraled around its length. The camera snake-fed into the open toilet in the corner of the bare bathroom, disappearing into a liver-colored puddle at the mouth of the bowl at a rate of about one inch per second. The procedure was eerily medical in appearance. A three-by-three screen on the console played the camera view creeping through a pipe of cloudy water glowing night-vision green, an odometer-like counter marking off the distance.

"How far's it go?" asked Maddox.

"Twelve hundred feet," said Ripsbaugh, sitting back in an unsteady chair pulled from the kitchen, its spindles broken underneath. "I get a fourth of my regular excavation fee for twenty minutes of sitting and watching TV."

The house as a whole had a trapped odor, its floors sticky like the

floors of an animal cage. Having talked his way in here with Ripsbaugh, only to be frustrated by Wanda's absence, Maddox leaned
against the wall to wait, trying to come up with some conversation.
"So what's the worst thing anyone's flushed?"

"The worst?" said Ripsbaugh. "I don't know. You hear about wedding rings, guys having to go into the tanks and get them. Feminine
products, you know, those things, they swell up with water five times
their size. What messes up tanks most is coffee grounds and bleach.
Coffee grounds because they clog up your outlet pipes. But bleach,
and all these antibacterial soaps they make now? Kills off the bacteria
in the tank. It's the bacteria that does all the work in there, eating
solids and breaking them down. People so busy chasing bacteria out
of their house, meanwhile this tank of waste is swelling up under-
ground, about to back up on them."

"Bleach is bad, huh?"

"When my father ran the company, he would pump out a residential tank once every five or ten years. You could go that long. Not anymore. You one-ply or two?"

"I don't know. Whatever's cheapest."

"One-ply is the way to go. Ladies like the softer two-ply, but it
breaks down slow, scums up the top of the tank. Flush down that
three-ply they make now, or a baby wipe, or one of them quilted paper
towels? Might as well pull off your shirt and throw it in there too.
None of it's going anywhere until I come by to suck it out."

The motor whined and the console clicked. The feeding stopped.
Ripsbaugh eyed the screen, toggled the joystick controls.

"Yep," he said. "We got a blockage. Right at the inlet. Something's
snagged there." He tried to prod at it with the scope, to no avail. He
patted his knees and stood. "Have to crack her open outside."

Maddox stopped in the kitchen, the linoleum crackling under his
boots. Prescription bottles and dirty dishes and soft packs of GPC cigarettes. Losing lottery scratch tickets facedown in the trash. A still life
in crumb and stain. He could feel it here, he could almost smell it: the
malaise, this enfeebling despair that radiated like a contagion through-

out Black Falls. The breakdown of law and order was, in a sense, a reflection of this mental breakdown.

Outside, beyond a tattered blue tarpaulin covering last winter's unused firewood, Ripsbaugh held the head of a wide green hose unwound off his whirring Cold River Septic truck, the thing twitching as it sucked from a hole in the yard.

The stink was rude, richly awful, just shy of disgusting. Closer, Maddox saw a half-moon slab of concrete overturned next to Ripsbaugh's trusty shovel, revealing a crescent hole smiling out of the earth like a dark mouth, wide enough to swallow a child.

"Thousand-gallon tank," Ripsbaugh said. "That's small potatoes. I remember yours, when I did the Title Five inspection on your mother's house?" Prior to the sale of any property in Massachusetts, the state environmental code required that the septic system be inspected and certified. "That was an old six-by-six vault. Way over capacity for the house size."

Ripsbaugh pulled up the dripping hose, offering Maddox a glimpse below. A muddy white inlet PVC pipe came from the house, jutting into the tank in a modified T. Below it lay a solid coat of thick, white-gray fluff.

"That mess on the top there, that's the paper, sink food, detergents. Below that, all wastewater. People think their septic tank is full of shit, but it's not. Waste dissolves pretty quickly. 'Effluent' is the term."

This was by far the most he had ever heard Ripsbaugh speak at one time. But everybody in this world is an expert on something. Maddox looked down at the meringue of undissolved waste shimmying on the surface. "Effluent, huh?"

"Dribbles off into the leeching fields. Seeps back down through the rock and soil, reentering the water table. Then you pull it back up through your well and drink it, start the whole cycle over again."

"Yum," said Maddox.

"Earth is the best filter there is. All these other towns on water bans now, because of the lack of rainfall? That's public sewers. Piping out all their water instead of returning it to the ground. These new developments go up and bleed the land dry, just so that residents don't have to face the once-a-year stench of getting pumped out. People want to believe in magic white bowls that make everything disappear."

Maddox looked back to Ripsbaugh's rumbling tanker. "And from here . . . ?"

"Treatment facility over in Aylesbury, they burn it clean." He left the thirsty hose sucking air on the dirt lawn, picking up a long, flexible wire tool with a two-pronged end. "I don't take it all out, though. You leave the sludge on the bottom, the bacteria that feeds on the waste. Breaks it down. The dirtiest part of the tank, that does all the work." He lay flat on the ground and reached into the smelly tomb with the tool in his gloved hand. "That's nature in action."

He worked by feel, picking around inside the PVC pipe, then pulling back sharply as though hooking a fish. Fluid from the unclogged pipe disgorged into the tank.

Ripsbaugh brought the tool out of the mouth of the chamber and deposited the dripping obstruction on a clump of dead grass. Maddox glanced back at the front door. This went beyond snooping through the Tedmonds' garbage, closer to a necropsy of their home.

The matter was sodden and soiled but not mucked brown. Some prodding and separating with Ripsbaugh's tool revealed the bulk of it to be gauze strips and first aid tape. A swollen packet that looked like a fat, cotton wallet was an absorbent bandage, and threaded into it were faint traces of black.

"Blood," said Maddox.

"That's what people flush," said Ripsbaugh, picking through it some more. He poked out two tiny, waste-streaked, zippered plastic envelopes, small enough that their only legitimate use could have been stamp collecting.

Maddox looked at Ripsbaugh, and found Ripsbaugh already looking at him. "That what I think it is?" Ripsbaugh said.

"I think so," said Maddox.

"Probably soaked too long in there for any drug trace to show up in a lab."

The guy knew his cop shows. Maddox looked back at the house again.

Ripsbaugh said, "Search ain't legal anyway. 'Plain view' is the rule. Bathrobe Bill gave his consent for you to be inside, but this goes beyond discovery."

Maddox played it down, shaking his head. "I'm not here as a cop."

Ripsbaugh looked at him, the wire tool dripping to the ground. "Then what are you here as?"

Maddox tried to come up with a good answer for that.

Ripsbaugh said, "I heard you asking Bathrobe Bill about Wanda. She still go around with Bucky Pail?"

Maddox said, "She does."

His tone let Ripsbaugh know that he would not go any further. The empty sucking of the dirty vacuum hose was the only noise as Ripsbaugh absorbed the information he had gleaned.

Maddox's back pocket started to vibrate. He pulled out his pager and checked the number.

No. Not Sinclair. Cullen. Maddox ignored it.

"Nice pager," said Ripsbaugh, watching him return it to his jeans.

"My girlfriend," Maddox said.

Ripsbaugh looked surprised.

Maddox added, "She's not from around here."

Not a good lie, but whether he believed him or not, Ripsbaugh let it go. He bent to pick up the dripping hose, about to return it to the hole. He pointed at the gauze and the little dope bags on the ground. "What about this?"

They were indeed worthless to a lab, and unallowable as evidence. Maddox nodded, and Ripsbaugh used his hungry hose to suck them up into his tanker.

The nozzle went chugging back into the septic tank, and Maddox stepped away. No more waiting for Wanda to come around to his side, he decided. No more paying out rope. He needed to find her or Frankie as soon as possible.

A voice came out of his patrol car, the police radio calling his unit number and his name.

40
HESS

HESS WAS A HIT AT cocktail parties. Homicide investigators usually are, because of the gritty glamour the television-watching and moviegoing public associates with them. The imagined car chases, the Mexican standoffs, the psychological dance of cop and criminal: all that sweet nonsense. Married women especially, for some reason, would gang up on him in the corner, or sit close to him on the sectional, white wine shining in their eyes as they plied him for more stories. And Hess performed for them, he gave them what they wanted, all his best tales and others he'd only heard, selling them on the danger of the job, the pathos, the trauma. They wanted to be lifted out of their cycle of playdates and school buses and once-a-month trysts with distracted husbands; they wanted their romantic imaginations fired. They dropped "tells" like clumsy poker players, twisting at the chains around their necks, finding conversational excuses to reach out and touch his arms. Hess lived in an upscale town near the Amherst universities, but on a state policeman's salary—though a homicide investigator, his rank and pay grade remained that of a trooper—he could not compete with his neighbor's tennis weekends and sporty third cars. So while the husbands gathered around the pool table in the finished basement talking golf clubs and consumer electronics, Hess remained upstairs mind-fucking their wives. A cocktail party gigolo, flexing his cop persona like his biceps, flashing them the goods before leaving them in the lurch, returning for good-byes with lovely Janine on his arm. Better than bedding any one of them was knowing that he was the "other man" in a hundred imagined infidelities of overprivileged women who secretly wished they were married not to their husbands but to him.

The thing he always started off telling them, which was not a story per se but rather an operating principle, and which happened to be absolutely true, was that every case he worked was essentially the same. Every unattended death was the Case of the Broken Vase. A body, or traces of it, lay broken on the floor. Most of the pieces were right there, and his job was to reassemble what he found, then track down the rest. By the time he had the vase glued together well enough to hold water again, he usually knew who had knocked it over and how, and whether its shattering had been an act of carelessness or calculation.

Here Hess had a vase that would not come together. He could stand a flower in it—Dillon Sinclair—but water kept spurting out on all sides. Now was the time to start looking more closely at the people he had handling the pieces for him, making certain they were reconstructing this thing the correct way.

His mistake all along had been in pretending to treat the locals like cops. They were more like informants and that was how he decided to approach the Black Falls PD now. Hess had come upon a significant chunk of vase, and he wanted to see firsthand how they processed it.

He went out to bring them in from the front room of the station. Bucky Pail was sitting on the floor, falling asleep with his cap in his hands. Maddox stood apart, looking out the front window at the academy trainees milling about the lawn, dressed in their spiffy blue shirts, navy Dickies, and regulation boots, swigging water while they waited for the school buses to return them to New Braintree. But the faraway look on Maddox's face was more like something you'd see on a man standing at the edge of an ocean.

So maybe he did have aspirations after all. From what Hess had been able to learn about him, hiring on to any real police force would be a tough sell. A trip through Maddox's tax returns going back ten years—highly unauthorized, another favor called in—showed fringe-type jobs, low-wage, nothing steady. W-2s from all over: a roofer, a mover, a landscaper, a pool cleaner. Short stints as a bartender in three different parts of the state; a car wash in Lowell; Domino's pizza delivery in Taunton and Brockton; cab driving in West Springfield; road painting in Fall River. He had worked as an asbestos stripper in Worcester and in the boiler room of a Cape Cod high school. The only tie-and-shoes job he'd held was as a stereo and TV salesman, and only for three months.

To Hess, it read like someone who was hiding, or even halfway on the run. Maddox's name also popped up as a reference/co-signee on bail bonds for three different people, two of them arrested on drug charges—one simple Class B possession, third offense, one for Class A possession with intent to distribute—and one for breaking and entering with intent to commit a felony, as well as, in the Commonwealth's parlance, "possession of burglarious tools." But no arrests himself—which Hess already knew, given that Maddox had been cleared on a Criminal Offender Record Information search before getting hired on as a cop, and had passed the routine background check that went along with his gun license application.

Still, it was a very unusual résumé for a part-time cop. What it showed Hess was that Maddox was a washout, like most of the lost souls in this town. He wanted to grill Maddox about his background, make him squirm a little, but had decided to hold on to that card awhile longer. Sweating Maddox, though potentially quite pleasurable, was not the point. At least not yet.

Pail too had clouds circling about his head. The assault charge against Sinclair, obviously, but there were other whispers: abuses of power, sexual transgressions, even an alleged indecent assault right here inside the station. Other charges brought against him along the way—exposing himself to a female motorist, simulating masturbation in front of another—had all been quickly dropped, reeking of intimidation and witness tampering.

And then there was the case of Hugo Ibbits. A California fugitive stopped for speeding in Black Falls, he was first said to have been arrested and jailed by Pail, but then, after his death three nights later in a fiery car crash in the hills above town, the story changed. The death was briefly investigated by the U.S. Marshals office, which has jurisdiction over fugitives, but later dropped without a finding. This was before Pail got caught beating a handcuffed Sinclair during a traffic stop up in those same hills.

Inside the reports room, Hess took up a position at an angle from the laptop so that he could observe the two cops' reactions. Bryson sat before the screen.

"We found Sinclair's camera," Hess announced, "half buried under leaves in the Borderlands. CSS took a biopsy of the forest, digging up everything within two cubic feet of the find, all of which they are currently processing. The memory card was installed and intact. Seventy-nine images, of which we have here a quick DVD burn. A privileged peek at a sliver of Sinclair's own memory. And, no surprise, it gets pretty fucking weird."

Bryson worked the touch pad, starting the slide show in reverse order, from the most recent images back to the oldest.

The first sequence of pictures were dark, taken at night and without a flash. Tough to make out anything at first. Hess had needed four or five passes in order to see it clearly himself.

The photographs had been taken through a window: that much was evident. Part of the silver casing of the camera was visible in some shots, reflected in the moonlit glass, if you looked for it. The subject of each of the first six images was a boy lying on his belly, asleep in a bed with his arms tucked under him, the covers kicked away. Spiderman pajamas, the waistband of his underpants showing above the top of red and blue shorts. A match head of bright orange hair.

Bryson paused the slide show there. Hess watched Bucky squint, still trying to see what was on the screen.

Maddox stared heatedly, looking spooked. "One of the Heavey boys," he said.

"Heavey," said Hess, "being the guy who found footprints behind his house. Who saw someone he thought was a woman running off into the trees."

Bucky saw it now. "What the *fuck*."

Maddox's mouth tightened. Bryson worked the mouse to resume the slide show.

There followed images taken through a different window, of a different young boy in another bed, this one blond and sleeping only in his underwear. The images were nearly identical, taken in rapid succession.

"There," said Hess.

Bryson stayed on the image. Hess's eyes stayed on the cops.

It took them a moment to see what was different. The camera was positioned farther back from the window glass. In the reflection, visible behind and around the silver camera, was a hand. A forefinger on the shutter release. And, to the side of that, long, straight strands of black hair.

And—just barely on the other side—a closed eye winking beneath a hairless brow.

"Fuckin' *freak*," said Bucky, leaning forward to see. His upper lip curled back like he could smell Sinclair.

Maddox's brow dropped low over his eyes.

More pictures flashed, most of them peeping shots of young boys asleep in their beds, though not all. One artsy image showed a deer crossing Main Street at dawn, snapped from the vantage point of Sinclair's second-story balcony. Another one Hess waited for was an early-morning shot from the same perch, looking down on the roof of a car turning the corner. A patrol car. The unit number was eight.

Bucky looked fast at Maddox. "That's him," he said to Hess. "That's Maddox's car."

Maddox's surprise was pure and convincing.

Bucky stared at Maddox as though he was owed an answer.

Hess said, "Any reason you know of?"

Maddox shook his head.

Bryson went on. In another peeping shot, Sinclair had experimented with holding the camera away from his eye. In the dim reflection of the glass, his face appeared like an eerie double exposure, a ghost without eyebrows superimposed over a sleeping boy.

Hess said, "So he was dressing up in black, riding his bike around after dark, and sneaking into backyards to snap pictures of little boys sleeping in first-floor bedrooms. Until twelve forty-three A.M. on June twenty-fifth, the time and date stamp of the last picture."

Bryson said, "One week before the night the insurance salesman, Heavey, said he heard a shot in the forest, near where this camera was recovered."

Hess said, "And then there's this."

There followed five flash-lit images of a basement in an apparently abandoned house, the paneled walls kicked in and defaced: spray-painted devil's horns, various "666" designs, and, in dripping red like a comic-book howl, the words, *Black Falls is Helllll!*

Hess said, "Recognize any of this?"

Bucky and Maddox took turns shaking their heads.

"Cult stuff," suggested Bryson.

Hess watched Maddox's face sour in disagreement.

Then came more early images, many of them unclear, either too dark or with the sleeping child obscured. Sinclair learning by trial and error.

When the next one he wanted came up, Hess said, "Stop."

A two-story house at dusk, the image taken among trees across an otherwise empty backyard. The house had a rear deck, and the bit of the front yard visible around the left side looked like wetlands.

Bucky leaned in. He got right up over Bryson's head, examining the screen. He straightened and looked back at Maddox.

"That's his place," said Bucky, pointing. "That's Maddox's damn house."

Maddox was still absorbing the image. He did not deny Bucky's claim.

Hess said, "Maddox?"

Maddox said, "Looks like it."

Bucky said, "Scarecrow was fuckin' taking pictures of you?"

Hess asked, "Why would he take a picture of your house?"

Maddox shook his head, as much out of disbelief as I-don't-know.

Bucky Pail pulled back, formed a wide grin. "'Cause he's fuckin' gay. They're gay together. You and Scarecrow got something going, Maddox?"

"Yeah," said Maddox, turning to Bucky. "He likes me to handcuff him and slap him around. Says you taught him."

Hess said, "All right, all right."

Bucky's eyes were dead, staring at Maddox. But Maddox's attention had already returned to the screen. Figuring out this house mystery was more important to him than jousting with Bucky Pail.

Hess said, "Maddox, what do you have to say about this?"

"I have nothing to say. I'm looking at this just like you. I don't know what the hell it is."

"Sinclair's a fan of your work? Your own backyard paparazzo?"

"I have to answer for him?" Maddox said. "What do you want me to say?"

"It disturbs you."

"Sure it does. But not as much as those pictures of the sleeping boys."

Hess nodded, having gotten what he wanted out of Maddox. "They looked quite dead, didn't they."

Maddox looked up fast like he hadn't thought of that.

41
VAL

VAL SAT IN HER WHITE yard chair at the long edge of the white resin table on the back porch. The turf beneath her slippers was a fuzzy green indoor-outdoor carpet, and two citronella candles were set in the middle of the table, near the empty umbrella hole, both jars blackened, the wicks burned down to the bottom. The back porch was screened in, but insects were still a problem, because of the smell. The septic company garage out beyond the low chain-link fence at the edge of their property drew gnats and mosquitoes and chits and no-see-ums out of the surrounding woods. Blue-bulb zappers hung from three corners of the roof, snapping and sizzling all day and night.

She had taken a glass and a half of rosé at about ten and only another small glass with lunch, so she was certain he couldn't tell. Donny Maddox sat at the shorter end of the table, his back to the yard. Keeping his distance because of the kissing in his car. She watched the smoke feather up off her cigarette and then ribbon in some mysterious, unfelt crosscurrent. This was where she did her thinking. Later she would revisit the conversation as though he were still sitting here, veering off into unexplored dialogues, playing with alternate endings.

She already remembered the way he had looked at the plastic tray of annuals on the newspaper in the sunniest corner, when he first joined her out here. The flower petals parched and dead. And the memory of his look—so recent it was more of an echo than a memory—already colored her responses. She didn't want him turn-ing that same look of pity on her. The unplanted violets represented the flare of a good morning some weeks before, a few hours of get-my-life-in-order-starting-with-this-house energy, which, as always, soon burned itself out.

She turned the cigarette over in her hand to disrupt the smoke stream. "This is my weight loss program," she told him. "My exercise regimen and my portion control." She inhaled, savoring the hit. "Best part is, it works. Kane hates it. Hates the smell, which is ridiculous, coming from him. But I need it. Anything to cover up this." She pointed across the side lawn to the septic garage.

Donny turned to look, just being polite. He seemed reluctant to tell her why he had come.

Val said, "Dill didn't do what they say he's done. You know that, right? He's a lot of things—he's sick—but he's not a murderer."

Donny nodded, still fretting. "You still have no idea where he is?"

She shook her head. "I go back and forth now between hating him and pitying him. He was always so lost and different and weird inside—but not evil. How I think of him now is like a piece of fruit left out too long. Parts of it are still okay, but the parts that are black and spoiled, you can't eat around them." She smoked. "They still try-ing to make something out of his magic? Cults and black masses and that?"

Donny said, "How'd you know?"

"The head trooper, when he had me in there, asked if I was a witch."

Donny frowned, either at the notion or at the mention of the head trooper. "What do you think of that?"

"It was just tricks. Stupid tricks. He was a lonely little boy cutting cards and waving scarves down in our basement. Obsessed with it. And my father—God, he hated it. Taunted him mercilessly. Humili-ated him. I mean nightly. Calling him a fairy. So of course, what does Dill do but practice that much longer, that much more obsessively. Started dressing in black, you know, playing up the part. Living it.

Becoming this kid his father hated." She picked at a ridge in the table with her fingernail. "Just tell me you'll try to help him, if you find him."

"They found a camera in the Borderlands today. His camera. You're not supposed to know about this—no one is. But inside, taken over the past few months, were these pictures of sleeping boys."

Val showed him that she was not shocked. "That's what you came here wanting to know about? Are you asking for that trooper? Or for yourself?"

"Just me."

She sat back. "I feel like everything with Dill, everything, is this attempt to get back his childhood."

"Get it back? From where?"

"I remember one time I found him in our basement with a noose all tied, elaborately coiled like in the movies, strung up over one of the ceiling supports. He said he was working on an escape trick. Sure he was. I told him at the time, I said, 'Don't leave me here alone.' That was my biggest fear. Now I know he would have been better off."

"Alone? But what about your father?"

She let stillness settle like night.

Donny started to ask, then thought better of it. He sat back a bit in his chair, not knowing what to say, what to do.

Val flicked some ash, surprised he hadn't known already. She smiled, not happily, and looked past him through the screens, through years. These were things she saw from this porch table.

"But then he did leave, he ran off to Boston. I threw myself into the scholarship as my way out. And then, after I lost that . . . I guess now I can say that I had a collapse. I didn't see anyone, I didn't do anything. Didn't eat or sleep. All I did was go on these marathon walks. With my sketchpad and a little bottle of water, anything to get away from my house. One day I wandered out near the dump. But instead of garbage, I smelled mulch. Wet, fragrant mulch, and it drew me. And there Kane was out in front, spreading it with a pitchfork.

A steamy hot day, just like this one. Putting in a little stripe of garden in front of the dump, and I thought, you know, how perfectly *odd*."

She felt a smile bunching her cheeks. Not the sweetness of memory, no, but rather the wisdom of a girl grown so much older.

"I was heavy into contradictions then. Pretending I could still be an artist, live like an artist, *see* like an artist. The contrast, the poetic futility of the garden—all that appealed to me. Like when you find something in the outside world you think perfectly reflects what you're feeling inside? You respond to it. And I remember thinking to myself, about Kane Ripsbaugh, That guy looks exactly like how I feel."

She licked her lips in an effort to douse the bitter smile, then swallowed, as though memories were food you could chew down once and for all.

"You were nineteen," said Donny. "He was—forty? Older?"

"Well, marrying for love—do you know how new a concept that is? There are marriages of advantage and there are marriages of convenience, and I wanted out. If not from the town, then, at the very, *very* least, from my house. From my father. Kane owned his own house, and he wanted me. He promised me things. He even seemed to love me—who would have guessed that? The scrawny little mess I was at the time. I think I imagined I'd be like the heroine in some thick French novel, a peasant girl who claws her way out of the mud of the countryside into Paris society. I'd start with the septic man and move up, ruthlessly. Only, there never was any up."

"Kane's a good man," said Donny. "I mean, he may not be . . ." He was wise to give up on that. There were numerous things Kane Ripsbaugh wasn't: handsome, sweet-smelling, tenderhearted, talkative. Interesting. Young. "Nobody's perfect. But he'll stand by you."

"He took me back, you mean."

Donny didn't want to go there. Val stubbed out her dying cigarette, already wanting another. "There are these hinge moments in life, you know? I sit out here, and I think about them. Critical turning points where your life could have completely changed, one way or the other. You know?"

"Well, sure."

"You're thinking I'm going to bring up the scholarship again." Another smile opened up her face, this one bittersweet. "You won't even remember this, but—Lynn Gavel's party? For the yearbook staff, our senior year? We were right in the heat of our rival thing, and my ride, she had left without me, and you had your mom's car so you were going to give me a lift home? And it was getting late, and I knew you wanted to go, but I was being all pouty and . . . do you remember, I wandered off down to the pond at the end of her street, and you had to come looking for me?"

"I do."

"I wanted you to come after me. I went off on purpose—I even sent my ride home—so that you would have to leave the rest of them and come to me. I was a pout because I couldn't figure out how to get you interested. Interested enough to kiss me."

He started to say something else, then settled for, "No, I never knew."

"Of course you look at me now and you think, Thank God. But that's the thing. I would be different if I had wound up with you. So different. Not straitjacketed here. I always felt close to you, Donny. Like we had a connection. If only it weren't for that . . . that damn scholarship . . ."

She blotted her eyes with a knuckle, harshly. She watched him try to come up with something to say other than I'm sorry, fail, and glance at the porch door.

"I'm scaring you off, huh?" Her words came out on a weird laugh.

"No, no," he said. "It's just that, I have to get out to see Pinty."

"Do you ever think about what your life would be like if I had won the scholarship? Your life in this town, what it would have been?"

He nodded, begrudging her nothing. "Every day since I came back."

"You'd have been a cop, right? Probably. And with you in there, maybe the Pail family wouldn't have taken over. Things might be a lot different. For everybody. Probably you would have married someone in town."

"Maybe."

"Maybe someone . . . like me."

"But you wouldn't have been here, right? You would have won the scholarship." He got to his feet as though afraid she would try to kiss him again. "You'd be long gone."

"That's right," she said. "Long gone."

She reached for another cigarette, knowing that, as soon as the door shut behind him, she would begin spinning their conversation around and around inside her head, her mind like a spider threading a web so elaborate, it could catch even imaginary prey.

42

BUCKY

THE CLASSICAL MUSIC record popped and crackled on the old hi-fi turntable. The album was one of a boxed set of six that Bucky's mother had ordered from the television soon after he was born. She bought it to play for him and Eddie in the afternoons, hoping it would somehow calm them down. *Arthur Fiedler and the Boston Pops Play Your Timeless Classics,* it was called, the cover showing a bloody sun setting behind the tuxedoed conductor, who was some Einstein-looking guy. Oh, how he and Eddie used to hate it. Used to jump around the room just to hear it skip. Tried scratching it up with the needle when they were big enough to reach. Played it on 78 rpm and whipped pillow cushions at the stereo. But those goddamn thick old wax discs were indestructible.

The records found their way back out of the cabinet after his mother died. Daddy played them at night to help him fall asleep in his chair. And if Eddie or Bucky ever turned it off, the man woke up in a rage. Daddy never slept in a bed again.

Now Daddy was gone and Eddie and Bucky had split up the albums, Bucky sticking Eddie with the faggy piano pieces and keeping the *Apocalypse Now* music for himself. They didn't live together. Pails had owned Jag Hill for almost as long as there was a town named Black Falls, two separate family homesteads set on opposite slopes of the otherwise undeveloped hill. Eddie stayed in the larger house a half mile away, the one they had grown up in, because Bucky preferred his uncle's old place, which had started out as a hunting lodge and still had a pair of antlers nailed to the front door. Still had the curing shed and the old camper out in back.

Bucky was cooking up a late lunch of toasted bologna, watching the edges curl off the browning bread through the window of his toaster oven, and thinking about that freak-ass Scarecrow. When Frond first turned up dead enough to bring the staties to town, Bucky had been pissed. Everything had to be put on hold, he figured. But now he welcomed the distraction. It was perfect. Everyone running around looking for Scarecrow, the town whipped into a frenzy. And once they found him and left, then Bucky's position in Black Falls would be stronger than ever. Pinty would be gone, along with his pet Maddox, leaving no obstacles in Bucky's way. Total freedom to finish his "experiments" before moving on to the next stage.

This town was nothing more than a laboratory to him now. A proving ground. When he was through with Black Falls, he would toss it at Eddie's big feet like a bone gnawed clean. This was going to be a town full of zombies by the time Bucky was done.

They say summer colds are the worst, and a bad one was spreading through town. A cold that was to become a countywide flu, which would eventually burn through all of New England like an epidemic.

Bucky saw now that Ibbits had come to him as a kind of prophet. A hobo prophet, appearing out of the desert as they often do, living in his car, on the run from California. A carrier of the disease, and yet, at the same time, a doctor, a medicine man. But a prophet first and foremost. Of doom. Bearing *script*ure, in the form of a pre*script*ion—in the form of a recipe. A simple little recipe with simple, everyday ingredients.

A recipe for plague.

Ibbits said meth was the perfect drug if you only did it once. Trick was: How? How do you win a fortune with one pull of the slot machine lever—and never walk into a casino again? Fuck the hottest chick on TV—and never expect to touch her again? Learn the most mind-shattering truth of the universe—and never allow yourself to think it again?

And yet, Bucky did. He had. One time only. Or rather, nine times over the course of one bullet-fast three-day weekend. One seventy-two-hour run. Nine smoked foils. No sleep. No food. *No need.*

Most of the rush of the first day he had spent working on his cars. Pure gear-head heaven, twenty-four hours straight through without a break, compulsively immersed in the hobby of all hobbies. Mind and hand and wrench and engine: one. Connected. It was all-American nirvana. It was bliss.

Nothing would ever be anything like that first blaze. When eventually he got horny, he'd called Wanda and smoked a foil with her and she went off like a comet. They fucked for hours, a fuckfest beyond human capability, superhuman sex, orgasm upon orgasm, each exploding with intensity. Universe-creating orgasms. Big motherfucking bangs.

That were so good, so right, so complete, so *out there,* that he couldn't be bothered now to fuck without it. They had tried a couple of times, Wanda tweaking up alone and then begging him, pleading for his dick. But meth turned him from the ultimate pussy hound into what he thought of as a meth monk. It just wasn't there for him anymore. You go to the moon, you visit the fucking stars: What was left in Black Falls that could please him? He didn't need it now, not the way he used to. Or rarely, anyway. Certainly not from bony Wanda. Meth had messed with the switchboard in his head. He was getting off on something else besides sex now. Something—the Idea—had taken its place.

The Idea was what he had caught on to that third day. What the meth had showed him. What it revealed.

A clarity.

Everyday people, he had realized, would kill to feel the way he did. Would slaughter their own parents for a taste of this. Would trade away their kids.

That was when he saw his future. That was when he knew.

Knew immediately that he had found the thing he had been looking for all his life. Not a drug to get high on—no. Every drug that had come through town, that had found its way into lockup, he had test-driven like an impounded car. Even regular speed—nothing was like this shit. Nothing came *close*. Nothing had this cosmic giddyup.

What he had found here, without searching for it, without even knowing it existed, was a tool. What in other hands was a toy, was in his hands a sharp knife. A cunning weapon.

A low-priced alternative to cocaine, even cheaper than heroin. A high that lasts longer and burns hotter than 'shrooms or acid or anything else out there. A drug that doesn't take you out of the world but, like a great fuck, plunges you deeper into it. That makes you invincible, immortal, and that's better to screw on even than coke.

Meth is a blow job for the brain, a hand job for the ego. It writhes naked and moaning in the swelling lap of your soul, bouncing on your hard-on, squeezing your balls, making you come and come and beg for more.

That first high, anyway.

The virgin ride of pure intensity, which Ibbits said you never quite get back to again, but which many people devote the rest of their lives to chasing. Ibbits told him about the effects of the drug on people out west, where he was from: men walking away from their jobs, women from their children, losing houses and cars and selling off everything, including themselves. Religion promises you something glorious just around the corner? Meth actually lets you glimpse it. Lets you hear the angels sing.

Bucky still felt tempted all the time. Especially working these long hours cooking up the stuff. But he saw now another thing the meth had showed him: this was what life is. Chasing your virginities. Chasing your infant satisfactions. That pure bliss of first love (mother). The bewildering, earth-shuddering majesty of your first orgasm. You want it all back. You want to be born again. Life as pure nostalgia.

Everybody everywhere is looking for transcendence, for deliverance, something to devote themselves to. And meth gives you that. At first. Then it starts to reduce you. Bucky had already seen it here in Black Falls. Meth turning men into monkeys. Part of the drug's joy is that it peels you back to your animal instincts; it strips out higher, more complex emotions such as regret and anxiety. Your needs become meth and sex, in that order. And then eventually just meth. You want nothing else. You know no future, you feel no past. Shame loses its drag on you. Your body doesn't matter anymore. Only what you put in it. You are a zombie.

Bucky pulled out his toasted bologna and laid it sizzling on a paper towel. He squirted mustard on it, and while it cooled, he wiped his greasy hands on his shorts and changed up the record, laying in his old Kiss *Alive II* album. Track two: "King of the Night Time World."

After the revelation, Bucky had gone back to the station lockup to see Ibbits, held there over the long weekend, waiting for a trip out to the county judge on Tuesday. Bucky was all fired up on the confiscated meth, and Ibbits saw this. Bucky let him out and brought him back to his home to pick the man's brain. He offered him freedom in exchange for information, and, after a liberal hit off his own stash, Ibbits was only too willing. He wrote out recipes and supply lists. Everyday stuff—hydrogen peroxide, acetone, Heet, Pyrex bowls, coffee filters, denatured alcohol, hot plates, cold medicine—much of which Bucky already had around the house and garage, except for the iodine. Against the cost of this, he priced out the product at $100 per gram to start, $1,200 per ounce, $15,000 per pound. He even drew up a business model, a pyramid design, declaring the New England states to be virgin territory, and growing more and more animated at the prospect of the two men going into business together.

At some point around the fourth or fifth time Ibbits was repeating himself, Bucky unwound the AM antenna from his stereo receiver and strangled him with it. He lay Ibbits out on the floor by the fireplace, then returned to poring over the lists, refining the plans in his own mind. Bucky never listened to AM radio anyway. Later he had Eddie drive him back to the station, where he picked up Ibbits's Escort. The crash, he arranged himself, as he did the fire.

Another big reason for Bucky not to dabble. His taking meth was like pouring napalm on a grease fire. Of all the things the drug had shown him that weekend, the most revealing was Bucky Pail himself. He found out that he had been living behind a secret identity all these years: that of Bucky Pail, Black Falls police sergeant, son of Cecil and Verna, brother of Eddie. But what he was inside, the real deal within the hollow shell he wore, was something beyond extraordinary.

The proof of this was that he had never lost focus since that long weekend. Not once. Every step since then, every move he had made, only brought him closer to his goal. Buying fuel, tubing, and glassware to outfit the old curing shack in back, then later the camper. He started off buying up Sudafed for the pseudoephedrine, and he still had Wanda clear out the Gulp whenever they got in a new shipment. But his search for a reliable, local source of iodine had led him to the fruity vet Dr. Bolt and a genius solution. He ordered road flares by the case for the red phosphorous they contained, and then it was on to the cook.

Cold medicine and household poisons cooked to a powder. That's all it was. Easy to bake as chocolate chip cookies, Ibbits told him. Problem was, Bucky had never baked chocolate chip cookies in his life.

But he learned. How to vent the shed so that the fumes didn't get to him. How to dip the flares in acetone, loosening up the phosphorous for scraping. How to tube out the dope. How gourmet coffee filters worked better than the cheaper, no-name brand.

Internet recipes are all bunk, Ibbits had declared. The Man had gotten to them somehow. The cook sites that turned up at the top of the big search engines directed you straight to the Drug Enforcement Agency and registered your computer number. Lots of disinformation out there. And even if you did stumble upon a good recipe, it would be like trying to follow a chef on one of those TV cooking shows where they have all the time-consuming stuff prepared ahead of the taping. Sometimes, in the boredom of a cook, Bucky imagined he was before a TV camera, taking viewers through the process. Showing them his hot plate and mason jars and Pyrex bowls all set up on the counter. Gallon jugs of muriatic acid and Coleman's fuel, cans of Red Devil lye. Him donning his mask and gloves, and, as he boiled and filtered, the studio audience pruning up their noses at the bitter smell.

He tested his batches on Wanda. She was his willing lab bunny. Through her he introduced it into the margins of this marginal town— teenagers, mostly, some rats she had met at the Gulp—test-marketing the product, rolling it out slowly. It was everything Ibbits said it would be and more. Bucky's stockpile grew as he awaited the right moment to release his stores full bore to the public. Then he would watch meth spread like a contagion, consuming its consumers, his own personal army of zombies marching forth, the drug spreading, spreading, and the money riding up the pyramid to the source at the top.

Other opportunists would soon vie for the attention of this new class of customers he was creating—and let them. Let them take over the risk and the blame. Because by then he would have made his wad. Already, he was sitting on about $100,000 worth of product. He would play it out until the moment felt right, and then ditch this used-up town for good. Turn it over to Eddie, let him pick his ass in that run-down station, in a town full of the undead. Let him preside over the final throes of Meth Falls, Massachusetts. Bucky would be down in Daytona, retired at age twenty-six in the land of spring break and NASCAR, wet-T-shirt nights and fat-boy Harleys and fun in the fuckin' sun. College honeys, not the country bush he saw here. Party girls looking for a man with money to spend and maybe a little meth to get them off. Why not dabble, set up a little lab behind his mansion pool house, keep his hand in? This magic dust was his ticket to the world.

This was all part of his pregame ritual, how he got himself fired up to head back out and cook up another hot batch. He was minting money out there, and soon, very soon, he would be able to start throwing some of it around.

He was already at the back door when the front bell went off. Wanda knew he didn't like her coming up here uninvited. She was getting more and more strung out, but he couldn't cut her off now. A six-teenth of a gram was all it took to keep her happy. If only she knew how valuable she was to him. If only she knew how much bank he was going to make off her skinny ass.

He was grinning to himself and chewing the last bit of bologna toast when he opened the door.

43

MADDOX

PINTY IS DEAD.

That was Maddox's first thought as he approached the central station on Pinty's floor, seeing the duty nurse waiting to intercept him.

Instead, she said, "He's been asking for you."

Inside Pinty's room, the dying plant the town had sent over had been moved to the windowsill in a last-ditch effort to revive it. Pinty was asleep, his mouth tube gone, the oxygen line still under his nose. Maddox reached for his left hand where it lay curled across his chest.

Muscles tugged at Pinty's cheeks. His lifting eyebrows signaled a tectonic shift, and his eyes rolled open.

Maddox waited for Pinty to find him there.

"Greggy," Pinty said. He was hoarse and stiff-jawed from sleep and the tube.

"Pinty," said Maddox. "It's me. It's Donny."

Pinty stared, trying to make him real. Trying to make him his son. "Greggy."

So Maddox just nodded, holding his hand until he went out again. Pinty's cold fingers were rigid, locked in a curl. Maddox realized they were palsied from the stroke.

He stayed with him awhile, but Pinty remained asleep.

Later, on his way back out through the emergency room lobby, he saw an ambulance unloading a woman on a stretcher, the accident victim clutching her handbag and trying to talk on her mobile phone with a bandage wrapped around her head.

The EMTs wheeling her in were the same two who had reported to Black Falls the night of the teenagers' car wreck. Maddox watched them go, then followed them inside the ambulance entrance, getting an idea.

He found a woman reading a fat paperback behind the service window. He showed her his badge—the jersey alone wouldn't do it—and asked for the release forms from that night, giving her the accident date and location. "Two minors," he explained. "We have some property we need to return to them."

She clicked keys on her computer with long, jeweled nails, eyeing Maddox while the pages printed silently behind her. A Portuguese woman with dark eyes and a broad nose. Line-thin eyebrows and a faint scar beneath her left ear, riding over her jaw. She handed him the copies and said, "You don't remember me."

Maddox went cold.

She said, "You're wearing a uniform now."

Lowell, he remembered. Eight years ago. Her name would come to him. Her hospital ID was on her belt, too low for him to read.

She said, "I was Bobby Omar's girl."

She was alone inside the window, and there was no one in the hallway within earshot. She seemed as interested in keeping this private as he was.

Maddox said, "I didn't recognize you."

"You haven't changed. Much."

He had to be careful. So many different ways this could go. "I guess Bobby's upstate now?"

"I guess so."

"You don't visit?"

She shook her head, earrings tinkling.

"Glad to hear it," he said.

"He trusted you, you know. He always said he was never sure

about the others, never sure about anyone. Even me. Why he kept that wolf on a chain in our crib. But he was sure about you. Mad Dog Maddox."

She seemed to mean this as a compliment. Maddox folded and refolded the pages in his hands, stopping once he realized he was doing so.

"It was a lifetime ago," she said. "Who I was then. The anger I had for everything, for everyone. I was in so deep." She looked away, curling her tongue. "I'm out here with my sister and her husband now. I have this job. I'm dating one of the drivers."

He sensed her eagerness, her need for his approval.

Back outside, past the ambulance, he made his way to the reserved parking for police vehicles. Maddox would have to find another way into the hospital from now on. His life was like that, whole towns and city neighborhoods, entire regions of the state, walled off to him.

Once he left the overhang and the bright sun hit him, he remembered the pages in his hand. He smoothed out the wrinkles and skimmed the forms. He noticed that the boys' addresses were identical: that of the Ansons, the foster family in town. The same family responsible for Frankie Sculp.

Below that, the person who signed the boys out from the hospital had checked off "Guardian" next to her name. The signature was illegible, but the name typed next to it read, "Tedmond, Wanda."

THE ANSONS' RANCH house looked outwardly normal in the same way a shaken can of soda looks fine until you crack it open. The weedy land was once a thriving apple orchard and seasonal farm stand, now a remote foster farm for Department of Youth Services residential placements.

It was late in the day when Maddox arrived. The school bus was gone from the driveway, meaning that Mrs. Anson was not at home. The man of the house finally responded to Maddox's knocking, Dan Anson seeing the uniform and looking for an accompanying social worker. He wore an oily T-shirt and sweatpants apparently without underwear. "Going camping?" Maddox said.

"What's that?"

"Are you planning a camping trip?"

Anson blinked his blitzed eyes. "Not that I know of."

"Because you already pitched a tent."

Anson looked down at the lazy erection pressing against his gray cotton sweats as Maddox stepped past him into the house.

Inside was no less humid than outside. "I spoke to your wife last time," said Maddox.

"She said. You still looking for Frankie, right? We don't know where he is. Kid's a professional runaway."

"I'm looking for two others now. Carlo and Nick. They went joyriding recently, cracked up a stolen car."

Anson played at thinking. "No," he said, "I haven't seen them."

Maddox walked into a living room of magazines and catalogs fluttered by window fans. A boy about eleven, one of the Ansons' two biological kids, stared at the TV, barely registering him. Maddox went to the kitchen, checked the contents of the refrigerator. Predictably not much. He went back up the hallway opening doors.

"Uh, excuse me, what is this?" said Anson, moving sideways, peering into each room after Maddox did. "I said they're not here."

Maddox opened the door on what appeared to be the Ansons' bedroom, the sheets tossed, window shades drawn down. He saw a computer on a student-sized homework desk. The modem lights were working, but the monitor was off. Maddox switched it on.

Anson stayed by the door, scratching at his unshaved neck. "You can't really do that."

While the screen was warming up, Maddox noticed a lightbulb behind the monitor, its screw base, wires, and filament all removed.

Anson said, "Yeah, that lightbulb burned out."

The fat end was blackened inside. "Pretty spectacularly," said Maddox, picking it up and hazarding a waft. He did not see the accompanying straw.

Maddox checked the monitor. It showed the home page for a fantasy football site.

"See?" said Anson. "Everything's cool."

Maddox reached for the warm mouse, dragging the cursor over the BACK button and clicking. The previous page visited showed a naked guy shackled up in leather restraints on an S&M rack, curse words and racial epithets scrawled over his chest in purple lipstick, his left nipple about to be burned with the lit tip of a cigarillo by a chubby she-male wearing a Nazi helmet, infantry boots, and a monocle.

"Look, I was just killing a little time—"

Anson ducked as the lightbulb shattered against the wall behind his head, glass tinkling to the floor.

Next to the PC was an open two-liter bottle of Mountain Dew Pitch Black grape soda. Maddox pressed buttons to open the CD trays and made ready to empty the contents of the bottle into them.

Anson threw out both hands from his crouch. "Jesus, man, what the fuck?"

"Carlo and Nick, where are they?"

"I'd know, man? How can you keep track?"

"That's supposed to be your damn job." Maddox splashed soda across the room, fizzing like black acid on Anson's shirt. He dribbled a little into the computer.

"You wouldn't. You can't!"

"Say it loud again," said Maddox. "How you don't know where they are. Maybe they didn't hear you."

A bang like a loose door snapping shut. Maddox carried the bottle of soda across the room and hauled down one of the shades, rod and all, from the window.

Two boys were racing away across the backyard into the old orchard.

Maddox looked back at Anson, shrinking against the wall. Maddox moved fast to the desk, glugging soda into the CD slots while Anson covered his head and groaned. "I'll be back for you," said Maddox, rushing past him, cutting down the hall to the living room, past the kid at the TV to a back door leading to a short flight of rickety stairs outside.

Maddox ran fast and angry. The kids had a head start, but the two burnouts hadn't seen anything like exercise in months. They looked back and saw him coming and veered off into what remained of the apple orchard. Never even occurred to them to split up. Running lockstep, they cut between trees and across lanes, unable to shake Maddox's pursuit. Seeing he was about to catch them, they slowed.

Maddox did not. He tackled both at full speed, throwing them hard to the dirt and spoiled fruit and scavenging ants.

Both teens had the same choppy home haircut. Maddox got his knees into their spines.

"Why are you running?"

"Because," said one.

"Because?"

"Of Frankie," said the other.

They were trying to look up at him, but Maddox was kneeling on their backs, forcing their faces into the ground. "What because of Frankie?"

"He said cops were looking for him. Were looking to do him."

Paranoid tweaker. "Where is he now?"

"Hiding, I guess."

"Who brings in the meth?" said Maddox. "Him to you or you to him?"

One teen remained silent. The other said, "What?"

Maddox grabbed their home haircuts and mashed their faces into the dirt. Not a good day to cross him. He asked again.

"Him," said one.

"Him to us," said the other, spitting dirt.

Maddox said, "And you deal to Anson back there?"

One tried to rise up in protest. "That douche bag?"

"He steals," said the other. "Took half our stash. To protect us, he said. Otherwise he'd turn us in."

Maddox said, "Where does Wanda figure in to all this?"

Blinking. Swallowing. "Wanda who?"

Again, Maddox ground their mouths into the dirt and ants. "You're teenagers, lying's supposed to be a *talent*."

They coughed up truth. They'd seen her around, but the hospital was the first time they'd met her. She'd introduced herself as a friend of Frankie's. That was all they knew.

Maddox floated Bucky's name but neither of them so much as blinked.

"I'm asking again. Where is Frankie now?"

"We don't know."

"We might, though," said the other one.

His partner winced at that.

To the talker, Maddox said, "Out with it."

"We followed him this one time."

"We were just curious," said his partner.

"You wanted to take him down!" said the talker.

"Show me," said Maddox, standing, pulling them to their feet.

MADDOX BUZZED THE office door first, because it was closest to the driveway. DR. GARY BOLT, VETERINARIAN, read the sign. A window sticker said, HILL'S SCIENCE DIET SOLD HERE. He gave the button two quick pushes but didn't wait, the office dark, just like the house attached to it.

It was late, the sun gone now, summer light straggling in the western sky. He left the kids in the back of his patrol car and followed the rock path to the front door of the house. The bell was an old one you twisted like a key, but it did not ring. He knocked. While he waited he heard a muffled thump inside like someone tripping, then the sound of something dropping to the floor and rolling away.

Maddox moved to the side of the door. He kick-knocked with his hiking boot, the old training coming right back to him. He sized up the heavy door and figured he was as likely to dislocate a shoulder as he was to break it down. He backed off and started around the side of the house, under a picture window, looking for another way in.

He heard a feeble tapping as he neared the bulkhead doors. A block of wood was jammed under the handles, and Maddox drew his revolver, kicking at the wood, once easy and then harder, popping it free and stepping back, waiting to see who came up.

One door was pushed open, stretching out spiderwebs and shaking loose rust, revealing the arm and scared eyes of a man in his fifties.

Dr. Bolt looked at Maddox's handgun and POLICE jersey as he climbed the stairs out of the basement. "Thank the good Lord."

Maddox grabbed him, helping the older man onto the grass. He wore an undershirt and boxer shorts and a pair of old rain boots he must have found in the basement. He carried a mayonnaise jar under his arm with a few ounces of fluid swishing inside it. "Who's in the house?"

Dr. Bolt made a grand gesture of defeat. "His name is Frankie. He locked me in the cellar."

"Frankie Sculp?"

"Yes."

"What's he doing in there?"

"What *isn't* he doing?" Dr. Bolt looked at his house as though it were a family member in jeopardy. "Just please get him out. He's paranoid, hallucinating. He sees people who aren't there. You can't talk to him."

Maddox looked at the stone basement steps, revolver in hand. He thought about calling for backup. "Does he have a gun? Any guns in the house?"

"No. He has a steak knife in the back pocket of his shorts. He thinks you are coming to kill him, the police. He said he hears SWAT teams in the air-conditioning ducts. I don't even *have* air-conditioning ducts."

Maddox needed to talk to Frankie before anyone else could. "My patrol car is in your driveway. There's a radio under the dashboard. Give me five minutes, then use it. Tell them the situation and your address. The cellar door is locked?"

"A chair wedged under the knob, I think."

"What's in that jar?"

Dr. Bolt held it low at his side. "My urine. I've been down there all day."

Dogs started barking inside. Howling. Dr. Bolt looked stricken.

"The kennel?" Maddox said.

"In back."

Maddox went down into the cool, dusty basement, two dim lights buzzing. He passed an old croquet set under the stairs and took the red-striped mallet, his revolver out in front of him as he climbed the old plank stairs. He gave the door at the top a test shove with his foot, then brought the mallet head down a few times against the ancient doorknob, which cracked apart. He stood the mallet in the corner and kicked open the door.

The chair went crashing against the opposite wall. Maddox jumped out and swept both sides of the short hallway in a two-handed stance, grateful for the light from the basement.

The house was a mess inside. No light switches worked. Broken glass crunched under his boots on the rug.

With the dogs barking madly in the rear, his sweep was perfunctory, throwing open doors and checking rooms. He crossed into the adjoining office, clearing the front counter and the examining room, then moving through a door to the barking dogs in back.

The room smelled of pet shampoo. Three occupants in eight large aluminum sleeping pens, all of them stomping and howling. Maddox zeroed in on a low, open-doored supply locker at the end of the row, and was making his way toward it when a clatter erupted behind him. He turned to metal pans tumbling off the top of a high cabinet and a figure springing from a narrow hiding space beside it.

Frankie Sculp, knife in hand. Maddox had time and cause to shoot him but did not. Frankie, screaming incoherently, brought the knife blade down again and again in a slashing motion, cutting his own chest and legs through his T-shirt and shorts.

Maddox holstered his revolver and lunged with both hands for the knife. He got Frankie's wrist and drove the kid back against the high metal cabinet, bringing more supplies crashing down on them. With one hand on the knife wrist and the other around Frankie's throat, Maddox spun and dropped him face-first to the floor.

The knife popped free, twirling away along the gritty tile. Frankie was howling and bucking, not fighting Maddox, exactly, though the violence amounted to the same. Maddox bent both his wrists behind him, twisting and yanking up on his thumbs, putting a knee into his back and holding him there, letting him kick the floor and wail along with the dogs.

Maddox yelled for Dr. Bolt and then tried to get Frankie's attention. The kid kept squirming, smearing some blood on the floor, but no fast-flowing pool. Incredible, how much heat was coming off him.

"Is he hurt?" said Dr. Bolt, appearing in the interior doorway.

"Not badly." Maddox looked around, trying to figure a way to immobilize the possessed teenager. "Handcuffs. I left mine in my car."

Dr. Bolt looked on, the jar of urine still in his hand, its contents gently swaying. "I might have a pair," he said.

He returned from his bedroom with nickel-plated handcuffs and handed them to Maddox by the linking chain. Maddox clasped them around Frankie's wrists and stood, pulling Frankie to his feet, hooking an arm around his bent elbow and then pushing him, headfirst, through the vet's office and back into the adjoining house.

Dr. Bolt righted a table lamp in the main room out front and screwed in a lightbulb, finding a bare wall socket to plug into.

The interior of the room was demolished. Meticulous destruction: the bookshelves stripped bare, tables upended and their legs unscrewed, sofa cushions removed and unzipped and unstuffed, pictures and photographs taken from their frames, the ceiling fan pulled apart to its wires. An upright piano in the corner had been completely disassembled, frame, keyboard, strings, everything.

Maddox set Frankie down on his side to get a look at his wounds.

Sweat-drenched ribbons of T-shirt hung over the bloody streaks criss-crossing his chest. Subcutaneous but not life-threatening. Just enough to mark him for life.

For his part, Frankie was feeling no pain. He sneered at the lamp, addressing the shining light. "See? Now they're going to bind my feet and throw me in the river like a puppy in a potato sack, and *you just look the other way!*"

Maddox tried to find a telephone he could reassemble. He located the base and the speaker for the interior of the handset.

"He cut the wire outside," said Dr. Bolt, slumping into an easy chair with no cushions, the jar in his lap. "I'm going to lose my practice."

Maddox assessed the scene: a room in shambles, a bloody guy handcuffed on the floor muttering at an unshaded lamp bulb, and an older man in boxer shorts sitting with a jar of his own urine. "Want to tell me what's going on here, Doctor?"

"I'm relieved." Dr. Bolt stared straight ahead. "I am actually relieved now. That it's over. Finally over."

Frankie told the light, "You said you had to get them or else they were going to get you. You were going to show them *all.*"

Dr. Bolt said, "I'll hire a lawyer. A good one." He looked at Maddox across the destroyed room. "Why did I ever let it get this far?"

Maddox said, "There's something you need to tell me, Doctor."

"He knew I had iodine and iodine tincture for horses. He knew that already."

Maddox took a step closer, starting to understand. "Do you keep a supply of pseudoephedrine here, Doctor?"

"It's prescribed for canine incontinence. A Schedule Five controlled substance. He had me order the maximum legal amount every month from my supplier. He was blackmailing me, holding things over me. Yes, I faked point-of-sale documentation. I committed multiple frauds. Every gram of it went to him."

"Doctor, I know who it is. All I need is to hear his name. From you."

"This is going to be very bad for me. I need protection. Real protection. Protection *from* the police. He'll want to do away with me."

Maddox said, "The best way I or anyone else can protect you from this person is to arrest him first. All you need to do is say his name, and this is over just like that. All over. You'll be safe. Just give me his name."

44

HESS

HESS WAS HEADING HOME for the night and some well-earned downtime. He'd phoned ahead to his wife, who had already slipped the two boys some Benadryl and uncorked a bottle of red. He thought it was her when his Nextel lit up blue, his ring tone playing Rhythm Heritage's "Theme From *S.W.A.T.*"

Bryson instead. "You'll want to know this, Leo. Just took a call from Maddox on the local band. Requesting two units, one to the office of a veterinarian, and another for some backup for himself. Said he's making an arrest."

"Arrest?" said Hess, squinting at the highway in front of him, the lane markers zipping past like white bullets. What now? "He hasn't got Sinclair, has he?"

"No, not Sinclair. Something else. Wouldn't say over the radio."

"And he wants *us* backing him up? Not his own? Who does this guy think he is?"

"I was going to ask him myself, but then the DA called. Not her office. Lady DA herself."

Hess felt a cool rush, like a slow pour of water over him. "Saying?"

"Back up Maddox. Whatever he needs."

Hess switched on his wigwags and grille blues and punched the gas, cutting across two lanes to the next exit. The thought bubble he had of Janine answering the front door in her black lace teddy was replaced by Maddox answering it in his junior league Black Falls police getup instead. Hess said into the phone, "I will be right fucking there."

45
MADDOX

THE DRIVEWAY WAS UNMARKED and unnumbered, coming up on him quick in the darkness of Jag Hill. Maddox's patrol car raised a squall of dust, state police cruisers trailing him as Bucky Pail's house appeared around a bend in the driveway, a short ranch with twin carports on the left and junkyard vehicles extending around back.

Maddox stopped, getting out with his flashlight. Bucky's house was dark. The troopers took their time putting on their Mountie hats.

The front door wore a pair of antlers. Maddox knocked and waited. He wanted to feel a certain level of satisfaction, the kind he had anticipated throughout five months of working this case, but the end had come up on him so suddenly, all he cared about now was an expedient arrest. To close the book on this case and this period in his life. To finish the job.

No answer. He stepped back, jumpy, peering in through a small, four-pane window, seeing nothing. Maddox's worst-case scenario: Bucky holing up inside, armed and squirrelly.

One trooper stayed in sight of the front door while the other followed Maddox around the side, underneath the carport, keeping his flashlight beam wide of the house: four or five more cars, a motorbike without tires, and what looked like a speedboat engine dismantled on a black tarp.

The back door was open. Maddox crept up to it. He would not knock this time. No need. Bucky was either sleeping or hiding.

His boot snagged on something near the door, an extension cord, leading from an exterior outlet into the dark backyard. Maddox left the other trooper at the door and followed the wire with his flashlight. It was three lengths of cord plugged together, threading through the dirt and ending up at a portable radio set on a stack of milk cartons next to a small car with its hood up. The radio dial glowed faintly, but nothing played.

Maddox heard something, though. A low, doglike growling coming from the other side of the car, where the trees began to crowd in. He moved around the front bumper with his light, stopping fast.

His beam found a dog pulling at something with its teeth. Not a dog at all, but a coyote, tearing hungrily at a man's face. The face was eaten open to muscle and cartilage, chewed back to the ears and around a full set of crooked teeth. The naked corpse lay on its belly in the dirt, arms behind its back, its wrists handcuffed.

The coyote turned slow, lupine eyes reflecting Maddox's light. It backed off a few steps, baring bloody teeth as though flashing the grin it had just eaten off Bucky Pail's face. Then, resentful yet unashamed, it slunk away along a narrow path back into the trees.

PART IV
MANHUNT

46
CULLEN

CULLEN FOUND MADDOX sitting on a slab inside one of the two holding cells where Bucky Pail should have been locked up now. "I've been looking all over."

Maddox's head was back against the wall, his cap in his hands in his lap. He looked very much like a man doing time. "Only quiet place in the station."

He was right about that. Cullen closed the outer door on the clamor. "We need to talk. We could be in some deep shit here. You saw the handcuffs. Just like Pail handcuffed him when he beat him up."

Maddox closed his eyes, nodded.

"I just came from there. Saw Hess, but ducked him. Guy's in his glory now. The blood trail starts inside the front door. Then into the kitchen, where Pail's clothes were found, sliced off him along with some skin. That's where he was cuffed and killed. They found the dagger there. The one missing from the witch's house."

"Athame," Maddox corrected him.

"Stabbed so hard, the tip was broken off inside him. There was a little toaster oven pulled out, and a squeeze bottle of mustard on the counter. They think Pail had been making some sort of lunch when Sinclair arrived, using a paper towel as a plate. They found flecks of paper inside the corpse's teeth. The thinking is that Sinclair, before dragging the body outside, stuffed the greasy paper in Pail's mouth in order to draw animals."

Maddox offered no response, turning his cap over and over in his hands like thoughts inside his head.

"Look," said Cullen, stepping inside the open cell, "I know this is a blow, but we've got to talk strategy here. Hess is ramping up big. He's got everything he needs, multiple homicides, a killer on the loose. A murdered cop, even if he was dirty. That's an immediate threat, a killer out of control."

"This is about covering our asses on Sinclair?"

"We built up a slam-dunk case against Pail. Problem is, our arrestee is dead. And he happened to have been killed by our informant."

"Small snag."

"So let's accentuate the positive. On the plus side, everything else is bingo. We're talking a historic drug bust for this region. We've got well-trod paths in the back of Pail's house leading out to a shed and an old camper. Piles of empty cans of lye and driveway cleaner behind them, along with cases of stripped road flares. And lots of bare patches in the scrub where he must have buried waste. He's contaminated acres of his own property. I'd be amazed if those holes don't glow green at night. Two HAZMAT teams are en route. You know that stink they talk about around meth labs, like the piss of an asparagus-eating cat? It was immediate at the shed. I couldn't get any closer than the door, but both structures were meth kitchens, it's plain. The guy had grocery bags full of product stockpiled, and I mean pounds of it, ready to go. At fifteen grand a whack? He's been a busy little beaver. He was starting up a business, the first serious meth franchise in New England. Doing the product launch here in Black Falls. He started off in the shack, and it looks like he cooked there until the place became basically uninhabitable. Also looks like he had a serious fire, which probably occasioned his move to the camper. Jars of pharmaceutical-grade pseudo, the supplier's seals and government warnings still on them, along with the vet iodine. The animal doctor is in some serious shit, but he's not the face on this. Bucky Pail is, and you can't bring a dead man to trial. Except, of course, in the press. Which has been tipped and might even be up there already.

Good visuals, the chemicals laid out behind the shack, HAZMAT astronauts removing waste. Oh—and the brother. He showed up while I was there."

"Eddie," Maddox said.

"Right. Was all fired up, tried to badge his way in. You don't tie him to this? He lived on the damn hill with his brother. He must have known."

Maddox shook his head, rolling the back of it against the wall. "Not that I could find."

"But he knew about his brother and Ibbits, right? He knew that Ibbits was in lockup that weekend he supposedly wasn't, before he disappeared."

"Seems that way, yes."

"Okay. Prosecution-wise, it's a short jump from there. He and the others can come in for conspiracy and intent to distribute. Those are our arrests, for the perp walk. Grand jury ends up not handing down indictments? Well, that'll be months from now. Nobody remembers." Cullen loosened up his shoulders. "All right. Now I'm starting to feel better about this."

Maddox didn't move, didn't agree, didn't say anything.

Cullen said, "You still thought Bucky Pail had something to do with killing Frond, didn't you?"

The door opened on the station noise. Hess stepped inside, followed by Bryson, the trooper Cullen had talked to at the murder scene. Hess wore the mad-dog expression of a lifter in mid-rep. He reminded Cullen of the middle school football coach he would see one field over from his son's soccer practice, a guy muscled all out of proportion to his job.

Bryson closed the door, Hess stopping at the entrance to the cell. Staring. Waiting.

Maddox lifted his head from the wall and shrugged.

"Why the fuck didn't you tell me?" said Hess. "How about some fucking professional courtesy, instead of trying to make me look like a fool? Maybe if you'd clued me in to things here, I'd have taken a sharper look at Pail. That occur to you yet? Maybe your catch wouldn't be quite so dead right now. And you not so shit out of luck."

Cullen watched Maddox sit there.

"No," Hess went on. "You wanted that bust all to yourself. Golden boy comes home, makes good. I like the psychology of you UC guys. The homo hidden-life thing. This is your big coming-out party, isn't it. You're out of the cake now. Big splash."

Hess turned and looked at Bryson, as though checking to make sure he was watching. In doing so, Hess discovered Cullen. "You. You were at my homicide scene. You DA?"

Cullen attempted an introduction, Hess ignoring his outstretched hand.

"You're his leash?"

Cullen said, "I have oversight of the Mitchum County Drug Task Force. Looks like we had two investigations on parallel tracks that intersected last night."

"Last night, bullshit. They intersected with Sinclair. *That* was the time to tell me." Hess turned back to continue dressing down Maddox. "Before your investigation cross-infected mine."

Cullen said, "We had a CI implicating local law enforcement in corruption, misconduct, abuse of power, and possible narcotics involvement."

"Sinclair? Your confidential informant is a killer. I hope you don't expect me to keep quiet about that fact."

"Hold on now. Don't forget, we're the aggrieved party here, in terms of results. Your suspect killed our collar. Our *huge* collar. You know anything about methamphetamines, Trooper? Crystal meth?"

"That's the next big scare drug? The one that's going to hollow out our cities, turn children into prostitutes, grandmothers into gang-bangers?"

Cullen said, "This is the one."

"I'll be sure to head for the hills, just as soon as I catch my killer."

"Meth isn't just a ghetto drug or a city drug. It's backyard. It's everywhere. It eats away entire communities—"

"Save the horror stories for your constituents. All I want from you, right now, is a time line. This whole Sinclair thing from *A* to *Z*. Along with whatever else you've been holding back."

"Simple," said Cullen, transferring his folder from one armpit to the other. "You know that Sinclair was assaulted by Pail during a DUI stop."

"And pled out to a nickel license suspension with no prison time in return for dropping assault charges and civil claims," said Hess. "He got his deal. So why would he flip and start working for you?"

"He had a grudge, he had information—some. He brought it to us. That's why we believed him. Because he had nothing to gain. It was the mention of meth that made us really jump. That scourge, burning up the rural West and Midwest for some time, is all but unknown here. Thing is, even he didn't know the extent of it. He figured maybe the Pail brothers were taking a cut somehow, looking the other way."

Hess, having calmed down somewhat, looked at Maddox. "You would meet with him?"

"That's right," said Maddox.

"How often?"

"Nothing regular. Now and then. He would page me."

"That's how you communicated."

"We issued him a pager," explained Cullen.

"Are you his lawyer?" Hess snapped, and Cullen held up his hands and backed away. Hess continued with Maddox. "Has he been in touch with you since he disappeared?"

"Of course not."

"'Of course not,' sure. Because we're all on the same team, right? You would have run right down here and told me. Professional courtesy." Hess frowned hard, looking like every gym teacher Cullen had ever hated. "When was the last time you two met?"

"A week before he disappeared."

"What'd he tell you? What was his attitude?"

"He was using. He was tweaked up."

"But you didn't bust him."

Maddox scoffed; Hess knew better. "I told him he was a fuckup and I walked out. He did page me several days later. A Friday, could have been the day he disappeared. Set up another meet for that next week."

"Where?"

"The top of the falls. Where we always met."

"Sounds romantic."

"The river runs about a half mile back of my mother's property. I could walk there. No one would see us."

Hess was satisfied but still smarting. "For the record, I was right about Sinclair. He did stay. Right here, in this area. Now we step it up big-time. Sweep through this place, flush him out fast."

Maddox said, "One man's death is another man's resurrection."

Hess looked at Maddox with something close to amazement. Even Cullen was a little shocked at Maddox saying that.

Hess said, "We really don't like each other, do we?"

"You've been tripping over your shoelaces this entire investigation."

"Thanks to you tying them together." Hess checked Cullen, as though to say, *You believe this guy?* "You still don't think it's your boy, do you?"

Maddox said, "That last page to me, he indicated he was onto something. That he had something for me, which was unusual, because ten out of our total maybe twelve meetings were bullshit. Most of the work here I did on my own."

"So what was he good for, then? What *did* he give you?"

Maddox, instead of answering him, stood up quickly. As though he had just now found himself sitting inside a jail cell. "Oh, fuck."

"What?" said Cullen.

"Wanda." Maddox looked at Cullen with true alarm, that of a man who had overlooked something of critical importance. "Pail's girl-friend—sort of. She was dealing for him. And using." He put his cap back on his head, moving past Hess.

Hess said after him, "Whoa, hold on."

But Maddox didn't lose a step, walking right out the door into the chaos of the station.

Hess looked at Bryson, sharing his disbelief, then turned his glare on Cullen, as though Maddox were *his* fault.

Cullen patted the air between them in an appeal for patience, his tone turning confidential. Covering for Maddox was covering for himself. "Look, he had a thing go bad on him, his last assignment."

"How terrible," said Hess, starting out fast after Maddox. "Cry me a motherfucking river."

47

HESS

THEY TRAILED MADDOX'S clunker of a patrol car into the hills above the town, Bryson driving. Hess had gone after Maddox in anger, but now regretted it, feeling paralyzed in the passenger seat with no phone and nothing to do, the investigation at a stage where it could easily wriggle away from him. With the HAZMAT alert, the situation in Black Falls rated automatic "critical incident" status with the MSP, meaning that the Incident Management Assistance Team—command post specialists in coordinating lost and missing person searches for the Bureau of Tactical Operations—was already on site. It also meant that the Mitchum barracks' Special Emergency Response Team had been roused, heavily wooded wilderness searches being their specialty. It meant too that the MSP Air Wing Unit was being scrambled, helicopters in the air over Black Falls by noon. Hess had an afternoon of handshaking and name-remembering before him.

"I wonder if he's in that state forest somewhere," said Hess, looking into the trees blurring past. "A cave or a hollow. Deep in, but close enough to make nighttime excursions into town."

"Kind of like a gay Rambo."

Hess's look brought Bryson stammering.

"No, no, hey, I'm with you, I only meant—"

"Or else he's holed up in one of these homes." The trees occasionally gave way to secluded cabins and cottages. "Maybe already killed again, and is hiding out."

Bryson nodded dutifully and drove on.

"These UC guys, huh?" said Hess, nodding at Maddox's car. "Twitchy. Can't trust them because they see both sides and forget sometimes which one they're on. They develop sympathy for the devil, and in this job having too much compassion is like having too much fear."

"Ten years undercover," said Bryson. "The guy's won performance awards he couldn't even show up to collect."

Bryson with stars in his eyes. He had come to Hess highly recommended, but now Hess didn't know.

They slowed at the intersection of two ropy roads. Maddox pulled up in front of a wreck of a house, the roof moldy, the front screen door torn. The homeowner's solution to either a water leak or critter invasion had been to cap the chimney with an upended blue plastic trash barrel.

Maddox was out of his car fast. Apprehension was a new look for him. He didn't even react when Hess and Bryson caught up with him inside.

A grizzled guy in a thin brown bathrobe sat back in a pilled easy chair like slum royalty. Maddox was asking him about this Wanda, and the guy, Bill was his name, sat there like Hugh Hefner's bitter half brother, saying she was sleeping.

They crowded up the narrow hallway, Maddox pushing the door open on a room with an empty bed. He stripped back the sheets in one motion, something small and light flying out and flitting to the floor beneath a small, three-loop radiator.

Two small drug bags.

Maddox pushed past them into the tight hallway and tried another closed door. When the knob didn't turn, he banged on the unpainted wood grain with the flat of his hand, calling her name.

"Who is that?" came a sleepy voice.

Hess watched Maddox's head bow with relief. Apparently, he had thought this Wanda was dead. "It's Maddox."

"What are you . . . doing here?"

Lots of movement inside. A classic stall.

Maddox stood in that sideways manner people have of speaking through doors. "I need to see you."

Water was running. "I'm gonna be a couple of minutes. . . ."

"Right now."

"It's your turn to wait for me for a change, how's that? This is lady business in here."

"Wanda."

They heard the flush. Hess showed Maddox his impatience.

"Wanda."

"Hold your horses."

"Wanda. I'm going to kick it in."

The knob had a slot keyhole in its center, and Hess motioned to Bryson for the Leatherman tool he usually carried. Bryson gave it to him and Hess unfolded a knife blade and jiggled it in the knob.

"I said I'm coming—"

Hess turned the knob and Maddox pushed in fast through the door. Wanda was a string-haired rag doll in terry-cloth shorts, a washed-out Celtics ring tee hanging off her shoulders like a nightshirt on a little sweaty girl. She was bent over the sink as though hiding something, and Hess first thought she was fixing up. But when Maddox turned her around, her hands were empty except for the two damp sweatbands she was pulling on over pad bandaging.

The white walls of the sink were bloody, and on the rim, near the torn-open box of bandages, were a pair of tweezers and nail clippers, both stained red. The woman's eyes were glassy as she bent to protect her arm, but Maddox, after his initial shock at the sight of the blood, tugged off the sweatbands, and the bandages beneath came away.

There was a puff of stink that smelled almost cadaverous. Wanda's forearm above her wrist was a mess of chewed flesh. She had been using the grooming tools to pick at her wounds, one abscess dug down to the tendon, its ridges black with spoil. The burnlike lumps of skin looked boiled from beneath, maybe from unabsorbed poisons eating their way back out of her body. The sight reminded Hess of Bucky Pail's face, and how the coyote had torn into him.

She cradled the arm as though it were precious, an infant unswaddled. "I have an infection," she said.

Hess rippled with a shiver. "Good Christ."

Wanda looked at him like a corpse turned suspicious. "What's this?" She turned to Maddox for an explanation, but Maddox, holding her gaze, said nothing.

"This is an arrest," said Hess. "You have the right to remain silent. . . ."

Still holding her gory arm at an odd angle, she looked from Hess back to Maddox again. "Donny?" she said, the reality of her situation slowly sinking in.

Maddox looked dazed. He stared into the middle ground between them.

Hess, disgusted but trying to get through this, said, "Anything you say—"

"Where's Bucky?" she said, starting to panic.

Hess held up his hands to calm her down. "Anything you say—"

"No!" she yelled at Hess, reeling backward as though he were attacking her. "*No!*" With nowhere else to go, she wedged herself between the small sink and the dirty tiled wall, shaking her rag-doll head.

They weren't even police to her. They were the embodiment of the pain of withdrawal that was to come. Agents of dopesickness. That was the fear behind her hazy eyes. And the wild betrayal when she looked at Maddox.

Hess realized he could not grab her wrists. With nothing to handcuff, she wasn't going to go easy. Why the hell am I dealing with this now? he asked himself.

"Bryson," he barked. "Get in here and arrest this woman."

48
EDDIE

EDDIE BURIED HIS brother right after the autopsy. He thought that putting him in the ground—reminding people that a police sergeant had died here—would also lay to rest all the talk. So there was no wake, no service, just this graveside observance. They couldn't do an open casket anyway, and whatever religion the brothers once had was buried here with their mother, with the beads tangled up in her folded fingers.

His grief wasn't wet. It was dry like ice, angry and focused. No throwing his hands up at the sky. No cosmic "Why?" God had nothing to answer to Eddie for. Only two people did.

Scarecrow, of course. That twisted little would-be abortion. Using Bucky's own handcuffs on him (*How could you let that little shit get the drop on you?*) and feeding him to the wolves. Eddie wiped his nose on the sleeve of his father's old suit jacket, the double buttons on the cuff like teeth rubbing across his lips. Thinking about any aspect of the murder made him want to tear at his own skin, made him want to claw at the earth—but the one thing Eddie kept focusing on, the one thing that sickened him in the pit of his being, was Bucky's clothes being taken off. That freak seeing his brother naked. Getting his jollies. Eddie's fists weighed down his jacket pockets like two hot stones.

And then Maddox. Where was he now? Sure, he had a grudge against Bucky, and vice versa. But this disrespect? Not showing up for a fellow officer? Unforgivable. Bucky had been straight-up right about that guy, not trusting him, not liking him. And now all this drug nonsense on the news, in the papers—Eddie couldn't help thinking somehow it was Maddox's doing. They called it a "lab." What they didn't know was that Bucky got his first chemistry set at age seven, and that he had always been a dabbler. As kids, the two of them used to use his compounds to blow up stumps and things on their hill. They even made their own fireworks, Bucky experimenting to learn which powders made them spark red or green or blue.

And how was it Maddox had been the one to find Bucky's body? He'd sure never been to the house before that night. And where had he been hiding since? Didn't he know Eddie had questions?

It was Maddox's house they were heading to after this. Eddie was going to get his father's suit dirty, maybe. Maddox had a lot of talking to do.

A *whup*ping noise drowned out the pastor's voice, and suddenly a helicopter with state police markings on its belly crested the trees, beating low over the graveyard, loosening petals from the condolence bouquet and flapping Bible pages in the pastor's hand. The same helicopter that had buzzed Jag Hill last night with its searchlight beaming down, searching for Scarecrow.

The flyby was almost like a tribute—*should* have been a tribute—with the mourners shading their eyes from the sun, which, to Eddie, looked like a military-style farewell salute. Bucky deserved such a tribute.

But so few mourners. Where was the rest of the town? Didn't they know that Bucky had taken a stand for them? Who was it who first roughed up that little freak when he had the chance? And in doing so, put his life on the line for this town? This was his thanks? This was the respect they gave him? This turnout was like a vote of support for his killer.

He looked down to the low stone wall along Number 8 Road, the state police troopers grouped there. They didn't care. It wasn't one of theirs dead. Eddie looked to the side, the vehicle path that ringed the cemetery. He saw Ripsbaugh standing by his Bobcat, shovel in hand. No respect. Not even the courtesy to take a break during the ceremony. The Grim Reaper over there, couldn't wait to bury him. Like this service was holding him up.

Eddie's brother. His baby brother. Pails had lived in Black Falls almost since the beginning, and they had plots throughout this cemetery, from the thin, cracked, pre-Revolutionary-era stone markers leaning like bad teeth in the front row to the broad, modern headstones in the rear. Eight or nine separate markers here with PAIL carved into them.

Eddie was the last one now. Eddie was all alone.

People were looking at him, Big Bobby Loom nodding. Eddie hadn't been paying attention. It was his turn. He took Bucky's cop hat and set it on top of the casket, then cracked open two cans of Bud, sipped the foam off his, and set the other at the edge of his brother's open grave.

Eddie stayed down on one knee, head bowed.

Help me, Bucky. Bring me Scarecrow. Bring him to me, brother. I dedicate the rest of my life to avenging you. To clearing your everlasting memory and our proud name. And to punishing this town for turning its back on you today.

When it was over, Eddie lingered while the mourners wandered away. He stared at the coffin as though he could see inside, his brother's faceless head nestled in padded white satin. Mort Lees and Stokes and Ullard gathered at his back. A good feeling, them united. Eddie turned away his hazy eyes and they started off together, as one.

The uniformed troopers detached from the stone wall. Eddie thought they were at last coming to pay their respects, but then he saw their faces. The troopers stopped, blocking the way to the road.

"You don't want to make a scene now," said one of them, thumbs hooked inside his gunbelt.

"What scene?" said Eddie, Mort at his side. "What is this?"

The trooper said, "All of you, raise your hands, lace your fingers behind your heads."

This broiling heat. This beating summer sun. Eddie felt himself going wild inside. "This is a graveside observance."

"Graveside observance is over, Jack. Feel lucky we let you have that. You want to maintain some dignity, you comply with my command now and come along quietly. Hands up and behind your heads. Let's go."

Eddie saw one trooper move his palm flat against the butt of his sidearm, another with his fingers holding open the flap of a pouch of Mace. From that point on Eddie was blind with rage. The fight occurred as much inside him as around him. He unloaded his despair. Wanting to hit and be hit. To hurt and be hurt. Mace burned his eyes, and the name he yelled as they pulled him to the ground was Maddox's.

49
CULLEN

"**B**OLT DID INDEED GO OUT and get himself a good lawyer," said Cullen, sitting on a thin-cushioned divan inside Maddox's mother's house, casually bobbing the shoe of his crossed leg, the hand of his outstretched arm plucking at the stiff crocheted slip covering a wheel-shaped pillow. "A smart lawyer who convinced him to roll over fast. Had no choice, really. With Pail dead, they knew Dr. Bolt was the one we would go after, get his face on TV, make an example of. And it's an easy case to prove. This way, we get what we want—Pail the archvillain, whose crimes die with him—and Bolt gets what he wants—to play the victim. Which is less than a half-truth, but it gets us close enough to the full story. He'll plead out early to avoid a jury. Take short time, some token like thirty months, long probation, and register as a sex offender."

"Sex offender?" said Maddox.

"Bolt occasionally hired some of the foster kids to do odd jobs around the kennel. Some of them he fed ketamine hydrochloride, which I understand is a dissociative anaesthetic for animals."

"Special K."

"What you call it on the street. Himself, he'd take some Internet Blue. Viagra." To Maddox's scowl, Cullen said, "Yup. Bolt stresses it was 'only a few times,' as though he should be eligible for further sentence reduction for not doing it to hundreds or thousands of kids. Good Sergeant Pail found out about this somehow, and instead of taking him down, used it against him. Which raises the question of how did Bucky Pail know that veterinarians handled not only pseudo-ephedrine, the main ingredient in making meth, but the other govern-ment-restricted precursor, iodine?"

"Ibbits," said Maddox, seated across from him in a chair uphol-stered in brocaded rose blooms. The ticking came from a ceramic clock on the otherwise empty mantle behind him. Everything else was in open boxes, half packed, and probably had been for months. It was an old house with attendant aches and pains. Including the irregular wood creaks Cullen kept hearing upstairs.

"Ibbits indeed," said Cullen. "A fugitive from justice, a nomad with the epic misfortune of cutting through Black Falls on his way to nowhere. Of being pulled over in one of Bucky Pail's notorious speed traps. Hugo Ibbits was Patient Zero for meth here in Mitchum County. Like a spore floating on the air, who landed inside our throat. He did spend time in lockup, brother Eddie finally confirmed it. Bucky came and got him out on a Sunday night, though Eddie still insists his brother released him. He truly believes that Ibbits cracked up his own car and died in the fire. And he still backs his brother's innocence one hundred percent on the meth lab. When we showed him printouts from his brother's Internet searches, seeking property in Daytona Beach, Florida, Eddie actually broke down. Guy cried."

Maddox nodded but demonstrated no sympathy.

Cullen rounded it up quickly, tired of the details he had spent the last forty-eight hours assembling. "Wanda moved it through Sculp and others via a drop at the vet's. Sculp dealt to the other kids at his house, and the kids further seeded it around town. The supply chart was growing, doubling every eight to twelve weeks. The tipping point was approaching soon, where Bucky would have to turn it loose. Sculp dealt to Sinclair. Don't know how they connected originally, and unless Frankie gets a grip on himself after detox, we'll have to wait for Sinclair to get caught to find out."

Maddox sat forward. "They need help here for this. We have to go through town and figure out some way to deal with these people, reach out to them. They've had a taste of it now. We need to get in here and address this before it occurs to somebody that they can cook this shit themselves, in the trunk of their car."

"Well," said Cullen, "I'm with you on that, but let's be honest. That's the mopping up that never gets done. The message is always, 'Mission Accomplished,' through the press, and, yes, through my office. Drugs confiscated? Problem solved. That's the only story people want to hear. I just don't see us getting much support. Especially with the Sinclair hysteria ongoing. You following that?"

"Not really." Maddox had been out of action since Wanda Tedmond's arrest.

"Sightings all over town," said Cullen. "A twelve-year-old kid walking home from a friend's house yesterday saw Sinclair beckoning to him from some trees across the street. People've seen him cutting across their neighbors' backyards. Calls come in to nine-one-one saying he's down in the basement *right now.* Or their kids' toys were moved around in the driveway—maybe it was Sinclair." Cullen smiled in amazement. "It's a legitimate phenomenon. We have a saying in the DA's office: Awaken the fears of a parent and you awaken the fears of a community."

"Police radio last night said something about coyotes—"

"Roaming the streets, it's true. A couple of them got shot and killed. The Air Wing helicopter with its thirty-million-candlepower searchlight rousted them all from the state forest. Or maybe they were drawn here by the scent of fear. Of course, having state police strike teams in full ninja tac skulking through your neighbor's pasture, clearing old barns and outbuildings—that doesn't exactly help calm things down. Doesn't ease much anxiety. My way over here, I passed people out on their front steps, hunting rifles across their laps. Guy shot out his own patio window last night, thought he saw a shadow. They're pulling down antique Winchesters from over the fireplace, riding around with loaded handguns on the passenger seat. Massachusetts has the most restrictive firearms laws in the country, but enforcing those statutes tonight would mean packing half the town into two small jail cells. This is a holiday for people, a once-in-a-life-time opportunity to lock and load in public, maybe even bag them-selves a gen-u-ine child molester."

Maddox said, "Wonderful."

"So you can see how well martial law would go over. State police actually imposed a curfew, but nobody knows it. How do you alert a community without a Web site or cable TV channel or even a town newspaper? This is why you need to stay on. In name only, just until Sinclair is brought in. Can't totally disband a town's police depart-ment during a crisis like this. Plus, my boss's perspective is, there's one thousand seven hundred fifty-eight potential votes here, so don't mobilize taxpayers by pissing them off."

"Nobody here votes."

"Still, she doesn't want a lawless town on her register. Just let Hess and his bunch do their thing, and wait this out. Play the small-town cop for a couple more days."

Maddox nodded unhappily. "And after that?"

Cullen shrugged, flapping his tie out over his lap. "That's up to your brass. You might as well know, no matter how this Sinclair shit storm falls, I'm recommending you back with full confidence."

"Actually," said Maddox, "I was asking about the town."

"You mean their police?" Cullen shrugged again. "That's a little beyond our purview, isn't it? I'm sure they'll work it out, hire on replacements. What other choice do they have?"

Maddox accepted this quietly. He had seemed uncomfortable since answering the door, but only now did it occur to Cullen that Maddox was impatient for him to leave. Another subtle creak upstairs drew Cullen's eyes to the swirled pattern of the plaster ceiling, then the detailed molding around the edge.

"One thing I've been meaning to ask you," said Cullen. "I saw the pictures from Sinclair's camera. The one of your house here. What was that?"

"I don't know. I don't think I want to either. You ever crack open an egg and get a bloody yolk? Crack open Sinclair's head, and that's what you'd get."

"But what do you *think*? Was he fixated on you?"

"I don't know how he saw me. I had a secret. A secret job, a secret life. He was drawn to that. I think he wanted that for himself. A great secret existence."

"Maybe he found one. I'd watch yourself, anyway." Cullen patted his own knee, uncrossing his legs. "And now I get to go home." He stood, returning the wheel pillow to the corner of the divan, reaching for his file. "What about you? What's the night hold?"

Maddox shrugged, getting to his feet.

"Alone with your thoughts, eh? Well, enjoy your downtime. God knows, it never lasts."

The moment had arrived either to shake hands or not. Cullen tapped Maddox lightly on the chest with the file folder, then nodded and started away. Sometimes it ended that way. No finish-line string-breaking or end-zone spike. There was an excellent chance they would never even see each other again.

On his way out through the garage, Cullen took another look at the old Ford pickup. Its rusted wheel wells and dinged sides and mud-browned tires marked it as a true, working truck, a farm rig, and, as such, unsuited to Maddox's needs. Cullen checked the front seat through the driver's window and saw a package of breath mints, a garage door remote control, and a paperback with a pink and blue cover he recognized as being one of his wife's book group novels.

A pickup truck and chick lit. Cullen was only sorry he'd never been introduced.

50
TRACY

TRACY WENT DOWNSTAIRS after she heard the car drive away.

Donny, alone in his kitchen, turned and raised a "there you are" smile.

"Sorry," he said. "I didn't know he was coming by."

She shrugged. "That's okay."

"I'm not used to mixing work with my private life. Not really used to having a private life at all."

"Okay," she said again.

"He's from the Mitchum County District Attorney's office. I don't know how much you heard. . . ."

"Was I supposed to be listening?"

He shrugged like it was all right if she had been.

"Most of it," she admitted.

He nodded. "I never, ever lied to you. To everyone else but you."

"You never told me much truth either."

"I know. But I'm about to."

Tracy stood against the dishwasher to steady herself. This buildup was too much. She folded her arms protectively, to stop herself from trembling. "Okay."

"This isn't my first job in law enforcement. I've been with the state police for just over ten years."

Tracy had guessed as much, listening from the foot of his bed upstairs. But hearing him say it now blew holes in her ears. "You're a state trooper?"

"Never actually wore the uniform. Not for one day on the job."

Tracy stared, trying to picture him in the shirt, the hat, the boots.

"Issued me a gun too, but I never carried it. Both have been in storage since the academy. They pulled me out right before graduation to work undercover. Which I've done continuously ever since."

"Undercover?" she said, a term she thought she knew from the movies, but which, when applied to Donny Maddox, had no meaning for her at all.

"Narc work, mostly. I think it started off as an experiment. They wanted someone with a clean background, who could walk around with a real name and a real social security number with real mileage on it. So I kept no personnel file with the state police. Only one captain and one major within the organization knew my cover. My police salary was always paid out into an account under my mother's name so that I never drew a paycheck. It wasn't very much anyway. Unlike uniform troopers, I couldn't pad my take-home with detail work."

He shook his head like he was rambling.

"I kept what I earned working my cover jobs, lived off that. That was the life. All real jobs, lots of bars, day labor, some under-the-table stuff. Building up visibility and street cred. Every step of the way, I was wheeling and squealing. And always managing to be somewhere else when the cops came knocking.

"Most undercovers go four, five years max. It's a fast track to promotion. But with me, it wasn't something I dipped in and out of. I was always in it. Birthdays would come and go, and I'd think, This year, this is the last. Only to see another one come around again. I used to blame the SP, but it was me just as much. Fact was, I liked it. It was what I knew, and it came easy to me. Until the job before this one."

He cleared his throat. He was telling her everything and it was too much at once. Tracy prepared herself for the worst.

"An OxyContin ring operating out of Haverhill. You know what

Oxy is, right? Pharmaceutical painkiller. Heroin users love it because it's control-released. A sustained high over time. These were bad boys, taking off pharmacies at gunpoint. Ran down a Haverhill cop once on a getaway, the guy died of a heart attack. I worked them through this girl I had conspired to meet, a roommate of one of their sisters. A good girl, basically, with a good heart, but kind of tragically naive and gullible. Perfect for me. I contrived to get myself kicked out of my own apartment, knowing she would take me in. That was how I was trying to break in with her friend's brother. But it was slow going. I would hit up this girl for information, things she'd heard. These guys were all Latins, and 'roid ragers, paranoiacs. When things started to go bad for them, when they had to shade off some jobs because they picked up on stakeout heat at the scene, they went on a witch hunt. One night I came home and she was gone. No word, nothing. Turned out they had fingered her for the leak instead of me. Her body was found underneath a bridge. They'd force-fed her a couple of crushed-up Oxy, which, outside of its control-release capsule, delivers a twelve-hour high in one bolt. They took turns urinating on her as she was dying."

Tracy's arms were crossed so tightly she could hardly breathe.

"Yeah." Donny cleared his throat again. "I knew how it happened, I knew who did it, but had no proof. So I poured myself into it that much harder, breaking in with them in order to seal this murder rap. But to get there, to run with these scumbags and earn their trust, I had to do some things. Things I wouldn't ordinarily do. The rules of the game that are meant to be bent? Well, I really bent them. Tied them in knots. But as far as I was concerned, the end more than justified the means."

He was nodding hard. He looked sick.

Tracy felt paralyzed.

"The other side of it was, I knew my mother was ill. She would tell me she was okay, and I let myself believe her because I couldn't get out to see her anyway. I was living with these guys by then, this hyper-paranoid bunch—totally insular was how they rolled, you never

mixed with anyone outside the crew—and everything was coming to
a head. So I put off seeing her, and put it off, and fucking put it off.
It was right after I got these guys picked up in the act of knocking
over a CVS in Salem, New Hampshire, that she had her fall.

"There was real static coming my way after the case, the rules I
broke, and I was at a point where I just didn't care. So I quit. The day
after my mother's funeral, in fact. Tried to, anyway. Then they came
to me about Sinclair, who had been beaten up by Bucky Pail during a
DUI stop. He had made some narco allegations against the Black Falls
police, and Pinty had already been to the DA's office about corruption
in the department he once ran. It was my hometown, it was a good
fit, so they offered me this probationary rehab assignment, a straight-
forward fact-finding case of possible rogue cops running amok. I
didn't really care about making good myself. It was for Pinty I did it.
Aside from my mother, he was the only one who knew what I was—
knew that this was the reason I never came back after graduation,
never served my scholarship time. He got me hired on to the force
here, and I've been working this case ever since."

"Sinclair?" Tracy said, trying hard to understand. "You were
his . . . ?"

"He was my informant, yeah. I had that distinct privilege. He was
just starting to figure out that this thing was bigger than even he had
originally thought when he disappeared. Now, somehow, my small-
town criminal conspiracy case has dovetailed into a double-murder
investigation."

She was breathing hard like she had been running the entire time
he was speaking. Running away from what he was saying and at the
same time racing to keep up with him. "So then, Wanda . . ."

"She was the only one close to Bucky Pail. That's what that was all
about. But she stayed loyal to him. Or rather, she stayed loyal to his
drugs."

Tracy said, "In the movies, undercover drug agents, sometimes
they have to take drugs themselves. To prove they're not police."

"Yeah."

She waited. "That's all you're going to say?"

Donny said, "Yeah."

She felt weird, her hands and legs tingling. *Drugs. Donny.* She looked at him standing across the kitchen, suddenly realizing that she might not know this man at all. "Did you wear wigs, disguises?"

"No."

"You used your real name?"

"Mostly. Twice I got loaned out to DEA short-term, they tagged me with a phony background. But predominantly, it was just me."

"And you've put away a lot of people?"

"A good few, yeah."

"Don't you worry about them coming back to find you?"

"Not really," he said.

This was his first lie to her, she realized with a chill. "These people . . . you would live with them, gain their friendship, trust? Knowing you were going to turn on them in the end?"

"It's the second-dirtiest game out there, right after the drug trade itself. But there is no other way. The only way to fight street crime is with street presence." She watched him try to come up with some way of illustrating it so that she would understand. "There are people who are good at doing drugs. That may sound strange to you, but there just are. They can handle it somehow, they can manage their life. What I was good at was this. Undercover. I tried not to question it beyond that. And generally I had success. Until Haverhill." He could see that he was having trouble getting through to her. "Can you see now why it was so important to me that no one knew about us?"

Tracy felt cold. And scared, and suddenly heartsick. She felt squeezed. "What was her name?" she asked.

Donny didn't understand at first. Then he looked down at the floor. He was thinking about that girl, remembering her. "Her name was Casey."

She watched him so closely, needing to read his face for the answer to this question. "Were you in love with her?"

"No," he said. "I wasn't. But isn't that worse?"

This was like trying to wound him by ripping out chunks of herself and throwing them at his head. "You were playing a role."

"That's right."

"Are you playing a role now?"

A weird buzzing ended the charged stillness. Tracy looked at the corner of the counter where he routinely dumped his wallet and keys. His pager was creeping sideways, vibrating.

Donny picked it up, checking the message screen. He looked confused at first, then alarmed. He pressed a button, read something more. "It's him," he said.

He started moving, past her and around the corner to the hall closet.

"Who him?" she said, following.

From the top shelf he brought down his leather holster, unsnapping it and pulling loose his gun. "Sinclair."

"*What?*" She took the pager from him to see for herself.

The sender's SkyTel address was displayed along with the header and the current time. *Meet at pulp mill. Urgent. ALONE.*

"How do you know it's him?"

Donny used a key from his ring to undo the trigger lock on his gun. "Three people have that pager number. No—four. The assistant district attorney, who just left here. You. Wanda, who's in lockup. And Sinclair." He took the pager out of her numb hands, and, before slipping it into his back pocket, showed her. "That's his account number. This was sent from his pager."

The two halves of the lock spilled onto the counter. He popped open the barrel to check the load, then closed the gun back up again and tucked it into his holster. He undid his belt strap to his right hip, threading the holster onto it, fixing the belt and buckling it tight.

Tracy said, "You're not going there alone. He's already killed one policeman."

Donny grabbed his wallet and pocketed his keys. "It's nothing like that."

"How do you know?" She looked to the window, the night outside. "Call your state police."

"They would scare him off. You read the message. Look—it's just not like that. I don't have time to explain right now."

He started away, then came back fast.

"Stay here. Wait for me, okay? Please. And don't open the door for anyone but me."

"Don't open the—Wait! What if you don't come back?"

He hurried down the hallway. "I'm coming back."

51
MADDOX

MADDOX WAS ALMOST an hour in, and still no sign. He had gone through every desolate room on three long floors, painstakingly clearing the crumbling mill, not wanting any surprises. Every single window had been smashed, stones lying where they landed on the floor after having been launched by kids on the other side of the river.

He went back outside via the same kicked-in door. A few decaying bales of paper stock remained in the adjoining lot, and he stood among them looking up at the big former polluter, an ominous industrial carcass looming over the river's edge. He had forgotten how much he used to dread these secret meetings with Dill Sinclair. How, after all the schemers and psychos who had crossed his path over the years, he had to come home to meet the one guy he literally could not stand to be around.

He remembered their last meeting, farther north along the bank of this same river. Sinclair emerging from the trees at dusk, the hood of his black shirt pulled over his balding head despite the heat, pocketed hands tugging it down. "Shall we do the secret handshake?"

Maddox, despising his dripping familiarity, said nothing in response. Behind him the river rushed to the small island that divided the flow at the edge, the twin cascades plummeting to the natural rock basin seventy feet below.

"Ever come here as a kid?" asked Sinclair, moving to the edge. The right cuff of his loose black jeans was still tucked into his sock above his black-and-white Chuck Taylor All-Stars high-top, to keep the fabric from tangling in his bicycle chain. He looked out over the drop into the lower valley, the water cutting a path through the trees as it wound south. "I did. I used to look down on the town and wish I could hop in this river and ride it right out of here." He glanced back at Maddox with a smile. "Do I make you nervous, standing out here? Some say people have a natural aversion to heights, but I don't think that's true. I think people are actually drawn to heights. They're *drawn* to the edge, and I think *that* is the scary part. People keep back for fear they might be tempted to take the leap." He looked way down to the churning pit below. "The ease of it. One step. What would it feel like, falling? You never wonder?"

Maddox stood his ground some twenty feet back. He could have rebutted that people with nothing to lose tend to find precipices just about anywhere they looked.

"The water, the way it crashes down there, forms a whirlpool." Sinclair scooped up some loose stones, dropping them one by one over the edge. "You wouldn't have a chance to drown. The force of the water would destroy you first. Tear off your clothes, your skin. Mash you up against the rocks. Obliterate you, leaving no trace."

Maddox said, "If you're waiting for me to talk you down from there . . ."

Sinclair snickered, tossing the rest of the stones and brushing dirt off his hands. "Nobody would cry, right? Nobody would shed one tear. They'd be happy. They'd be thrilled. It's almost funny. If the people in this town only knew."

"You don't do this for them."

"No? That's true, I guess." He turned back to Maddox. "But then again, neither do you. I wonder sometimes, who hates this place more—you or me?" He rolled his head to one side, rubbing his neck. "Who would ever have guessed that the two of us together would join up to save these hicks from themselves?"

He seemed to be smiling. Remarkable how much the absence of eyebrows cut down one's range of expression.

Maddox said, "You brought me out here for nothing, didn't you."

"I'm *trying* to be good," Sinclair said. "I am. But it's so fucking lonely when there's *nothing to do*." He chewed his nail. "Except go crazy. Okay, so nobody wants me to be happy, right? So, fine. I can't even find anybody to be *miserable* with. How do you get by? You met anyone here?"

Maddox didn't like Sinclair's look—didn't like it because he couldn't fully read it. Did he know about Tracy? Had he been watching Maddox?

"Okay," Maddox said, and started walking off.

Sinclair's voice sounded bewildered behind him. "Where are you going?"

"I can do this myself. You think you're playing games with me? You give me *nothing*."

"It's my life on the line here," Sinclair said. "We can't just talk? Have a goddamn conversation like normal people?"

"I'm not your friend. You find out something I can use, you page me. And next time don't show up here tweaked."

That silenced him. Until Maddox was almost to the trees.

"I *will* have something," Sinclair said. His voice wasn't cracking, but it was strained. He hadn't moved from the edge of the falls. "You'll see."

"Right," Maddox said. "Promises."

"It's big. More than you know."

Maddox kept right on walking.

That had been the relationship. A rat-and-mouse confederacy, like the strategic alliances that form within a dysfunctional family. *You and me against the others.* And Maddox exploited that.

Which was why acting disappointed was sometimes enough to motivate him into action. In that respect, Sinclair was like Maddox's damaged twin. He wanted his better half's approval. Wanting to do well, to succeed, to shine in someone's eyes for once: that was Sinclair's greatest secret.

His greatest failure was his inability ever to do so.

More minutes passed. A car drove by, Maddox watching it from the dark corner of the lot, crossing the bridge and turning onto Main Street, pulling away. Now he was getting pissed.

Maddox brought out his pager. Nothing further. He checked the original message again. It had been sent from Sinclair's pager, there was no doubt. But the text. He reviewed it now that he had more time.

Meet at pulp mill. Urgent. ALONE.

Sinclair's messages were long and rambling, not staccato bursts. Granted, the guy was on the run. But also there were no misspellings. Sinclair was notorious for that—whether he was dyslexic or just sloppy, Maddox didn't know. "Pulp" would be "plup." "Urgent" would be "ugrent." It was constant, every second or third word.

And why wait so long to contact him? If he had in fact been carrying the pager with him all this time, why hadn't he used it? Why hadn't he responded to any of Maddox's earlier messages? Why ignore him until now?

Maddox suddenly felt exposed, standing half visible in the moonlight behind the old paper mill, looking at the trees across the river and farther south along Mill. He was beginning to think that coming here had been a terrible mistake.

52
TRACY

S HE DREAMED A MEMORY: the afternoon her parents had sat her down in the sitting room, where all the serious conversations took place, and told her thirteen-year-old self that they were breaking up for good. Her father was not deaf, so it fell to him to utter the words—through a smile, as though everything were going to be okay—while her mother sat next to him, hands angrily mute in her lap. Tracy had cried that day, more out of confusion than anything, the distress she felt from her parents. As soon as she could, she excused herself and went into her room and shut the door. The next thing she remembered was her mother shaking her shoulder, and Tracy feeling a surge of bliss, as though waking from a terrible dream. Her relief vanished as soon as she saw the look in her mother's dark-rimmed eyes. Her mother left the room silently and Tracy felt her reproach, though she did not understand why until she was older: her mother had seen her slumber as a careless act, the betrayal of a much-needed ally.

So now, bolting awake to the rumble of the opening garage door, Tracy felt that same moment of pleasant disorientation, of consolation—only to be brought down crashing by the shameful realization that she had once again fallen asleep. How was this possible? Emotional exhaustion? Or simple cowardly escape? She chastised herself for her weakness, rubbing hard at her cheeks and her eyes, her skin feeling like it had aged a year during that nap. Her face turning into her mother's face.

She had been sleeping with an undercover state trooper. She knew nothing about the man she had fallen for. It came back to her in a bolt: who Donny was, where he had gone, whom he was to meet. So when the garage door started to close, fear woke her completely. Was this him? She went and stood half hidden inside the bathroom doorway, feeling more useless than ever.

He walked in, his holster already off his belt, his keys and pager in his hands. He shuffled his boot treads on the thin mat and shook his head when he saw her. "Nothing. He never showed."

"Never showed?"

"Two hours I waited. Wandered all over that rotting place." He walked past her and dumped his stuff on the counter where the pieces of his trigger lock remained. She could smell the old building on him, sawdust and decay. "I'm sorry, you were probably worried."

Could he see that she had fallen asleep? "But why would he . . . ?"

Donny pulled a jug of water from the refrigerator and poured himself a glass and drank all of it. "Stand me up? I don't know. Any number of reasons, I suppose."

"Okay. But."

He poured himself another full glass and closed the refrigerator door. "It was this feeling I had there. While I was standing out in back, by the riverbank. Like I was being watched."

"Watched? Why would he be watching you?"

"He wouldn't. But what if someone else had his pager? Say they wanted to find out who had been paging him? That's how you'd do it. Set up a meet and draw that person out into the open."

"But you're losing me," said Tracy. "Now you think someone else has his pager?"

"I don't know." Donny paced, looking angry with himself. "The physical evidence that Sinclair did these killings—it's overwhelming, it's obvious, it's damning. I know all that. But it still doesn't fit the person. Walking those creaking boards around the mill, I remembered him more clearly than I have in a while." Donny's face shriveled in distaste. "He's a . . . a craven little sneak. A skinny sleaze with no eyebrows, hyper-needy, loopy. I've met all kinds of people, some of the worst you could know. You don't make it that many years undercover without developing a pretty accurate radar. And, yes, there is something dripping and waxy and cold about him that is very real. Sinclair is a creep in every sense of the word. But he's not a killer. Vindictive, passive-aggressive, self-pitying, narcissistic—all those things. But without a speck of actual violence in him. Only want. He picked on kids. A total coward."

"What about being on drugs?" said Tracy.

"I've seen him that way too. I can't say it's not possible. Anything is." Donny threw up his hands, there being no final answer. "In some weird way, I feel responsible for him. For what's happened."

"That's crazy."

"He was my informant. I was his keeper, in a sense. His handler. Waiting for him out there sort of confirmed it for me."

"Even so—what can you do about it?"

He looked back at his pager as though hoping it would buzz again. "Nothing, now."

He walked around a little, Tracy standing still, watching in silence. She felt it too, the impulse to keep talking about Sinclair, to go on about it all night. Anything to avoid what they really had to say to each other.

"I'm sorry I had to leave you like that," he said.

The only way to override her guilt at having fallen asleep was to speak to the source of her distress, to say exactly what was on her mind. "How soon until you leave here for good?"

He took time selecting his words. He was being too careful. "I don't know exactly. I'm here at least until they find Sinclair."

"And if that is tomorrow?"

He struggled through a pause. "Tracy, look. With the life I've lived up to now, it's tough for me to think about committing to anything."

She stopped him right there with a sad nod disguised as an angry nod. "That's fine," she said.

"No, wait."

"It's fine." She was already going.

He didn't follow. She climbed into her truck, opening the garage door with the remote he had given her, then cocking her arm as though to throw it out her window and smash it to the cement floor.

Of course, she did not. She could not.

Not yet. There was still hope.

She pulled out of his driveway into the dark night, bleary-eyed and oblivious to everything beyond the haze of her distress, paying no attention whatsoever to the small, unlit car parked on the shoulder of the road.

53

HESS

"So you went there alone," said Hess.

"That's what it said to do."

"You send back any reply?"

"No."

"Nothing?"

"I sent nothing."

Hess switched his spearmint toothpick around his mouth, chewing on Maddox's story. Dealing with him in his softball team POLICE jersey and ball cap was like dealing with a guy doing summer theater.

Hess said, "Tracing the page got us no fix on the location of his two-way. Pager transmits by radio wave to a tower, then up to a satellite and back down again. Why people favor pagers in places like this where there's no cell reception."

Maddox nodded, evidently knowing this already, and Hess worked the pick some more, sucking off flavor as he appraised him. He did not buy this prompt reporting of Sinclair's page as an attempt to make peace.

Hess said, "You thought maybe it was me. Thought maybe I'd gotten hold of his pager number and was testing you."

"It crossed my mind."

Hess smiled. "UC. Don't know who to trust, so you don't trust anyone. That part of you gets worn down. It's why people don't trust *you.*" The desk phone rang, Hess ignoring it. "What were you going to do if he showed up?"

"Bring him in."

"You two don't have any previous agreements or anything?"

"No way."

"Sinclair have a thing for you?"

"He better not."

"You never met at this abandoned mill before?"

"Never."

Hess thought some more. "I think we got him on the run. We got him reaching out, and it's about time. About time he made a mistake."

"How'd the Pail crime scene come in?"

Hess scowled, people still second-guessing him after the Ripsbaugh thing. "We got more of the same sneaker treads outside in the dirt, where the body was dragged. We recovered fibers from the kitchen and an old ottoman Sinclair brushed past on his way to the back door— the same black cotton we recovered from Frond's."

Maddox said, "He's wearing the same clothes?"

"The guy's on the run."

"Yeah, but—it's been close to a month."

Still being fucking challenged every step of the way. "Guy's mental, all right? He's lost it. Why change clothes?" He shrugged and went on. "No latents, but who leaves fingerprints anymore? Talcum powder instead, as before, indicating gloves. Maybe even the same ones he wore at Frond's. Found talcum in a couple of different places. The handcuffs were novelty grade, available at any toy store. Purely for show. But it's Pail's fingernail scrapings that had them doing high-fives in the lab. Skin cells. Nice ones. Matching Sinclair."

"*Matching* Sinclair?"

"As in, irrefutable. What, am I the bearer of bad news?"

Maddox shook his head. So transparent. So Hess decided to nudge him even further.

"And then there's the pinecone."

Maddox looked up. "The what?"

"Pinecone. Medical examiner found it jammed up inside Pail's keister. Humiliating the corpse, you know? That's some kind of informant you were working there."

Maddox said, "Christ."

"CSS profiles him as taking his revenge upon the town that shunned him. Enjoying the game of it, the commotion he's causing here, the choppers circling overhead. Getting his rocks off. Maybe even fucking with you in particular." Hess pointed to a geological survey map of the town tacked up on the wall behind Maddox, the cleared areas of the Borderlands shaded red. "We've been over and through those woods and he's just not there. I mean, he's not some ultrasurvivalist anyway, right? Not some gay Rambo." He checked to see how Bryson's line played with Maddox; it did not register at all. "He's getting help somewhere in town. Someone around here is helping this guy. We went back through his voluminous Internet activities again, his e-mails, instant messages. Picked up the words 'Hell Road,' a term we didn't know during our first go-round. He had set a rendezvous with someone he met in a magician's chat room. Someone local. At midnight on the night we now think he disappeared."

Maddox said, "Did you trace it back?"

"To the Brattle Public Library, one town over. But as a protest against the Patriot Act, they have a policy of not keeping records of online activity or computer users. Bottom line, it was a hookup, a date. A booty call for gay sex in the woods. That was the premise, anyway. Now that meeting—I'm sure it wasn't you."

Maddox flat-eyed him. "You want to get back at me, and that's the best you've got?"

"Just wondering if you might be jealous, him hooking up with someone else." Hess started past Maddox and opened the door. "Oh, and from this point forward? He contacts you again, I want to know about it as soon as you do."

54
MADDOX

T HE TOWN CEMETERY up on Number 8 Road was an ancient patch of sloping sod shaded here and there by great weeping willows and fronted by a low stone wall. Across the road, four steps of locally quarried granite led nowhere, high weeds and odd, blazing flowers growing out of the foundation of the old Congregational church that had burned down one hundred summers before.

He walked along the upper lanes of newer stones to the one that said MADDOX. His mother's name, MARGARET, and the dates of her birth and death were newly engraved. He squatted and touched the lettering, so dry and sharp compared with REGINALD, the name of the father he had barely known, above it. It was not his way to pray, but Maddox spoke to her in his head just as he did sometimes when sitting alone in her empty house.

I'm sorry.

Every town family was buried around him. He went and found PINTOPOLUMANOS, Pinty's last name engraved in a narrow font in order to fit across the stone. Mrs. Pinty's name and dates were filled in, as was Pinty's name, Stavros, below hers, awaiting an end date. Next to Gregory's name and dates was a carved icon of the American flag.

Pail's grave, a perfect dirt rectangle, awaited its stone marker.

Two fat bales of sod stood near. The can of Bud remained, lying on its side, the open top being visited by flies.

Maddox located the Sinclair stone marker and stood before the grave. No headstone, just a slab set into the grass. Jordan was the father's name. The family had arrived in Black Falls without a mother, already the jagged piece of a whole no one had ever seen. Jordy Sinclair had briefly been a cop—they eased out bad apples back then—before going full-time into contracting and developing, putting in cul-de-sacs around town in the early 1980s before the mill went under. After only a few winters, his houses began falling apart: shifting on their foundations, joists warping and sagging, walls cracking under overweight roofs. Shoddy craftsmanship and substandard materials. At the time of his death—he was the victim of a one-car, midday drunk driving accident—he had been at the wrong end of several lawsuits.

Maddox turned to see the orange highway department pickup truck pull in. Ripsbaugh rolled along the ring road, getting out, pulling his shovel from the truck bed and carrying it in that familiar way of his. "Don," he said, coming toward him down the lane.

"Kane," said Maddox, wondering why the man never tied his bootlaces.

Ripsbaugh stopped, set his shovel blade down in the grass. "Got to finish sodding Pail's grave. Final touches."

"I saw."

"Is it true, what they say? About the coyote?"

"Sure is."

"Suits him. And a meth lab? Scourge of rural America, according to the TV."

"I guess we got lucky," Maddox said.

Ripsbaugh squinted under the sun. "I guess you did. Looks like you're the last cop standing." Ripsbaugh regarded the Sinclair marker, the grave at their feet. He stared a moment as though saying a little prayer, then launched a gob of saliva at the ground. "All this grass here should be black."

Maddox forgot sometimes that Ripsbaugh was Sinclair's brother-in-law. "Why did the father leave Dill all his property?"

"He didn't leave either of them anything. The mill houses you're talking about, he had them all in Dill's name for legal reasons. As a tax dodge, and so they couldn't be attached to any lawsuits. Dill didn't even know he owned them until after the death."

"So why didn't Val ask for some of that?"

"Didn't want anything to do with it." Maddox could see that Ripsbaugh was proud of this. "She always says the best thing her father ever did for her was die in that car crash."

Maddox nodded, ready to drop it, head on home.

"See, the problem with Val," Ripsbaugh continued, thinking it through, "the problem with Val is that she's smart. So smart, and highly intelligent people suffer more than others. When she's right in her mind, she can do anything. But she just can't maintain it." Ripsbaugh nudged at the grave sod with the tip of his spade, cutting little divots. "And sometimes she puts that blame on me. As the source of her problems. Sometimes I think it's why she married me in the first place, to give her this excuse. A stone for her chain. She asked me to marry her, did you know that? I always figured I'd end up, you know, adopting a wife from Russia or Cambodia or someplace. Just for a companion. I never knew I could get so lucky. But someone offers you a bargain like that, you don't think twice. You take it."

"Sure," said Maddox.

"So why don't we have children, right?"

"No," Maddox said. "I wasn't—"

"She doesn't like it. The act of sex. Physically, she gets sick."

Maddox wasn't going to say another word. Until confusion overtook discomfort. "But so, how—?"

"Frond?" he said, the spade making little *snitch-snitch* sounds in the soil. He spoke with the forbearance of a man taking the pain of another person's ailment onto himself. "It's acting out. That's her pattern. She does me wrong, then lets me find out—then hates herself all over again. She punishes me in order to torture herself."

"A pattern," Maddox said, thinking, There were others?

"But when she's clear, once she's healthy again—she *thanks* me, can you understand that? She's *grateful*. For me standing by her. For what I put up with. Even calls me her hero." He looked off at the nearest weeping willow. "You ever been called a hero, Don?"

Maddox said, "No."

"As a life, it ain't always easy. But what we have together, it's enough for me. Oh, it's plenty." Ripsbaugh nodded. "You're looking at me like—"

"No, no. No."

"You never been married. There's more to it than sex. Lots more. You want to know what she does for me? So dirty I get sometimes, coming home at the end of a day? She runs me a bath. She kneels by the tub, and she bathes me. You ever been bathed, Don? Anyone ever run a warm washcloth over your shoulders? Since you were a kid, ever been shampooed? Her fingers in my scalp—I'd take that touch over any other kind, any day of the week."

Maddox nodded, trying not to tip his embarrassment. "You don't have to explain yourself to me. Or to anyone."

"Sure I do. Thing is, she's my wife. You sign on, you sign on for life."

Maddox admired that, even admired Ripsbaugh, at the same time he pitied him. His openness, though a bit unnerving, stirred something in Maddox—beyond his desire simply to change the topic. "I want to run something by you, Kane. Have you tell me if I'm crazy or not. You follow the forensics shows and that sort of thing, right?"

"A bit," he said, defensive at first, as it was this interest that had helped get him into trouble. "This about Dill?"

"The blood evidence is the main thing. I mean, they do have hairs. But hairs can be moved around. And they have sneaker tread impressions, but shoes can get around also, it seems to me. And if you have the guy's shoes . . . well then, right there you have fibers from his residence. So it comes down to the blood, essentially."

"Okay." Ripsbaugh was starting to get it. "But if it's not Dill—"

"Just talking here. Thinking it through. Tell me about blood. What could someone do with it?"

"Well," said Ripsbaugh, "it congeals fast—that much I know. It clots, making it tricky to handle. If you don't have a live donor . . . you can store it cold, I guess. Maybe forty-two days, something like that."

"Can't you freeze it?"

"Sure. It freezes."

"Because—and then you wouldn't even need liquid blood. If all you wanted was for it to be discovered in a sink trap, you set it there frozen. An ice cube of blood. Then you torch the house, knowing that the heat traveling along the pipes will melt it. All you need to show up there is a trace."

"Well, I suppose. But hold on. Who's doing this?"

"My point is only that the blood, even skin cells, *could* have gotten to these crime scenes some other way than directly from Sinclair being present. Stressing 'could.' "

"I guess," said Ripsbaugh. "But then, where is Dill?"

"Say he's compromised in some way. I don't know. Someone holding him hostage or something."

"Okay. But why?"

"I don't know. You got me there."

"No fingerprints?"

"No. Talcum powder, though. As from the inside of latex gloves."

"Okay. But there would only be powder if he took off his gloves."

"I hadn't thought of that."

"Talcum powder used for anything else?"

Maddox shook his head. Because he didn't know, and because now he was starting to reconsider the whole thing. Verbalizing his speculations had made him sound half desperate. What was he clinging to? Why couldn't it be Dill Sinclair? And why the hell did he care? "Sounds crazy, right?"

"It's a theory, I guess."

"Anyway," Maddox said. Enough of this graveyard conversation. "That's all someone else's problem right now."

Ripsbaugh squinted at him in the sun. "I don't suppose you're staying on here."

Maddox thought of Tracy walking out on him the night before. He shook his head.

"How soon?"

"Soon," said Maddox.

"And after you go, then what?"

The thought occurred to Maddox as he stood there. "You know what, Kane? You should join up."

Ripsbaugh scowled. "Too old."

"You kidding? They'd bend the rules. They can't afford to be choosy."

"Val wouldn't like it. Her father having been a cop and all."

"You have the interest in police work. And what does this force need now but an honest cop who knows the town and cares about its future? The way Pinty was back in his day. A steward of Black Falls." Maddox stepped back, convinced, before starting away. "It's a good fit. At least think about it."

"Hey," said Ripsbaugh after him. "If I guessed DEA, would I be wrong?"

Maddox smiled but did not look back. "Think about taking the job."

55
MADDOX

H E PARKED IN HIS driveway, but instead of going into his house, found himself walking down the street. It had been a July of constant humidity, like living inside a cloud. Tomorrow the weather reports promised an afternoon downpour and electrical storm to jolt the atmosphere and rearrange air quality, the way an electroshock treatment alters chemistry in the brain.

This road he had grown up on, Silver Leaf Lane, rated little traffic, its houses set well apart, most of them tired 1970s-style split-levels and wood-sided ranches with stone chimneys and one-car garages. The last house before a stretch of undeveloped land emptying onto the cross street had been the Sinclairs'. It sat dark and dead on a plot of dry gray turf, a small Colonial with an unattached two-car garage. The mortgaging bank had seized the property after Jordy's death but failed to resell it: because of the Sinclairs' notorious name, because of plummeting home values in town after the mill closing, and because Jordy Sinclair had built it himself, the house having serious structural flaws.

Maddox started up the cracked, weed-sprouting driveway, drawn by his curiosity about Dill Sinclair, and curiosity about the past in general, about this street he had lived on, the world at that time. All the secrets he never knew.

The first-floor windows remained boarded up, the brick stairs crumbling, the gutters long ago raided for aluminum. The garage at the head of the driveway was swaybacked like a falling barn, a faded real estate sign lying among its dead brown hedges.

The backyard was narrow, its grass long and weedy and tired of growing. Maddox remembered the tree house where his mother had found Dill smoking her stolen cigarettes, and located it some ten yards back in the trees: open-faced with a slanted roof of surplus lumber and ladder steps, nail heads crusted with sap.

He returned to the yard, intending to complete a full loop of the house and be done with it. But a concentration of buzzing flies drew him to the rear corner, where a dead toad lay rotting in the basement window well. Maddox backed away from the flies, then noticed some zipping back and forth between there and the bottom plank of the nearest boarded window.

The plank did not sit flush with the rest. When Maddox touched it, it moved.

He tugged and the entire board pulled away in his hand.

The one above it came away just as easily, both planks simply propped up there on the sill. He could see where the pointed ends of the carpenter nails were twisted, the wood, at some point, having been pried away.

The revealed window was without glass, the frame itself ripped out. Someone had broken the seal on this place. Someone had been inside.

He waved off the flies and peered in. Dark, because of the boarded windows, but after a moment he could make out the vague contours of an empty room, with flattened moving cartons on the floor and an empty cardboard roll of packing tape.

Maddox ducked back out again, hassled by the flies. He looked around the side of the house, wondering if he should do this. Then he hoisted himself up over the sill.

Headfirst was the only way in. His hands found the floor, dusty but clear of broken glass. He got his legs through, the soles of his Timberlands thudding hollow in the gloomy room. Two rooms, actually, open to each other, running the length of the house. Dust floated up as he moved, grit stirred by his presence like a ghostly thing trying to resurrect itself out of ashes.

A short passageway took him past a bathroom alcove into the kitchen, empty except for an old refrigerator, stove, and pulled-open trash compactor, mouse droppings peppering the countertop.

Continuing clockwise, he moved through another doorway into a small dining room with a fireplace of blackened brick. Cobwebs formed filament shelves in the corners, fist and heel holes cratering the walls.

He arrived at the bottom of a staircase, almost back where he had begun. The balusters along the bottom were all karate-kicked in half, the wooden handrail ripped out of the wall. He started loudly up the steps, proclaiming his presence.

The second floor was four more empty rooms. Some small animal had hoarded niblets of what looked like Indian corn; the nylon webbing of an old umbrella left behind in one of the open closets had been shredded and chewed. The plaster walls were cracked under the weight of the roof.

Back downstairs, Maddox retraced his steps to the short passageway between the kitchen and the first room. A door stood ajar opposite the bath, its unpainted edge showing the grain of the original wood inside. The hinges gave with a rusty whine, Maddox smelling basement. It was dark down there, a low-ceilinged stairway hooking ninety degrees at the halfway point. The cellar from every horror movie ever made.

He listened. He waited.

"Police!" he barked. Worth a try. *"Who's down there?"*

He heard nothing except the open-channel static of anxiety in his head. He wished he had brought his flashlight. He tried the light switch inside the door, as though it might magically work for him. It did not. But like a gamer needing to sweep every corner of every virtual room before moving on to the next level, he pushed ahead down the dark plank steps.

"I'm coming down," he announced.

From the bottom step, he scoped out the area on either side, spotting a pair of glinting eyes that turned out to be two crushed beer cans. The window wells admitted just enough sunlight to see by. He moved along the edge of the underside of the stairs, something big and bulky appearing behind the base of the chimney like an animal rising up: a rusty oil tank on four legs.

His boot toe nudged another can, which he kicked away as if it were a rat. The acoustics were unsettling, and there was a trapped smell here, less an odor than a vapor. Maddox's hand found the wood grip of his revolver. He hesitated leaving the perceived safety of the underside of the stairs, but did so, turning, the side wall of the basement revealed.

Its paneling was marked with spray paint. The boldest of the graffiti read: *Black Falls is Helllll!*

One of the images from Sinclair's camera's memory stick. Suddenly, Maddox felt him here. Felt Sinclair's presence. In this basement where he had practiced his magic routines obsessively. Where Val had once found him playing with a hangman's noose. Sinclair had returned here recently, at least once, standing right where Maddox stood now, camera in hand. Going over old ground like a dog on a short tether, looking for reasons or explanations. Looking for answers. Just as Maddox was doing now. What was it Val had said?

I feel like everything with Dill, everything, is this attempt to get back his childhood.

Would he kill to get it back?

Maddox heard a creak. A gritty scrape. A thumping, muffled; something moving overhead.

Footsteps on the floor above him. Someone else was inside the house.

Maddox's revolver cleared his holster. He moved silently to the bottom of the stairs. He started up slowly, the handgun thrust before him like a flashlight, turning at the bend, making for the brighter dimness of the open door at the top.

He caught a hint of shadow. Someone in the kitchen. He crept ahead, wincing at the little wooden groans beneath his boots.

The house was silent up top as he crossed the threshold into the hall. The piece of the kitchen he could see was clear. With his revolver closer to his chest now, he rounded the corner, sensing movement in the dining room and whipping toward it hard.

He saw the wide-brimmed campaign cover first, then the silver whistle and badge. He pulled off his aim, and the trooper in front of him howled and did the same with his sidearm, then spun off and ripped a string of curses.

"Okay, okay," Maddox said, settling himself down, his heart kicking at his chest.

"What the *fuck* are you doing here!" howled the red-faced trooper, angry and scared at how close he'd come.

"Easy." Maddox was conciliatory. "Easy. Hold up."

The trooper stabbed his still-drawn Sig Sauer P226 toward the floor. "Fuck you, 'hold up,' you fucking dickhead! Almost got your ass killed! The fuck are you doing in here?"

"The fuck am I doing?"

"I'm responding to a call, motherfucker. Like a real fucking law officer. Joke-ass local yokel. Get out of my face."

The trooper thrust his sidearm back into his duty belt holster and strode out of the room.

As Maddox climbed back out through the missing window, the high branches of the backyard trees began to shudder. Leaves twisted and blew down as a concussive *whup*ping rose up overhead. The roaring flutter of a Massachusetts State Police Air Wing helicopter.

The trooper had his hat off now, a uniform violation for a road trooper in the MSP. He was snarling into his shoulder radio. "Nothing showing . . . some local dink playing cop, snooping around . . . false alarm."

A neighbor must have seen a man—Maddox—walking toward the

abandoned Sinclair house, the entire town being in this hysterical state of alert.

"What are you looking at?" demanded the bareheaded trooper, turning on Maddox again, unable to let this go. "The *fuck* are you looking at?"

Maddox thought of the K-9 dogs all fired up after a search, seeking to sink their teeth into something, anything. He could ding this road guy, drop a letter in his performance file for abusive language as well as the removed hat, dock him some vacation time. But instead he just stood there and absorbed the trooper's contempt for a small-town cop.

THE HELICOPTER moved on and Maddox returned to his driveway, finding a tan Corolla parked behind his patrol car.

Val stepped out of the driver's side. She looked relieved, almost elated, as he approached. "Where were you?" she said. "I tried the doorbell, I knocked."

He was startled. "Is everything okay?"

"Okay?" She held her arms away from her sides as though modeling the new Val. "Everything's great. Can't you tell?"

She wore a loose, grape red top over denim jeans. Her black hair was washed and brushed out, styled similarly to the way she used to wear it in high school, a little bit of makeup setting off her winged eyes.

"The smell," she said. She presented her hands and arms for examination. "The septic stink. It's already going away."

"Oh," Maddox said. "That's . . . good."

"So you're leaving now?"

"This moment? No. Don't look so happy about it."

"But I am. I'm happy to give you the chance to redeem yourself."

"Okay." This sudden ebullience looked strange on her. Strident, like a flower in overbloom, its pedals curling back too far. "Redeem myself how?"

"I've been packing some things already. Quietly getting ready."

"Packing for what?"

"To tag along with you. If you'll have me, that is."

She said the last part like she was ribbing him. Maddox fumbled for the right facial expression, never mind words. She saw this and jumped in.

"Just as friends, of course. I mean, at first. We wouldn't have to . . . I'm not looking for anything right away. Just a friend, a helping hand. From there? You never know, right?"

"Val—"

"Everything's going to change. Everything. You wait and see. No more drinking during the day. No more pining away out on the back porch. No more *dwelling*. I'll join a gym. I'm going to be so healthy. You can help me."

Maddox could only look mystified. After a few moments her smile started to wilt.

"You must know," she said, "this is no snap decision on my part. I've thought it all through. Believe me."

He nodded, trying to find a way into the conversation.

She said, "Think about it. *Think* for a moment. It would be like . . . like taking a potion. Like all these lost years since high school, they never happened. Like throwing luggage off a plane, watching it shrink and disappear. We'll be *free*."

"That would be wonderful, Val. For anybody. In theory."

"Okay." Her smile tightened like a press squeezing the last bit of sweetness out of an orange half. "What?"

"To start with? You have a husband."

She stared at him as though this was the most hurtful thing he could have said. "I know I have a husband," she said. "I have fifteen *years* of bad decisions behind me. Of wasted life. This I know, Donny. That's what this is all about."

"Don't you think you should talk to him about it?"

Now she squinted, as though trying, really trying, but ultimately failing to see the logic. "Do you think someone who is part of the problem would accept such a radical solution?"

"Because, Val, if this is truly what you want—leaving town, starting over—you don't need me. You can go."

"Bullshit. I do need you. It *has* to be you. Can't you see that?"

The inflated smile was gone now, supplanted by something like panic and dying pride. He didn't want to be too sharp with her, afraid she might go off flying around his driveway like a stuck balloon. "No, I can't."

"Can you ignore the fact that you owe me?"

"Owe you?" It took him only a second. "The scholarship."

"*Yes,* the scholarship. *Yes,* that is what I'm still talking about. Poor me, right? Still clinging to this—*right?* Do you *know* what it was like? To have this whole entire town against me, for who my father was, and my freak brother? No one wanted to waste that scholarship on me. They wanted to give it to their favorite son. Somebody who'd make something of himself, who'd *amount* to something. Not an art student from a bad family. What's she going to bring back to Black Falls?"

"Val."

"But who wound up wasting it? Who was the one who squandered that opportunity—for the town, and yes, for himself? Only to bounce back here fifteen years later with *nothing* to show for it? That chance you burned, you let slip through your fingers? That was my *life,* Donny. That was *mine.* Do you deny that you could never have won that scholarship without Chief Pinty behind you? Without his hand on your shoulder? Can you deny that now?"

"It was one-tenth of a percentage point, Val."

"You don't understand. You should *want* this. You should *want* the chance to make this right. As a *man.* This is why you came back here in the first place—don't you know that? *This is why you came here.* Righting a wrong is the closest thing we have to going back in time."

Maddox thought of Ripsbaugh, what he had said about her needing a stone for her chain. "I'm sorry, Val. I am. But I don't think I'm responsible for whatever—"

"Is this about the farm girl?"

"What did you say?"

"You heard me." Her face was twisted now, as though a mask had been snatched away but the adhesive still stung. "I came by here last night, or tried to. Saw a truck leave your garage. Saw *her* behind the wheel. You don't think she's a little young?"

"Have you been watching me?"

"Are you going away with *her*? Going to have *babies*?"

"Val." The anger in her face chilled him. "Jesus."

She shoved hair off her face so that he would have an unfettered view of her contempt. "You owe me, Donny Maddox. You *owe* me a chance."

Maddox felt heat coming up his neck. How quickly compassion can turn to enmity when someone forces her mania on you. When someone assigns you responsibility for her own frustrations. This came to him in his driveway like a lesson.

Val said, "You could live with yourself? Leaving me here? The same way you left your mother?"

He nodded, not in answer to her question, but in acknowledgment of her audacity in throwing down the kicker: the Queen of Spades with his mother's face on it. "That's the way to hurt me, all right."

"Hurt you? *Hurt you?* How can you be hurt? You're *skating* through life. Hands behind your back, *gliding* along."

"Go home, Val."

"And talk to my husband, right? *Discuss?* You think Kane knows me?"

"I'm sure no one knows you."

"That's *exactly* right."

She looked at him with the pity of a madwoman, throwing open her car door and driving away.

Part V
AN INSTRUMENT
OF VENGEANCE

56
MADDOX

NEXT MORNING, WHILE waiting for his toast to come up, Maddox heard a thump. A goodly weighted noise, followed by a lesser bump, coming from the rear of his house. An unnatural thump.

The mind takes unexpecteds such as these and tries to shape them into something understandable, tries to assign them meaning.

The mental image Maddox assigned to this noise was that of Dillon Sinclair stepping onto his back deck.

So powerful was the force of this image—the black wig and clothes, the eyebrowless eyes—that Maddox moved to his closet, getting down his holster from the top shelf. He undid the trigger lock in what seemed to take an inordinate amount of time, then moved to the sliding glass door off the serving area.

He stepped out into the wet heat, his revolver at his side. No one on the deck, the backyard empty. He scanned the trees around the yard and listened for movement. Then he saw the twisted black lump on the deck.

Closer, he made out the velvet fringe of wings. A dead crow, eyes and beak still open, its neck broken.

Maddox looked at the near trees, his mind still jumping with implications—*Who threw a dead bird onto my deck?*—until he realized that the thump, so solid and quick, had been this bird striking the window. The bump that followed was its dead body falling to the wood.

You want omens? he thought. We got omens. A town full of them.

Deer running antler-first into your car. Crows flying full speed at your house. Nature dispatching its assassins.

He carried the revolver back inside and returned with a shovel from the garage, scooping up the dead crow and walking it to the deepest part of the yard, pitching it into the woods near the spot from where Sinclair had snapped the photograph of his house. Maddox stood there a few moments, the weight of the shovel in his hands, looking into the trees. He realized that the crow indeed had flown out of the woods to tell him something. Something important.

It was time to let Sinclair go. To give up needing to believe in his innocence. Maddox's fear of the thump reminded him that Dill was as capable of murder as any man. Whatever his father had put him through, whatever had happened to him in that house at the other end of the street: it happened to Sinclair, not to Maddox. Dill had made his own choices since then. The rest was up to Hess.

Maddox went back inside. He picked up the phone and called Tracy. "Let's talk," he said, inviting her for dinner. He could sense, in the way she so casually affected to resist him, the hurt infecting her like a cold. But she did agree to come over that evening, then hung up without saying another word.

Outside, the air was stifling, the humidity at its breaking point, and yet Maddox felt good suddenly. He felt a change in the wind.

On his way to Pinty's house, he came upon Ripsbaugh patching a pothole and pulled over. Branches waved overhead, leaves flippering behind the sweat-drenched man. "About as bad as it gets, huh?" said Maddox through his rolled-down passenger window.

Ripsbaugh bent over to see inside, shovel in hand. "You can taste the lightning coming."

"Hey, about yesterday at the cemetery. My grand theories? Just forget about all that."

"Yeah? How so?"

"It is what it is. I'm not sure why I had to try and make more of it."

Ripsbaugh looked almost suspicious. Maddox worried that he had awakened a conspiracy theory. "Just forget it altogether."

"I have."

Maddox thought about saying something to Ripsbaugh about Val's visit yesterday. But enough. Val had made her choices too, whether she could admit it or not. Maddox drove away, leaving Ripsbaugh leaning on the long handle of his shovel under the darkening sky.

Inside Pinty's house, a stillness hung like the moisture. On a desk inside the upstairs bedroom that used to be Pinty's home office, an oval-framed photograph showed a younger, bare-armed Pinty standing with his hand on the shoulder of his towheaded, ten-year-old son, Gregory.

Maddox sat down in Pinty's chair, holding the photograph. Every community, it seemed to him, lost its "innocence" on a fairly regular basis, usually once per generation. Each new age required its own poignant milestone, its pedigreed moment of loss, marking the passage of child into adult. A dividing line between the way things used to be and the way things are now. Maddox's father's murder thirty years before at the hands of Jack Metters had been such an event. But Black Falls never recaptured its putative innocence. What followed instead was one loss after another, a decline growing more precipitous with each successive year. All tracing back to that one fatal moment in time.

Maybe the town's regenerative powers were gone for good. Maddox thought of Metters's gun blasting its way through his peacoat pocket, the rounds cutting hot into his father's chest, thudding into Pinty's hips and waist—and their trajectory continuing through the years, right into today.

57
TRACY

ROSALIE WAS JITTERY, what with the wind blowing through the barn and the early darkness and thunder heralding the coming storm. Tracy had come out to the old cowshed to sit with her, to console the pregnant llama with her presence as they prepared to weather the cloudburst together. She leaned over the stable door to touch noses with Rosalie, as the females liked to do, Tracy smelling the sweet hay and the dung of Rosalie's stall and the sweaty essence of her coat, reaching up gently to stroke her long, proud neck.

What did Donny want to meet for? What could they possibly have to talk about? *Hey, it was great, it was fun, let's keep in touch?*

Part of her personal theory of reverse therapy—where she tore herself down instead of building herself up, the idea being to get so low that there could only be betterment ahead—involved making short, punchy "No More" lists:

No more lazy nights together.
No more rum and Diet Cokes (negative taste association).
No more curling up with him on the sofa.
No more deep, half-remembered conversations while watching bad TV.
No more allowing herself to get silly in front of him, or anyone—ever.
No more falling asleep in Donny's bed.

No more of his lips on her back and shoulders.
No more Donny.

The warm body she had once clung to like a life raft: he had been her dream of a man. No background. No past history, no baggage. No family to impress or avoid. He came perfectly shaped, and perfectly empty, to be filled up any way she liked.

Now he had a past. Now he had a history and regrets and short-comings. Now he was real.

This was the only way it could end. His departure had been pre-destined, like a merman needing to return to the sea.

But really, she shouldn't be sullen. She had been warned, hadn't she? And repeatedly—every goddamn step of the way—something he would no doubt remind her of yet again tonight. *It was temporary, it was short-term, it was going to end.* Her bad for falling in love. Wish him well, and hope he remembers her fondly as he goes off on his merry journey back into the world.

She was sick of being the gracious loser. Sick of being kept back in life and expected to accept it as her lot. The farm and her mother and this land. Who else was she ever going to meet in Black Falls? Who else was going to blow into town except those already banished from the world? Who else but lepers visited this colony?

If only she were hard enough to stand him up tonight. To be as cruelly dispassionate. But she didn't even bother with retributive fan-tasies because, pathetic little hopeful bird that she was, she would go, she would listen, she would hope, she would let him feel better about himself, and then she would hug him good-bye as he ground his heel into her chest.

Rosalie nodded like she understood. Tracy admired the llamas; their fierce protective instincts when guarding herds of sheep, goats, cows, or horses; their tireless work ethic; the aggression they dis-played when sensing a threat. They were popular guard animals because they were fearless about hurtling their three-hundred-pound bodies full speed at any predator, be it dog or coyote or wolf or even small bear, wailing a high-pitched alarm. What they lacked in grace and refinement, they more than made up for in pride and attitude and strength. Even a yearlong pregnancy never got Rosalie down. She didn't need a male companion to make her feel whole, or special, or loved.

Though she had needed one to get pregnant.

Lightning flashed on the barnyard dirt outside, Rosalie emitting a throaty groan. Tracy worried that the storm might trigger her labor. No Dr. Bolt to check her over now. Tracy was going to have to see Rosalie through this one all by her lonesome.

Rosalie got to her feet, a warble rolling in her long throat. She shuffled back and forth in the stall, jutting her head over the door. Her hooves scraped the hay-strewn flooring, Rosalie growing agitated. The same way she had been a few nights before, when the coyotes ran out of the forest and the hills, loping through town.

Tracy reached out to pat her head but Rosalie bucked away, stomping the planks. "What is it, girl?" said Tracy, looking out the open door.

Another high, cloud-smothered ripple of lightning created a shadow that appeared to retreat from the wood ramp leading outside.

Rosalie warbled and hissed.

"Mom?" Tracy said. She was not in the habit of calling out to her deaf mother, but thunder and lightning will do that to you. She walked to the doorway where the old ramp was hinged and peered around the corner. Another pulse of suffused cloud lightning moved shadows under the trees, but there was no one in sight.

She saw the sink light on in the kitchen, the stained-glass sun she had made in fourth grade hanging from a suction cup inside the window. Tracy hopped down to the dirt, needing to see if her mother was indeed inside.

She was. Blond hair marbled with streaks of white she refused to dye. Rinsing vegetables in the sink. Tracy watched her mother catch sight of herself in the mirror the interior light made of the window. Staring, just a moment, her wet hand coming up to touch her softly wrinkled neck. Then returning to her vegetables, as though nothing had happened.

Those were the moments Tracy would find most difficult to endure. The reveries that led straight to regret.

Rosalie raised another cry, lightning rippling again, but brighter this time, putting Tracy's shadow down on the dirt—and another shadow, this one rising behind her. She turned just in time to see the figure emerge from beneath the ramp, long dark hair whipping in the wind as it raised some sort of weapon.

Tracy never felt the blow. She tasted dirt, a pair of hands pulling at her back as she attempted to crawl toward her mother. Then something fell on the back of Tracy's neck, and she went out.

58
PINTY

PINTY SAT UP AGAINST the many hospital bed pillows. His toes under the sheet at the end of his dead legs seemed a mile away.

Another thunderboomer outside his window, rain falling fast and hard. He watched with fascination, part of the new regard he had for all things since waking up. The perfect yellow packets of sugar that came on his meal tray. The colored pushpins in the wall. The elegant sweep of the clock's second hand. The whispering of the nurses' shoes. Everything had a place and a function and a beautiful simplicity.

It was raining in Rainfield.

Donny sat in the padded chair pulled beside the bed. He looked all right. He had been passing himself off as Pinty's son in order to gain family visiting privileges, a ruse Pinty was only too happy to support. Beautiful in its simplicity. Everything with a place and a function.

"Thank you for this," Pinty said, his walking stick lying across his lap.

He wanted to touch the smooth silver grip with his right hand. Doing so was like trying his luck at a carnival game of chance, that one where a number of identical strings are hooked, threaded, and tangled around a spoked grid in such a way that you cannot determine by sight which one to pull in order to raise the door that releases the prize. You have to guess, and then proceed by a process of elimination. Sometimes Pinty got it on the second or third string. Sometimes the strings didn't work at all.

When his hand moved, it came up quaking, fingers curled. "Twelve weeks of rehab," he said. "Just to hold a pencil steady."

Maddox said, "You'll do it in eight," and Pinty smiled at his faith. The smile came easily, without thought. First string.

Speaking was getting easier too. Like recovering from frostbite, his jaw thawing out a little more every day. It was raining in Rainfield. "What was that you were asking me about?"

"The scholarship," said Donny. "I won it fair and square, right?"

"By one-tenth of one percent, as I recall. Skin of your teeth." An odd question he was asking. "Why are you wondering about that now?"

"But it was fair. I mean, I won it."

"Sure you did."

"You didn't pull any favors. Didn't shake anybody's hand too hard."

"No, no, no." Pinty didn't know what he was after here. "I may have gone around to a few of your teachers, sure, just letting them know what you had riding on your midterms, how hard you were studying. That a full scholarship for the son of a police officer killed in the line of duty was at stake. Future of the town, and all that."

Donny blinked, getting quiet, looking at his hands on the blue armrests.

Form. Function. Simplicity. A chair, a bed, a window. Old man, younger man. Weak and strong.

Pinty went on. "I never begrudged you that, by the way. I always held out the hope, maybe even the knowledge, that you'd find a way to make good on your pledge. And now look. Years overdue, but you've given Black Falls a new start. Given it a fighting chance. That scholarship turned out to be worth every penny we raised."

Donny was squinting into his lap now, like he was working over some puzzle Pinty could not see. "Righting a wrong is the closest thing we have to going back in time."

Pinty agreed. "That's as good a way to put it as any."

Donny looked up as though he'd been poked. He shifted in the big chair and slipped a device out of his back pocket, that pager he carried around with him everywhere. Pinty heard it buzzing.

Donny read the display and looked charged. He got to his feet.

"What?" said Pinty.

"Sinclair," Donny said, reaching for the telephone on the bedside tray. "Wants me to meet him on Hell Road."

59
HESS

THE RAIN CONTINUED in earnest after the thunder and lightning had moved off, drumming on the roof of the Hummer. The windows stayed cracked because they couldn't run the defrost, because they couldn't run the engine, because they were hiding in a turnout a thousand yards from the Borderlands trailhead. The Special Tactics and Operations team leader sat beside Hess in the wide backseat, his head tipped back, eyes closed but nowhere near sleep. Hess kept swiping water off his own face from the drops smacking the top edge of his window and spitting into his eyes.

The wire in Hess's ear sizzled. *"He's walking out."*

The STOP team leader lowered his chin and opened his eyes. "What do you mean? Just walking out? Alone?"

"That's a roger. What do we do, advise?"

The leader looked at Hess. Hess frowned, shook his head.

"Bring it in," said the STOP leader. He reached forward and patted his driver's shoulder, the Hummer's engine roaring to life.

They were the first ones back to the trailhead, pulling in next to Maddox's parked patrol car. Hess got out in the rain, watching a man in a poncho exit the fire road entrance, walking determinedly toward him through the puddles. Maddox stopped in front of Hess, shrugging back his glistening hood.

Hess said, "What gives you the authority to pull the plug on this thing yourself?"

"I stood in there for an hour and a half," said Maddox. "He's not coming. Not going to let himself be trapped like that."

Light beams came bobbing out of the trees as the mud-soaked STOP team emerged from the fire road behind Maddox, faces camo-painted, assault rifles outlined beneath their vented ponchos.

"He's playing with us," said Hess. "Seeing how high we'll jump."

The STOP leader came over, his driver holding a black umbrella. "Air Wing's still on standby, on the ground," he reported. "Rainfall messes with heat imaging anyway."

"He was never here," declared Maddox, stripping off the assault vest beneath his poncho.

Hess said, "It's time we sent him a return message. Give me an hour to huddle, think about what to say."

"Here," Maddox said, handing over the pager. "I'm done. Knock yourself out."

Hess watched Maddox climb into his car and pull out. Maddox's headlights briefly illuminated Bryson crossing the lot, looking ridiculous in galoshes and a rain hat knotted under his chin, as though his mother had dressed him.

"Another missing-person report," Bryson said. "A young woman this time."

The sixth such alert of the day. The first five had each ended happily, products of miscommunication and town hysteria. But the MSP would respond as they always did, quickly and conscientiously.

Hess started toward Bryson's car through the thumping rain. "Who made the call?"

"No call," said Bryson. "Woman came straight to the station." He tapped his ear. "She's deaf."

60
MADDOX

MADDOX PULLED INTO his driveway, hitting the button on the visor-clipped remote control and watching the door go up on Tracy's Ford truck parked inside.

He had completely forgotten about inviting her over. He tipped his head back against the headrest, cursing himself, then jumped out and ran through the rain into the garage. His peace offering had turned into an insult. Now he had to salvage this somehow. He shook out his soaked legs but didn't even take time to remove his wet boots, walking through the door into the first-floor hallway.

"Tracy?"

The house was dark. He hit a light switch and continued down the hall toward the closet.

"Tracy?" he called out, louder. "Trace?"

Must be upstairs. He slid his holster off his belt and was reaching to store it up on the top shelf when something made him stop. The silence in the house, certainly. Also, a smell now, one he had been in too much of a rush to notice before. An odor deeper than the coppery smell of the rain. Earthy, like that of the llama farm, but less pleasant, more stinging.

Maddox stopped calling her name. He went quiet, sliding his revolver out of the holster and moving to the intersecting end of the hallway. He looked to the locked front door, rain spilling off the gutter outside.

He went to the bottom of the stairs and stood there looking up.

He did not turn on the light.

He started up. At the top landing, he just listened and let his eyes adjust.

He heard breathing.

Someone was standing at the far end of the hallway. Not hiding there. Just standing. Waiting.

It wasn't Tracy. Maddox held his gun ahead of him, trying to see.

The figure moved, shifted its weight. Maddox made out long hair. The wig.

"Dill?" Maddox said.

He lowered his gun and took an angry step forward.

Dill started toward him. With the darkness throwing off Maddox's depth perception, he did not until too late see how fast Dill was coming. He was further distracted by the shovel that Dill held in his hands.

As Dill closed the distance between them, Maddox got his gun up and fired two quick shots. Both rounds rang off the back of the shovel, ricocheting into the ceiling and the wall.

Dill's body crashed into him, the shovel headfirst batting back the revolver, then swinging up to crack him near the temple.

Maddox fell hard. A warm feeling spread inside him from his head and neck through his back, relaxing him against his will. The house tipped as Dill stood over him, wild hair swaying. Then everything closed up and went dark.

IN THE DREAM THAT wasn't a dream, Maddox stood in the trees beyond his backyard, the spot from where Sinclair had snapped the photograph. He saw his house exactly as in the picture, except for the presence of his mother, sitting alone on the back deck in her housecoat. Maddox yelled to her but she could not hear him. Then Tracy appeared in a second-floor window, banging on the glass with both arms, screaming, but Maddox heard nothing. A twig cracked and he turned and saw Sinclair next to him, drawn and dopesick, wearing his wig and a Black Falls patrolman's outfit, the camera glowing around his neck like an amulet.

MADDOX AWOKE MOANING. He could not hold his throbbing head straight, a pulsing pressure on his skull. He was dizzy and on the edge of nausea.

He could not move. He thought he was still in the dream.

His mother's kitchen was set before him like a still life, a picture in a frame he could step into. He expected her to walk in, smile, say hello.

He was shivering. Wet clothes.

Someone moved in the room behind him. Someone not his mother.

He was tied to one of the kitchen chairs with blue nylon line from the garage. His hands were numb behind him, his ankles knotted tight to each front leg of the chair. He could turn his head, but not enough to see behind him.

"Dill!" he yelled, the word accompanied by a bloom of pain.

On the counter he saw his keys and coins and beeper. His pockets had been turned out. There was his holster also, but empty.

In the near corner stood a spade with a long wooden handle.

Maddox picked up movement reflected in the sink window. He saw him. The black wig. His face blurred, standing back, watching Maddox from behind.

A hand gripped his right shoulder. Not a normal hand, as his eyes strained to see it. The fingers and palm were glazed over somehow, inhumanly smooth. Not gloved, but coated. Mannequin-like.

The hand left his shoulder and Dill came around to stand before him. He wore the rumpled black sweat suit that had shed fibers at Frond's and at Pail's.

But Maddox realized that his build was all wrong. The sweatshirt was stretched tight across his shoulders and chest. He saw the black Chuck Taylor All-Stars, but the sneakers had been sliced up the top, the canvas stitched back together again underneath the laces in order to fit larger feet.

Then the face below the wig. Just like the hands, it bore the smoothed-out finish of a man of pure wax.

But with eyebrows. Or something like eyebrows, taped down underneath the mask, or whatever it was he had over him.

This was not Sinclair at all. The blurred face.

Maddox got the smell now. All at once, the clinging sewer odor. He was still trying to make out what was over the face—skintight but with holes for his eyes, nostrils, and mouth—not masking its appearance as much as . . . as . . .

Kane Ripsbaugh said, "You figured it out pretty good."

Heart pounding, brain screaming, Maddox focused on Ripsbaugh's coated face beneath the black wig.

Ripsbaugh examined his hands as though they were someone else's, not his own. "Liquid latex. Dries fast and solid, like a thin rubber. Seals me in. So I don't leave any of me behind. Only him."

The Scarecrow. Ripsbaugh's costume looked like clothes overstuffed with a man instead of straw. "Where is he? Where's Sinclair?"

"He's right here."

Either the latex deadened Ripsbaugh's already flat expression, or it was some kind of calm insanity. All of Maddox's breath caught in his throat.

With two bald fingers, Ripsbaugh extracted a pager from his pocket, laying it on the counter next to Maddox's. "Identical to yours. I noticed that. But I had to call you to the old pulp mill to be sure." He swept some hair off his shoulder, a horridly casual gesture that only showed how much time he had spent wearing the wig. "Frond told me the state police had promised to send someone. Sinclair was your informant, wasn't he?"

Maddox did not answer, seeing, in the center of the sweatshirt stretched out over Ripsbaugh's chest, a small tear about the size of a bullet hole. "You shot him."

Ripsbaugh looked down at the hole. "A clean kill."

"In the Borderlands that night. You needed his clothes."

"I needed *him*. A bogeyman. When I drove out of Hell Road,

coming up on you standing over that deer, I knew right away something was up. Your shooting stance. You were no amateur. But it was too late. I had already taken that first step."

Maddox thought back to Ripsbaugh's headlights coming up bright in his eyes. "You had him in the back of your truck?"

"We've both been working undercover here, Don."

Maddox shook his pounding head. "You pulled blood from him. You bled his *corpse*?"

"It wasn't difficult."

"Your wife's *brother*?" Maddox tried to think it through. "You knew how CSS worked. You *knew* they'd pull the sink traps. So you directed them there—wiping out the sink, making it look like someone had cleaned up. You gave them everything. Sneaker prints, wig hairs, fiber transfers from his clothes. Skin cells?"

"Scraped his arms. Collected them in a paper bindle, just like they do."

"You planted them in Bucky's fingernails. As though he got them from fighting with Sinclair."

"Like laying out crumbs." The latex glaze over Ripsbaugh's face could not mask his triumph.

"You sealed yourself away in this . . . this . . ."

"The adult video store in Rainfield sells it by the quart. Clear or colored." He flexed his hands, the latex giving like a second skin. "No latents. No oils, no hairs. No transfers except from Sinclair's clothes, his wig, his sneakers."

"And the talcum powder?"

He touched his fingers together. "So the latex won't adhere to itself. A rip or a breach just wouldn't do."

"That cut on your arm?"

"Self-inflicted. Good insurance, as Walt Heavey would say. In case anything showed up linking Val to Frond. If not for those letters, they never would have suspected me."

"So you cut yourself, just in case." Maddox saw it now. "If they did suspect you, you wanted to force their hand. Make them commit."

"Make them eliminate me early. They got greedy with the DNA, like I knew they would. Because we're all just hicks out here, right? Too dumb to live anywhere else. Too stupid to cover our own asses."

His latex fingers wiggled at his sides. Maddox tried flexing his leg and arm muscles against the rope, the nylon tied tight. Where was his gun?

Don't ask him what he's going to do to you. Don't give him a reason.

Keep talking.

"Val was with Bucky too?"

That soured Ripsbaugh. "Sometimes she gets stuck. She gets in a rut, because she's so smart and the rest of the world is not."

"But . . . *Bucky Pail*?"

"She's vulnerable, and people take advantage of that. But you don't trade in your wife when she gives you trouble."

Maddox said, "You fix it with murder instead?"

"Killing is easy when someone hurts the one you love. The one person in the world you pledged to protect. Frond and Pail, they aren't where they are now because they wronged me. They're there because they wronged her. They took advantage. Using her. Like her father all over again. Taking whatever they could get, thinking there would be no consequences." His hands squeezed into smooth, seamless fists. "I am their consequences. I am a reckoning."

Maddox strained against the ropes, trying to get loose without Ripsbaugh seeing him trying. "That include the pinecone?"

Ripsbaugh straightened, looking freakishly proud in his long wig. "Sex offenders commit sex crimes."

Humiliating the corpse, Hess had called it. Ripsbaugh was over the edge. "This is like trying to cure Val by going around killing off her symptoms. You can't kill away her depression."

"She doesn't want to do these things with other men." He spoke with the conviction of the quietly unhinged. "She hates herself for it. So I do what I have to in order to make her clean. With these."

His hands again.

"She's sick, Kane. Toxic. And being around her, it's made you sick too."

"What about you?" Ripsbaugh said. "You've been meeting her."

"Meeting?" said Maddox, at first confused. "No. No, it was—"

"She came to me. Told me everything. How you talked about going away together."

Maddox's shivering stopped. For the moment, he gave up testing the rope. "Now hold on."

Ripsbaugh's eyes were tight, knowing and bright. "Your high school sweetheart."

"Kane. You've got it all wrong."

"Together again after all these years."

"Kane."

He was a different man now, the wig and the latex coating giving outer expression to his psychosis. "I always liked you, Don. I did. But you should have left her alone. She can't help herself. Why she needs me. To help her. To make things right."

Ripsbaugh considered his palms again. He was working himself up into a killing.

"You don't know what it means," he went on, "to make someone a part of you—and then feel them suffer. Feel them trapped inside a hell they did not create, and do not deserve. And all you can do is watch." His voice became disturbingly calm. "You can't know what that's like, Don. Can you?"

Something in his stare hooked Maddox. Something behind his smoothed face.

Something indicating that this was not merely a rhetorical question.

Maddox tuned into the emptiness of the house. He remembered arriving home. Seeing the pickup in his garage. Walking down this very hallway, calling out to her.

"Tracy?" Maddox whipped his aching head around, trying to see as much of the downstairs as he could. "Trace!"

Ripsbaugh said, "It's good here, where you live. Isolated enough. The rain outside eats up your voice."

"Tracy!" Maddox uttered the word with force and panic. He flexed his arms and legs against the cutting rope. "What have you done?"

Ripsbaugh walked around behind him, gripping the chair, tipping it back. The rear legs gouged the wood floor like claw marks as Ripsbaugh dragged the chair down the hallway with Maddox in it.

Maddox struggled ferociously, the ropes giving a little now—his angled weight putting stress on the chair.

Ripsbaugh stopped and turned the chair around before the closed bathroom door.

Maddox felt a new wiggle in the back splats, more give in the dowels. He was struggling to exploit these weaknesses as Ripsbaugh opened the bathroom door and wheeled out a large machine: the very same video diagnostic system Maddox had seen him use at Wanda's.

The motor was quiet, the spindle still. The red snake cable trailed off with the thinner silver wire coiled around its length, disappearing into his open toilet.

At first, Maddox did not understand.

The three-by-three view screen on the control console showed vague patches of night-vision green against a blur of black. Maddox strained against the ropes to lean closer, to see better.

Something was there. Visible only in contrast. Barely moving.

A head, shoulders, half a chest. Light-colored hair against a darker T-shirt. In water up to her midsection.

The green on the screen. Tracy. Arms raised out of the septic tank water, her eyes wide and glowing, lips moving, calling out.

Maddox could not believe it. His mind would not accept it, any of this. Not the hazy image on the screen. Not Ripsbaugh standing in his house wearing Sinclair's clothes.

"The smell will be long gone before anyone thinks to come around looking," said Ripsbaugh. "The rain is already smoothing out the dig marks in your yard."

Dig marks.

No.

Impossible.

In Sinclair's cut-and-stitched sneakers, Ripsbaugh walked to the open toilet. He flushed it, holding down the handle with his inhuman fingers until the bowl emptied.

The snake twitched as the rush of the water tugged on it.

On the display screen, the camera view trembled. Maddox could do nothing but watch.

Water splattered forth. Glowing green, it vomited from the mouth of the pipe, spraying Tracy's face.

She covered her nose and mouth and her eyes glowed wide as she screamed into the darkness.

Maddox heard a muffled cry, as from someone calling out from miles beneath the ground.

"There's air, but it's bad air, and going fast. No light. She doesn't know where she is."

"Get her out!" The chair shook beneath him, Maddox pushing with every muscle, eyes locked on Tracy on the screen. "Get her out! *She has nothing to do with this!*"

Tracy's hands stayed up near her muck-streaked face, eyes wild. Her screaming was so far away.

"You want to save her," said Ripsbaugh, turning on the sink, full power. "To deliver her from that place, from that pain." He ran water in the tub, opening the drain. "If only you could."

More water flowing past the camera, obscuring the view.

"That is why I am showing you this, Don." He walked away, back down the hall, to the kitchen. "Now you understand." Maddox heard him open the sink tap. "Now you know what I go through."

Maddox was underneath that bridge in Haverhill again. Standing over Casey's naked corpse, knowing it should be him lying there and not her. Knowing that no amount of vengeance would ever be enough, and going a little crazy inside.

Ripsbaugh returned. "They'll find her truck pulled over on one of the hill roads. Keys inside, though not your garage door opener. Thousands of young women disappear every year. They'll come here, they'll search your house with lasers and filtered vacuums. They'll search it good, the residence of a missing state trooper. But they'll never think to search the septic tank." Ripsbaugh brought his glabrous face close, so close that a few strands of wig hair brushed against Maddox's cheek before Maddox could jerk away. "They won't ever find her."

Maddox rocked the chair with everything he had. "Kill me, get it over with," he said. "But *let her go!*"

Ripsbaugh watched him struggle. "One problem with that, Don. With killing you. Sinclair's next murder will be his third. Do you know what that means?"

Maddox swelled his chest, pushing against the seat. He felt some separation in the wood beneath him. Or imagined he did.

"Three victims, that meets the FBI criteria for a serial killer. And I sure don't want the FBI here."

Maddox could bend his elbows a bit, giving him more leverage.

"So you're going to have to disappear. Sinclair will be suspected, of course. They'll find this kitchen chair pulled out from the table. Abrasions in its sides, some rope fibers. Rounds from your gun lodged in the wall and ceiling upstairs. Sinclair was in your house tonight. But, as with the girl, your disappearance will remain a mystery."

Ripsbaugh stepped into the parlor, pinching a bit of sleeve with his coated fingers and rubbing the fabric against the corner of the divan. Another Sinclair transfer.

"Sinclair's legend will only grow. Because he is going to disappear tonight with you. His work here is done. But Sinclair will live on, longer than you or even I, haunting the woods around Black Falls. A town needs a good bogeyman. Fear is like religion that way. It galvanizes a community. Makes them care. Black Falls is already coming back to life. You feel it, can't you?"

Maddox had earned just enough rope slack to lean forward onto the balls of his feet, tipping up the back legs. With all that he had, he rocked back down, driving the chair legs into the floor.

A good blow, but not enough. There was no crack, though his feet were looser, allowing him even more leverage. He rocked violently side to side, trying it again.

This time, the rope shifted, still holding him fast, but giving him a few more precious centimeters with which to work.

Ripsbaugh watched dispassionately. "If I've gone on too long, it's only because, as I said, Don, I always liked you." He looked at his smooth hands again, as though awaiting their command. "I always liked you."

Maddox sprang up with all his might, driving his hips down and hearing wood crack as a splat fractured behind his lower back, one of the legs on the left side giving way.

Maddox was on the floor. On his side, still lashed to the broken chair. But loose inside the ropes.

Ripsbaugh did not move at first. Maddox had no time to be shocked, kicking free of the splintered front legs, squirming with his hands still bound behind his back.

When Ripsbaugh did finally reach out to stop him, Maddox flailed, jabbing at Ripsbaugh's knee with a loose foot, kicking him back. Maddox writhed madly, his wrists getting looser, his knees pulling free.

He felt a new tension pulling on his waist. Ripsbaugh had taken up one end of the rope. He fashioned a loop with it and came at Maddox, meaning to slip the noose around his neck.

Maddox, helpless against a strangling, dug in with his heels and spun himself around, keeping his head away from Ripsbaugh, swinging another kick at his legs.

Ripsbaugh looped Maddox's foot, catching it. The broken chair back scraped against the floor as Ripsbaugh pulled the rope hand over hand, reeling Maddox in. His smooth, blank fingers.

Maddox went limp a moment, tempting Ripsbaugh with slack. Ripsbaugh took the bait, yanking back on the line, looking to bring Maddox close enough to fall on him with the rope and finish him.

But Maddox jerked as Ripsbaugh hauled, the line pulling taut, the rope ripping right through Ripsbaugh's fingers. Ripsbaugh let go, but not fast enough.

Ripsbaugh brought his hands up in front of his face as though they had been burned. Strips of shielding latex hung like layers of dead skin, baring his fingers beneath.

Maddox dug into the floor with his heels. He scraped away on his back, down the hall, away from Ripsbaugh. He knocked over the shovel by the kitchen counter and dragged it along with him, the ropes pulling looser with every movement.

Maddox got to one knee. Both wrists were free of their knots, his arms still tangled in the rope and chair behind his back. He shrugged one arm loose and used that to start on his legs. In the kitchen to his right, the sink was running.

Ripsbaugh remained at the other end of the hall, doing something with his exposed hands.

Maddox worked maniacally, shredding skin off own his fingertips as he stripped away the last of the rope and the chair. He picked up the shovel with the intention of running down the hall and braining Ripsbaugh with it, but the angry crack of a handgun froze him.

Ripsbaugh held Maddox's revolver in his peeling hands, having fired it into the floor. He raised the smoking barrel now, leveling it at Maddox.

"All right," said Ripsbaugh. "That's about enough."

61
RIPSBAUGH

PULLED FROM THE BACK of his waistband, the revolver felt cold against the bare parts of Ripsbaugh's fingers. He could almost feel his skin oils adhering to the wood grip. He had to be so careful now.

Maddox stood at the other end of the hallway, wild with desperation.

Ripsbaugh had to remain clearheaded. This was a critical time. This was where killers made their mistakes—in haste. In going off plan. Part of him was exposed, but he still had control of the scene.

He had the gun. He was okay. Nothing had gotten away from him yet.

"Put down the shovel."

Ripsbaugh didn't want to be too close for the kill shot, if it came to that. He wanted the round to lodge inside Maddox and not kick out. Not get lost in a wall somewhere with Maddox's DNA on it.

Maddox was doing something to the fingers of his hand. He was picking at the tips. A few drops of blood fell to the wood floor.

"That's for the FBI," said Maddox. He flicked tiny droplets into the kitchen. Up at the ceiling. He smeared some on the handle of Ripsbaugh's shovel. "Now what? What's this do to your master plan?"

Ripsbaugh knew that, even if he could find and clean every drop, there were chemicals that brought up old bloodstains. "Now that there's blood evidence, what's to stop me from shooting you?"

The plan had been to march Maddox through the woods behind his house to the top of the falls. Let the force of the water dispose of him without a trace. Then throw Sinclair's clothes in after him, the wig, the pager—everything. Flush the evidence. Flush Maddox and Sinclair. Leave nothing linking either of them to Ripsbaugh.

But, as with Frond and Pail, things wouldn't go exactly as planned.

All Maddox was doing here was making more work for him. Ripsbaugh didn't look forward to shouldering his dead weight all the way to the falls. But hard work was hard work. And he had found that killing—doing it right—was just about the hardest work there was.

The arteries of the chest. Same place he did Sinclair. Plenty of muscle to catch the round.

"It's for Val I do this," he said.

But Maddox dropped the shovel and darted fast into the cross hallway, the shot missing him. Ripsbaugh put another quick round into the intervening wall, tracking Maddox about shoulder high. Then he cut through the sitting room, beating Maddox to the front door.

Maddox wasn't there. Instead Ripsbaugh heard footsteps pounding up the stairs.

He was going to the bedrooms to hide. He was trapped and running scared.

Ripsbaugh started up after him, coming to the top in darkness. He had to be very careful not to leave anything of himself behind. Only Sinclair. That was of supreme importance now.

One door was open in the hallway. He heard bumping inside, and it occurred to him that Maddox might have another gun in the house.

Ripsbaugh peered through the doorway into the stripped-down master bedroom. The far window had been pushed open, screen and all, letting in the rain.

Ripsbaugh rushed to it. He thrust his gun hand out the window to cut Maddox down. Below was the steep roof over the kitchen, runoff coursing down the shingles to the deck below.

Maddox was not there.

Ripsbaugh realized his mistake too late.

He was pulling back into the room when the blow came from behind, shoving him halfway out the window. His hip struck the sill hard, his feet leaving the floor, the heel of his gun hand coming down heavily against the wet shingles.

Amazed he had not tumbled right out, he looked back and saw his free hand gripping the side of the window frame. The bare patches of his fingers pressed against the smooth wood— dirty oils sizzling his mark onto the painted surface.

Another body blow, so hard that the sill cracked beneath him, and his hand released the frame. The elbow of his gun arm was wedged beneath him against the shingles. His legs remained inside the house, kicking blindly, hitting nothing.

He twisted, trying to get the gun free of his own weight. Trying to aim the muzzle behind him. One shot was all he needed to push Maddox back. One bullet was all he had left.

He was half turned when the third blow came, upending him, shoving him through.

Tumbling down the roof, Ripsbaugh swung his arm around, firing wildly at the window.

Crack.

Not even close. Ripsbaugh let go of the gun to try and stop his fall. The rough shingles shredded more latex off his hands, everything coming apart now.

A rattling sound. The gutter.

He was off the roof. Twisting, falling.

It was hard, hard work. Maybe the hardest.

62
MADDOX

MADDOX RACED OUT of his mother's bedroom, the hallway listing like a ship in a storm. He grabbed the handrail and tripped down the stairs. If his choice was to finish off Ripsbaugh or save Tracy, then there really was no choice at all.

Rain thumped the spongy grass. Beneath his feet, he heard her screaming.

"Tracy!" he yelled, lowering his shoulder and hitting an ornate stone pedestal planter like a linebacker. It shifted off its base and fell, Maddox sprawling over it, then getting up and seeing the exposed tank cap, a concrete slab split into two half circles.

Maddox got good purchase around Ripsbaugh's dig marks. He pried up one half of the heavy slab with his bloodied fingers, sliding it aside.

The stench, the aching screams. It was like uncapping a tunnel to hell.

Maddox had no flashlight. He yelled her name, but she could not hear him over her own screaming. The white PVC outlet pipe was disgorging water, the camera end of the snake sticking out of the downspout like a lizard's tongue.

He pried off the other half of the cap, her head coming fully into view. Her upturned face, muck-streaked and fright-wild, finding light.

"Donny?" she shrieked. *"Donny!"*

The water was up to her chin. Maddox lay out on his chest, his face in the stench. Reaching down to her. Her slimy hands grasped his, but she slipped away before he could haul her up. He tried again, but could not hold the grip.

The stench gagged him and he lifted his head out, looking around the yard for something, anything. He wished he had taken the nylon rope with him.

He yelled down, "I need something to pull you out with!"

"Don't leave me!"

"I won't! I'm not! I'm coming right back! You hear me?"

"Where am I? What's happening?"

She was drowning in filth. He had to tear himself away. He jumped up.

"Donny!"

He sprinted around the house toward the driveway, praying he had left the garage door open.

63
TRACY

T RACY SCREAMED AT the open mouth that screamed rain. The mouth of the monster.

Her throat was so raw from puking and screaming that she had no sense of taste anymore, no smell, the ungodly stench having burned out her mouth and nose. Breathing this foulness was like eating it, taking it into her body. The belly acid of the beast that had swallowed her.

The water was at her earlobes now. She kept her face upturned. The opening was all she had. The sky was up there. Air. Light. Escape. Rain spattered her eyes but she did not blink.

It grew darker above. A shadow falling. Her hope rose.

"*Donny!*"

No.

Someone else standing over the hole. Looking down. His face in shadow.

Long black hair.

She remembered now.

Sinclair.

She screamed. And screamed. And shrank away from the mouth.

64
MADDOX

Yes—he had left it open. He rushed between Tracy's pickup and the side of the garage where the storage shelves were. Old tools, baby food jars of nails and screws, twine and tape—

Clothesline. From when his mother used to hang out wet sheets in the backyard, a hundred years ago. He would play hide-and-seek in them with her.

He grabbed it, and a knob-handled, needle-bladed scratch awl—the sharpest, nearest thing he could find—and ran back out into the rain. He raced to the hole in the yard, sliding the last several feet over the soaked grass like a runner going for third, yelling down to her.

She was just a floating face now. The effluent up to her ears, her arms reaching for him.

"He's up there!" she screamed. *"Look out!"*

Maddox scanned the front yard, the adjacent wetlands, the house. She was delirious. They were alone.

He knotted a loop and lowered the rope into the riser. Tracy pulled one wrist through, gripping the line, and he braced his feet against the mud around the rim. He hauled her up, hand over hand, the clothesline burning his palms and bloody fingers.

She emerged from the narrow hole, head and shoulders, clawing at the grass with her sludge-streaked hands like a corpse from a grave. She kicked her dripping legs free and then, saved, collapsed onto him, slimy and foul-smelling, squeezing him tight.

She twisted around, amazed to see his house in the dark rain, the hole in the yard. She was bewildered as to how she had gotten there. Maddox helped her to her feet and was pulling the rope off her arm when Tracy screamed.

Ripsbaugh, wig hair flying, came running at them across the yard with his spade in his hands.

Maddox shoved Tracy aside. He rushed Ripsbaugh just as the shovel came around, Maddox avoiding the blade, the wooden handle cracking against his raised left arm and sending him sprawling over the open tank cap.

"Run!" he yelled to Tracy. But she was already doing that.

Ripsbaugh appeared over him, shovel raised. Maddox rolled away just as the blade buried itself sideways in the wet turf where his head had been. He scrambled to his feet as Ripsbaugh pulled the spade from the sucking ground. Ripsbaugh lunged and swung, and Maddox, off balance, thought he was far enough away.

The dirty blade sliced through the meat of his upper left thigh, a gouge of pain that spun Maddox sideways, dropping him to one knee.

Ripsbaugh reset himself, eyes determined as he wound up for a beheading shot.

The clothesline lay on the grass around Ripsbaugh's feet. Maddox grabbed the loose ends and yanked back.

Ripsbaugh's legs came up, crashing him to the ground, his head smacking back.

Maddox, grunting in pain, pulled the awl from his back pocket and buried it deep in Ripsbaugh's left thigh, to the bone.

Ripsbaugh's howl was monstrous. His leg kicked so violently that Maddox lost his grip on the knob. Maddox looked up just in time to see the blunt top end of the shovel handle coming at his face.

It struck him full in the cheek, snapping back his head. He brought his hand up to cover the point of impact and felt the left side of his face droop, the bones cracked and loose inside.

Ripsbaugh was writhing and trying to get up, the knob of the awl jutting from his thigh. He still had the shovel. Maddox had nothing but a broken face and a bad leg.

Tracy.

Maddox got to his feet and took off, each step a burst of flame, hobbling hard to the other side of the house, opposite the direction in which Tracy had run. He looked back with his hand covering his face and saw Ripsbaugh with the awl blade out of his thigh, limping after him, shovel in hand.

Tracy was free. That was all that mattered. Whatever happened now, no one else would die needlessly because of him.

65
TRACY

T RACY RAN BLINDLY INTO the driveway, right past Donny's patrol car before stopping. She turned back and saw Sinclair in the front lawn, limping badly after Donny around the far end of the house.

The driver's door was unlocked. She jumped inside, slamming it shut after her, locking it with her slimy fingers, reaching across for the passenger door and locking that one too.

No keys. She saw the radio under the dash and picked up the handset and ran her disgusting hands over the knobs.

Nothing. Then she saw the on/off switch.

The dial lit up white, reassuring lights blinking red and green.

She held the handset with both hands so it wouldn't slip away like a bar of soap and she pressed down the talk button and yelled for help.

"Who is this?" came the radio voice, angry.

She met fire with fire, blasting her name back at him.

"The missing Tracy Mithers?" said the voice.

She told them where she was. She told them Sinclair was there and he was chasing Don Maddox. Don Maddox, the state police trooper.

"Stay right where you are," said the voice.

She eased up on the handset and it slipped to the floor. She checked all the door locks again, and the windows, making sure she was sealed in. She looked back at the radio and noticed a panel of switches above it. With her mucky fingers, she flicked every one of them.

Blue lights blazed across the house and the driveway. The siren screamed.

She saw something in the rearview mirror then. Just her own hair. She twisted the glass down so that she could fully see herself, and her screaming nearly topped the wail of the siren.

66
HESS

HESS WENT RACING through the station. "Get that chopper in the air!" he yelled at Bryson.

The STOP team was lying about on the front porch, kicking back, rifles dangling from their shoulders. The leader sat up as Hess went past with his Sig drawn.

"A UC in town," said Hess. "He's State. Sinclair's at his house *right now*." As Hess hit the driveway, he yelled back over his shoulder, "He's one of ours!"

67
RIPSBAUGH

RIPSBAUGH PUSHED THROUGH the trees after Maddox. His thigh was screaming at him to stop—goddamn awl hurt more coming out than going in—but Maddox was hurt too, and unarmed, and just a few trees ahead. Ripsbaugh had lost the awl when he stumbled in the backyard, but he still had his shovel, its grip and weight as familiar to his hands as any tool could be to a man. He held it ahead of him, swatting branches aside and dragging his leg along as fast as he could.

There was still time. Time to finish this, and do it right. The llama farmer was gone, but she didn't know it was him. She only knew Sinclair.

Finish Maddox, then get back to the house. Wipe down that window frame in the upstairs bedroom, get rid of the handprint. Then tidy up the rest, seal the septic tank outside, haul the machine away before the police came. And find Maddox's gun. And the bloody awl.

Much work to be done. But he could still get away. Everything else said Sinclair. Still enough time for everything to be all right. To finish this. For Val.

All of Ripsbaugh's secrets would die with Maddox.

The sudden peal of the cop siren spun him around. He saw blue lights through the trees. Police.

Couldn't be. Not yet.

No—Maddox's patrol car.

The girl.

For the first time, Ripsbaugh felt things slipping away. He realized that all his good work here might come to nothing in the end.

He stood looking back and forth, torn between the house, where the incriminating evidence still needed to be destroyed, and the snapped-branch trail left by Maddox, who had wronged him. Who had wronged his wife.

A vision swam into his mind's eye: Val on all fours, looking back at Maddox grunting over her. Her eyes heavy-lidded with confusion and pain and desire.

Protect Val. Kill the secrets.

With a howl of determination, Ripsbaugh launched forward, pulling himself tree by tree after Maddox.

68
MADDOX

CRASHING THROUGH THE woods with his galloping limp was less like running than controlled falling. His sliced leg was warm and rubbery, but somehow saw him through. Maddox protected his broken face with his hand, branches and briars pulling and slashing at him: one lash for every lie he had ever told, for every person he had ever deceived or put at risk.

The woods opened to a broad clearing, the Cold River flowing left-right, swift with fresh runoff. Its banks were rugged, lined with current-smoothed stones all the way to the edge of the falls.

The clouds were breaking up overhead, the rain ending. The full moon peering through, bleak and glowing like a nightmare sun, transforming the river into a vein of silver.

Maddox looked back at the trees. Ripsbaugh came hobbling out, closer to him than Maddox would have guessed. He was using his shovel as a crutch, his wig hair jerking behind his head with each hop.

Maddox gimped along the slick stones. No chance of crossing the Cold: too wide, too deep, too fast. He heard the unsuspecting water, which had coursed so proudly out of the highlands and down the broad river basin, howl with betrayal as it launched over the precipice into the brink. Wading any deeper than knee-high would mean getting sucked in by the current and whisked over the edge.

He had no strength for another run into the trees. This was where it had to happen. Maddox searched the ground for good-sized stones to throw, removing his hand from his sagging face, waiting for Ripsbaugh with his back to the river.

Ripsbaugh came up to the bank of stones. Branches had ripped open his black-cotton sleeves and shoulders, revealing shiny skin; Ripsbaugh wearing full latex coating underneath. The wig had shifted back from his forehead, steaming body heat escaping from the cap, giving his peeling face the effect of a smoking skull.

Ripsbaugh eased off his shovel, gripping it like a weapon now, turning it over and over in his hands. Rocks versus shovel. Ripsbaugh had the advantage, but not at that distance.

Maddox hurled stones at him. One after another, any he could get his hands on, but baseball-sized rocks if he had a choice. He couldn't get as much speed on them as he wanted, throwing almost one-leggedly. But they went fast enough that Ripsbaugh could not protect himself or bat them away with the shovel, taking blows in the gut and arms, one sharp-edged rock opening the side of his neck.

Ripsbaugh had to overcommit. Shielding his face with his arm, he came staggering at Maddox over the wet stones. Maddox closed him up with a rock to the midsection, then lunged as hard as his bad leg permitted, shoving Ripsbaugh off balance.

Ripsbaugh went over sideways, holding on to the shovel with one hand. Maddox started kicking that hand with his boot heel, from a squatting position so that the thrusting strength came from his arms braced against the stones behind him, not his other leg.

Ripsbaugh, unable to rise, could not protect his shovel hand. Maddox battered and crushed his knuckles until his fingers gave up the grip. The shovel clacked off a few stones, the blade dipping into the water, tasting it like a steel tongue. Ripsbaugh grabbed after it, but too late. The current seized the tool by the blade, snatching it away from his reach, rushing it out to the edge and over.

Maddox got one more good kick in, to Ripsbaugh's ribs, before Ripsbaugh caught his boot, twisting his leg and throwing Maddox backward against submerged river rocks. Maddox tried to right himself but could not get any traction on the slippery stones. So he crabbed backward, dragging his own bad leg as Ripsbaugh pursued him on his, hunched over, furious and determined.

Maddox felt something through the ground. A thumping, a vibration. Like the pounding bass beat of distant music.

A helicopter crested over the precipice of the falls. The State Police Air Wing search-and-rescue unit. Ripsbaugh stiffened, hearing the bird but not daring to turn around. Wet wig hair hung over the latex peeling off his face, his eyes flaring.

He knew. There was no getting away now.

"Give up, Kane," yelled Maddox over the noise.

Ripsbaugh stared at his empty, shredded hands, hope gone like the shovel over the edge of the falls. He had nothing left to lose.

He curled his tattered hands into fists and came hard after Maddox. Maddox kicked, but Ripsbaugh caught him by the ankle and, with great strength, began dragging him over the lumpy stones, into the river.

Maddox felt the current start to pull. Delirious pain as his bad leg bumped over the stones, water whipping into his face from the approaching Air Wing's rotor wash.

He saw land behind Ripsbaugh brighten as the helicopter swung around, its searchlight a cone of immaculate brightness.

Thirty-million candlepower. That was what Cullen had said. Chased the coyotes out of the Borderlands.

Maddox grabbed the last stone before the open water and held on, hugging it close. Ripsbaugh kept hauling on him, lashed by river spray as the spinning helicopter righted itself overhead.

Maddox shut his eyes, turning away just as the searchlight hit.

69
RIPSBAUGH

RIPSBAUGH WAS ABOUT TO pull him loose when Maddox closed his eyes.

Closed them like he understood. Like he accepted his fate. Like he would let go of that last rock and they would both wash away together.

The thought of leaving Val alone in this world emptied him.

Then the searchlight hit, and everything went white.

Ripsbaugh blinked. He blinked again but there was no black to go with it, no alteration in the white. The searchlight had burned right through his eyes. He raised his hurt hand to cover his face, but much too late.

Maddox kicked hard, shaking loose of Ripsbaugh's grip. Ripsbaugh started to fall, the river already pulling on his legs. The bad one gave way, and he grabbed blindly after Maddox, at where Maddox had been.

He caught hold of something. Something smooth. The toe of Maddox's boot.

The current sucked at his lower half. The river wanted him. It wanted them both. Hungrily, the water whisked away Sinclair's sneakers from Ripsbaugh's feet. With his other, busted hand he made a lunge for Maddox's ankle, getting a two-handed grip. It was Maddox's bad leg. He could feel Maddox's agony.

Ripsbaugh lifted his face out of the water, blindly trying to see how close he was to pulling Maddox in with him. That was when the blow struck. A boot tread, crushing him full in the face. His hands released at once, and the water took him fast, sweeping him along like he was nothing, running him out to the edge and over, flushing him away.

Oh Valerie.

70
MADDOX

CLINGING TO THE RIVER ROCK, Maddox remembered what Dill Sinclair had once said at this same overlook, about people staying back from the edge, not because they were afraid of falling, but because they were afraid of the temptation to leap.

Ripsbaugh screamed all the way down the falls until the clash and spray pulled him into the pit churning below, the mashing vortex devouring him whole.

71

HESS

THE CRAMPED OFFICE-GARAGE of Cold River Septic was a small, cluttered building set on the edge of Ripsbaugh's property, fed by a dirt lane off the driveway, carved away from the house and yard by a short chain-link fence.

Searing heat inside at midday, but they couldn't open the windows because of the flies. It wasn't that the place smelled bad inside, it actually smelled too good. The disinfectant Ripsbaugh used on his equipment had a flavored scent, sticky and sweet like cough syrup, drawing the swarming bugs.

Hess didn't like getting beat. But if he was going to get beat, at least it was by somebody with a real serious fucking game plan and not just some blunderbuss. This guy Ripsbaugh was playing a game no one else could see. Getting arrested in order to clear himself? Psycho balls. And Ripsbaugh hadn't just beat Hess. He'd beat CSS, he'd beat the crime lab in Sudbury. And he'd beat Maddox.

"So this liquid latex," said Hess, silence killing him like the heat. "That's a new one."

Maddox, forthcoming on every other aspect of the murders and the man who had committed them, remained stubbornly circumspect regarding Ripsbaugh's character. Crazy people have crazy motives, but Ripsbaugh's rationale—cleaning up his beloved town by creating this bogeyman killer to mobilize the residents and bring down the corrupt cops—seemed ambitious in the extreme. Maddox might have been holding something back. Because of some lingering sense of trauma, after all he had been through, the beating he'd given and taken. Or, and this was Hess's gut, maybe it was something a little more personal. Something between him and Ripsbaugh, like pity for the guy. Or, God forbid, something like respect.

They had found Ripsbaugh's tanker truck pulled in behind trees around the corner from Maddox's street. On the plastic-lined front seat lay the garment bag Ripsbaugh used to keep Sinclair's clothes and wig pristine. Fucking diabolical.

"TV teaches," said Hess. "Millions of people watch, but all it takes is one who's not only listening but *learning*. All these forensics shows and B-movie crime reenactments and jazzy serial killer documentaries? To him it was one long instructional video. A four-year correspondence course to Murder U. One guy out of a million with the will and the drive to apply the techniques he sees."

Maddox nodded, watching Ripsbaugh's video diagnostic contraption through his unbandaged eye, the whirring cable snake feeding slowly into a toilet bowl inside a folding-door utility bathroom. A technician from SwiftFlow Environmental Systems, Ripsbaugh's former regional competitor, operated the controls, watching the pipe camera's progress on a three-by-three monitor.

Hess stood with Maddox before a wired-in laptop, the search being recorded by CSS. To Hess's eye, the perspective was that of a coal miner, a green helmet light illuminating a foot or two of dark tunnel ahead. When it reached the open end of the pipe, the view dipped down, revealing a moonscape of glowing green curd.

"Keep going?" asked the SwiftFlow technician.

Maddox said, through a mouth still swollen, "Keep going."

The crust proved soft as the camera dipped through it. The view dimmed below, like an underwater camera in a murky pond. Hess was amazed they could see anything. "Where's all the shit?"

Maddox, and not the SwiftFlow technician, answered him.

"Sludge at the bottom of the tank breeds bacteria that breaks it down into wastewater. The effluent rises, dribbling off into the leeching fields, where it seeps back down through rock and soil, reentering the water table. You bring it back up through your well, and the cycle continues."

Maddox knew a lot, it seemed. A good guy, all in all, but weird. Seemed to Hess his own well was dug pretty deep.

The SwiftFlow technician said, "Holy Mother of God."

It came to them on the screen, a cloudy form taking shape.

A body. A human being suspended in fluid, naked, curled on its side. Like an oversized fetus in amniotic broth. A stillborn stuck in a polluted womb.

The corpse was startlingly well preserved, except for the outermost layers of derma. The small dark hole in the center of his chest looked to Hess like a gunshot wound.

Dillon Sinclair.

So this is where you've been hiding all this time, you son of a bitch.

"I'll be goddamned," Hess said. He had seen a lot of things in his career, but this particular image would never leave him. "What a town."

Maddox stepped back after a long look, gimpy on his sore leg. He was about to leave.

"Maddox," said Hess. He stuck out his hand. "What do you say? Two guys trying to do their jobs, right?"

Maddox thought about it a moment, then reached out and shook. "Thanks for that helicopter."

72
VAL

THE TANK OFF THE SEPTIC garage had already been excavated and dismantled, the pit filled in with loam just that afternoon. Then peace and quiet for an hour or two, until, late in the day, Val heard his tires on the gravel.

She answered the doorbell with a tissue balled in her hand. It was Donny, still in his Black Falls PD uniform, his face bandaged, leaning on a cane like old man Pinty.

Her face was puffy. She had been doing a lot of crying, and the rawness at the rims of her eyes added to their uncertainty as she looked at him.

His mouth was off-kilter from the swelling, the bandages making his expression difficult to read. She wondered if it would be okay to hug him.

She went ahead and did so, gently. It was not reciprocated.

"God," she said, sniffling into his shoulder. "It's all such a nightmare."

"It's pretty bad," he allowed.

She pulled away, still unsure. He stepped over the threshold on the cane, favoring his left leg. The bridge of his nose was deeply bruised, the color of the sky on late summer evenings.

She said, "So you were state police? All these years. That's what you've been . . ."

"That's right."

"I don't know what to say," she said. "I'm so glad you are all right."

"Of course you are," he said, wincing, maybe from the pain.

She turned her head a few degrees as though for better reception, his flat intonation putting her on edge. "I am," she said, working the tissue in her hands, smiling out of confusion. She backed to the stairs, sitting down on the third step. "So much he hid from me. I think I never understood him."

"He understood you."

Donny was not going to make this easy. She looked up at him, waiting for some sort of signal. Some indication of release, of absolution. She always had trouble reading men. Except Kane.

"You wanted out of Black Falls," Donny said. "Now you can go."

"Yes?"

"And now you will go."

She blinked, looking at his uniform. "Are you saying that as . . . ?"

"As a policeman?" said Donny. "Yes. You will take whatever you can pack in a bag, right now, and you will go away from here. That is the only deal I'm offering. Leave everything else behind and go. Right now. Tonight."

She searched for some sort of glimmer in his eyes, anything. "But, Donny—"

"You knew," he said.

Blinking bewilderment. "I didn't."

"Frond and Pail. You tried to talk them into taking you away from here. Both of them turned you down. Just like I did."

"Donny, I—"

"So you confessed to Kane. You told him everything, after the affairs were over. To clear your conscience, right? *Wrong*. To overload his. To punish him for your misery."

"But how could I have known—"

"You didn't. Not for the first two. You knew it would hurt him. You knew it would eat at him over time. But not so that he'd take it upon himself to do something about it. Something nearly heroic in its lunacy. Trying to make you happy again by killing off your sadness."

The cool dispassion he had walked in with was gone. "But when you told him about you and me? And about Tracy? You knew, Val. You knew exactly what you were doing. You were *sending* him to me."

His glare was a hand around her throat.

"You had a killer in your pocket," he went on. "An instrument of your vengeance. Your revenge on this town that you hated. This town that he loved—almost as much as he loved you. I don't even think you want to leave. I think you want to stay. I think you need this place as an excuse for your misery. A place and a people to blame. But now you will go from here, tonight, and you will never come back."

Donny's hands were squeezed tight at his sides, the same way Kane's used to get. Seeing that emboldened her, and all pretense fell from her face like glass out of a shattered window. She reached for the handrail, waiting for the trembling to go out of her lips. She wanted to be standing when she said this. Wanted him to see her pride, her triumph.

"I have lived with monsters all my life," she told him.

Donny turned and limped away. "That is why I'm letting you go."

73
MADDOX

Tracy stood with both forearms on the stall door inside the old cowshed. She and Rosalie, the mother llama, watched with equal pride as the new cria tottered around on spindly legs.

"Samantha," said Tracy. "I picked it because it's a happy name. You can't say it without smiling. Try."

Maddox eyed her legs beneath the strings of her cutoffs, tanned down to the tops of her boots. Clean now. He wondered how many showers and baths it had taken. How much soaking and scrubbing before she had begun to feel normal again.

"*Samantha,*" he said, feeling soreness in his cheek between the second and third syllable. It hurt to smile. "And what about you?"

"What about me?"

"You feeling happy?"

Under her straw cowgirl hat, her pretty eyes lacked the sparkle they once held, her spirit of mischief. Maddox felt as though he had taken that away. "I'd like to feel happy," she said. "I'm trying."

Footsteps scratched the dirt outside. Mrs. Mithers coming. Tracy looked at Maddox, but without any trepidation or nervousness. She was past all that now.

Instead it was Maddox who readied himself, standing as straight as he could with the cane.

Mrs. Mithers looked in with a smile of greeting, walking up the cow ramp. Maddox presented himself, Tracy signing the introductions.

Maddox took a good look at Tracy's mother's face. As with the rest of her generation, she had come late to sunscreen and straw hats. But there was beauty beneath the striations of age and divorce. Enough to make one wonder what difference a good marriage might have made.

Mrs. Mithers signed, and Tracy translated: "How's your cheek?"

"Not so bad," he answered. "In a way, after ten years of working undercover, I think I kind of had it coming."

Mrs. Mithers didn't know what to say to that.

"Do it too long," Maddox went on, "and you either burn out or burn up. That's what I told them at the state police barracks yesterday, when I resigned."

Tracy turned. She stared at him. "Resigned?"

"They wanted me on a desk. I never did wear the uniform. Seemed strange to start now."

Tracy kept staring, and Mrs. Mithers had to touch her daughter's elbow to get her attention. She signed, and Tracy stammeringly translated the question she could not bring herself to ask: "So what are you going to do?"

"Well," he said, bypassing Tracy and addressing Mrs. Mithers directly, "undergo a little reconstructive surgery, that's the first thing. Beyond that, it looks like Pinty's going to need some help getting around for a while. Never mind putting together a competent police force here. I suppose it's no secret that I still owe this town five years."

Tracy said, "Five *years?*"

"Less six months, for time served. So, four and a half. But after that, believe you me—I am *gone.*"

Tracy was still staring at him.

To Mrs. Mithers, he added, "Unless I meet someone. You know. Fall in love. That old trap."

Tracy pulled her hat off her head and rushed up and squeezed him so tight he staggered back on his cane. She kissed his good cheek, quaking in his arms, crying or maybe laughing. Either way, it was happiness, and Maddox, sore as he was, felt better than he had in a long time.

He buried his nose in Tracy's hair. She smelled clean and pure.

ACKNOWLEDGMENTS

For aiding and abetting, thanks to Richard Abate, Colin Harrison, Susan Moldow, Robert Shulman, and Trooper John Conroy of the Massachusetts State Police.

Scribner proudly presents

Sugar Bandits

By

Chuck Hogan

Coming soon from Scribner

Turn the page for a preview of
Sugar Bandits . . .

THE LOT

A cold night in November.

Neil Maven stood on the edge of the parking lot, looking up at the buildings of downtown Boston. Wondering about the lights left shining in the top-floor offices, who does that, and why. A thumping bass line made him turn. A silver limousine eased around the corner, its long side windows mirrored, allowing the less fortunate to see what they looked like as they watched extreme wealth passing them by.

Maven stuffed his hands deep in the pouch pockets of his blanket-thick hoodie, stamping his boots on the blacktop to keep warm. Another Saturday night, the city getting along just fine without him.

Nine months now. Nine months he'd been back. Nine months since demobilization and discharge, like nine months of gestation, waiting to be reborn into the peacetime world. Nine months of transition and nothing going right.

He had already pissed through most of his duty pay. The things you tell the other guys you're going to do once you get back home—grow a beard, drink all night, sleep all day—he had done. Those lofty goals he had achieved. The things the army recommends doing before discharge, to ease your transition—crafting a résumé, lining up housing, securing employment—no, those things he had let slide.

A lot of businesses affixed yellow "Support Our Troops" ribbons in their front windows, but when you actually showed up there looking for work, scratching your name and address on an application pad, they saw not a battle-tested hero but a disability claim in the making. Hiring a guy with more confirmed kills than college credits was a tough sell. Maven wasn't mistrusted the way, say, felons are mistrusted—not at all. But he could feel people's suspicion, their unease. Like they heard a *tick, tick, tick* going inside his head. Probably the same one he heard.

Barroom conversations took on a closed-captioned-like subtext. "Let me buy you a drink, soldier," meant, *If you wig out and start shooting up the room, spare me, I'm one of the good ones.* "You know, I came *this close* to enlisting myself," meant, *Yeah, September eleventh pissed my pants, but I pulled myself together and haven't missed an episode of* American Idol *since.* "I supported you boys one hundred percent," meant, *Just because I have a ribbon magnet on my car doesn't mean you can look at my daughter.* "Great to have you back," seemed to mean, *Now please go away again.*

He finally did drop by the VA for some career guidance, and a short-armed woman with a shrub of salt-and-pepper hair sat down with him and banged out that magical résumé, diligently omitting any reference to combat experience. (Since coming back, everything was about writing off what had happened. What he considered to be his only true accomplishment in life, aside from not getting maimed or killed in action—namely, passing the six-phase Qualification Course at Fort Bragg and earning his Special Forces tab in the run-up to the Iraq invasion—was neutered to a bullet point on the "Skill Sets" section of his résumé: "Proficient at team-building and leadership skills." But not man-killing.) The resulting document was a skimpy little thing that whimpered, "Please hire me." He had fifty of them printed on twenty-four-pound paper at Kinko's, and seeded another seventy-five around the city via e-mail, to a great and profound silence. This three-nights-a-week parking lot guard job, he landed through an ad on Craigslist. A yen for 9 A.M. Red Bull had led to him pulling a hand-scrawled "Help Wanted" notice out of the window at the City Oasis convenience store four blocks from his apartment and presenting himself at the counter for minimum wage employment.

The owner of the parking lot was a builder looking to add a spire to the city skyline, another shiny pin in the Boston pincushion. The property manager who hired Maven, a square-shouldered navy veteran of two tours in Vietnam, clapped him on the back fraternally before telling him that he would break Maven's hands if he stole so much as a penny.

After a week or two of long hours standing out in the bitterly cold night, warding street people away from soft-top Benzes and Lexus SUVs, this threat eventually took the form of a challenge. Every shift, Maven showed up for work thinking he wouldn't steal, only to soften after standing around in the lonesome marinade of night. $36.75 Flat Fee, Enter After 6 p.m., No Blocking, Easy-In/Easy-Out. He kept it to one or two cars a shift, nothing serious. Latecomers always, inebriates pulling in after midnight, exulting in calling Maven "my man" or "*dude,*" and never asking for a receipt, never questioning why he lifted the gate by hand. All they wanted was to tuck their silver Saab in close to the downtown action, so that nothing disrupted the momentum of their weekend night.

This was funny money, the $73.50 he skimmed, and he wasted it accordingly, opening up the gate at quarter to two and hustling a couple of blocks over to Centerfold's in the old Combat Zone, dropping his ill-gotten gains on a couple of draft beers and a table dance before lights-up at two. Maven was in a bad way. Any money he had left over after last call, he would take with him two blocks over to Chinatown, ordering a pot of "cold tea" along with the club zombies and the Leather District poseurs and the legal college seniors too cool for Boston's puritanical 2 a.m. closing time. Maven would sit alone at a cloth-covered table, the piped-in Asian music trickling into his beer buzz like soft rain as he drank down the teapot of draft Bud and popped pork dumplings like soft, greasy aspirins. Then he overtipped, tightened his boot laces, and strapped on his shoulder pack for the run home.

Home was Quincy. Quincy was eight-point-two miles away.

Running was a purge and a meditation. His thick boots clumped over the cracked streets of dodgy neighborhoods. Along dormant

Conrail tracks and under expressway bridges. Past dark playgrounds and suspicious cars idling at corners, traffic lights blinking yellow, people calling out to him from porches and stoops: *"Who's chasin' you, man? Why you runnin'?"*

Quincy is home to beautiful ocean-view properties, seven-figure marina condos, and the original family property of this country's first father-son presidents, the Adamses. Maven's converted attic apartment was nowhere near any of these. It had sloped ceilings in every room, a stand-up shower with zero water pressure, and stood directly under the approach path into Logan.

This was his life now.

Sometimes, during his run, he thought about the dancers and the way they eyed themselves in the strip club's wall mirrors as they worked the stage, so unashamed and even bored by their public nudity, as though they were just part of the spectacle, and not, in fact, its focus. This was Maven's attitude toward his own life now. He was observing a man slowly slip away, and curious as to how it would all turn out, yet untroubled by the fact that this man was him.

It had been just six nights since he'd nearly killed a man.

The rain came down hard that shift, hard enough to wash away the sounds of the city around him, the normal symphony of the downtown weekend: no laughter from passing couples; no Emerson students doing their gloating in packs; no polite debate from the scarf-wearing, *Playbill*-toting theatergoers; no club-hoppers tripping over sidewalk cracks and laughing their asses off.

There was a small booth for him at the gate, but with the rain pounding on the roof like fists, it was easier for Maven just to stand outside. Stand outside and let the rain rap his poncho hood and shoulders, blowing down in sheets from the high security lamps like the shimmering folds of a great tent weathering a storm. He felt like a rock beneath a waterfall, which was not unpleasant; no man comes back from war without a little Zen in his psychic portfolio.

People think it never rains in the Arabian desert, but it does: an eerie occurrence, like applause inside a church. Desert rain tastes silty and leaves dirty black tears down your temples and your chin. Boston rain, on the other hand, thanks to recycled industrial emissions, smells and tastes soft-drink sweet.

Since returning to the States, Maven had battled the so-called "reimmersion issues" common to discharged Iraq veterans. Heightened startle reflex, avoidance of crowded places, anxiety attacks bordering on panic. Discarded Coke cans, dead animals on the roadside, a man walking alone into traffic: in Iraq, these things had the unsettling tendency to detonate fatally and without notice. His time over there had been one of unremitting suspense met with unrelenting vigilance, and this vigilance was one of many habits he was trying to tamp down now, in hopes of one day switching off entirely.

Two things conspired to distract him from his usual wariness that night. The insulating rain was one of them. The other was a gleaming black Cadillac Escalade that pulled in around ten.

The Escalade is a big SUV, so the driver was sitting at about Maven's eye level. Nothing about him jumped out at Maven: black hair, a no-nonsense face, perfectly curved shirt collar, jutting chin. The dash was loaded with electronics, more than were in Maven's entire apartment. Windshield wipers flicked rain into his face.

As the driver went poking into the sun visor for some cash, a girl leaned forward from the passenger seat beside him. She threw a brief glance Maven's way, nothing more than a peek around a blind corner, just curious enough to put a face to the dark figure in the rain. The liquid crystal display of the radio and the navigational screen lit her green and blue like some beautiful android peering out from a different plane of existence. Maven glimpsed a neck without flaws, a delicately pointed chin, and a tantalizing shadow line of cleavage.

All in an instant. She sat back again, no spark in her eyes, no recognition, nothing.

"Messy night?"

It was the guy talking, a neatly creased fifty clipped between his fingers.

"Yeah," said Maven, slow to recover, his hands disappearing inside his deep pants pockets within the poncho, making change.

The guy accepted the wet bills and coins and spilled them into a cupholder. "Stay dry, man."

He pulled in and parked, and Maven watched them walk away arm-in-arm underneath a wide black umbrella. His gaze focused on her bare calves beneath the cut of her dress, the shoe straps tied like restraints around her ankles. Her heels picked at the sidewalk, the sound fading into the rain.

He knew her. Knew *of* her, anyway. A girl from his high school. Older than him by three years, a senior when he was a freshman, but as clear and fixed in his memory as the bikini models who used to smile down from the posters on his bedroom walls. Smiled knowingly, with one crooked thumb hooked in the side string of their bikini bottom, drawing it inches away from their cocked hip. That kind of memory.

Her name came back to him with the stinging slap of a snowball to the face: Danielle Vetti.

He said it aloud a few times in the rain, "Danielle Vetti, Danielle Vetti, Danielle Vetti," watching it steam and disappear. The memory, this one-second encounter—even if he was wrong, even if this was just his horny brain misfiring—the *taste* of her name in his mouth, all put a charge into him the likes of which he hadn't felt in a long, long time.

Danielle Vetti had been *the* girl in high school. Passing her in the hall was the highlight of your day, something you'd brag about to your seatmates in the next class. Guys at their lockers, guys in the bathroom you didn't even know, would pass the word: *Check out Danielle Vetti today.* Every eye, boy or girl, went to her when she passed. They just didn't make people like that in Gridley, Massachusetts.

Danielle Vetti.

He needed a better look at her face. For confirmation. Not to approach her or say anything; he reverted to his intimidated freshman self. No, just to satisfy his curiosity. To round out his high school experience. To see Danielle Vetti one more time.

That was why he had been out lurking near the rear bumper of the black Escalade, feeling invisible in the rain, paying no attention to the guy coming off the street.

"You see a little wet dog come through here, man?"

The guy's Latino accent didn't match what Maven saw of his face beneath the hood of his oily anorak. But this detail didn't jump out at Maven until the second guy did.

The blow came from behind, Maven down and rolling in a puddle. He was pulled up, head throbbing, and a thick strap went around his chest like the kind used to cinch down loads in a flatbed truck. It was ratcheted fast from behind, pinning Maven's arms against him inside the poncho.

The first guy showed a knife, low and silver, turning it so that it caught the overhead light. A fat three-inch blade. Maven's focus went in and out.

The guy behind him tugged Maven back between two cars, out of sight from the street.

"The money, man," said the one holding the knife. "I might cut you anyway, so give it up fast."

Steam billowed from the mouth of the guy holding the cinch strap, his breath smelling sour and chemical. Maven couldn't clear his mind, couldn't get any thoughts started. A cold automobile engine that wouldn't turn over.

They were pulling him toward the booth. The knife guy backed inside it, Maven getting a better look at his face there, his smile sharp and hungry, breath creeping through wide spaces in his teeth like fog through a broken fence. He pecked at the register keys with his empty hand, hitting the big button, the drawer shooting open.

The knife guy's smile faded. He came back outside, the knife low at his waist. He was keen to use it. He wouldn't go away until it was bloodied.

"Search him."

Maven's teeth set hard, his tongue pressing against his gums—and he felt the notch in its right front quadrant. He felt himself relax then. A kind of deadness crept over him, the prelude to combat readiness, a feeling he had once known so well.

Everybody who comes back has their one story. Even if they come back with more than one story, even if they have a couple of good stories that keep improving every time they tell them—there's still that one. The one story that gets you, that's *yours*. The one story you own; the one story that owns you.

It was a girl. Young, maybe fourteen, but hard to tell with her head wrapped in a kaffiyeh of gauze-thin cotton. Her best head wrap, soft and golden like caramel. Maven was working a sneak-and-peek at a house in Samarra with his fire team. These young girls would detour past American soldiers regularly, looking to draw a reaction while at the same time discouraging any real contact. So many there, especially the young, loved America—whatever "America" meant to them. So to be admired by an American, to be fancied by a westerner: it was like having your dream beckon to you.

Maven was posted at the front corner of the house and didn't even see her until she was maybe twenty meters away. She was smiling, but even at that distance Maven could tell that something was wrong with her smile. Her chest moved fast with shallow breaths, and she walked with her arms raised from her sides.

It looked to him as though she were in trouble, and Maven actually took a step or two toward her, moving into her kill range. She reached inside the loose sleeve of her robe and yanked down with a shiver, expecting to die.

Her hand held a broken wire.

She looked at Maven with surprised panic in her eyes, then reached back inside her sleeve fast.

Maven brought up his M16. He could have cut her down right there, a chest-pattern, three-round burst. *Brr-rrr-rrp.*

He did not. His finger never squeezed back on the trigger.

She bent over, working hard, reaching up into her armpit. Maven spun behind a parked Humvee just as she exploded. The windows shattered and sprayed his armor-plated vest and he was thrown against a fence. His fire team found him on the ground, on all fours, spitting blood, thinking he'd been hit. But it wasn't that. A warmth spread instantly over his gums, pooling in the right pocket of his cheek. He choked on something wedged in his throat, swallowing it down. He had bitten off a chunk of his own tongue.

It was a long time before he could talk right again. He saw many things during his tours there—worse things even—but for some reason it was always this girl who appeared in his dreams. Ended them usually, waking him up. Why she came at him, why she chose him, there was no answer. Insurrectionists had been hiring head cases to do pay-and-sprays on American troops, even strapping IEDs to noncoms against their will. Maybe the near-death experience of the first misfire made her change her mind. Maybe in those last frantic moments she was actually trying to get the device off her. No explanation consoled him because, in the end, what the fuck did it matter anyway.

The brutality of war, the random nature of man's existence: she didn't represent anything like that to him. All Maven got out of it was reinforcement of something he already knew: that he was a born loser, and a magnet for trouble. Fate had a way of jumping out at him every once in a while, just to remind him so.

As the tightened strap creaked behind him, the smoothed-over notch in his tongue pushed against the inside of Maven's bite. The second guy's free hand came around to pat Maven's chest and belly through the slick poncho. He felt Maven's waist, pausing at his side pants pocket, gripping what he realized was just a mobile phone, then continuing, the guy stooping now, his hand coming to rest over the cargo pocket along the lower left thigh of Maven's cammo fatigues.

The guy's molesting hand squeezed excitedly as he felt the wad of bills inside, his grip on the strap easing just a bit.

Maven kicked back the heel of his left boot. He was going for the chin but caught the nose instead, a crunch and a dull pop, like the bursting of the glass tube inside an old-fashioned fire alarm.

The knife came thrusting at him, Maven pivoting and kicking out, catching the guy hard in the gut. The guy missed with the blade and went sprawling backward onto the wet pavement, the force of the kick sending Maven down too, armless and hard.

The guy behind him, now doubled over, released the strap, holding his gushing face with both hands.

Maven rolled onto his knees, getting to his feet fast. He punted the guy with the knife before he could straighten, the guy twisting as he fell, almost landing on his own blade. Maven stomped his elbow, then squatted down on his arm, feeling for the knife with his hands still trapped inside the poncho. A heel to the head kept the guy still as Maven finally twisted the knife from his grip, running the blade tip inside the strap and poncho and slashing his arms free— just as a blow from the side knocked loose the knife and sent Maven tumbling.

Maven sprang up fast into a fighter's crouch, the second guy who hit him still holding his busted nose and bleeding face. Maven threw two low jabs, quick-quick, cracking ribs on either side of the guy's torso. The guy tried to crumple but Maven shoved him backward against the rear of the Escalade and drove the heel of his boot into the guy's crotch like he was squashing a tarantula. The guy's hands sprung open off his bloody face, a wail escaping his mouth like a man thrown through saloon doors.

The other one was back on his feet behind Maven, having retrieved the knife. Maven knew this because he saw him reflected in the Escalade's rear window, and when he turned hard, the knife guy seized up momentarily, thinking Maven's powers of perception were beyond human. He reset himself and led with the blade, and Maven side-stepped the clumsy thrust almost before it started. A sound made Maven turn, the other guy's fleeing footsteps, hobbling away off the lot. The knife guy came in with a wild, diagonal slashing move, its tip catching the fabric of Maven's poncho beneath his raised arms, slicing it as Maven pulled away.

The other guy's face sharpened as though he had drawn blood, and not just ruined a seven-dollar surplus poncho.

It was this sneer of victory that made Maven snap.

The knife came at him again and Maven stepped into it this time, catching the guy's hand and twisting, rotating the entire arm. He peeled one finger back off the knife handle, then another, all the way down like the rind of a banana, fracturing both. He rotated the man's hand like the cap on a stubborn jar, cracking bones in his wrist. The guy was screaming and trying to fall but Maven would not let him go. Gripping the knife in the guy's own broken hand, Maven cut into his leg just above the knee, slicing upward and opening the guy's thigh as though with a zipper. Maven ignored his cries, bending the guy's arm back at the elbow and forcing the trembling knife toward the strained muscles of his screaming throat.

Another arm hooked Maven's then, stopping him as he was about to cut the man's neck. Not the guy who had run away; this was a good pro grip locking his arm. Maven's legs were pushed out from behind, putting him off-balance, taking away his leverage.

Maven never saw the face of the third man behind him. Only the woman in front of him, standing a few cars down from the Escalade, a man's black jacket draped over her shoulders, her silver dress shimmering like rain within the rain.

It was Danielle Vetti, her hand covering her mouth.

Maven released the knife guy, who had already fainted anyway. The other man released Maven, and Maven backed away from the mess he had made there in the parking lot, turning from Danielle Vetti's sight, wanting only to get away. He started walking, then jogging, until soon he was running, so hard that even the rain couldn't catch him.

About the Author

Chuck Hogan abandoned his career as a video store clerk when his first novel, *The Standoff,* became a bestseller and was translated into fourteen international editions. His most recent novel, *Prince of Thieves,* was awarded the Hammett Prize for literary excellence in crime writing. He lives with his family in Massachusetts.

$\begin{smallmatrix} 8 \\ 1.50 \\ x \end{smallmatrix}$